The Island of Whispers

A Novel by
Brendan Gisby

A McStorytellers publication

http://www.mcstorytellers.com

For all good rats everywhere.

Contents

Part One:

The Threat

Chapter One

It was near the end of his watch. For the last time that night, Twisted Foot sniffed the air, slowly scanned the terrain below him and listened intently. As his narrow eyes moved gradually from left to right, his sleek black body quivered and bristled in the early autumn breeze. Far out into the estuary, a faint ribbon of yellow was spreading along the horizon, creating a thin wedge between the dark night sky and the even darker waters of the River Forth.

Nothing stirred on the island. There were no sounds save for the gentle slap of water on rocks and the wind that whispered through the slitted windows of the crumbling monastery. Soon, though, the stillness would be shattered by the first northbound express as it thundered over the giant steel bridge which loomed high above.

Twisted Foot smelled a sharpness in the air. It would not be long, he thought, until the Cold Cycle began: the time when the winds grew into shrieking, biting monsters which swept over the outside world; when the waters round the world boiled and frothed, sending up huge white creatures to batter and shake the rocks; and when hard white water clung to the high ground on which he now squatted. The hunting packs would stop then, and there would be little work for the Watchers, only the occasional solitary vigil to guard over the secret world deep below.

He would spend much more time in the underworld during the Cold Cycle, content in the warmth and security of the Watchers' lair. Yes, it was a time for relaxation. There would be long mating sessions with the lair's she-rats. Later, there would be games and frolics with the newly arrived offspring. There would also be those enthralling periods in the Common lair when Long Snout and the other elders of the Inner Circle recounted stirring and often harrowing tales from the history of their hidden world, a history which spanned many, many Cycles from the early struggle to colonise the island through to the stability and comfort of the present society.

Yet, despite his anticipation of the pleasures brought about by the coming Cold Cycle, a sense of foreboding had crept into Twisted Foot's thoughts, causing him to shiver more pronouncedly in the pre-dawn chill. As well as the mating, the games and the stories, that time, he knew, heralded the Selection, when the less robust and less purely formed young from each lair were sought out and imprisoned by the Protectors to await slaughter for the hungry mouths of the Inner Circle. It was true that many of the youngsters selected would be the weaker she-rats, who were regarded as unsuitable for future breeding, and the more deformed of the he-rats, who were not fit for training as Protectors or Hunters or even Watchers. Nevertheless, the Selection was a time of immense sadness in the lairs, a time of sacrifice for the greater good of the society – and for the continued wellbeing of the ruling Circle.

Twisted Foot recalled the trauma of the Selection during his own first Cold Cycle when, as a trembling youngster, he had observed Broken Tail, the Chief Protector, scurry through the Watchers' lair, sniffing out the weak and the handicapped, and marking each across the snout with a swipe of his sharp claws. He remembered vividly the great fear that had pervaded the lair, the squeals and shrieks of his young playmates, and the enticing tang of blood from their freshly inflicted wounds. He remembered, too, a feeling of profound relief when the deformity from which his name was derived had gone undetected by the Chief Protector.

A faint scrape from among the rocks below him brought Twisted Foot's thoughts jolting back to the present. The hunting pack was returning!

Raising his snout to the night sky, he uttered a shrill warning call. The answering call came almost immediately from out of the darkness. Moments later, silently and as if from nowhere, Torn Coat, a scarred veteran from the Hunter's lair, appeared beside him.

'Look sharp, dung-head!' snarled Torn Coat as he brushed past, his bared fangs showing traces of a recent kill.

Twisted Foot watched closely as the rest of the hunting pack moved stealthily towards him. First came the small slave-rats: there were six of them in all, but only three were fully employed. Each of the latter slaves dragged behind him one of the night's kills, jaws clamped over the limp and bleeding neck of a young gull. Moving noiselessly behind the slaves, four more Hunters slid past Twisted Foot, this time without acknowledgement. Finally, the familiar shape of Fat One, a fellow Watcher, lumbered into view.

'Another fine feast for White Muzzle and his lot,' he grumbled to Twisted Foot.

The new day's light crept tentatively up the estuary as the two Watchers followed the hunting pack in the direction of the old monastery. Unlike the quiet, efficient pace of the Hunters, their progress was clumsy and almost comical, reflecting the awkward bulk of one and the grotesquely twisted hind foot of the other.

Chapter Two

The small monastery had been abandoned more than six hundred years before, when its last occupants had slipped quietly and sadly away from the island, only a handful of survivors from the ravages of the vile pestilence that had spread through their devout community, wreaking its black, contorted death. For centuries afterwards, the rocky, whale-shaped islet was known to people on both sides of the Forth as Plague Island: a place to be avoided, a place of ghosts and demons and eerie, whispering winds.

In time, though, the notion of a haunted island receded, as did the memory of the fearful, rat-borne disease that had laid waste to the former inhabitants. Gradually, the island regained its formal name of Inchgarvie. Gradually, too, men returned to Inchgarvie: grey-haired historians to pick over relics of the deserted monastery; bearded, top-hatted engineers to supervise construction of the nearby Forth Railway Bridge; local fishermen and seal-catchers; occasional naturalists; and others attracted to the mysterious island out of plain curiosity. Their visits had been brief, lasting a few hours usually and a day or two at most. Only once more during its history was Inchgarvie occupied by humans for any period of length: they came at the outset of World War Two to build – and later to man – the anti-aircraft gun emplacement that was sited on the east-facing point of the island to help thwart Germany's long-range bombing sorties in the area.

Now, in the last decade of the twentieth century, visitors to the island were few and irregular. Even the multiplicity of craft that plied the Forth steered clear of Inchgarvie, deterred more by swirling, unpredictable tides than by fear of lingering ghosts. After more than fifty years, the concrete gun emplacement remained virtually intact, but centuries of neglect and exposure to the elements had exacted a more telling price from the low-built monastery which occupied the western half of the island; its roof had collapsed long ago, little remained of its internal walls and several ragged holes punctured its thicker external walls.

The returning hunting pack re-entered the dank, rubble-strewn interior of the monastery through one such narrow aperture near the base of the east wall. Their re-entry was greeted instantly with a short screech from a point among the rubble a few yards ahead of them. Uttering his own sharp call in response, Torn Coat moved swiftly towards the Watcher, whose small, pointed snout poked out cautiously from a gap below some broken masonry.

'Pass, warrior,' croaked Small Face.

Without further response, Torn Coat also slid under the masonry and abruptly disappeared down a deep cleft between two ancient flagstones. One by one, the others followed Torn Coat. As Fat One squeezed his unwieldy rump through the cleft, Small Face, easily the tiniest and most timid of the Watchers, called out to Twisted Foot.

'Think of me when you're curled up snugly in the lair,' he wailed.

'Never mind, comrade,' Twisted Foot retorted, 'we'll keep your nest warm for your return.'

Then he, too, vanished down the tunnel that led to the underworld, leaving Small Face to maintain his lone daylight vigil.

The tunnel was long, narrow and very steep. Its roof had been rounded and smoothed by the passage of bodies over many years. By contrast, its floor was bedrock: hard and sharp, and constantly wet from seeping rainwater. Like those in front of him, Twisted Foot slithered rather than crawled down the tunnel.

Eventually, the ground levelled out and broadened, marking the entrance to the underworld. Here, as usual, crouched two surly Protectors, who observed the return of the hunting pack menacingly, but without comment or movement. Behind the Protectors and to their left was a shallow pool of murky rainwater, where the Hunters stopped briefly to lap while Fat One and Twisted Foot guarded over the slaves. Resuming their formation, Hunters and slaves moved off at speed along the wider, higher tunnel leading to the Common lair. Their work now over, the two Watchers also drank from the pool and then proceeded leisurely in the same direction.

As always, the utter blackness of the underworld and its familiar scents and sounds brought reassurance to Twisted Foot. On the world above, he felt exposed, vulnerable. There was that continual sense of anxiety, that fear of imminent intrusion by the Two-Legs. Around the outside world, the strange creatures controlled by the Two-Legs caterwauled through the air and sea and boomed across the giant bridge, threatening and unnerving him. Here in the welcoming blackness those fears were quickly forgotten. Here there was concealment from the Two-Legs, and the promise of warmth, sustenance and companionship.

The Watchers emerged from the tunnel into the Common lair. Unlike the rest of the underworld, this place was spacious, almost cavernous, easily accommodating the normal Assembly of some three hundred he-rats from the Inner and Outer Circles. The floor of the lair was oval-shaped and level for the most part. The centre of the oval was dominated by an outcrop of rock, flattened at its top to create a broad, circular platform. The walls of the lair sloped gently inwards to form a dome-like ceiling, the pinnacle of which was located directly above the platform. Along the walls, a series of low, narrow tunnels led off to the other lairs. To the right lay the abodes of the Watchers and Hunters. To the left, a gang of Protectors kept constant guard over the entrance to the Scavengers' lair, ensuring that the bedlam and violence within did not spill out. The tunnel at the farthest end of the Common lair gave access to the home of the Protectors. From here, another tunnel led to the sanctity of the Inner Circle's lair, a place that was also guarded continually, but for entirely different motives. A final tunnel led from the Protectors' lair to the outside world, emerging at a point not far from the western wall of the monastery. Barely known to the other members of the underworld, this tunnel provided the Inner Circle and their Protectors with an escape route in the event of flooding, insurrection or other such calamities.

As he and Fat One moved through the Common lair towards its central platform, Twisted Foot noted that most of his Outer Circle comrades had already gathered for the Assembly. The returning hunting pack had created the usual stir among them, and more than a hundred pairs of greedy, slit eyes were now fixed on the pack's kills, which had been placed enticingly in the middle of the platform. Bristling and growling, a ring of Protectors surrounded the platform, ready to pounce mercilessly on any who might dare to breach the circle.

The appearance of Long Snout at the entrance to the Protectors' lair brought the commotion to an abrupt halt. Twisted Foot and Fat One scurried through the throng to join the ranks of the Watchers. The Assembly had begun.

Chapter Three

Flanked by two rows of Protectors, the long procession of Rulers led by Long Snout crossed the Common lair and stepped up to the platform. Close to one hundred of them crowded its flat, smooth surface. Most kept to the edge of the circle, while the spacious nucleus was occupied by the elders, together with White Muzzle, the King-rat, and his immediate family.

Like his now hushed companions, Twisted Foot gazed in awe at this spectacle. The superior bearing and sheer majesty of the Rulers never failed to fascinate him. There were so many features which set them apart from his own kind. In stature, they were broader and much longer, with skinny tails that stretched the same distance as their bodies. In contrast to the uniform blackness of the Outer Circle, their coats were lighter in colour, varying in shade from the dull stone of the lesser Rulers to the rich earth that signified royalty. Their eyes, too, were very different: rounder and fuller, and always seeming to reflect the blood colour of a dying sun.

From the centre of the platform, Long Snout, ancient Chamberlain of the underworld, stood erect on his hindquarters and slowly surveyed the audience around him. Now pointing his muzzle to the roof and revealing his yellowing, but still fearsome, fangs, he emitted a long, piercing screech, which reverberated round the Common lair, reinforcing and accentuating the stillness therein.

'Comrades of the Secret World!' he began. 'Countless Cycles ago, our forefathers came to this place on a Two-Legs vessel which had crossed many dark, cold waters from a land far away. Searching for a new home, they braved the icy water to reach the world above. There, they came upon the black Scavengers and their vile, warlike ways. Our forefathers were few and the Scavengers were many, but the Scavengers were defeated and enslaved.'

'Not that story again,' Fat One sighed to himself. His eyelids drooped heavily as he settled his bulk between Twisted Foot and Long Ears, resigned to what threatened to be yet another protracted Assembly.

'Comrades of the Underworld!' the Chamberlain continued. 'Our forefathers drove the slaves to create this warm and secret place, this world of darkness and sanctuary. But much more was required. Our forefathers were ageing. They had need of many loyal warriors to protect them, to feed them and to keep watch on their enemies. Careful breeding with the she-rats of the Scavengers produced a race of strong, black-furred warriors. Thus evolved our present society: the Inner Circle of Rulers and the Outer Circle of Protectors, Hunters and Watchers.'

Long Snout paused to sniff the air. Eyes ablaze, he scoured the Outer Circle rats, compelling their attentiveness. His whole body stiffened suddenly when he spied Fat One, now fast asleep in the midst of the Watchers.

As the Chamberlain pushed through the others on the platform to obtain a closer view of this transgression, both Twisted Foot and Long Ears were desperately prodding Fat One with their snouts.

'Wake up, you fool!' cried Long Ears in his familiar, high-pitched squeal.

In the same moment, Neck-Snapper, a particularly sadistic young Protector, leapt snarling into the ranks of the Watchers.

'Let me wake the fat idiot,' he growled and then lunged towards Fat One.

Old Sharp Claws, the Chief Watcher, moved nimbly to block the path of the Protector.

'Back!' warned Sharp Claws through bared teeth. 'I'll deal with this!'

Neck-Snapper hesitated for some moments, snorted in disgust and retreated slowly to the ring of Protectors.

Sharp Claws then turned to glare at a thoroughly shaken and wide-awake Fat One. 'Later!' he hissed.

Fat One shivered. The punishment, he knew, would not be a violent one, but he would still pay dearly. Many long, freezing watches on the outside world would be a worse fate.

Satisfied that a penalty would be paid, and content that the incident itself had succeeded in rousing his audience, Long Snout returned to his place in the centre of the platform. His Inner Circle colleagues, on the other hand, had watched the episode with their usual disdain. Matters like this one were commonplace and irksome, serving only to interrupt the Assembly – and to delay the feast that lay ahead.

The Chamberlain resumed his oration.

'Comrades of the Dark World! The society created by our forefathers has endured many hardships through many generations. Yet it has survived – and it has prospered. It has survived because we are a disciplined society and because we are ever-vigilant. Yes, discipline and vigilance: these are the rules which govern our every way.

'Discipline and vigilance,' he repeated slowly, this time directing the words at a very attentive Fat One.

'Comrades, our secret world remains hidden from the marauding Two-Legs because our lives are disciplined. Our presence on the world above is controlled carefully, kept to only a few Hunters and slaves each time – and always when darkness covers the land. Our time here in the underworld is spent in comfort. We do not allow our numbers to overrun the lairs. Unlike the Scavengers, who couple incessantly, we mate only during the Cold Cycle. The Selection also rids us of the weak and useless among our broods, keeping our society strong and able.

'In the same way,' continued Long Snout, 'our sources of food are managed carefully.'

His words acting like a trigger, the attention of the Outer Circle rats switched immediately to the heap of gulls sprawled between the Chamberlain and the handsome forms of White Muzzle and his two sons, Red Coat and Fire Eyes.

'Yes, comrades, our Hunters plunder the nests of the white birds. But they do so sparingly. Because the kills are not excessive, the white birds remain on the world above, a constant source of tender young flesh for the Inner Circle.

'So it is with the grey-furred swimmers who emerge from the waters during the Warm Cycle. Only the weakest and least defended of their young are carried off by the slaves. There is no alarm, no fear. The No-Legs always return to breed again.'

Long Snout paused now to regard the six Scavengers who had accompanied the hunting pack on its recent foray. Quivering, terror-stricken, surrounded by fierce Hunters, the slaves huddled together, seeking some solace from their closeness. They had been to the outside world, had learned its secret. They had sensed freedom there. Their fate was clear – and imminent.

'Warriors of the Outer Circle!' cried Long Snout. 'Your source of food is also plentiful and controlled with care. The Scavengers are the slaves of our society. They carry for us and dig for us. They are also your sustenance. We allow them to breed freely and to infest their lair. They devour each other to still their hunger. But those who survive are strong and well-fed, their flesh well able to satisfy your own appetites.

'However, we must never forget, comrades, that the Scavengers are warriors like us. There are many of them. They must be watched over constantly here in the dark world and on the world above. Remember, warriors, without vigilance there will be insurrection by the Scavengers! Without vigilance there will be discovery and destruction by the Two-Legs!'

Sensing that the Assembly had come to a close, many in the Outer Circle began to shift restlessly, eager for their share of slave meat.

'Hold, comrades!' screeched Long Snout, the sheer ferocity of his cry commanding renewed attention.

'Recently, our Watchers have reported sightings of many Two-Legs – many more than usual – on the giant which steps over the waters and casts its shadow on our world. We sense danger. We fear the prying eyes of the Two-Legs. Until the danger passes, more Watchers will be posted on the outside world. Be vigilant, Watchers! Keep us informed of the Two-Legs' movements.'

The Chamberlain paused, his eyes locking on Sharp Claws. The Chief Watcher bowed curtly, signifying his acknowledgement of this new command.

'Now, comrades!' Long Snout cried with a flourish. 'The Assembly is over! Let the feasting begin!'

Chapter Four

Excitement spread through both Inner and Outer Circles, although the cause of the excitement in each case was quite different. On the platform, White Muzzle, as befitted his rank, was first to claim a gull, seizing the bird in his massive jaws and dragging its carcass closer to Red Coat and Fire Eyes. There, the King-rat and his princes proceeded to rip open the bird's soft belly and then bury their muzzles deep in its exposed and spilling stomach. In similar fashion, some of the elders led by Long Snout claimed another of the gulls, while the last was snatched away and set upon by a group of lesser Rulers. Salivating freely, the remaining members of the Inner Circle waited eagerly, ready to pounce on the carcasses once the others had taken their fill. Later, the remnants of the carcasses would be carried through to the Inner Circle lair to be picked clean by the she-rats. The bones would be chewed on, and the feathers would be used to line the Rulers' nests. Nothing would be wasted.

Events on the floor of the Common lair were no less exciting. As the Outer Circle rats looked on in anticipation, a band of Protectors closed in on the trembling Scavengers. At the head of the band were Jagged Fangs and Neck-Snapper, both skilled executioners. Once slain, three of the slaves would be claimed by the Protectors, whose lair numbered more than a hundred rats. The carcasses of the other slaves would be shared by the smaller lairs of the Hunters and Watchers.

Jagged Fangs was first to move. Jaws snapping, he leapt at the throat of the nearest slave. His victim struggled momentarily and then fell limp, blood gushing from its gaping neck. In the next instant, Neck-Snapper lunged towards another slave, but this time the intended victim was too quick. Side-stepping the attack, the slave sprang suddenly at the Protector's eyes. A great shriek of pain erupted from Neck-Snapper. Just as unexpectedly, the slave sprang away from the line of Protectors, literally propelling its body into the startled crowd of Hunters and Watchers, and then flew past them towards the tunnel that led to the outside world.

Quick to recognise their route to salvation, the other slave-rats also leapt into the crowd. Desperately clawing and gouging any who blocked their way, they, too, broke free and sped towards the tunnel. In total uproar, almost two hundred Outer Circle warriors raced after them.

'Wait!' screamed Long Snout.

The power of his command seemed to bounce off the walls of the lair, overwhelming the din from the chase. The pursuit came to a sudden halt.

'Fools!' he roared, his muzzle still dripping blood. 'By now, the Scavengers will have escaped to the outside world. It will be too light – and therefore too exposed – to hunt for them. We must wait until darkness.

'One Eye,' he turned to the Chief Hunter, 'send your best warriors when darkness falls. Bring the slaves back to me!

'Until then, more Watchers are needed above. Sharp Claws, make sure you send your best. I want reports of the slaves' movements!'

With an angry snort, the Chamberlain returned to his carcass.

Chapter Five

Long Snout had been right. The return to the Common lair of the two entrance tunnel guards, bleeding and shamefaced, confirmed that the slaves had made good their escape. Now the worst was feared for Small Face. The tiny, unsuspecting Watcher would have stood little chance against the onslaught of five vicious and desperate Scavengers.

Sharp Claws chose three Watchers for the daylight duty. To mark the start of his period of punishment, Fat One would replace Small Face at the top of the entrance tunnel. The tasks assigned to Twisted Foot and Long Ears were more wide-ranging and dangerous. Their job was to scour the island, locate the escapees and observe their activities. Before nightfall came, they would return to the underworld to report on what they had seen. Quietly, efficiently, the Hunters would then move in for the capture.

Although he was deformed and still very young, Twisted Foot was noted for his keen intelligence and for his coolheadedness in the face of danger. These qualities had impressed Sharp Claws on more than one occasion. Like Twisted Foot, Long Ears was barely two full Cycles. Although on the small side, he was nimble and quick-witted. As his name implied, his ears were exceptionally large, rendering his appearance floppy and comical. His ears, though, were also his greatest attributes, providing him with a sense of hearing that was second to none in the Watchers' lair.

Heaving and groaning, Fat One clambered up the long tunnel. He was tired and hungry, and certainly not relishing the prospect of this extra watch. Behind him, Twisted Foot and Long Ears were also apprehensive.

The mission, they knew, was important to the underworld. It would be arduous and perilous. To succeed, they had to get close to the Scavengers. The slaves had already demonstrated their prowess, had tasted the blood of fellow warriors; discovery by them would spell certain death. Exposed in the brightness of day, the Watchers would have to exercise great caution and stealth.

With a final grunt, Fat One squeezed through the gap in the flagstones, emerging into the half-darkness created by the overhanging debris. Twisted Foot and Long Ears appeared moments later. Soon, all three were sniffing through the rubble in search of Small Face. A trail of fresh blood led them to a dark corner of the monastery and a narrow crack at the base of the stonework where the walls met.

Twisted Foot peered excitedly into the crack. 'Small Face?' he cried. 'Are you there?'

A weak, muffled squeal came in response. Some moments elapsed, and then slowly, cautiously, Small Face stepped into the light. Shaken and hurt, he blinked furiously in recognition of his three companions. Blood still seeped from an angry gash along his side.

'I – I'm sorry,' he whimpered. 'I couldn't stop them.'

Fat One nuzzled into Small Face. 'You did well to stay alive, comrade,' he consoled.

'Return to the lair now,' Twisted Foot said softly. 'Tell Sharp Claws what happened. Rest up. We'll take over here.'

As Small Face began his painful descent to the underworld and Fat One concealed himself beneath the rubble, Twisted Foot and Long Ears set off gingerly from the relative safety of the ruins. Needing a vantage point, they travelled in parallel paths up to the high ground on the east of Inchgarvie. From there, they would have a clear view of all sides of the island.

They climbed with their backs to the railway bridge, fearfully aware that their progress might be observed by any number of inquisitive Two-Legs. Fortunately, the terrain was strewn with rocks, which provided plenty of cover for the two Watchers. Darting from the shadow of one boulder to the next, each paused, listened, watched and then repeated the manoeuvre. It was some time, therefore, before they reached the top of the slope. Nervous, breathing heavily, they crouched side by side, Long Ears pointing to the west and Twisted Foot to the east. Now utterly exposed, they pressed their bodies flat to the ground.

Long Ears craned his neck to peer down the slope that he had just ascended. His gaze swept over the monastery and the jagged strip of rock that jutted into the sea behind it, and then shifted up to the immense orange-red superstructure of the Forth Bridge. Just as the Chamberlain had warned – indeed, as Long Ears himself had observed on previous watches – gangs of Two-Legs were active along the length of the bridge. Thankfully, the presence of the Watchers seemed to have gone unnoticed by those closest to Inchgarvie.

Long Ears resumed his search of this side of the island, scanning the craggy slopes to the north and south, examining and re-examining the ruins of the monastery. Except for the occasional flap of a white bird, there was no movement.

Twisted Foot's scrutiny took in the steep rock-faces which dropped directly in front of him and to his left and right. This was where the white birds dwelt – and where the Hunters stalked in the dark of night. With gulls now taking off, wheeling and landing in rotation, there was a great deal of activity among the recesses and crannies, but so far no sign of the fugitive slaves. Further ahead of him, he could see the flat, moss-grown roof of the concrete gun emplacement which perched on the island's promontory. Beyond that was the empty sea and the faint outline of another larger island on the horizon.

Patiently, as still as the ground beneath them, the Watchers waited for their quarry to emerge.

Chapter Six

Although not particularly cold, the day was a dull one. Oppressive grey clouds filled the sky. Rain was not far off. The sea was also dirty grey and sluggish, its surface barely ruffled by the light morning breeze. Familiar sounds vied with each other along the estuary: the monotonous growl of traffic on the road bridge, drowned suddenly by the rush of an express train over the nearby rail bridge; the distant, steady thrum of passing vessels, punctured by the shrieks of swooping gulls.

Crouched on the crest of the island, Twisted Foot and Long Ears attempted to block out the sounds of life around them, to concentrate on the terrain immediately below, straining to catch some unfamiliar noise or to glimpse some unusual activity. Both came in rapid succession. A flurry of movement at the foot of the eastern slope was followed by the raucous call of a gull in distress and then the sharp crack of wings beaten against rock. Hearing the gull's cry in the same instant as his companion, Long Ears shifted round quickly to join Twisted Foot in his search of the lower slope.

Flapping and croaking, the gull tumbled out from the rocks. A slave-rat clung to its back, while another tugged furiously on the bird's neck. Others danced around the melee, dodging the wing swipes, waiting to pounce. The struggle was over in seconds. Its gullet now torn open, the bird uttered a last wheezing rattle and then became still.

Another flurry of activity ensued as the five slaves proceeded to half-carry, half-drag their prey away from the rocks and across to the flatter, more defensible surface of the gun emplacement's roof. Once there, the onslaught was violent and noisy. Growling incessantly, clawing and tearing through the feathers, greedily devouring great chunks of bird flesh, the Scavengers seemed totally unconcerned about any dangers that might lurk near them, only occasionally raising their heads to glance about or to regard with lazy indifference the circle of gulls which hovered high above, sending down screams of empty challenge.

Twisted Foot and Long Ears watched the slaves' activities with considerable envy. Neither had eaten for some time, nor had they ever tasted the succulent flesh of the white birds; that pleasure was only enjoyed by the ruling Circle. In their eagerness to obtain a clearer view of the carnage, both stretched out over the ridge, but a casual glance up the slope by one of the Scavengers had them promptly shrinking back. Twisted Foot, his heart thudding, knew that their incaution might prove fatal. They were a long way from the underworld. The slaves were fast: if they gave chase, Long Ears might just make it to safety, but his own halting pace would not be enough. With growing dread, he peeked over the edge. The Scavengers were still on the roof, their attention completely absorbed in the gull's entrails. Twisted Foot drew back again, this time breathing easier.

His relief was short-lived. Only moments later, Long Ears was prodding him urgently.

'Look!' his companion whispered. 'Over there!'

Twisted Foot followed the direction of Long Ears' gaze. Not far off, a small, brightly coloured Two-Legs vessel was cutting through the placid water at speed, the sound of its engine overpowered for the time being by the thunder of a passing train. The vessel was heading straight for the weather-stained wooden jetty on the south side of the island.

Twisted Foot had observed Two-Legs visitors on several occasions in the past, but never from a place so open and vulnerable as this one. His first impulse was to scuttle in panic down to the monastery, where he and Long Ears could join Fat One in the security of the shadowy ruins, but the impulse was denied by a superior power. Their orders from the underworld were to maintain vigilance over the fugitive slaves: that was what they must continue to do. If we keep as flat and as still as possible, Twisted Foot began to reason, we may not be seen by the Two-Legs. Besides, the visitors hardly ever ventured up to the high ground, usually keeping to the narrow footway which ran round the lower parts of the island. His panic subsided for the moment.

The two occupants of the lime-green dinghy stepped up on to the jetty's greasy surface. Wearing bright orange lifesaving jackets on top of shiny yellow anoraks, their appearance matched the gaudiness of the dinghy. Both were bareheaded, clean-shaven and young. One carried a plastic box containing a powerful drill; the other a satchel full of short aluminium tubes. Theirs was no casual visit to Inchgarvie: they had business to perform.

Hardly glancing to their left or right, the two men set off immediately for the crest of the island. Regretting their earlier decision to stay put, the Watchers now sunk closer to the edge of the ridge, ready to slip down the steep face of the northern slope. The visitors had climbed only a few steps when a chorus of shouts and whistles from the direction of the bridge halted their progress – and at the same time sent Twisted Foot and Long Ears scrambling over the edge.

Attracted by the din of the hovering gulls, about a dozen workers on the bridge had gathered to watch the slave-rats' feast. Except for the occasional murmur, they had observed this spectacle in silent fascination. The arrival of the two men on the island now provoked a more excited reaction from them. As the workers shouted, stamped and gesticulated, one of the visitors, mistaking these actions as signs of a jocular greeting, grinned and raised his arm to wave back.

'No!' cried a worker. 'Over there!' He pointed down to the gun emplacement and then cupped his hands round his mouth. 'Rats!' he boomed. 'Hunners o' them!'

The worker's exaggeration ringing in their ears, the men moved round the slope with mixed feelings of curiosity and trepidation. In moments, they had a clear view of the oblong concrete building and the rat pack on its roof. They stood quite still, open-mouthed, not daring to get closer. Whoops and catcalls continued to rain down from the bridge.

Undeterred by the constant shrieks of the gulls high above them or by the clamour of the equally distant Two-Legs, the Scavengers had proceeded to gorge on the flesh of their victim. The freedom that had been snatched so recently from their captors; their daring escape from the very jaws of death; the excitement of the kill; the scent of fresh blood in their nostrils: all these sensations combined to intoxicate them. They felt strong, invincible. The sudden appearance only yards away of the brightly clad Two-Legs brought a swift challenge to this new-found confidence.

All five Scavengers stopped abruptly to watch the visitors. Like the visitors, they remained stock-still, unable to decide on their next action. The strange giants showed no outward sign of threat, but, instinctively, the Scavengers sensed immense danger from their presence. A loose rock dislodged by one of the visitors rolled noisily down the slope, breaking the stalemate. Each of the Scavengers flew off in a different direction, scurrying down from the roof and slipping through one of the emplacement's high slit holes into the safety offered by the building's dark interior. The men stared for some moments at the bloody mess of bones and feathers abandoned by the rats. Then they returned hastily to the jetty. To a fresh chorus of cheers and whistles from the bridge, the dinghy's engine spurted into action. The two visitors left the island just as quickly as they had come.

From their precarious perch near the top of the northern slope, Twisted Foot and Long Ears had witnessed the flight of the slaves and had listened to the sounds of the retreating visitors. Some time later, they observed the dispersal of the gang of Two-Legs on the bridge. Cautiously, they crept back to their original position. A steady drizzle had broken free from the heavy skies, accentuating the greyness and bleakness of the scene below them. The rest of the day was uneventful. The slaves remained hidden in the gun emplacement. There were no more visitors to the island. When dusk fell, the Watchers picked their way carefully down the wet slope. They were tired, cold and very hungry – but they had much to tell Sharp Claws.

Chapter Seven

Neck-Snapper winced. He curled more tightly in his nest, seeking some relief from the excruciating pain that stabbed into his head. He had come off badly in the incident with the fleeing slave-rat. The attack had left a deep score down the right side of his muzzle and a gaping, bloody hole where his right eye had been. A lost eye was normally an impressive battle scar, one which drew looks of admiration and envy from the younger warriors, but the whole of the Outer Circle knew that his injury had been caused by a lowly Scavenger. He had been humiliated in front of them. His failing had led to the slaves' escape. He would never again be trusted to carry out executions; guard duty would be his lot from now on. Fuelled by the blinding pain, anger and resentment boiled within him, on the verge of exploding. The appearance in the Protectors' lair of the Chief Watcher and his crippled comrade triggered the waiting explosion.

With a great roar, Neck-Snapper leapt from his nest and charged at the Watchers. Twisted Foot cowered back in alarm, but old Sharp Claws stood his ground, arching his back and facing square on to the crazed and drooling attacker. Others in the lair had also leapt from their slumber and were now assembling behind Neck-Snapper. The crowd quickly parted, however, as the burly form of Broken Tail pushed through from the back.

'Enough!' cried the Chief Protector. 'Get back to your nests!' he ordered.

The onlookers slunk away; none dared defiance. Even Neck-Snapper, in spite of his demented state, could not ignore the command. Before retreating, he directed a final menacing glance at Sharp Claws.

Twisted Foot shivered, recognising the meaning of that look. There will be another time and another place, comrade, it said, when we will meet alone.

Broken Tail now turned his attention to the intruders. 'Why have you come here?' he rasped. 'You know that this is the time of rest.'

'We have news from the outside for the Chamberlain,' Sharp Claws responded quickly. 'Grave news,' he emphasised.

Broken Tail pondered for some moments. He had little regard for the Watchers, but he did have some respect for Sharp Claws' wisdom and experience. The news must surely be important, he judged; important enough to rouse the Chamberlain.

'Come,' he commanded. Then he wheeled round and led the Watchers to a tunnel in the centre of the lair's left wall.

Still shaken by Neck-Snapper's sudden onslaught, Twisted Foot stayed close to the Chief Watcher as they headed towards the tunnel. The surroundings were new to him. Peeking round nervously, he could see that the lair was much bigger than his own one. Although many bodies occupied the nests, he guessed that the place was not as full as it would be normally at this time. Security in the underworld had been increased substantially since the escape of the slave-rats, with extra guards having been posted along the entrance to the Common lair and outside the tunnel leading to the Scavengers' lair. Here in the Protectors' lair, guards also squatted round the tunnel now directly ahead of the Watchers. A last, timid glance backwards gave Twisted Foot a blurred glimpse of another group of Protectors at the far end of the lair, but he had little time to think about or question their purpose.

They moved quickly through the long, low tunnel, emerging into another spacious lair, home of the Inner Circle. Rows of comfortable, feather-lined nests took up the greater part of the floor area. Some of their occupants looked up sleepily, blinked several times, yawned and then settled down again. Rainwater glistened on the wall to the left, collecting in a shallow pool in a corner of the lair.

Twisted Foot watched the slumbering forms of the Rulers with much envy in his heart. Compared with the luxury of this place, life in the Watchers' lair was cramped and austere. He had faced considerable danger that day. He was still cold and bedraggled from his time on the outside world. He had had no rest, and hunger gnawed at his belly. These experiences, he realised, were alien to the Rulers. Here there was comfort and absolute security, and the certainty of food and rest. For the first time in his short life, Twisted Foot was conscious that he was becoming resentful of the favoured lifestyle of the Inner Circle. The resentment that had crept into his thoughts was abruptly ousted by fear, however, when the Chamberlain rose from his sleep.

Long Snout was wide awake and on his feet. His eyes glowed fiercely. There was anger in his voice.

'What is the meaning of this disturbance?' he hissed, towering over the visitors.

Broken Tail replied for the group. 'News, Chamberlain,' he bowed, 'from the outside world.'

'Well?' Long Snout asked sharply, directing his stare at the Chief Watcher.

Just as they had been reported to him only a short time ago, Sharp Claws recounted the events witnessed by Twisted Foot and Long Ears. The Chamberlain listened carefully. Occasionally, he turned his cold gaze to Twisted Foot, causing the young Watcher's heart to kick each time. When Sharp Claws had finished, Long Snout remained silent for a few moments longer and then turned again to look at Twisted Foot.

'You are certain that you were not seen by the Two-Legs?' he asked.

'Y-yes, certain, Chamberlain.' Twisted Foot stumbled over the words, fighting to control the tremble in his voice and body.

'Good,' pronounced the Chamberlain.

After some further deliberation, he spoke in urgent tones to Broken Tail: 'Go quickly! Take word to One Eye. Tell him that the Hunters must remain in the underworld. Let the fugitives enjoy their freedom – for the short while that they will have it!' The last words were spoken with venom.

As Broken Tail scurried off, Long Snout now directed his commands to Sharp Claws: 'Send up your Watchers when the next light comes. The Two-Legs will return for the Scavengers. Let me know what takes place.

'This young warrior,' he indicated towards Twisted Foot, 'should lead the watch. He shows some promise.'

Twisted Foot was too tired to react to the Chamberlain's praise or to consider the consequences of another daylight watch. Completely drained, he followed Sharp Claws out of the lair. As he passed the line of nests, he caught sight of a sleepy-eyed White Muzzle, curled up snugly between the dozing figures of two red-furred she-rats. The King-rat's hefty girth and shining coat exuded health and wellbeing. Dark resentment returned to Twisted Foot's thoughts.

Chapter Eight

The small dog sprang effortlessly up to the jetty. It remained there, surveying the island, sniffing in the scents of this strange, new territory. Its owner stepped up from the boat to join the dog in its scrutiny. The man was tall and lean and slightly stooped. The wind coming from the east tugged at his mane of grey hair and sent billows running through his loose overalls and shabby green jacket. An unlit pipe protruded from his close-cropped silvery beard.

Skilfully, the man struck a match and placed it in the bowl of the pipe, alternately sucking hard on the newly glowing embers and exhaling great puffs of thick smoke, which were immediately snatched up and dispersed by the wind. The man kept his gaze on the island, exploring the contours, seeking out movement. His eyes were also grey, and hooded like a bird's. His face bore a calmness, an expression that said: I've seen it all before; there are no surprises left. Unhurriedly, he set off for the footpath on his right. His height dwarfed the dog, which now trotted lightly behind him, its nose pointing close to the ground.

As he walked, the canvas bag which hung from the man's angular shoulders swayed and rattled in the breeze. Although it was shaped like a plumber's satchel, Tam Proudfoot's bag contained only the paraphernalia of his particular trade: a large torch; an array of traps with strong steel springs and deadly shutters; poisons of all kinds, in bottles, tins and small cardboard boxes; and foul-smelling offal, wrapped in Clingfilm and kept in an old biscuit tin. The tools of the rat-catcher's trade were crude and simple, but always effective.

Tam reached the gun emplacement, climbed the rocks at its rear and then stepped down on to its roof. The little Jack Russell terrier sped past him, anxious to inspect the bird remains scattered over the roof. Another gull had fallen victim to the rats during the night. Tam's examination of the carcasses was much less thorough than the dog's close-up sniff. He sucked on the pipe again, looking out to the swelling sea, a hint of humour in his eyes. The visitors to Inchgarvie the day before had returned to spread alarm in the community about the hundreds of fierce rats which infested the island. He had lived here all his life; rats were his business. The story, he knew, was exaggerated. Not deliberately, of course, but magnified as usual by peoples' natural horror of the creatures. There were rats on the island, that was true; but he was confident that they, too, were visitors, not inhabitants. Tam took a final pull at the pipe and then slid the heavy bag to his feet.

'Right, Nipper!' he shouted to the dog. 'Let's dae our job!'

Tam went to the edge of the roof and crouched down. He was now directly above the building's entrance. The stale, damp smell which rose up on the breeze confirmed the dankness within. Tam placed his hand on the flat of Nipper's head.

'Down there, boy,' he said, using his other hand to point at the ground outside the entrance.

The dog understood. It leapt from the roof, landing lightly and twisting round to face the entrance.

'In there, boy!' Tam shouted. 'In there, Nipper!'

Ears pricked, tensed, the dog stepped cautiously into the gloomy interior. Tam stood back from the edge. After a short period of silence, the place erupted suddenly in a cacophony of loud yelps, squeals and fierce growling. Rats began to spring from the slit holes, scrambling up to the roof and then bounding away to the safety of the rocks. Tam counted four fleeing bodies. The yapping from below had subsided, but the growls persisted. He looked down to see Nipper emerging backwards from the building, a fifth rat caught by the neck between the dog's small, powerful jaws. Nipper shook the rat violently, hammering its struggling body repeatedly against the ground. The squirming ceased abruptly as life went out of the creature.

'Here, boy!' called Tam. 'Up here, wee boy!'

Nipper carried the prize up to the roof, dropped it at Tam's feet, and then danced and yelped with delight.

'Good boy, Nipper,' said Tam as he stooped down and picked up the limp rat by its tail.

He peered at the body. Black, he remarked to himself. Not like the local ones. Better fed, too. Probably from some ship that's been to foreign parts. West Africa, maybe, or the Mediterranean. A visitor, right enough. With a sudden heave, he tossed the rat far out into the sea.

Tam chuckled as he set about his next task. 'Hundreds o' rats!' he laughed.

He knelt down and selected four traps from the bag, together with the biscuit tin. Warning the dog to stay back, he placed the traps at intervals along the roof. He returned to each trap, priming it with a chunk of pungent offal and carefully setting its stiff shutter. Carrying the bag in one hand and the tin of bait in the other, he left the roof and entered the gun emplacement. Nipper followed him, but kept at a discrete distance.

Tam crouched down again, placing both bag and tin on the ground. He pulled the heavy torch from the bag and snapped it on. The solid beam cut through the darkness, revealing rubble, cobwebs, dried bird droppings, some feathers, but little else. Tam nodded. The absence of a nest confirmed his theory about the rats' origins. He tossed the last piece of offal into the centre of the building and then covered it with the contents of a box of poison pellets.

With the torch and bait tin stowed away, and with the bag slung back on his shoulder, Tam stepped out of the gloom.

'That'll do it for the now,' he said to the waiting dog.

The rat-catcher re-lit his pipe, stood puffing for some moments and then returned slowly to the jetty. The tiny dog pranced playfully at his heels.

As the noise of the rat-catcher's boat became a distant drone, the Watchers at the top of the island relaxed only slightly. Danger still lurked in the rocks below. The Scavengers were well concealed down there, but they could re-emerge at any moment.

Twisted Foot and Long Ears had left the underworld at dawn. Shortly afterwards, they had watched the events unfold at the gun emplacement, this time without the noisy accompaniment of the Two-Legs on the bridge. With its resounding cry and strange, mottled coat, the Four-Legs held them mesmerised. Neither had seen a creature like it before. The ferocity of its attack on the slave-rat was something that they would not forget easily.

The Watchers now tried to concentrate on the lower part of the slope leading to the gun emplacement, but the tantalising smell of offal, carried up to them on the wind, kept drawing their attention back to the building's roof. The food left by the Two-Legs puzzled them. Whatever its purpose, though, however enticing it seemed, they regarded its presence with significant mistrust.

The Scavengers were not so sceptical. One by one, lured by the pungent scent, their small dark heads appeared above the rocks. All four moved forward stealthily until they crouched together on the edge of the roof. After some moments of hesitation, the bravest (or greediest) of them darted to the first of the traps and snatched at the bait. The bait would not give. The Scavenger tugged again. This time the trap's shutter hammered down with a loud, sharp crack, crushing the Scavenger's neck and driving a steel spike through the back of its brain. The others fled from the roof. It was not long, though, before they were back again, first devouring the offal that had eluded their dead companion and then moving on to examine the next trap. In seconds, another victim had been claimed, and the process began again. On this occasion, despite the more cautious, joint approach of the two survivors, a swift double-kill was scored by the snapping shutter.

The young Watchers had flinched each time a trap shut. For a long time afterwards, they gazed down on the corpses of the fugitives, still marvelling at the cunning and treachery of the Two-Legs, equally astounded by the utter foolishness of the Scavengers. The excitement was now over; the immediate danger gone. Another long day on the outside world loomed ahead of them.

Chapter Nine

It was a Sunday, the last day of September. The estuary was quiet. Passing trains still rushed through the calm, but the intervals between their intrusions were longer. On the bridge, the intense activity of the past week had dwindled to a handful of strolling maintenance men, their orange helmets bobbing just above the fretwork of the central parapet. Around midday, the wind dropped to a gentle whisper, pale blue sky peeked from gaps between the clouds, and the sun appeared overhead, tentatively at first, and then strong and dominating, as if making a last, defiant stand against the encroaching chill of autumn.

As its brightness grew, the sun seemed to invigorate the landscape, transforming the immobile grey sea into sheets of dancing, glistening ripples; bringing a new sheen to the dull paintwork of the rail bridge; re-discovering and enriching the yellows and greens of the fields and woods on either side of the river. Sunshine also spread over the little island in the lee of the imposing bridge, penetrating the gloomy interior of the monastery, where Fat One slumbered among the debris, and glancing off the backs of Twisted Foot and Long Ears, who crouched on the high ground like twin, ridged boulders.

Twisted Foot welcomed the warmth on his back; it made the waiting easier. For the first time since the killing, he looked away from the corpse-strewn roof. The stillness of the scene below had been disturbed only once, when a lone gull had alighted briefly to gloat over the contorted bodies of its foes. As it flew off, the cries uttered by the bird had been mocking and contemptuous.

Twisted Foot's gaze swept over the shimmering sea and took in the newly brightened shoreline to the north. Somehow, the shore seemed closer than before. Behind it, trees, fields, hills: all had become more distinct. Were there societies like his one over there? he asked himself. Societies which lived underground and hunted above? Societies constantly under threat from the Two-Legs? Societies with Watchers and Hunters and Protectors, and fearsome Rulers like Long Snout? He remembered how the Chamberlain had looked the night before: awesome, angry, spitting out orders. He remembered his own feelings of smallness and insignificance. But Long Snout's harsh ways had brought success, he admitted. Thanks to Long Snout, the Two-Legs had left, satisfied; the Dark World remained undiscovered. Discipline and vigilance had been observed. Discipline and vigilance ruled their lives.

The Watcher's thoughts returned to the adjacent shore. He wondered if the societies there were ruled with the same harshness. Perhaps not. Perhaps the menace of the Two-Legs was less. He sensed space, openness, distance from the Two-Legs, food in plenty. Perhaps...

'Perhaps there is a better life over there,' said the soft voice close to him.

Startled, Twisted Foot looked quickly at his companion. It was as if Long Ears had crept into his mind and listened to his inner thoughts. He felt uneasy, insecure.

'I – I don't know,' he stammered at length.

For the remainder of the watch, Twisted Foot focused his gaze on the terrain below, but his thoughts kept drifting back to the land across the estuary.

Chapter Ten

It was Narrow Back who brought the news to the underworld. Breathless, his tongue hanging sideways from an open mouth, he came scampering through the Watchers' lair in search of Sharp Claws.

'The giant!' he cried, his eyes wide with excitement. 'The giant is awake!'

Sharp Claws rose from his nest. He had woken immediately from a sound sleep. Despite his age, he looked bright and alert.

'What is it, Watcher?' he asked.

Narrow Back scurried back and forward, impatient, agitated. 'The giant,' he repeated. 'The giant in the water,' he expanded, as if the elaboration told everything.

'What about it?' Sharp Claws said quietly. Narrow Back was easily aroused, not noted for his calm and intelligent thinking.

The Watcher's thin body shook with impatience. 'The giant awakes!' he exclaimed. 'It – it glows brightly! It grows larger! Come! Hurry!' The words gushed out in a torrent of excitement.

Not waiting for a response, his tongue still lolling wildly, Narrow Back rushed out of the lair. With a sigh, Sharp Claws followed briskly behind him.

Exhausted after a third daylight vigil, Twisted Foot peered drowsily at the departing figure of the Chief Watcher. He shifted slightly in the nest, careful not to disturb the young she-rat who pressed close to him, still fast asleep. Others in the lair were also peeking out from their nests. Some had already forsaken the warmth to confer in soft murmurs on the floor of the lair. Like them, Twisted Foot found it difficult to put any shape or substance to the cause of Narrow Back's agitation. Together with Long Ears and Fat One, he had returned to the underworld in the early evening, leaving the skinny Watcher to take up the night post at the monastery. That was some time ago. It would be dark up there now. The hunting pack and its Watchers would be about their work.

Twisted Foot yawned, dismissing the notion of joining the huddle on the floor. He was very tired. It had been another long day on the high ground. The rat-catcher had come back with his strangely coloured Four-Legs. He had been pleased with his examination of the traps and his search of the gun emplacement's interior. Long Snout had also been pleased: smug was perhaps a better description. He had decreed that the Hunters should venture above ground again after an absence of two nights. Until Narrow Back's noisy entrance, it seemed that life – above and below ground – had returned to normal.

Twisted Foot yawned again. Whatever had upset Narrow Back would be explained soon enough, he decided. He burrowed his muzzle into the she-rat's warm, soft belly. Soon, the rhythmic breathing of Watcher and mate was as one.

'Look sharp, Watchers!' The cry came like a crash of thunder in the stillness of the lair.

Immediately, bodies spilled from the nests, heading quickly for the tunnel opening. Sharp Claws squatted there, grim-faced, blocking their progress. The two Watchers who had accompanied the hunting pack were on either side of him, their expressions equally grim.

'Hold!' Sharp Claws roared. 'There will be no Assembly yet! But gather close to me, I have much news for you.'

He moved into the centre of the lair, allowing the crowd to form round him. Even Small Face, still weak after his encounter with the slave-rats, left his nest to join the she-rats and youngsters at the back of the crowd. Excited murmurs filled the lair.

Sharp Claws rose up on his hindquarters until his full height towered over the audience.

'Quiet!' he commanded. The buzz ceased abruptly.

'Comrades,' the old Watcher began, 'a grave event has taken place on the world above, an event which threatens the existence of our society.' He paused, giving the audience time to grasp the full weight of his words. He looked suddenly tired and sorrowful.

'For many days, we have watched the Two-Legs busy themselves on the giant which looks down on our world. The purpose of their activity is now known to us. Lit by countless fires along the length of its great body, the giant began to glow in the darkness. After a while, its brightness filled the sky, turning the darkness of our world into light. Such was the brightness that every rock, every stone, every piece of ground glowed like the giant. The Hunters and the brave Watchers with them were forced to conceal themselves. The white birds were also startled by the brightness, and many of them flew from their roosts. Even when darkness returned to the giant a short time ago, the few remaining birds proved too restless for the Hunters to make their kills.'

Sharp Claws' expression grew grim again.

'Comrades,' he continued, 'we do not know why the Two-Legs caused this evil. We do not know if they will cause it again. We fear that they will. At this moment, the elders of the Inner Circle are considering what steps should be taken to protect our society from this grave threat. The Assembly will be called when they have decided. Remain in the lair until that time.'

Long after Sharp Claws had departed to await the emergence of the elders, many of the Watchers remained huddled together, discussing the news and its implications. At their centre was Narrow Back, who had returned, still wide-eyed, from the night watch to tell and re-tell the story of the awakening giant. The story grew more elaborate with each re-telling.

'There was another strange event up there,' Narrow Back mentioned at one point. He paused for effect, scanning the faces of his companions.

'It was some time after Sharp Claws left me to report to the Chamberlain. I decided to creep down to the place where the rocks narrow and reach out to the water. You know the place I mean. I wanted to take a closer look at the giant's fires, you see. As I got nearer, though, I could see that a familiar figure had reached the place before me.'

He stopped again, this time waiting for a response.

'Get on with it, Narrow Back!' boomed Fat One. 'Tell us who you saw.'

'It was Broken Tail,' he whispered. 'The Chief Protector.'

There were looks of puzzlement among the audience.

'The thing is, you see,' he continued rapidly, 'the mystery is, I – I don't know where he came from. I'm sure – absolutely certain – that he didn't come up the tunnel. Then he disappeared, just vanished.'

There were further looks of puzzlement.

'A mystery,' said Narrow Back. 'A real mystery.'

Something – a faint memory, a blurred image – nudged Twisted Foot's thoughts. He tried hard, but the image wouldn't focus.

Chapter Eleven

The tremors travelled down from the high ground, spreading through the underworld and causing dust to fall from the roof of the Common lair. The occupants of the other lairs became still: a thousand pairs of slit eyes looked upwards. A faint rumble came in the wake of the tremors. The disturbance stopped briefly and then began again, the tremors renewed, stronger, the distant whirr grown to a deep whine. Youngsters abandoned their games, rushing back to their mothers' sides. Protectors at the pool looked up, startled, from their lapping. Hordes of Scavengers surged towards the tunnel of their lair, panic in their actions. In the lair of the Inner Circle, the elders broke off from their debate, fear in their eyes. Long Snout seethed with anger. 'Two-Legs!' He spat out the word.

On the world above, the two brightly clad young men had returned to complete their business. They occupied the crest of the island, now confident that the threat of rats had been eradicated. The heavy drill operated by one of them bit through the rock with a jarring screech, a rush of dust and sparks marking its path. The other man hammered metal tubes into the holes made by the drill. Soon, a shiny frame began to take shape.

In the course of the men's work, more visitors arrived on the island. One of them installed an electrical circuit, while the others unloaded about a dozen large cartons and then proceeded to fill the upright tubes with the contents of the cartons. Their final tasks were to seal the tubes and to cover and secure the frame with sheets of strong polythene.

The time taken to erect and prime the contraption lasted four hours. By mid-afternoon, all of the visitors had gone from the island.

The Assembly was called at long last. He-rats streamed into the Common lair. Many were shocked and jittery, the continual pounding from above having taken its toll. The Protectors outside the Scavengers' lair rested uneasily after prolonged efforts to keep the rioting slaves at bay. As they stepped up to the platform, the members of the Inner Circle also looked uneasy. This would be no ordinary Assembly. There would be no stirring words to fortify the hearts of the Outer Circle; no great feast of bird flesh ahead for the bellies of the Rulers.

Long Snout dominated the centre of the platform, as cold and grave as ever.

'Comrades of the Secret World!' he began solemnly: there had been no need to call for silence. 'These latest intrusions by the Two-Legs have confirmed our worst fears. The threat is upon us. For the first time in many Cycles, our society faces discovery. Remember, comrades, with discovery comes destruction. But discovery may yet be avoided if we are careful, if we are more vigilant and disciplined.'

The Chamberlain scoured the tense faces below him.

'Yes, comrades, harsh measures will be needed to preserve our secrecy.'

He turned to his left and then to his right, each time regarding the Rulers who crouched close to him. Some were older and more gnarled than Long Snout himself. Finally, he swivelled round to look directly at White Muzzle.

'The King-rat and the elders have decided what measures will be taken,' he announced, turning back to the Outer Circle. 'As of this day, the Cold Cycle will begin! The hunting packs will cease! Mating may commence!'

A faint murmur rose up from his audience. Many in the Outer Circle relaxed visibly.

'Understand this, comrades!' Long Snout snapped. 'The Cold Cycle will last as long as the threat to our world remains. That may be a long time – much longer than has been experienced for many generations. During that time, we must be sparing with our food supply. We must control our numbers carefully.'

The audience was suddenly silent again.

'During that time, there will be Selections – frequent Selections. We have decreed that none will be exempt from them. The Selections will be complete!'

Long afterwards, in the quiet of the Watchers' lair, Twisted Foot was roused gently by Small Face.

'Twisted Foot,' his tiny companion whispered. 'What did Long Snout mean when he said that the Selections would be complete?'

An eerie voice came from the nest next to them.

'It means, comrade,' said Long Ears, 'that for as long as they decree we shall keep on breeding our young for the mouths of the Rulers.

'Just like the Scavengers do for us,' he added.

Twisted Foot's heart jumped. Again, it was as if Long Ears had been listening to his innermost thoughts.

Part Two:

The Plot

Chapter Twelve

Some called it the Eighth Wonder of the World; they were struck by its imposing splendour and majesty. Some were more impressed by the mechanics; a great feat of human ingenuity, an engineering miracle, they enthused. The statistics held others in awe: the many tons of steel which clothed its vast structure; the countless rivets which fixed the steel in place; the endless gallons of paint which kept corrosion at bay. A rare few found ugliness in the colossus: a rich man's folly, a vanity, it had broken men's backs in the making, had sent not a few plummeting to their deaths. To admirers and denigrators alike, though, the old bridge was a daily familiarity, a fixture unconcerned with the passage of time or mortal lives, a constant in a world of change and turmoil.

For a hundred years, the Forth Railway Bridge had straddled the banks of the estuary, a permanent bond between the ancient burgh of Queensferry to the south and its identically named neighbour across the river. A century of sunrises had woken the giant, beginning afresh its sovereignty of the landscape. Across the decades, it had looked down imperiously on the ebbs and flows of human development: unflinching in 1939 when the Luftwaffe came so very close to success; indifferent to the demise of the sturdy steam locomotives which had crawled, chugging and panting, through its massive belly; still defiant in 1964 when a rival road bridge sprang up on its horizon: a sleek, modern pretender to its vast kingdom. Now, in 1990, its centennial year, the old monarch remained aloof from the rush of activity along its mighty arches.

To celebrate the centenary of the bridge, the communities on both sides of the Firth of Forth had united to organise a series of local events. From March through to early October, there had been, among other activities, exhibitions, concerts and open-air plays. But the major events were reserved for the last day of the celebrations on Sunday, October 14th, the anniversary of the bridge's official opening. A million spectators would converge on North and South Queensferry that day. Above the estuary, there would be air displays and parachute demonstrations. In the towns, pipe bands and street performers would entertain the crowds. At night, the beams from powerful searchlights would split the sky above the bridge, just as they had done during the anxious War years. For the climax of the celebration, the giant silhouette of the bridge would be seen against a backdrop of cascading rainbows from a spectacular fireworks display. In the midst of this splendour, a switch would be thrown to inaugurate the permanent floodlighting of the bridge, its final birthday tribute.

With seven days still remaining, the preparations for the finale were well advanced. The logistics needed to cope with the expected influx of sightseers to the area had been worked out carefully. On the following Sunday, the local communities would be sealed off from normal traffic; temporary car parks on their outskirts had been designated for incoming motorists. Special trains would disgorge other visitors on either side of the bridge, but, for the first time in a hundred years, no trains would cross the bridge that day. After weeks of intensive work, the floodlighting was in place. A trial switch-on during the previous week had been successful. Now, the contractors were busy securing the miles of cable that had been threaded through the intricate arches of the bridge.

Some concern had arisen about the arrangements for the fireworks display. The organisers intended to mount the display from Inchgarvie, the small island close to the foot of the bridge's central arch. The fireworks would be stored on the island and set off by remote control from a safe vantage point. These plans were put in jeopardy, however, when it was discovered that the island was inhabited by rats. At first, there were reports of a huge colony of the creatures. Later, though, the local pest control expert advised the organisers that the scare was unfounded. In his view, Inchgarvie was incapable of sustaining a sizeable population of rats. His search of the island had revealed only a handful of stray 'visitors', and these had been swiftly exterminated. The fireworks extravaganza could go ahead as planned.

Chapter Thirteen

The two youngsters wrestled in a corner of the lair. There was much grunting and growling and scratching as they rolled over on the hard ground. Little puffs of dust were thrown up by the impact of their squirming bodies. Jaws open and fangs showing, each tried to gain purchase on the other's throat. Both were almost fully grown, their grappling more in earnest than in play. A sudden lunge by one of the youngsters sent his opponent sprawling backwards. Another lunge, and needle-like teeth sank momentarily into soft, exposed flesh, bringing the contest to an end. The loser uttered a sharp squeal of pain and then scrambled up and fled from the scene. With a great show of pride, the victor shook the dust from his fur and licked his fangs before strutting triumphantly back to the nest.

Twisted Foot nudged the youngster affectionately. This was his only son. Lithe, sleek and perfectly formed, he would reach his first full Cycle soon, ready to join the ranks of the Watchers. Sharp Claws would name him then. Soft-Mover, thought Twisted Foot; that name best described the youngster's sharpness and agility. Soft-Mover was a good name for a Watcher; it signified stealth and cunning. There was no hint of mockery in it, unlike the names that he and many of his companions had been given. Yes, Soft-Mover was a good name; a suitable name for a Hunter, perhaps. If the youngster proved his abilities, he might one day be accepted into the Hunters' lair. That would be a proud moment.

His prowess having been acknowledged by his father's nuzzling, the youngster now leapt away and began to creep along the neighbouring nests in search of another challenge. As he watched his son go, poignant memories of the last Cold Cycle returned to Twisted Foot. His mate had provided him with three sons and a daughter, all healthy and well-formed, his first offspring. The subsequent Selection had been particularly cruel, though, depriving him of all but one of the brood. The other young ones, although unblemished, had been wrenched away by Broken Tail and his thugs. There had been no cause, no justification. It had been a bitter blow, but in time he had come to accept the disappointment, to reconcile the indiscriminate and brutal nature of the process with the needs of the society. He had looked forward to the next Cold Cycle, to the next brood, and to another opportunity to raise strong and intelligent youngsters like Soft-Mover. Now, however, that dream had also been wrenched away by the Chamberlain's cruel proclamation.

The Cold Cycle is upon us, Twisted Foot thought ruefully, but it brings scant enjoyment while the threat of the Selections hangs over the lair. Even our mating has lost its pleasure. He recalled the words that Long Ears had spoken. Yes, he agreed, our breeding now has but one purpose: to fill the bellies of the Rulers. The image of Long Ears lingered in his mind, growing stronger, more solid.

'Time to go, comrade,' the soft voice said suddenly.

Twisted Foot blinked. Long Ears now crouched beside the nest, the image come to life. The watch, of course! Twisted Foot remembered. He sighed and left the nest reluctantly. The bitterness that he had felt after the last Selection had re-emerged, deeper and more virulent than before.

The four Watchers travelled up the long tunnel in silence. It would be dark on the outside world – and cold again. The effort to vacate their warm nests had been difficult for all of them, particularly now, when mating was permitted. Some of the young warriors down in the lair had no mates of their own; they would waste little time before pressing their attentions on the mates of the absent Watchers. A few might succeed in snatching brief moments of pleasure from the struggling she-rats.

Fat One cursed silently as he stumbled behind the others. He cursed the coldness into which he would soon emerge. He cursed his own stupidity for falling asleep during the Assembly, thus incurring this seemingly endless round of extra watches. He cursed the unattached young he-rats, who by now would be prowling hungrily round his nest. Most of all, though, he cursed Long Snout and the old tyrant's obsession with the Two-Legs. Punishment and extra watches aside, Fat One grumbled, the Cold Cycle usually brought less work, not more. The Hunters were now idle; they could stay cosy in their lair. With fewer Assemblies to guard and fewer executions to perform, the Protectors likewise had less to do. But the work of the Watchers had increased substantially. Still anxious about the menace posed by the glowing giant, still deeply worried about the flapping creature left by the Two-Legs, Long Snout had decided that, night and day, four Watchers must maintain vigilance on the world above. Since the great excitement of a few days ago, however, the giant had not come to life again. Nor had the creature on the high ground caused any harm; abandoned by the Two-Legs, it had merely flapped forlornly in the wind. Even the white birds had returned to their roosts, no longer afraid of the strange intruder. The high state of nervousness in the underworld had also been replaced by calm, albeit an uneasy calm. To all but Long Snout, it seemed that the threat of discovery by the Two-Legs had passed. Clearly, these long watches were so unnecessary, so unfair.

A blast of cold air from above signified that they had reached the end of the tunnel. Fat One shivered – and cursed again.

The members of the daylight watch left happily for the underworld. The dialogue with the sombre newcomers had been clipped, perfunctory. Twisted Foot and Long Ears set off for the western point of Inchgarvie, where they would be close to the shadowy bridge. Still grumbling, Fat One agreed to watch the east of the island. In a rare show of agility, he leapt up the monastery wall and squeezed his body into the space afforded by one of the oblong window holes. This perch gave him a clear view of both the jetty and the contraption on the high ground. The fourth Watcher, Digger, stayed inside the monastery, near to the entrance tunnel. Digger (so called because of his propensity for scratching the ground in search of worms and other tiny delicacies) was one of the lair's veterans, probably older than Sharp Claws, and certainly much frailer.

It was even colder than they had feared. A chilling wind swept down the estuary from the west, blustering through the bridge's giant arches and whipping into the faces of the two Watchers on the narrow point. Weak moonlight, intermittently obliterated by the passage of dark, fast-moving clouds, added a ghostly lustre to the battalions of jostling waves which besieged the rocks on either side of the ridge. The Watchers huddled together for warmth, their eyes closed to the merest of slits against the buffeting wind.

'At times like these, comrade,' Long Ears chattered, 'I would gladly be gone from this place.'

Twisted Foot was quick to recognise the jest in his companion's remark. Banter like this would keep them occupied for a while; it would alleviate the boredom and the miserable coldness.

'And where, apart from his nest, would a bold warrior go on a night such as this?' he quipped, playing along.

Long Ears didn't respond immediately. Instead, he peered across the estuary to the strings of twinkling lights on the northern shoreline.

'To the land over there,' he said at length.

Twisted Foot snorted, but something about the statement, the tone of Long Ears' delivery, told him that the jesting was over.

'There? But why?' he asked weakly.

His companion sighed and then regarded Twisted Foot for some moments. His outsize ears were quivering; his whole body seemed to tremble. Twisted Foot sensed that mounting anger, not the cutting wind, was the cause.

'For many reasons, comrade,' Long Ears hissed, his narrow eyes now filled with venom. 'Because I detest the oppression of our society. Because I am treated no better than a Scavenger. Because I don't want my youngsters devoured by the fat brown ones. Because I hate their smugness and their easy life.'

The tirade stopped abruptly. The tenseness in Long Ears' body disappeared, his rage expelled with it.

'These feelings,' he continued more softly. 'I sense – I know – that you share them; that you, too, are unhappy with the underworld.'

Twisted Foot was taken aback by the ferocity of the onslaught – not even Fat One's worst complaints had ever carried such hatred, such bitterness – but the stark truth contained in Long Ears' words also unsettled him. It was true: he did have similar thoughts.

'All right,' he said cautiously. 'Even if I do ... share your feelings ... what of it? It's just nonsense to speak about leaving here. The land across the water is nothing but ... a dream.'

'No, comrade, it can be done!' Long Ears was excited now. 'Look down there!' His snout twitched furiously as he motioned to the extreme point of the island. 'From there to the giant's foot is but a short distance. We could swim –'

'Swim?'

'Yes, swim! Aren't we told constantly that the founders of our society swam to this place from a Two-Legs vessel? Surely we can do the same to leave the place?'

'All right,' Twisted Foot nodded again, although he was still not convinced. 'What then?'

'Then we climb up into the giant's belly. I have seen the Two-Legs do this often. I know it can be done. We climb up during the darkness when the Two-Legs are gone from the giant. Then we crawl along the straight belly until we reach its end.'

The two Watchers now gazed up at the bridge. The sheer size of the structure was intimidation enough for Twisted Foot.

'I don't know,' he said. 'What about the creatures – the Two-Legs creatures which rush through the giant? Won't they be a danger?'

'Yes, of course. But if we do the same as the Two-Legs and keep well to the edge, I'm sure that we'll be safe.

'I know that it can be done, comrade,' Long Ears added quickly.

Twisted Foot stayed silent for some time. The plan was terrifying – but it could succeed. A jumble of thoughts and questions filled his mind. He tried to think clearly through the tangle. There had to be some tangible benefit, some hard justification, for such a perilous journey.

'This land across the water,' he said at last. 'What do you know about it? What does it offer? Won't there be many dangers over there?'

Long Ears grew excited again.

'You remember the stories told by the Chamberlain? The stories about the land from which the forefathers came? Their land had trees and grass; waters running down the sides of hills; lairs built deep under soft earth; birds of all kinds and small Four-Legs on which to feast. I think – I'm sure – that the land across the water has all these things.'

'But the Two-Legs? Won't there be many of them?'

'Perhaps, comrade. But the land is so vast. It can't be too difficult to find a place far from them.

'Think, Twisted Foot!' Long Ears was insistent now. 'No Rulers or Protectors! No Selections! Mating when we desire it! Bird flesh for the taking!' The words were cajoling, persuasive.

Twisted Foot had caught the excitement; many more questions were on the point of tumbling from him – Who should undertake this journey? How would they begin their new society? Who would lead them? – but Long Ears was already giving the answers.

'There must be others in the lair – young Watchers like us – who would be happily gone from here. I'm sure there would be little effort to persuade them. We should go with our mates and our young ones: we couldn't form a strong society without them. But –' Long Ears stopped now. He needed to choose his next words with care. He looked away from Twisted Foot and back to the far, twinkling lights.

'Our flight from this place must be well planned,' he said eventually. 'The venture is a dangerous one. We are doomed if the Rulers suspect us; Long Snout will feed us to the Scavengers. Yes, we need a careful plan. And we need someone – a brave and intelligent warrior – to lead us. A leader who will decide our steps and keep us from discovery.'

Long Ears turned to stare directly at his companion.

'Twisted Foot, comrade,' he spoke softly. 'Will you lead us?'

Transfixed, Twisted Foot returned the stare. The excitement left him, ousted suddenly by cold fear.

'Me?' he squealed. 'But – but I'm just a cripple. Not strong. I couldn't lead...' The words trailed off. The coldness seemed to clutch at his insides, constricting his breathing.

'It's not strength that we need, comrade.' Vehemence and insistence were back in Long Ears' words. 'It's cunning and courage and intelligence. You have all these qualities. More so than any of us. You are our natural leader!'

Twisted Foot's heart thudded. Iciness was crawling through his bowels.

'I – I don't know.' The voice was weak, whispering. 'I must have time to think...'

It was his turn now to stare at the distant shoreline.

Chapter Fourteen

She moved swiftly and lightly through the Common lair. The place was quiet, deserted except for the guards outside the Scavengers' dungeon. Her passage seemed to have gone unobserved. When she reached the pool, the Protectors at the foot of the entrance tunnel regarded her silently, indifferently. She drank greedily from the pool, stopping every few seconds to glance about. Only her lapping disturbed the eerie stillness. She sensed danger. She knew that it was unsafe to be here alone at this time. Her companions were all sleeping soundly, exhausted after another night of furious copulation with their mates. Her own mate was keeping the night watch above. She had been thirsty and had crept out of the lair, not wishing to wake any of the other she-rats. She would be away only a short time.

Shaking her dripping muzzle, she glanced once more at the immobile Protectors and then left the pool. The tunnel going back seemed longer, more threatening. She quickened her pace. In the darkness of the Common lair, she could see a darker shape moving towards her. Another dark form came close behind the first. She stopped, crouching very low, ready to spring away. Grave danger lurked in those forms. The trip to the pool had been a terrible mistake, she realised. She should have stayed safe in her nest, waited for the others to rise.

The first Protector crept closer, sniffing her scent, until she could feel the hotness of his breath.

'And where do you belong, pretty one?' he asked. The tone was light, but she recognised the menace in it.

She decided on a bold approach. If she showed no fear, they might let her pass unharmed.

'The lair of the Watchers,' she replied defiantly.

'A Watcher, eh?' The tone was mocking now. He had moved even closer, his snout rubbing against her own as he spoke. 'What about some pleasure for a lonely warrior? After all, it is the time of the mating.'

'But I have a mate already,' she answered quickly. 'Twisted Foot,' she added, the tremble in her voice belying the show of boldness.

The sudden, harsh guffaw made her start in terror. She spun round. A third Protector had slid behind her.

'The cripple?' he boomed and guffawed again.

The first Protector spoke again. His body was pressed hard against her.

'What you need, pretty one, is a real warrior on your back.'

She knew now what they intended to do. At first, she attempted to leap away, but the Protectors had her hemmed in. In desperation, she began to hiss and snarl, lashing out with her bared teeth. The effort was futile. Two of them gripped her head and neck in their powerful jaws. The third pinned her down from the back. She squealed as his sharp claws dug into her flesh. She felt his rough entry, his heaving body and then the rush of his seed inside of her. He slid off with a grunt, but the ordeal was not over. She struggled a second time and a third time when the others leapt on her back in turn.

The Protectors darted away from the still hissing she-rat. 'We'll be over here if you want any more,' one of them shouted from across the lair: the final insult.

Whimpering, hurting, the she-rat stumbled towards her own lair. One of her ears was badly torn, and blood seeped from the deep scores along her back. Her thoughts were bitter, vengeful. The pain would go, the injuries would heal in time, but the memory of this shame, this defilement, might never fade.

Small Face slunk back to his nest. He was anxious that she should not see him. He had watched her leave, had been concerned about her safety. He had gone to the edge of the Common lair, waited for her to return. Frightened, powerless to help, he had witnessed the rape. She had fought back bravely. They had hurt her, just like the Scavengers had hurt him. If he had gone to her assistance, the guards would have brushed him aside, hurt him again. I'm not a coward, he insisted, but he was ashamed of his weakness.

The she-rat crept into her nest and then curled up in a tight ball close to her youngster. Poor Grey Eyes, he thought. So young, so pretty. She will keep silent about her ordeal, lest Twisted Foot tries to take revenge. The Protectors would surely kill him – and take pleasure in it. Small Face shuddered. He, too, would say nothing. Twisted Foot was a valued companion, a kind friend; his loss would be cruel and tragic.

Grey Eyes was sleeping now. Soft whimpers escaped from her trembling body. Small Face felt sadness. He looked round the other nests. All was quiet, serene. What a strange and brutal world we live in, he mused. Here in the Watchers' lair there is peace, order. Sharp Claws is a respected and compassionate leader. There is a strong bond of comradeship between all of the Watchers. Out there, though, it is different: no compassion, no friendship. The Protectors roam the underworld, killing, raping, maiming. The Hunters are no better; they, too, are cold and cruel. The Rulers – the protected ones – are even worse. They condone and encourage the brutality so long as they are kept fed and warm. It is as if... as if the Watchers are not included in their society: a society apart, an inferior race to be spurned and ridiculed like the Scavengers. Yes, a society apart, he repeated the notion. But, alas, that is the sum of it. We can't change things; we can't fight them. There is no escape. He felt tired, helpless. No escape, he sighed and drifted into sleep.

Chapter Fifteen

The dreams kept waking Twisted Foot. At first, there were bright, sharp images of a clearing among the trees. He didn't know where the clearing was, only that it was far away, deep in the woodlands. The sun was shining. They were basking in its warmth. Grey Eyes was there; and young Soft-Mover, his jet-black coat glistening as he moved through the tall grass. Fat One was dozing under a tree. His other companions were in the clearing with their mates and young ones. There was an aura about the place, a deep glow of happiness. It seemed that if he reached out from his dream he could touch the glow, let the warmth course through him. Then the shadows always fell. Cold, dark images came to oust the brightness. The scenes were blurred, frightening: Long Snout towering over the clearing, the blood of newly born young congealed on his enormous fangs; Neck-Snapper hissing and spitting death, green pus festering in his ragged eyehole; Grey Eyes surrounded by snarling Protectors, her small body lacerated and bleeding. The images of light and darkness vied with each other, struggling for dominance, like a battle between good and evil. The confusion of the tumult threatened to overwhelm him. He had to break free from the dream, to awake, shivering and miserable, in the empty nest. Anger and bitterness greeted each awakening, building quickly to a helpless rage which sent convulsions through his body, until it, too, was almost unbearable. He had to close his eyes, to shut out the dark, violent thoughts. Then the cycle of dreaming and waking began again.

It had been like this since he returned from the watch to discover Grey Eyes' plight. He had known instinctively what had occurred; he hadn't needed to ask. She was away now, being consoled by her companions. His fellow Watchers had tried to commiserate with him, but he had wanted to be alone, to nurse his wrath. Sleep eased the anguish; his dreams subsumed it, but only to clear the way for another kind of turmoil, the one created by his need to decide whether to set off on the perilous journey to a new life or to stay here, suffering the hardships and indignities of the present society. As the dream conflict wore on, the shining images of the sun-warmed clearing in the trees grew stronger, more appealing, more attainable.

In his nest close by, Long Ears also slept fitfully; dozing when Twisted Foot closed his eyes, suddenly alert when Twisted Foot awoke, watching, waiting for some sign. He recognised the torment in his companion's movements; he knew that the decision would come soon. He had bared his thoughts to Twisted Foot, his plans for a new society. Twisted Foot was the most able of the young Watchers; of that, Long Ears was certain. He was clever, with an inner strength that transcended his deformed body; the one who could lead them away from this hostile place, their saviour. The others won't take me seriously, Long Ears told himself. I am too weak, too afraid. But they would listen to Twisted Foot. They would follow him. Long Ears concentrated his thoughts, willing Twisted Foot to wake, willing him to decide.

The dream had broken again. With a start, Twisted Foot opened his eyes, meeting Long Ears' gaze. It is time, he decided. He rose wearily from the nest. There had been no rest for him, but he was calmer now, more sure of his actions.

'Come to the pool,' he said to Long Ears. His voice, like his actions, was firm, resolute.

They made their way to the pool. There was a silence between them, a tautness, Twisted Foot deep in thought, Long Ears in quiet anticipation. As usual at this time of the day, several groups of he-rats clustered near the water's edge. Twisted Foot chose a quiet spot away from them. The two lapped for some time and then shifted back from the water to crouch close together. Twisted Foot looked round the tunnel, making sure that he would not be overheard. He spoke quietly and forcibly.

'All right, comrade, I will lead you and the others to the land across the water.'

Long Ears emitted a long sigh of relief, but he said nothing.

'First,' his companion continued, 'we must decide who should go with us. They must be our closest comrades. Those we know best and can trust most.'

He stopped for some moments, rehearsing the details in his mind.

'Fat One, certainly, and Small Face: they will want to go. Narrow Back, too. He is a very nervous and talkative Watcher, I know, but we will need him for the knowledge he possesses.'

The last remark puzzled Long Ears. Again, though, he stayed silent.

'The others are either too old or not well enough known to us. Besides, we must keep our group small, easy to handle. We will also be taking our mates and our youngsters. Already, our number is large enough.'

Long Ears nodded his agreement, excitement building within him. Twisted Foot huddled closer. His tone was urgent now.

'Our greatest danger at this time is discovery of our plan. Secrecy is all-important. So this is what we must do. You should speak to Fat One and Small Face. Separately. Not in the lair, where there are too many ears. But here at the pool or on the world above. I will approach Narrow Back. We must do this as soon as possible.

'When the plan is revealed to each of them, we must ensure that only our two names are mentioned. They must not know who their other companions will be, only that there will be a group of us. We must impress on them the consequences of discovery and the need for utter secrecy. Each of us will speak to our mates – again, as soon as possible – but our young ones must not be told until we are ready to leave –'

'When... when will that be?' Long Ears interrupted breathlessly.

'I don't know yet. I don't know how we will leave. I have still to work out a plan. But it will be very soon, comrade, very soon. Before our mates grow heavy with young. Before the Cold Cycle begins in earnest.'

Twisted Foot glanced round him. The place was more crowded now, more noisy. He shifted away from Long Ears.

'Watch for my sign,' he said quickly, 'then we'll speak again.'

He left the pool without Long Ears. He felt cheerful, light-headed, as if a great burden had been lifted from him. He wanted to comfort Grey Eyes; to snuggle close to her and give her his warmth. He would whisper in her ear, tell her of the plan to leave. That would be the greatest comfort.

Chapter Sixteen

Narrow Back was twitching furiously again.

'I've found it! I've found it!' he squealed. 'Come quickly!'

Twisted Foot gave out a sigh of exasperation and then scrambled over the rocks to join the skinny Watcher.

Narrow Back's whole body was quivering. His eyes flashed wildly in the darkness.

'Here!' he exclaimed. 'Just here!'

'Sh!' Twisted Foot snapped. 'You'll wake the underworld with your shrieking.'

His patience had been stretched almost to the limit. He had waited two long days for the opportunity to be alone with Narrow Back. He had volunteered for the watch, intervening on Small Face's behalf.

'Poor Small Face is not yet fit,' he had pleaded with Sharp Claws. 'Let me take his place.'

They had gone to the point of the island, where Twisted Foot had outlined the plan to Narrow Back. That was when the difficulties began. Narrow Back had behaved like a youngster: prancing, twittering loudly, filled with uncontrollable excitement. With panic rising in him, Twisted Foot had begged his companion to quieten down, had even threatened to leave him behind. It had taken a long time, but gradually Narrow Back became more restrained, his actions more sober.

The next task proved equally difficult. Twisted Foot had asked Narrow Back to locate the spot where he had spied Broken Tail on the night when the giant came to life.

'It's very important to our plan,' he had explained. 'Broken Tail didn't just appear from nowhere. There has to be another tunnel – a secret one – out of the underworld.'

To Twisted Foot's dismay, the prancing and twittering had begun afresh.

'A secret tunnel?' Narrow Back shouted. 'My goodness, a secret tunnel!'

After another period of pleas and threats, they had set off to find the spot, but Narrow Back's excitement seemed to have blurred his recollection. With mounting frustration, Twisted Foot had followed the eager Watcher's zigzag path across the sharp rocks and had listened to his incessant babbling. They were getting nearer the monastery. The watch was drawing to a close; the search more haphazard, the chattering more incoherent. At last, though, Narrow Back had found something.

Twisted Foot peered anxiously at the cluster of boulders. He was not surprised that the tunnel had gone unnoticed by countless passing Watchers. Its entrance was a long slit, kept permanently dark by the overhang of the largest boulder. Even in daylight the slit would be hard to detect. He understood now why the search had taken so long.

'You did well, comrade,' he said. The appreciation was genuine; his earlier impatience forgotten.

Narrow Back looked pleased with himself.

'What now?' he whispered, trying his utmost to keep his eagerness in check.

'Listen carefully,' Twisted Foot also whispered. 'I'm going into the tunnel. I need to be sure where it ends. I'll be as quick as I can. Stay here and keep watch – quietly. If anything goes wrong, if I don't… return, go back to the underworld with the others. Say that I disappeared; nothing else. Remember, nothing else.'

He was grateful when Narrow Back merely nodded. His companion was suddenly quiet, as if he understood the danger.

Twisted Foot slid under the boulder and through the slit. The blackness inside was complete. He was alone now and very afraid, but he had to finish this task. The tunnel was much wider than the one which ran from the monastery. Built for the Inner Circle, he surmised; their escape route. Well, with luck, it'll soon be our escape route.

He moved cautiously at first. The floor of the tunnel was also much less steep than the other one. He sniffed the dank air. The scent of he-rats was very faint, indicating that the place was seldom used. There was little time to spare. He crept more quickly down the tunnel, but stopped dead after only a few yards. The Protector's tail was a mere inch away from Twisted Foot's snout. He held his breath, stayed rigid. The Protector lay with the back half of his body inside the tunnel. The gentle rise and fall of the rump confirmed that his sleep had not been disturbed. Beyond him, inside the lair, two other dozing forms stretched across the tunnel mouth.

Twisted Foot hadn't realised how short the distance would be. Very slowly, very quietly, he stepped backwards until the Protector's tail was out of sight. He halted briefly, listening for movement. He was shaking uncontrollably now, gasping for air. Thankfully, the guards hadn't stirred, but disaster had been so very close. He turned and scurried back up the tunnel. For once, the outside world would be a welcoming sight.

Narrow Back's agitation had returned.

'Well?' he squealed as Twisted Foot re-emerged.

'Sh!' Twisted Foot hissed. 'Not here.'

They travelled further up the slope. When they reached the monastery wall, Twisted Foot spoke quietly and urgently.

'Listen again, comrade. The tunnel leads into the lair of the Protectors. When we go, we will leave by that tunnel. When the next Assembly takes place, watch for my sign, be ready to follow me. Tell your mate to wait outside the Watchers' lair. She won't be alone. There will be others. Tell her to follow them. Now, do you understand all of that? Do you understand that nothing must be said to anyone – only your mate?'

'I understand,' Narrow Back nodded. 'But –' He hesitated now. 'The tunnel. Isn't it –'

'Yes, it is guarded. But it won't be during the Assembly, not when the killing begins. Twice now, I've watched the guards come out for the killing. Don't worry, it will be safe for us.'

Twisted Foot looked upwards. Ragged patches of light had already infiltrated the leaden sky.

'Come,' he said. 'The watch is over. Let's join the others.'

They climbed into the monastery. In the midst of the rubble, Narrow Back stopped abruptly. He was still hesitant.

'Just – just one last thing,' he squeaked. 'I – I don't know if I can swim.'

Twisted Foot cuffed him lightly.

'Neither do I,' he replied and moved on.

Chapter Seventeen

It was an anxious time for the conspirators. They knew the details of the plan. They knew what was expected of them when the moment came, but the waiting seemed interminable. They knew the perils of their venture, and the horrors which would befall them if their flight was routed, but the waiting magnified their fears, increased their nervousness. The last Assembly took place many days ago. The underworld was growing hungrier. The next Assembly must be imminent.

In the deep of night, the Watchers' lair was hushed. Here and there among the rows of sleeping rats, an alert, concerned face gazed into the darkness. Sleep wouldn't come to them. They kept the vigil, waiting for the Rulers to wake, waiting for the Assembly to be announced.

Like his fellow plotters, Twisted Foot was restless. As he peered along the nests, he could pick out Long Ears, Small Face, Fat One. All awake, he observed. All here except Narrow Back, who keeps the night watch above. They trust in my leadership. The plan is a good one, I'm sure of it. Once in the Protectors' lair, we'll race through the escape tunnel, across the rocks and on into the water. The she-rats in the lair will raise the alarm, of course, but by that time we'll be far away. There will be no pursuit. Yes, the plan will work, but we must go soon, before fear overcomes our resolve.

His ears pricked suddenly when he saw old Digger slip into the lair and head straight for Sharp Claws' nest. There was a brief, murmured conversation, and then Sharp Claws left the lair quickly, with Digger scurrying behind him. Twisted Foot was more alert now. His three companions had turned to look at him, their eyes searching, questioning. Something – something important – had caused Digger to return from the watch. What had happened? Had the giant begun to glow again? Would this be an end to the plan? He felt dismay. Anxiety crowded his thoughts.

'What now, comrade?' Long Ears whispered to him, but he didn't reply.

It seemed like an age before Sharp Claws returned. The Chief Watcher was alone, his expression grim. He marched the length of the lair until he reached Twisted Foot's nest. He stared coldly at Twisted Foot and then at Long Ears.

'You two,' he boomed. 'Come with me. You're needed for a special watch.'

Twisted Foot's heart sank, his hopes with it. Before he left the nest, he nuzzled into Grey Eyes. He sensed her fear.

'Don't worry,' he said. 'I'll be back.'

They followed Sharp Claws out to the Common lair. Broken Tail waited there with a group of Protectors.

'Come with us,' he growled. 'The Chamberlain will have words with you.'

The Protectors quickly surrounded the two young Watchers. As the group moved off, Twisted Foot glanced back in panic. Sharp Claws was returning to the Watchers' lair. He looked old and sad, his eyes staring blankly at the ground. It was then that Twisted Foot realised the full terror of their predicament.

Terror had also set into Long Ears.

'Oh, no,' he squealed and began to tremble.

Twisted Foot pressed closer to his companion.

'Stay brave, comrade,' he whispered, although he knew that his own courage was rapidly deserting him.

Chapter Eighteen

As if in a daze, they stumbled along between their captors, passing briskly through the Protectors' lair and on into the sanctum of the Rulers. The guards took them to the centre of the floor and then retreated to block off the entrance tunnel. Broken Tail remained close behind the captives.

Long Snout squatted opposite the Watchers, glowering fiercely at them. Behind him, the Inner Circle rats looked out expectantly from their nests, like avid spectators hungry for sport to commence. On Long Snout's right, several Protectors crouched in a half-circle round a pool of blood. A lifeless, unrecognisable bundle of raw flesh and matted fur lay in the blood.

Long Snout stirred, baring his fangs, directing his words at the Watchers.

'So,' he hissed, 'here are the other brave warriors who wish to leave our society.'

The bundle shifted momentarily. It emitted a gasp of agony. Two glazed, pain-filled eyes opened, took in the scene and closed again.

'I'm sorry, comrades,' the bundle wheezed.

Long Snout nodded. A Protector dug into the heaving form at his feet, tearing away another strip of bloody fur. Narrow Back's shriek filled the lair. His body shuddered for some moments and then became still again.

A spasm of fear jerked Long Ears. Urine trickled from beneath him. Twisted Foot didn't move. Instead, his eyes fixed on Long Snout, matching the Chamberlain's cold glare. He hadn't killed before – that action was the exclusive domain of the Hunters and Protectors – but he could gladly kill now. Hate occupied his thoughts, keeping his own terror at bay.

Long Snout continued.

'Yes,' he sneered, 'your comrade – this pile of dung – has told us all about your plot. Tonight, the fool came blundering into the Protectors' lair. He came through the sacred tunnel. Your escape tunnel, warriors. As you can see, it was not too difficult to get him to reveal his secrets.'

He looked over to the guards by the tunnel.

'Get this useless creature out of here,' he commanded. 'Take it back to the Watchers' lair. Let it serve as a lesson for Sharp Claws and his traitorous scum.'

Two guards scurried across to Narrow Back. They proceeded to prod and nip him until he was conscious again.

'Move!' one of them screamed.

Slowly, painfully, Narrow Back slithered along the ground. Streaks of blood marked his tortured progress. He halted several times, and each time the prodding and biting were renewed. Finally, their patience gone, the guards grabbed at his flesh and dragged him, screaming and pleading, the rest of the distance out of the lair.

Long Snout turned his attention to the remaining Watchers.

'Now for the two other fools,' he spat. 'You! The small one with the big ears! Tell me who leads this plot. Give me the names of its members.'

Long Ears squirmed forward on his belly. He stared at the ground in front of the Chamberlain.

'Me!' he squeaked. 'It was my idea, Chamberlain. I am the leader. There are only three of us.'

'Silence!' screamed Long Snout.

Two Protectors rushed up to the trembling Watcher. Each took hold of one of his ears, pulling hard, tearing the flesh. The pain was excruciating; the squeals high-pitched and deafening.

'Now the truth!' Long Snout shouted over the din.

Twisted Foot continued to stare at the Chamberlain, the lust to kill even stronger now.

'He lies. I am the leader.' The words were uttered boldly, with no hint of fear.

The attack on Long Ears stopped. The Chamberlain stooped down, bringing his snout closer to Twisted Foot.

'Yes, you,' he hissed. 'The little cripple.'

He stepped back again and then suddenly lashed out with one of his front claws, slashing the Watcher across the top of the head. Twisted Foot stifled the scream. He tried to maintain his stare, but blood blurred his vision and stung his eyes.

Broken Tail stepped up from behind and seized the Watcher's neck in his jaws. Twisted Foot felt the fangs bite deep, his life slipping away. He had to struggle to speak.

'But there are... only three of us...' he gasped through the pain. 'Long Ears... Narrow Back... and me...'

Broken Tail's grip eased slightly. Long Snout appeared again through a red haze. Twisted Foot could barely hear the words.

'Put the traitors in with the slaves. They will be executed – slowly – during the Assembly. Their torment will be an example for the whole of the Outer Circle.'

Chapter Nineteen

Belcher saw them first.

'Visitors,' he said to Slayer.

Both Slayer and Slasher interrupted their feast to look down at the entrance tunnel. They recognised the huge frame of the Master. A group of the Master's underlings squatted some way behind him.

Slayer spat out a small bone.

'Let's go,' he ordered.

The three Scavengers climbed down from the high ledge. The wall was nearly perpendicular, but their descent was swift and nimble. As soon as they were far enough away, others on the ledge pounced noisily on the half-eaten carcass of the young she-slave.

When they reached the level ground, Slayer moved ahead of his companions to approach the Master. Their conversation was brief, but Slayer seemed happy with the outcome. Then the Master departed with all but two of his group. The prisoners he left behind huddled together, their expressions bewildered, frightened.

The place was not like any other part of the underworld. The walls of the lair were high and steep, descending to the left and right in a series of narrow ledges. Nests, crammed with slaves, occupied every inch of each ledge. The floor stretching out from the entrance tunnel stayed even for several feet and then dipped sharply into a deep pit. The bottom of the pit also teemed with rats, their squirming, jostling bodies almost obliterating sight of the murky pool at the far end of the lair. Gangs of he-slaves roamed the pit; clambering over their neighbours, they searched out the weak and undefended, raping, killing, squabbling over murdered corpses. Shrieks and cries rose up from the pit, combining with the constant chatter on the ledges to produce a single, deafening cacophony.

The Scavengers numbered more than twice the Inner and Outer Circle rats put together. The prisoners' senses reeled with the sights and sounds of the multitude. Nothing could have prepared them for this madness, this bedlam. They stared transfixed into the pit. The heaving black mass reminded Twisted Foot of the maggots that he had once seen in the belly of an old, decaying No-Legs which had been washed up on the rocks. There was that same sense of agitation, of mindless hysteria; that same blind frenzy.

Twitching snouts began to emerge above the mass. Eyes, hungry and violent, found the newcomers, recognised their vulnerability. A cry went up, and the mass surged forward suddenly. Bodies leapt from the crowd and clung to the wall of the pit. Twisted Foot and Long Ears cowered back, but the three Scavengers who had come to greet Broken Tail stood their ground.

Slayer glared down at those on the wall.

'Get back!' he commanded. 'Or the lair will feast on your miserable flesh tonight!'

There was a brief moment of hesitation, and then the leading slaves slid back into the pit. The crowd resumed its milling and jostling.

Slayer now approached the prisoners. Like his two companions, he was small and muscular. Old scars striped his coat, the harsh mementos of his struggle to dominate the lair.

'Welcome to my kingdom,' he said in a voice that was deep and rough.

Still quivering, the prisoners said nothing.

'Follow me,' Slayer barked.

They climbed up to the highest ledge on the lair's left, Slayer in front, and Slasher and Belcher taking up the rear. Slayer hissed fiercely, and the slaves occupying his nest shot away. Not much remained of the carcass that he had abandoned. He kicked the skeleton and scraps of hide into the pit.

'Settle here,' he ordered.

Twisted Foot and Long Ears crouched down in the nest. Slasher crept close to them, examining their wounds, licking the congealing blood.

'Let's kill them now,' he growled.

'Yes, let's kill them,' Belcher joined in.

Slayer pushed the eager Scavengers away.

'No,' he rasped. 'The Master wants them kept safe. They're to be executed.' His tongue curled round his large fangs. 'Then we'll have their corpses,' he added.

Chapter Twenty

Long Ears had stopped trembling some time ago. His heart no longer thudded wildly, and his breathing was now slow and measured. Warmth radiated from his sleeping body.

Twisted Foot had felt the tenseness slip away from Long Ears. He, too, had begun to relax, despite the incessant madness below. We're safe for the moment, he said to himself. A respite. But such a respite! They'll come for us soon, and then ... We had been waiting anxiously for the Assembly to begin. That was last night ... or is it still the same night? He couldn't remember. He knew only that the agony of waiting was worse this time.

He looked sadly at his companion. Poor Long Ears, he thought. He blames himself for the mess we're in. But it wasn't his fault. It was me – my mistake. I was wrong to choose Narrow Back. I should have been more cautious. Narrow Back paid dearly for his incaution. Twisted Foot shuddered when he remembered the bloody pulp and the horrific screams. The penalty for my failure will be exacted soon. But the others are all right, thank goodness! They've been spared. We kept our heads. We showed courage, at least.

He looked up, startled, from his thoughts. Slayer was prodding him roughly.

'Tell me,' he said. 'Why does the Master want to execute you? What have you done?'

The three Scavengers had crowded into the nest. Long Ears woke with a jolt. Twisted Foot found it difficult to concentrate, to form the words. He had to shout over the eternal din.

'It was because –' he croaked, 'because we wanted to leave this world to form a new society.'

'Leave this world? Go where?' Slayer looked amused.

Twisted Foot hesitated. I don't suppose it matters anymore, he decided.

'To the land across the water,' he replied defiantly.

'Land? Water?' Slayer was incredulous now.

Belcher pressed closer to Twisted Foot and belched loudly.

'He's a dung-head, King-rat!' he cried. 'He's mad!'

Twisted Foot began to understand. He took a deep breath. Then he spoke clearly and deliberately.

'Above this world, there is another world. A world with light as well as darkness. It has a sun and a moon, clouds and rain. It is surrounded by vast waters. Across the waters, there are other worlds. Lands with trees and grass and many strange creatures – creatures not like us. We had planned to go to one of those lands.'

'Dung-head!' Belcher shouted again.

'It's a trick,' growled Slasher. 'He lies. There is only one world. This one. We all know that. Kill him, King-rat!'

'Sh!' commanded Slayer. He stared at Twisted Foot for some time and then said, 'We know nothing of these strange words you speak. Perhaps you are mad, I don't know. But tell me, why – why you wanted to leave, why you wanted to go to this ... this so-called other world.'

'Because of the cruelty in our society,' Long Ears piped up.

'Yes,' Twisted Foot continued. 'We are Watchers, you see –'

'Watchers?'

'We watch over the outside world. There are also Hunters. They kill the white birds on the world above –'

'Yes,' Slayer nodded, 'we have seen these white creatures. The Master brings them to us from time to time. Go on.'

Twisted Foot was more confident now.

'There are also Protectors... guards. They guard over your lair. They are led by Broken Tail... the one you call Master. They serve the Inner Circle... the Rulers –'

'Rulers?'

'The large brown ones. The Rulers... our Masters.'

'Yes,' Slayer nodded again. 'The fat brown corpses. The Master brings them to us.'

Twisted Foot went on quickly.

'The Rulers eat our young. The Protectors molest our mates, and kill and maim us. We are treated no better than... slaves. Slaves... like you.'

'Slaves!' It was Slayer who was angry now. 'Explain yourself!' he demanded.

Twisted Foot gulped. He glanced furtively at Long Ears. His companion nodded, as if to say: Better to die quickly here, comrade, than slowly out there.

'They call you Scavengers,' Twisted Foot said carefully. 'But you are kept here as a food supply. The many warriors who are taken from your lair are killed... and devoured –'

'The cripple lies!' Belcher screamed.

'No, it's true! All true!' Long Ears cried.

'Kill them now!' Slasher hissed.

Slayer moved swiftly, placing himself between the Watchers and his angry cohorts.

'Shut up!' he commanded. He stared again at Twisted Foot. The look was thoughtful, pensive.

'All right,' he said eventually, 'we are scavengers, that's true. The Master gives us your dead to eat. In return, we give him our strongest warriors. It is a great honour for the warriors. They are needed for the ranks of the Master's underlings. That is what he says, anyway. You may be mad, I don't know. We haven't spoken to your kind before. I must think about these ... these stories you tell.' He paused, slowly bearing his teeth.

'But if you're lying,' he growled, 'I'll make sure both of you regret it!'

A sudden spark of hope fired Twisted Foot. He sensed that Long Ears was also roused. They shrank back from the threat nevertheless.

Slayer rose up.

'Come,' he said to Slasher. 'We have work to do.'

'Keep our visitors safe,' he ordered Belcher.

Twisted Foot knew that he had to be quick. He searched desperately for the right words.

'There's something else you should know,' he blurted. 'Your – your numbers here in the lair. They far exceed my own society. You – you don't have to stay here, you know. You don't have to remain as... slaves.'

The small King-rat stayed quite still. His fur bristled. He glared coldly at the wide-eyed Watchers.

'We have work to do,' he said brusquely. Then he leapt from the nest to join the melee down below.

Part Three:

The Revolt

Chapter Twenty-One

Like a great army, the storm clouds had assembled by stealth under the cover of darkness. When dawn came, they hung low and menacing in the sky, a vast grey pall above the landscape. The wind rose in angry, impatient gusts, signalling the start of the day-long barrage. Unleashed by their lofty grey marshals, eager battalions of stinging rain pellets darted in slants through the sky. The assault was fierce and relentless. The rain hordes swept down on the towns and countryside, rushing in torrents from roofs and along gutters, and gathering in muddy pools in the furrows and depressions of the land. Urged on by the wrathful wind, they drove into the heaving grey sea, creating myriad tiny eddies on its surface. Wounded and enraged by this incursion, the sea boiled and frothed round the forlorn little island in the middle of the estuary. Alone, exposed, the ancient rock seemed to hunch down, to prepare itself for another long siege.

It was Saturday, the eve of the finale. All through the morning and into the early afternoon, the storm battle in the Forth valley raged on unabated, unrelenting. The organisers were nervous. They had been promised fine weather for the big event: a bright, fresh day, followed by a crisp, clear night lit by a full moon. That was what they prayed for. Right now, though, the torrential rain was spoiling their preparations. On the outskirts of the towns, the fields which they had zoned for car and bus parking had rapidly become waterlogged. Even if much of the surface water drained away by the following morning, the prospect of a squelching, muddy trek into the towns was bound to deter many potential spectators. Of more immediate concern, however, was the fireworks display. There was no telling what damage the wind and rain were inflicting on the sophisticated display platform. The whole project could be ruined. The display was the highlight, the *pièce de résistance*, probably the biggest and most expensive ever staged in Europe. There was no choice: despite the treacherous conditions, a boat would have to go to Inchgarvie.

Deep below Inchgarvie, in the quiet of the Inner Circle's lair, the sounds of the storm came like distant whispers. Rainwater trickled more freely down the wall to seep silently into the lair's pool, but the rising level of the pool went unobserved by Long Snout. Irate, fretful, the old Chamberlain paced the ground, his thoughts taken up with more weighty matters. Throughout his many Cycles, he had encountered nothing like it: this sense of doom, of imminent disaster. The escaping slaves; the glowing giant; the Two-Legs creature on the world above: the events had accumulated with frightening rapidity. Now, intensifying the foreboding, there was this act of treachery by the brainless Watchers. Their plot had been foiled, of course, but the stench of their disloyalty lingered on in the underworld. Every trace of it had to be eradicated, swiftly and forcefully. A new, harder discipline had to be enforced; a new sense of loyalty forged.

Long Snout halted close to the spot where the blood had gushed from Narrow Back's wounds. The blood was dark and viscous now. He looked towards the rows of nests. White Muzzle slept soundly. In adjoining nests, Red Coat and Fire Eyes were also curled up with their mates. Unconcerned, as usual, he muttered to himself. The King-rat and his princes seem so ignorant of the lurking danger, as if they are no longer capable of using their instincts. Perhaps they are too well protected. They – and the rest of the Inner Circle – must be shaken from their complacency. They must learn to fear again, to be watchful and cautious.

This coming Assembly will be an important one, he decided. It must have two purposes. First, there must be stern words to rouse the Inner Circle; to spell out the mounting threat to their favoured existence. Then, for the Outer Circle, there must be action – firm action – to banish any further thoughts of disloyalty or insurrection. The public execution of the wretched Watchers will be slow and agonising; I will make sure of that. The whole of the Outer Circle, she-rats and young included, must be there to witness the torment, to comprehend and remember the penalty for treachery. Yes, he nodded, it must be a very special Assembly: stern words to rouse and unite the Inner Circle; harsh action to intimidate the Outer Circle; and then a great feast of slave-flesh to fill our bellies.

Long Snout grunted loudly. The moment was long overdue. It was time to summon the Chief Protector.

Narrow Back uttered a last, dying gasp. His torn, racked body became still, his eyes blank and staring. A mournful whine broke from Timid One, his mate. The others who had remained close to the nest began to whimper softly. Fat One and Small Face returned to their own nests in silence. Fear, more than grief, stilled their voices. Where were Twisted Foot and Long Ears? Why had this awful thing happened to Narrow Back? There had been no explanations, but each knew instinctively that the dream of escape lay in ruins. What now of their own safety? Were the mates and youngsters in danger? They could do nothing, but wait and watch and worry.

Old Sharp Claws looked down sadly at Narrow Back's stiffening corpse. He shook his head. Such a waste, he thought. Then he, too, returned slowly to his nest. Foolish young Watchers, he cursed. They think they know everything. They think they can run away and form their own society. Young fools! Look at what they've brought on themselves – and on the Watchers' lair. More misery, more ridicule, more scorn. As if things weren't bad enough.

He thought of Twisted Foot and Long Ears, defenceless and frightened in the midst of the Scavengers. He thought of his own early Cycles. Yes, it's true, he remembered, I dreamt of flight when I was young. But that's all it was: a foolish dream. I knew even then that the power of the underworld couldn't be broken.

He climbed wearily into his nest, shook his head again. He thought of the coming ordeal. Such a waste. I try my best to look after the young Watchers, to guide them, to protect them. Poor, foolish creatures. They'll be gone soon, destroyed like Narrow Back. I'll miss them. But it won't end there. Discipline will be increased; punishments more severe. Life for the Watchers will be harder than ever.

Sharp Claws sighed deeply. He kept his gaze on the entrance tunnel. Broken Tail would come soon, and the ordeal would begin. He had to stay strong, unflinching. The underworld had no place for sentiment.

Slayer crouched on the flat ground close to the mouth of the tunnel. He, too, waited for Broken Tail. On his left, in an excited huddle, were the ten young warriors whom he and Slasher had selected from the pit. The warriors were all fit and strong, his gift for the Master. On his right, Slasher and Belcher kept guard over the prisoners. The Watchers – or so they called themselves – seemed frightened, but they stayed silent, as if they were resigned to their fate. He hadn't talked to them again. Their words had been strange and confusing. Their notions had disturbed him. They had talked of a society ruled not by the Master, but by the fat brown ones; of fantastic worlds above their own; of slaves who were killed for their flesh; and of insurrection ... Was it possible? Could it all be true? He needed to dwell on the things they said. He had but a short time to do so before the Master returned.

The lair was unusually quiet. The chattering along the ledges had ceased for the moment. Even the multitude of rats in the pit had grown still, as if their constant milling and squabbling had brought them to the point of exhaustion. Twisted Foot kept his gaze fixed on the black mass. That way, he knew, lay escape. One leap, and he would be in the pit. The bodies would boil and froth again, but the disturbance would be momentary. Death would be swift and merciful; the torment ended. One leap, and then salvation. Long Ears recognised it. He, too, stared, mesmerised, into the pit, his body tensed, ready to spring.

Up on the ledge, in the slave-King's nest, there had been a glimmer of hope. They had waited for him to return, to signify that he would act on their words. They had followed his movements in the pit. The power that he wielded over his race was brutal and terrifying. Perhaps it was no wonder that he didn't respond. Outside the lair, the world would be strange and unknown. In here, he controlled life and death. In here, *he* was the Master.

When he did return to the nest, there was no acknowledgement, only a cold, hard stare. He had ordered them back down to the level ground. What little hope they had clung to perished with that order. Now, there was nothing left. Just the sea of black fur below. Just one leap. Then relief.

Without warning, dark shapes began to emerge from the tunnel. Twisted Foot caught the movement. His heart raced. He recognised Broken Tail and Jagged Fangs close behind. Three more Protectors hung back at the tunnel entrance, their forms still blurred.

The slave-King stayed where he was. The young slave-warriors became more excited. Broken Tail and Jagged Fangs crept closer. Now, Twisted Foot said to himself. It has to be now. One leap. That's all it will take. His breath was coming in short gasps. The pounding of his heart was deafening in his ears. He tried to lunge towards the pit, but a great, invisible weight pressed down on him, preventing any movement. He felt Long Ears' body grow stiffer. He saw his companion's eyes flash wildly in panic. One leap. They wanted to jump. They willed themselves to jump, but the weight pressed down harder, suffocating them, paralysing them,

Chapter Twenty-Two

Slayer stirred at last. He moved forward to meet the Master. Some of the more eager slave-warriors began to follow, but a sharp glance from the King-rat sent them scurrying back.

Broken Tail was first to speak.

'We will take the prisoners now,' he growled.

There was a pause. Slayer looked hard at the Master and then at Jagged Fangs.

'I am curious,' he said eventually.

'Yes?' snapped Broken Tail.

'I am curious about the prisoners. Tell me, what was their crime?'

Broken Tail was growing more impatient. He glared across at the Watchers.

'It's not important,' he snapped again. 'They're traitors. That's enough.'

'Yes,' Slayer persisted. 'But what exactly was their crime?'

Broken Tail snorted. He seemed to puff himself up. He glowered down at Slayer.

'Return the prisoners now!' he commanded through bared teeth. His size dwarfed the little slave-King, but Slayer was neither intimidated nor afraid.

'I shall,' he said. 'Presently...'

Slayer swivelled his head to regard the group of slave-warriors on his flank. He turned back to the Master.

'Here are the new recruits you asked for. All strong and healthy.

My gift to you.'

Broken Tail relaxed.

'I am grateful,' he grunted.

'Will they be murdered and eaten like the others?'

Broken Tail stiffened again. He stepped back slightly and then stared accusingly at the Watchers. The fur along Jagged Fangs' back began to bristle. The guards at the tunnel mouth shifted uneasily.

'What nonsense is this?' spluttered Broken Tail.

'Answer me!' Slayer hissed quickly, angrily.

No-one moved in the charged silence that followed. Slayer kept his eyes fixed on the Master. On either side of the prisoners, Slasher and Belcher tensed themselves. The young warriors stayed as still as stones. Alert faces, full of menace, watched from the ledges.

Broken Tail recognised his vulnerability. His gaze swept round the lair, taking full stock of the danger. Beside him, Jagged Fangs had begun to tremble. To his rear, the guards made ready to retreat further into the tunnel.

Slayer broke the silence.

'Kill them,' he said quietly.

In one sudden, concerted movement, the young warriors charged, snarling and spitting, towards the Protectors. On the right, Slasher and Belcher sprang forward. Both Broken Tail and Jagged Fangs spun round and raced for the tunnel. One of the guards scampered off to raise the alarm, while the two others remained just inside the tunnel, their backs arched, ready for the onslaught.

Jagged Fangs reached the guards first. Broken Tail, heavier and slower, hurled himself into the tunnel just as the two leading slave-rats leapt on his ample hindquarters. Screeching and squealing, the rest of the slaves clawed at each other in their eagerness to squeeze into the narrow entrance.

Slayer moved to the edge of the pit. His voice rose above the din at the tunnel and echoed round the lair.

'Come, comrades!' he roared. 'We invade the Master's lair! We kill all the Master's race!'

Immediately, a horde of rats swarmed down from the ledges, reaching the flat ground only moments later. Utterly terrified, the two prisoners cringed back against the wall. The horde swept past them. The black mass below had begun to move. Like a great, angry wave, it heaved up and then crashed against the side of the pit. As the first of the slaves scrambled up to the high ground, Slayer turned quickly to the prisoners.

'Go!' he boomed.

The paralysis had lifted. Reflex replaced terror. Without hesitation, the young Watchers plunged towards the tunnel.

His bearing stiff and proud and regal, the slave-King watched the bristling black mob stream from the pit. Then he, too, turned and charged into battle.

Chapter Twenty-Three

The Common lair rang with a crescendo of squeaks and squeals as rats in their hundreds jostled each other and chattered excitedly. It was difficult to tell what made them more excited: the gory horrors that would soon befall the two unfortunate rebels from the Watchers' lair, or the slave-flesh that would come afterwards, ending days of hunger. The presence at the Assembly of she-rats and trembling, wide-eyed youngsters was unprecedented, marking the occasion as special; the nervous voices of the newcomers added to the high-pitched clamour.

Fat One squatted silently at the back of the throng. His thoughts were dark and angry. So it has come to this, he reflected. The worst of cruelties. Our comrades tortured and killed before our eyes. Not even their own mates and young ones will be spared the spectacle. And then what? Who will be next? How many more Watchers will be dragged from their nests to face interrogation and slow death? We are not safe here. That's why we must go. That's why we must fulfil the plan.

He peered across the crowd to check that they were still there. He had told them to stay in a group, unobtrusive, close to the edge of the lair. When the time came, when he gave the signal, they would skirt round the edge and slip into the Protectors' lair. He would get there immediately behind them, make sure that they weren't followed. It would be just as Twisted Foot had planned it.

He could pick out Small Face. The little Watcher crouched slightly apart from the group. His anxious eyes met Fat One's, and his body shook with fear. Behind Small Face, Grey Eyes, by contrast, kept her head erect;

she looked proud and unbowed by the coming ordeal. Her son also had an air of defiance, although he stayed close to his mother's side. Fat One's mate, Bone-Cruncher, was in the group, together with her two youngsters, a fine son and a portly daughter. Long Ears' mate and daughter and Timid One and her son made up the rest of the group. All there, Fat One nodded to himself. Our new society.

It had all become so clear to him when Sharp Claws announced the Assembly and told of the awful fate planned for Twisted Foot and Long Ears. He had acted quickly, gathering together Small Face and the four mates, spelling out what might occur to them and their children if they remained in the underworld. They had all agreed readily to proceed with the escape plan. It was left to him now to ensure that the dream – the dream begun by his doomed comrades – was realised. He was the leader now, no longer the fat, lazy grumbler of the lair. First, though, he would have to stand by impassively while the Protectors destroyed his companions. He would have to show strength. He must not grow afraid; he must stay angry, hold his nerve, grasp the right moment.

The members of the Inner Circle had taken up their positions on the platform. The Chief Protector would return imminently from the Scavengers' dungeon with the rebel Watchers and slave-rats in tow. Long Snout rose up from the centre of the platform. He stood rigid and all-powerful. His fierce red eyes surveyed the rows of eager, upturned faces. Fat One stared into those eyes, directing the full force of his hate at them. He swore silently. Just one opportunity – a moment alone with the old tyrant – and he would rip the throat from him.

Long Snout's screech now filled the lair, stilling every movement, silencing every voice.

'Comrades of the Dark World!' he began the Assembly. 'Yet another threat to our society has shown itself. This time, comrades, the threat comes from within –'

He broke off suddenly to watch the commotion that had erupted at the entrance to the Scavengers' lair. The Protector who had shot out of the tunnel was still catching his breath. He was staring up, panic-stricken, at the platform.

'The slaves!...' he gasped. 'The slaves are coming!...'

In the brief, utter stillness which preceded the carnage, Fat One and Small Face locked eyes. The moment had come much sooner than they had expected.

Chapter Twenty-Four

The little plum-coloured boat lurched through the angry, swelling sea on its way from the Hawes Pier in South Queensferry to Inchgarvie Island. Big, spume-tipped waves sprang up from the sea to leap over the prow of the boat and crash into the narrow windscreen. Heavy rain slanted from the east, lashing the boat's starboard side and pummelling the flimsy roof of the cabin. Inside the tiny cabin, the three occupants stood close together, peering into the wildness of the day.

The two young men felt queasy. Their pinched pallor contrasted with the gaudiness of their apparel: shiny yellow anoraks and trousers; orange lifesaving jackets; and green Wellington boots. Their 'skipper', Charlie McNulty, thought that they looked like overdressed parrots. Charlie was a thin man in his forties; a six-footer with shoulders which seemed permanently hunched, a long face with a square chin, unruly black hair and wild, bushy eyebrows. It was his job to patrol the waters under the railway bridge in case any of the maintenance team fell into the sea. If they were lucky, they might still be alive after they hit the water. If they were even luckier, he might just get to them before they drowned or perished from the cold. No-one was working on the bridge today – the weather would have prevented it anyway – but he had been called out urgently to ferry the 'whiz-kids' from the exhibition company to Inchgarvie. Charlie had been on duty every weekend while the floodlighting was installed on the bridge. He would be on duty again during the whole of the next day's festivities. He wasn't too happy about this latest inconvenience, nor was he pleased about the storm which was tossing and buffeting his little boat.

Charlie lit a cigarette with one hand and steered the boat with the other. As it plunged under the first giant arch of the bridge and moved out into the estuary, the vessel began to lurch more violently. The two passengers clung, white-knuckled, to the rail under the windscreen. Their faces were even greyer now. Charlie puffed the cigarette and smiled a thin, malicious smile.

Digger hunched down and closed his eyes again as yet another blast of icy rain swept over the island. He felt cold and wet and exceptionally tired. He was an old Watcher, well past his prime, probably in his last Cycle. One day soon, he knew, he wouldn't wake up, and they would drag his corpse into the Scavengers' lair. It seemed to him that he had spent forever out here among the rocks, trying to shield himself from the worst of the storm. Darkness was an awful long time in coming. He alone kept guard over the outside world. The members of the daylight watch had been told to return to the underworld for a special Assembly. He came in their place. He was old and useless; he could forego the ranting of the Chamberlain on this occasion – and suffer the fury of the storm instead. He had been forbidden from seeking shelter under the debris at the entrance tunnel. He had to stay in the open, on the lookout for the arrival of Two-Legs. He had wedged himself below some large rocks close to the monastery wall, but the spot that he had chosen offered scant protection from the biting east wind and the driving rain.

Altogether, Digger decided, he was having a thoroughly miserable time. He felt very, very tired. He had already spent all night above ground. It was he who had been forced to report Narrow Back's disappearance from the watch. Poor Narrow Back. He saw later what they had done to him. Now, it seemed, Twisted Foot and Long Ears would get the same treatment. Well, that was one compensation: at least he wouldn't have to witness their demise. They were so foolish, the young Watchers. To rebel against the society. It was unthinkable. He had learned that a long time ago. So foolish and futile.

Digger shivered. He had to keep his mind on his duty. Duty must always come first. He tried to peer out from the rocks. The rain stung his eyes. He could barely discern the jetty down below and the frothing waves which threatened to engulf it. He closed his eyes. He was so tired. Sleep came like a stealthy predator, claiming his mind.

Chapter Twenty-Five

Jagged Fangs stumbled into the Common lair. There were bloody gashes across his muzzle and down his chest and forelegs. Broken Tail came limping behind him, his back and flanks lacerated and bleeding, the bone from one of his hindlegs gleaming white where the fur and flesh had been ripped away. The mangled corpses of the two guards lay back in the tunnel.

The first of the Scavengers appeared only moments later. The little warrior darted from the tunnel, paused, blinked, selected a victim and then flew at the target's throat. The others followed, one by one, snout to tail, often scrambling over each other in their eagerness for blood; an unending black torrent of bristling, sinewy avengers. The pattern each time was the same: a momentary pause to seek out a target, followed by a ferocious attack.

Shrieking and screeching, the Chamberlain's audience scattered in all directions. Protectors broke from their ring round the platform and raced to stem the flow at the tunnel. With amazing presence of mind, One Eye, the Chief Hunter, herded the members of his lair into the space by the pool and then set up a barricade of warriors to protect the she-rats and young. Sharp Claws also showed his calmness and quick thinking; pushing and prodding his charges, he began to move them back to the safety of the Watchers' lair.

There was great panic among the Rulers on the platform. Up on his hindquarters, Long Snout struggled to make himself heard over the mews and squeals of his colleagues. He wanted them to retreat to the

Inner Circle lair, but they seemed incapable of understanding or acting.

Wave after wave of Scavengers leapt at the wall of Protectors. The Protectors fought back fiercely. Before long, the ground outside the tunnel was strewn with slave corpses, but the Scavengers continued to surge forward; the flow of attackers was relentless, unstoppable. Several Protectors fell back with as many as five or six slaves clinging to each of them, biting, clawing, gouging at their eyes. Other slaves rushed through the gaps in the wall, springing into the open, immediately searching for new victims. Invariably, the cries and wails of the Rulers drew their attention. The fat brown ones were easy targets; so soft and juicy, so vulnerable. The wailing grew louder as drooling Scavengers began to propel themselves into the quivering mass on the platform.

Twisted Foot and Long Ears were swept along by the momentum of the rushing slaves. They emerged from the tunnel, breathing hard, with little time to take in the incredible noise and mayhem of the battle. Slayer sped past them and sprang straight at the eyes of a beleaguered Protector. The Protector screamed and stumbled backwards. Reflex took over the Watchers' actions. They slipped through the space left by the Protector and then headed across the Common lair.

'The tunnel!' Twisted Foot shouted. 'The escape tunnel!'

They raced past the platform. There was a blurred glimpse of Long Snout, towering above the rest, magnificent in his anger, a struggling Scavenger trapped by the neck between his massive jaws. As they rounded the platform, they caught sight of Small Face and the others, pressed hard against the wall, staring terrified at the squirming bodies just outside the entrance to the Protectors' lair. Twisted Foot recognised the burly shape of Fat One. His companion was floundering on the ground, trying desperately to dislodge the Scavenger on his back. Again, reflex dictated Twisted Foot's movements. He leapt into the fray, seized the Scavenger by the back of the neck and bit hard. The Scavenger gasped and shuddered. There was a horrifying, gurgling noise, and then hot blood spurted into Twisted Foot's mouth. He tossed the slave's body to one side.

Fat One scrambled up.

'Back from the dead, comrade?' he growled affectionately.

The others pressed round Twisted Foot. Grey Eyes and Soft-Mover nuzzled into him.

'Let's go,' he said. 'Quickly!'

Led by Fat One, the group moved off into the tunnel. Twisted Foot and Long Ears lingered at the back. They took a final look at the mounting slaughter in the Common lair. The black torrent continued to gush from the Scavengers' dungeon. The Protectors had all but lost control; snarling slaves were moving in on their mates and young ones. Up on the platform, the squealing, obese body of the King-rat toppled over as Slasher and Belcher tore greedily at his snow-white throat.

Sharp Claws prowled anxiously outside the Watchers' lair. Behind him, his warriors were bunched round the entrance tunnel. Most of the she-rats and youngsters were inside, safe for the time being. The slaves would come soon, though. The Watchers would fight bravely, but Sharp Claws knew that they would be quickly overwhelmed.

The noise of the battle was deafening, terrifying. His eyes scoured the Common lair, searching for stragglers amongst the carnage. He glimpsed Grey Eyes and her son as they fled into the Protectors' lair. Then he saw Long Ears, and Twisted Foot next to him. They were staring at the platform, as if transfixed by the sight of the Inner Circle in its death throes. Now they were turning, sprinting after Grey Eyes.

Escaping at last, Sharp Claws said to himself. He was glad. Whatever perils awaited them above ground could be no worse than down here. The society was doomed, and he along with it. He had been its loyal servant all this time; a true and faithful leader of the Watchers. Now, it seemed, he would die protecting the society.

He thought suddenly of his time as a young, fresh Watcher. The hardships. The humiliations. The cruelty of the Protectors. The smug, bloated faces of the Rulers. He had had dreams of escape then, but the power of the society had always held him back, kept him servile. Where was that power this day? What held him back now? He was old, yes, but he was still fit and strong, with Cycles yet to live. He didn't have to die here.

He looked again at the raging battle. Hordes of slaves had begun their assault on the Hunters. The Watchers would be next. There was no time for further thought. He sprang away from his warriors and then raced for the Protectors' lair. A small, lithe, muscular figure slipped down from the platform and moved silently behind him.

Chapter Twenty-Six

He awoke with a start. The pain was blinding him, burning into his head. He felt suffocatingly hot. He was panting hoarsely, shaking with fever, weaker than ever. It had been like this for many days: sleeping in snatches, jolting awake; each time the pain returning with renewed ferocity. His dreams were becoming more delirious, more frightening. This last one had been particularly bad. He imagined that huge, hideous monsters were in the lair. He could hear them snarling. He could see their large yellow eyes. He could feel their hot, fetid breath as they closed in on him. Then he had returned to consciousness; back to the stifling fever; back to the burning pain.

He held his breath for a moment and listened. The screams from the Common lair were muffled and distant. He remembered the special Assembly. He had been too weak to attend. In truth, though, he would not have wished to watch others perform his duties. Torture and execution: those practices had been his special province once – before this accursed affliction!

He listened again. There were other noises. Scratching noises. Here in the empty lair! He peered into the blackness. The pain stabbed at him. There was a blurred shape near the entrance. Then another. And another. Yellow eyes flashing. His heart thudded. Were these the monsters from his dream? He stumbled from the nest, his head swimming with the effort. The shapes became more blurred and then melted away.

There were voices now. Urgent voices. He couldn't see. He was confused. Were the voices in his own mind? He shook his head violently.

Excruciating pain jolted through him, almost stopping his heart. Nausea swept over him. Then suddenly his vision cleared. The shapes re-appeared. There were many of them. They were coming closer, coming into focus; hazy images transforming into fur and flesh. He recognised the faces. The fat, lazy one from the Watchers' lair. The little cripple at the back. The floppy-eared one. These were no monsters! Fear and blinding pain were quickly forgotten, replaced by blind rage. A great roar erupted from him. Then he charged at the intruders.

The demented Protector came at them from out of the darkness. The apparition was hideous. The whole of the right side of his head was horribly bloated and oozing pus. His long fangs were bared, gleaming white, dripping foam. There were shrieks of alarm from the Watchers. Small Face scuttled back with the mates and youngsters, but Fat One stood his ground. Arching his back and spitting, he forced Neck-Snapper to draw up. Twisted Foot and Long Ears raced from behind to join their companion. Growling loudly, Neck-Snapper regarded the three Watchers for some moments. The growling stopped suddenly. Then he reared up, ready to pounce.

The sea heaved up again and tossed the little boat against the wooden supports of the jetty. The sharp crack of the impact woke Digger. The old Watcher opened his eyes. Wind and rain whipped into them. He felt colder and more miserable than before. There was another crack. He peered down through tiny slits and saw the boat and the two brightly dressed men who were clambering out of it. One of the men slipped on the sea-lashed jetty. His companion helped him to his feet. Then they set off, struggling against the wind, heading for the high ground. The hoods of their anoraks were pulled down over their heads, almost completely concealing their frozen white faces.

Digger cursed. He should have stayed more alert. There was still time to redeem himself, though. He must return to the underworld at once. Special Assembly or not, he must find Sharp Claws and report the presence of the Two-Legs.

He squeezed out of his makeshift shelter and then moved stealthily across the slippery rocks. At least when he got to the underworld, he thought selfishly, there would be some respite from the foul elements.

Chapter Twenty-Seven

The voice was deep and gruff. It came from near the entrance tunnel.

'Over here, Neck-Snapper!' it shouted.

For the second time in only a few moments, Neck-Snapper cut short his attack. He looked in the direction of the voice. Sharp Claws moved further into the lair, closer to Neck-Snapper, placing the Protector between him and the young Watchers.

Neck-Snapper shifted round slightly, using his one eye to follow Sharp Claws' progress.

'You!' he hissed slowly.

'Yes, me.'

Neck-Snapper snarled. He turned round fully now and faced Sharp Claws. The young Watchers were forgotten for the moment. It was the old warrior whom he wanted. He had old scores to settle with him. Their bodies were only inches apart. Their meeting was long overdue.

Sharp Claws glanced at Twisted Foot.

'Make your escape now,' he said. 'Quickly!' Then he returned his stare to Neck-Snapper.

Twisted Foot hesitated. He was confused.

'But –'

Sharp Claws kept his eyes fixed on the Protector, watching for the slightest movement, ready for the lunge that would come.

'Go now!' he roared.

Twisted Foot nodded. He was still unsure, but he spun round and raced for the escape tunnel. The others scurried behind him.

Fat One watched them go. He wanted to stay, to help the old Watcher, but he knew that there was little time to lose. With a wrench, he moved off after his companions. He stopped at the tunnel mouth and glanced back. They hadn't moved. Each waited for the other to act, Neck-Snapper snarling and drooling, Sharp Claws calm and alert; sworn enemies savouring that taut, scary stillness before mortal combat.

Fat One slipped into the tunnel.

Neck-Snapper made the lunge. Sharp Claws dodged its impact, came up on the Protector's right side and gouged into his injured head. Neck-Snapper bellowed in agony. He jerked his head back, managing to dislodge Sharp Claws. Blood was pouring out of the re-opened eyehole.

The two flew at each other again, jaws agape, growling incessantly, each thrusting for the soft flesh of the throat. They toppled over in a deadly clinch, rolled across the hard ground and then crashed into the rows of empty nests.

The Scavenger's cold, hard eyes flickered in the darkness. The struggle no longer interested him. He licked his fangs and moved lightly past the noisy, writhing bodies.

Charlie lit another cigarette and continued to peer out at the island, a broad grin on his face. His two passengers had managed to get to the display platform. They were checking the structure now, making sure that it hadn't been loosened by the wind and that the layers of polythene which swathed it were keeping out the rain. One of the men was kneeling down, examining the base of the platform. Caught by a sudden gust, the corner of a sheet of polythene flapped up and wrapped itself round the man's head. He struggled to free himself and fell on his backside.

Charlie sniggered. It was pure comedy out there. He had watched them waddle up the slope, sliding and stumbling every few feet, like a pair of penguins. Earlier on, just before they left the cabin, he had ribbed them about the rats.

'Mind now, boys,' he had said with a straight face. 'Watch out for an ambush.'

The men had looked perplexed.

'Aye,' he continued, 'they rat bites can be awfie painful.'

It was just his wee joke, but they hadn't been very amused. Well, it served them right. They were the ones who had started the scare about the rats.

His gaze wandered away from the men and down to the monastery. He would be surprised if rats or anything else wanted to stay on the island. It was such a godforsaken place. He came past it in the boat almost every working day, but he hardly ever gave it more than a second glance. He knew very little about Inchgarvie's history, and he had been on the island only once, way back, when he was a youngster.

Something moved among the rocks. It was just a flicker, but it caught his attention. He got closer to the windscreen and peered out through the haze of grey rain. The thing moved again. It seemed to slide – no, to squirm – over the rocks. His face was pressed against the Perspex now. He wiped away the fog caused by his breath, screwed his eyes up, peered again. His first thought was a dog. But, no, not moving like that; not squirming. A cat, maybe. A big black cat.

The boat began to rock wildly. He lost sight of the creature for a moment. Then it re-appeared, creeping slowly, heading up towards the monastery. He wiped the Perspex again. He saw the long tail slithering over a boulder. A rat! The size of a cat!

'Naw,' he murmured. 'It couldnae be.'

The tail curled round another boulder. The creature's black body seemed to undulate as it slid through a gap in the monastery wall.

Charlie stubbed out his cigarette and zipped up his jerkin.

'Right!' he said.

He left the boat quickly and scrambled up to the jetty. The wind tore at his hair and clothes. Icy needles of rain stung his face. He struggled along the jetty, trying not to slip, wishing that he had stayed where he was. His smirk had gone. The joke was on him now.

Chapter Twenty-Eight

They were out in the open now, huddled together, shivering uncontrollably. The sea rose up on either side of them, wild and threatening, flinging its angry spray across the rocks. The he-rats were veterans of the outside world, past witnesses to its ugly, violent moods, but they were dismayed by the unexpected fury of the storm. It seemed as if the full wrath and vengeance of the Cold Cycle had been unleashed upon them in an effort to impede their escape.

For the she-rats and youngsters, this was their first terrifying glimpse of the world above their own. The sights, the sounds, the smells of this awful place were mind-numbing, beyond their comprehension. They had lived in permanent darkness, but here there was a lightness, a vast lightness which made them blink and want to hide; a great force which magnified all around them. Invisible creatures flew out of the lightness to strike at their bodies and sting them with armies of sharp, icy water. There were other creatures in the enormous expanse of water surrounding them: huge, angry white monsters which leapt up and battered the rocks. Theirs was a world of quiet, furtive movements; of warm nests and familiar scents. This world that they had fled to was harsh and squalling and hostile, with a jarring coldness which found its way into their bones.

Twisted Foot recognised their discomfort and bewilderment. He wanted to console them, to reassure them.

'It's not always like...' he tried to say, but the wind snatched away the rest of his words.

Long Ears pushed his snout into Twisted Foot.

'We must go, comrade!' he was shouting. His look was anxious, impatient.

Twisted Foot nodded. The time for explanations was past. They had to go now. He had to lead them into the sea. He looked round the others, silently rallying them. Then they moved off together down to the point of the island. As if understanding their intent, the hungry waves rushed up to meet them.

He appeared suddenly at Twisted Foot's side, bringing the startled Watcher to a halt. The little Scavenger seemed to have materialised from the greyness of the storm. Fat One was first to act. He rushed from the back of the group to challenge the Scavenger.

'No!' cried Twisted Foot as he sprang between the Scavenger and the charging Watcher. 'This is Slayer! The slave-King! He – he's coming with us!'

Fat One stayed still, growling, eyeing the intruder suspiciously. Slayer seemed more perturbed by the cold than by Fat One's growls. He was blinking and shivering like the rest of them.

'Well, Master,' he chittered to Twisted Foot, 'this surely is the strangest of worlds.'

Twisted Foot didn't reply. He turned now to watch the churning sea, to steel himself for the ordeal. The waves licked up, taunting him. The giant's foot seemed so far away. He had to go first. He had to show courage, determination. He teetered at the edge of the rocks and then plunged abruptly into the sea. The waves swept over him, immersing him. The shock of coldness came instantly, vice-like, compressing his lungs, expelling the air. He couldn't move. He was sinking into a deep black void. Then, suddenly, he could see light again. His head was above the surface. His front paws were threshing wildly. One of his back legs was jerking furiously, while the other dangled in the water, twisted and helpless. He was moving, bobbing on top of the sea, riding over the waves.

Slayer went next, fearlessly, without hesitation. Then Grey Eyes and Soft-Mover slipped into the sea together. The others followed quickly until only Small Face and Fat One were left on the rocks. Small Face looked pleadingly at his companion. He was stiff with terror. Fat One prodded him sharply.

'Go on!' he commanded.

Small Face hit the water with a loud squeal. He sank down and then re-emerged moments later, struggling, gasping for air. He was swimming, though; making progress.

Fat One watched them for a while longer. He had decided. He had to return. He would never be able to rest otherwise. He would never forgive himself. Old Sharp Claws deserved his help.

Fat One turned suddenly and sprinted back to the escape tunnel. Tossed back and forth at the whim of the restless sea, the ragged line of tiny black heads moved slowly towards the bridge.

For perhaps the hundredth time since leaving the rocks, Digger paused to listen. He was very close to the entrance tunnel now, nearly home. He had been inching his way through the rubble, extra-cautious because of the Two-Legs on the high ground. He tried to listen above the howling of the wind and the heavy splatter of rain. Nothing. He poked his head up, glanced round and then ducked down again. His heart gave a kick. Across from him, in the dimness of the monastery, was a darker shape. He had just glimpsed the Two-Legs. The giant was standing stiff and silent and staring in his direction.

Long Snout swept into the Protectors' lair. About a dozen blood-spattered Protectors rushed behind him.

'Quickly! Quickly!' Long Snout was shouting. 'We'll hold them off from here!'

The rest seemed to come in a flood, squealing in terror, clambering over each other until they were far enough into the lair; the surviving mates and young of the Protectors mingling with the torn, bleeding remnants of the Inner Circle. Another score or more Protectors came behind them to take up their positions at the tunnel mouth and to close the gap between slaves and survivors. Jostling bodies and shrill voices now filled the place. Attracted by the commotion, she-rats and youngsters were spilling out of the Inner Circle lair and joining the anxious throng.

The two combatants in the centre of the lair broke off from their struggle. Both were breathing hard, their bodies streaked with blood and saliva. They kept their eyes fixed on each other, conscious that the incoming rats were forming a circle around them.

Sharp Claws seemed dazed. It was some moments before he realised fully the danger that he was in. He began to back away slowly from Neck-Snapper, searching for a gap in the circle, ready to make a dash for the escape tunnel. By then, though, Long Snout had seen them.

The Chamberlain pushed through the crowd until he crouched next to Neck-Snapper. His presence silenced the hubbub of the spectators. His cold glare transfixed Sharp Claws.

'What's going on here, Chief Watcher?' he rasped.

It was Neck-Snapper who replied in a hoarse, wheezing voice.

'He – he's a traitor, Chamberlain. He – he helped the others – the other Watchers – to escape.'

Long Snout looked in the direction of the escape tunnel and then back at Sharp Claws.

'So!' he hissed.

Sharp Claws knew that he was trapped, that there was no escape now. He stayed rigid, staring up at the Chamberlain, waiting for death. He saw the jaws opening, the long yellow fangs reaching down for him. He felt sharp, momentary pain as the jaws snapped over his neck. Then blackness.

The jaws snapped again. Hot blood sprayed across the crowd. The severed head rolled off into them. The hubbub resumed.

Long Snout rose up and spoke quickly to the guards who had gathered round him.

'Go to the outside world! Find the traitors! Destroy them!'

Then he turned his attention to Neck-Snapper.

'You did well, warrior,' he growled.

Blood was still pumping in spurts from the crumpled, headless corpse of the Chief Watcher. At the mouth of the escape tunnel, Fat One was shaking violently. He closed his eyes to shut out the ghastly sight. When he opened them again, he saw the yellow slit-eyes of the charging Protectors. He moved too late. The leading Protector's fangs sank into his fleshy side. Fat One screamed and twisted away. There was a ragged, gaping wound along his left flank. The pain was incredible. He could hardly breathe. He began to scramble up the tunnel. He felt weak and exceptionally heavy, but the snapping, snarling jaws of the Protector drove him on.

Chapter Twenty-Nine

The inside of the monastery was dank and gloomy. The place smelled of decay. Charlie kept very still. He was numb with cold and soaking wet. His hair was plastered to his head. Rain streamed down his face, plummeted from the tip of his long, bony nose and rushed in tiny torrents down his jerkin to splash on his sodden trousers.

Up to Charlie's right, on the crest of the island, his passengers were still fussing around the display platform. Down below, Charlie stared into the debris, clamping his teeth together to stop them from chattering. He knew where the rat was. He knew that the rat had seen him. They were both waiting: hunter and prey at standstill.

Charlie decided to break the stalemate. He stooped down, snatched up a heavy chunk of masonry and hurled it in the direction of the concealed rat. The stone seemed to skiff across the debris before thudding into the opposite wall of the monastery. The rat sprang up, streaked across Charlie's left and disappeared through a gap in the base of the wall.

Charlie shuddered for just an instant. The rat was enormous, a monster. He picked up another large piece of stone and headed out to the point of the island. The two men up above watched him go. They looked at each other, baffled, and then shrugged and returned to their work.

Fat One pushed himself along the last few feet of the tunnel. He was in great pain. There was still a long way to go. Through the tunnel. Across the rocks. Into the sea. If he could just reach the water's edge, he would let the sea swallow him up, soothe this searing pain. They wouldn't follow him. He would be safe. He would soon join the others. But he had to move faster; he had to stay ahead of the Protectors.

He bolted out of the tunnel, back into the swirling grey day, and almost collided into the feet of the Two-Legs. The Two-Legs stood with its back to the tunnel mouth; a great, dripping giant with its arm raised and poised to strike. Trapped between the Protectors and this monster, Fat One knew that there was only one way to go. With a gasp of agony, he twisted round and began to scramble up the slope towards the monastery. His blood spattered on to the slippery rocks, but was quickly washed away by the pounding rain.

The Two-Legs completed its search of the south side of the point. Then it turned slowly to the north, head bowed, scanning the rocks, the arm still outstretched and menacing. The Protectors shrank back into the tunnel. They had seen the giant's evil white face and the great rock clutched in its massive fist.

He knew that he had made a terrible mistake. He had been so close to the entrance tunnel, only a few steps from home. But the attack by the Two-Legs had panicked him. He should have stayed in the monastery. Now he was out in the open, cringing among the rocks, further than ever from the underworld. The Two-Legs was here searching for him, ready to attack again.

Digger tried to stop his body from shaking and to regain control of his breathing. He had to concentrate on getting back to the monastery. He raised his head very slightly and peeked over the rocks. He could see the Two-Legs turning, its gaze sweeping the ground. Then he saw Fat One scuttling up towards him. The young Watcher seemed to be in pain. The whole of his left side was covered with blood. Where had he come from? Was the Two-Legs pursuing him, too?

As if trying to beckon to his comrade, Digger raised his head higher. He saw the rock before it hit him, a fleeting glimpse of something dark and solid. The impact lifted him off the ground. A sharp, blinding flash filled his head.

Charlie gave out a yelp of victory as he rushed up the slope. The rat was stretched out on its side, motionless. Thick blood was seeping from the wound in its head and spreading quickly across the wet ground. Charlie nudged the rat with the toe of his shoe. The rat didn't move. Its small, dark eyes continued to stare lifelessly into the rain. Charlie grinned, bent down and lifted the rat by its tail. He held the corpse at arm's length, feeling the weight, admiring his trophy.

'Ya beauty,' he murmured.

It is a monster, he thought. As big as a cat. But there must be others like it. As big as this one. Maybe a whole colony of them. The grin disappeared quickly. There was a frown on his face now. He glanced behind him. Where were they hiding? Were they lurking among the rocks? Watching him? The cold, grey island seemed suddenly more hostile. The sounds of the storm grew sinister, full of whispers, full of unknown menace. He could feel their eyes on him, following his movements. He had a vision of hordes of furry black vermin streaming down from the ruins, closing in on him.

Still clutching the rat by its tail, Charlie began to move back to the jetty, his eyes darting constantly among the rocks. His pace quickened as he got nearer the boat. He would never admit to it afterwards, but his legs were shaking uncontrollably.

Chapter Thirty

Twisted Foot could barely keep his head above the water. His eyes were almost completely closed against the stinging spray, and he couldn't feel the rest of his body. He was utterly exhausted now, but he knew that he must be very close.

A huge wave rose up in front of him. He didn't attempt to fight it. The wave swept him up, engulfed him in its spume and then spat him out again like unwanted jetsam, dashing his body back into the cold, murky sea.

Twisted Foot's head re-appeared above the surface. Water gushed from his mouth and ears. He was choking, sucking for air. He was clinging to something soft and slimy. But it felt solid underneath. Hard rock! He had reached the giant's foot.

He climbed higher until he left the seaweed behind and there was only rock under his claws. The waves leapt up in pursuit, anxious to reclaim him. He climbed another few feet, reached the top of the pillar and then hauled his aching body over the edge. He lay there panting, his eyes closed blissfully, the pounding of the sea still deafening in his ears. Safe.

There were four such circular granite pillars under this section of the bridge; each sunk deep into the River Forth and rising several feet above the surface like a giant steppingstone; each supporting a convergence of massive steel stanchions and arches from high above. The tops of the pillars formed the corners of a square. Inside the square, the seawater slapped and gurgled darkly.

When Twisted Foot opened his eyes, he saw the small, sleek form of Slayer crawling up to join him. The slave-King was shivering and panting loudly, but otherwise unscathed. The others came quickly behind him, each clambering up from the seaweed to find a space on the narrow ledge round the top of the pillar. They huddled together, seeking each other's warmth; a tightly packed semicircle of wet, shivering bodies.

Only Timid One was left in the water. She had fallen behind the others halfway through the journey, as if her strength and willpower had suddenly deserted her. Now a wave was picking her up and dashing her against the pillar. She clung to the trailing seaweed for some moments, looking up helplessly at her companions. Then she seemed just to let go, to yield to the hungry sea. The waves claimed her back, quickly sweeping her away from the bridge and out into the estuary. Her head vanished below the water and didn't rise again.

The others stared silently at the sea for a while, their eyes fixed on the spot where Timid One had disappeared. They hadn't been able to help her. Now they were too exhausted even to mourn her death.

The storm continued to rage around them, its fury unabated. The wind cut into their bodies. The driving rain added to their misery. From time to time, a frothing wave would curl up and crash against the pillar to remind them of Timid One's icy fate. At least we're safe for the time being, Twisted Foot thought. We'll rest here until darkness comes, he decided, and then continue our journey. He gazed up into the belly of the giant at the intricate network of crisscrossing spars. The first obstacle had been overcome. He sensed that the next obstacle would be no less dangerous.

His thoughts were interrupted by the sudden wails which came from Bone-Cruncher and her youngsters.

'Fat One!' Bone-Cruncher cried. 'Fat One isn't here!'

The others peered along the ledge, searching to their left and right. Then they stared down into the sea, as if expecting Fat One to emerge suddenly from the waves.

Small Face's voice came almost like a whisper.

'I... I th-think...' he stuttered, 'he w-went b-back to the underworld... f-for Sh-Sharp Claws...'

Twisted Foot's heart sank. He looked across to the island. His gaze travelled along the point, past the ruins of the monastery and up to the crest. There was no movement. Even the creature on the high ground had stopped flapping. A train was thundering overhead. The giant shook, and Twisted Foot along with it.

Tall waves crashed across the little boat's prow as it veered to starboard and headed back to the Hawes Pier. Inside the cabin, the three occupants were still cold and dripping from their experiences on the island. As on the journey out, the young men from the exhibition company clung grimly to the rail under the windscreen. Their task had been completed successfully. The fireworks display was safe.

Charlie's hair was still plastered to his head. His sodden, crumpled trousers stuck uncomfortably to his legs. He lit a cigarette and glanced at his passengers. The Thompson Twins without moustaches, he thought mischievously. The young men returned his glance. They had seen him raking among the rubble in the middle of the storm. Looking for ghosts probably. They thought he was crazy.

Charlie was grinning now. Still staring straight ahead, he said:

'You remember my wee joke aboot the rats?'

The men looked at him, but said nothing.

'Well, boys,' Charlie continued.

He left the cigarette dangling from his lips, reached down to a little cupboard on his right and pulled out the dead rat by the tail. He held up the corpse so that the rat's glazed eyes were level with his own.

'What d'you think o' this beauty?' he asked.

The young men blanched. One of them swore softly. The other began to gag. Charlie brayed with laughter. They thought that he sounded remarkably like a hyena.

Part Four:

Inside the Giant

Chapter Thirty-One

It was the sudden brightness that woke Twisted Foot. When he opened his eyes, he could see the sun facing him. It was away in the distance, peeping above the horizon, sending out its first rays to light up the estuary. The rays were washing over him and his companions, warming their damp bodies.

Twisted Foot felt the coldness and tiredness begin to lift from him. It had been a long ordeal up here on the narrow ledge. All through the dark hours the storm had raged. They had dared not move from the ledge, lest the wind snatched them away and plunged them into the frothing waters below or lest they slipped on the giant's dripping surface and slithered down to their deaths. They had stayed huddled together, shivering, waiting for the storm to break. And when it finally did, all they wanted to do was close their eyes and sleep.

He looked around at the others. They were all still asleep. He would have to rouse them. They had escaped from that accursed society over there, but they were out in the open here, exposed for all to see. Daylight or not, they would have to continue their journey soon or risk discovery by the Two-Legs.

He lingered for a few moments longer. He wanted to savour the warmth of the sun. Everything was so quiet, so peaceful now. Even the waters had ceased their constant turmoil to lay flat and placid, reflecting the light. He had witnessed this scene – the awakening of the world above – many times before when he came to the end of those long, lonely watches in the darkness. He knew that the tranquillity wouldn't last, though. The vessels of the Two-Legs would appear beside them soon. And the Two-Legs creatures would begin to rush back and forth through the belly of the giant. It occurred to him that he still hadn't heard the first of those creatures; it usually accompanied the appearance of each new day's light. He didn't know why this day should be any different.

After many hours of shrieks and squeals and growls and dying gurgles, quiet had also returned to the underworld. From his perch at the head of the pool, One Eye surveyed the aftermath of the battle in the Common lair. The floor of the lair was strewn with corpses. Although there were many Scavengers among the corpses, there were also many warriors and she-rats and youngsters from the Outer Circle. The carnage had been even worse on the platform in the centre of the lair, where the bodies of the Rulers were now piled, one on top of the other, almost all with their bellies split open. A few Scavengers still prowled around the bodies, gnawing at the spilled entrails, but most had gone, having already gorged themselves on Inner Circle flesh; tired, sated and thirsty, they had returned to their own lair, where they could quench their thirsts and sleep.

One Eye was pleased with himself for having had the presence of mind to guide the members of his lair to this narrow entrance to the pool. By making a stand here, the Hunters had not only denied the Scavengers access to the pool, but had also blocked their means of escape to the outside world. He was equally pleased with the performance of his warriors; they had successfully withstood wave after wave of attacks. Some warriors had been slain, of course, but most were still there beside him, alert, ready for the next onslaught. Behind them, sleeping fitfully round the edge of the pool, were their mates and youngsters. He turned to regard the sleeping forms. Safe for the time being, he nodded. Not like the Watchers. Having observed the slaves wander freely into and out of the Watchers' lair, he could only presume that they had all perished. They were a useless lot anyway, he muttered to himself; their presence in the underworld wouldn't be missed.

He returned his gaze to the Common lair. Directly across from him was the mouth of the tunnel leading to the Protectors' lair. His comrades over there had also fought bravely. They, too, had beaten back the slaves to protect their own mates and young, as well as what was left of the Inner Circle. He nodded again. It wouldn't be long before the Hunters and Protectors joined forces to regain control of the underworld. Together, they would drive the remaining slaves back into their dungeon, and they would ensure that none could ever escape from the dungeon again. That was the plan. All they were waiting for now was the order from Long Snout to begin the assault.

He had heard the details of the plan direct from the mouth of the Chamberlain himself. When he saw that the battle was ebbing, that the Scavengers were growing tired, he had gone immediately to the world above, struggling through the wind and rain to reach the sacred tunnel and make contact with the survivors in the Protectors' lair. Long Snout had been there; unbowed by the revolt, angry, defiant, as imposing as ever, the old Chamberlain was confident that, when it came, their counterattack would defeat the slaves. But first he wanted the surviving warriors to rest up, tend their wounds and regain their strength. In the meantime, there were other important matters to be considered. During the battle, the Two Legs had returned to the world above, their presence bringing to a halt the Protectors' pursuit of those wretched, young traitors. According to the Protectors, one of the Two Legs had killed a warrior. Its victim was a decrepit, worthless Watcher, but a warrior nevertheless. Although the Two Legs had departed in their vessel long ago, the Chamberlain was convinced that they would be back once more. With the traitors still at large, he also feared that that next visit could lead to discovery of the underworld and the destruction of their society. That was why the Protectors now permanently guarded the sacred tunnel from the outside. And it was why he, as Chief Hunter, had agreed to take on responsibility for watching over the rest of the outside world. Torn Coat, his most trusted lieutenant, was up there at this moment, with orders to go direct to the sacred tunnel to report any unusual activity.

One Eye yawned. Now it was just a case of waiting for the signal from Long Snout. He was tired. His only eye felt heavy. Perhaps he would also doze for a little while.

It had been many Cycles since he had ventured out on the world above, but when he heard the report from Broken Tail he had felt the necessity to come up here and witness the spectacle for himself. He was still blinking in the brightness, still gasping at the sharpness of the air, when he saw them. They were clustered around the top of one of the giant's feet: a bedraggled, sorry-looking bunch. From where he stood just outside the entrance to the sacred tunnel, he could make out the cripple from the Watchers' lair and the cripple's long-eared collaborator. The smaller, muscular one alongside the cripple must be the slave-King, he growled; Broken Tail had said that he was there. There was no sign of the fat traitor, though. The Protectors who chased him out of the underworld bragged that they had dealt him a mortal blow. Perhaps his corpse was somewhere among the rocks. Or perhaps he had drowned when he tried to swim across to the giant. No matter. It was the cripple he wanted. It was the cripple who was to blame for all of this. It was the cripple who would pay! As soon as he could spare them, as soon as this business with the Scavengers was over, he would pick out his best Protectors. Their job would be to find the cripple and bring him back. The traitor's punishment would be special, unprecedented!

Unable to contain his anger, Long Snout was growling and snarling so loudly now that he didn't hear the approach of the Two-Legs vessel. Torn Coat's sudden appearance at his side alerted him to the danger.

'Go back!' he hissed at Torn Coat. 'Let me know what the Two Legs get up to this time!'

'Pah!' he hissed again as he swept past the guard to return to the underworld.

Chapter Thirty-Two

As predicted by the weathermen, the Big Day had arrived in a blaze of sunshine and blue sky. Out of the storm that had raged for a whole day and a whole night, there emerged a bright, fresh autumn morning of the kind that are common in the east of Scotland. As soon as it was light, the organisers of the Big Day hurriedly reviewed the impact on their arrangements of the storm and the terrible deluge that had accompanied it. Not unexpectedly, parts of some of the fields which they had designated as temporary car and bus parks were still waterlogged, and frantic efforts were being made to drain the excess water. However, judging from the number of vehicles that were already converging on the fields, a bit of boggy land was not going to deter sightseers. That difficulty over parking aside, everything appeared to be still intact to cater for the estimated influx of at least a million visitors to the area.

By far the largest proportion of that number was destined to descend on South Queensferry, congregating in particular on the wide esplanade that extended from the eastern end of the town to the Hawes Pier. The esplanade gave commanding views of the old rail bridge, her road bridge neighbour to the west and the stretch of river between the two bridges. It was that expanse of water, along with the sky above it, which would form the main arena for the Big Day's events.

The esplanade was a hive of activity this early morning, with crowd barriers being erected along the seafront, the loudspeaker system being tested, the portable toilets being made ready for use, and the food and souvenir stalls and exhibition tents being set up. There was also much activity high up on the rail bridge overlooking the esplanade. Walking in single file along the narrow walkways on either side of the railway track, on the lookout for any storm damage, ensuring that all was shipshape for the old girl's birthday celebrations, two crews of maintenance men had begun to cross the bridge from south to north. Close on the heels of the maintenance men were two similarly sized crews from the floodlighting contractors on their final walk-through to check that all of the lamps and cabling were still in place. Train services across the Forth may have been suspended until the next morning, but the bridge was busier than ever today.

Down below, in the shadow of the bridge, a little plum-coloured boat was approaching Inchgarvie. The boat had departed from the Hawes Pier some time ago. On board again were Charlie McNulty and the two young men from the exhibition company. Charlie's passengers were visiting the island on this occasion to remove the polythene wrapping from the fireworks display platform and to give the apparatus a final check before that night's extravaganza.

Charlie stood on the jetty with the sun on his face. He lit a cigarette and yawned. The sunshine felt good, but his head was still very fuzzy, and the fumes from last night's beer were still in his nostrils. This journey over to the island at the crack of dawn hadn't done his hangover any good. Nor was he relishing the prospect of patrolling under the bridge for the rest of the day.

When he got back from yesterday's trip, it was as if the whole town had been in a party mood in spite of the storm. It was Saturday evening anyway, so he had gone to the pub and joined the party. He had vague recollections of relating his story about killing the monster rat and of no-one seeming to believe him. He didn't have the evidence with him, of course: it was still on the boat, wrapped up in a plastic bag to stop it smelling. And the two whiz-kids weren't there to back up the story.

He looked over to the crest of the island. The Thompson Twins were still fussing with their toy up there. He wasn't even sure whether the pair of them actually believed that the rat had come from Inchgarvie or whether they thought that he had dangled it in front of them as some sort of practical joke. Either way, they didn't appear to be phased about going back to the island. It was him, not them, who felt queasy this time; it was him, not them, who hung back at the jetty, not daring to go any further.

The young men were descending the slope now. Both of them had big smiles on their faces. One was carrying the folded sheets of polythene under his arm. The other was speaking into a walkie-talkie.

'All systems are go,' he was shouting.

Charlie threw his cigarette-end into the water and stepped down into the boat. As soon as this day was over and things were back to normal, he resolved, he would seek out old Proudfoot, the rat-catcher, show him his monster, hear what an expert had to say.

They were all awake now, watching the Two-Legs vessel cut through the calm waters below. The Two-legs intruders were departing in the vessel, leaving behind their creature at the top of the island. The creature was shining brightly, glinting in the sunlight, its purpose still a mystery.

Some of the youngsters had complained of being thirsty and hungry, and Bone-Cruncher was still softly mourning the loss of Fat One, but otherwise they were all resolute, all ready for the next challenge. Twisted Foot would lead the way. He had chosen the enormous steel arch to their rear as the safest and most straightforward way to go up. The arch travelled in a long curve from the giant's foot on which they rested until it reached a length of parapet at its top. Once they reached the parapet, they would crawl through it and into the belly of the giant.

Twisted Foot began the climb. Slayer came next. Then the others followed, all tentatively at first, until they became more confident of their footing. Long Ears had agreed to take up the rear so that he could encourage any of the group who faltered on the way. Their progress was relatively easy, and it wasn't long before the whole group was strung out along the lower part of the arch.

A short screech from behind him brought Twisted Foot to a halt. He recognised Long Ears' warning call. When he turned his head, he could see his companion quivering in panic.

'Two-Legs!' Long Ears was shouting. 'Two-Legs on the giant! Coming this way!'

Twisted Foot strained to hear. It was a few moments before he could make them out. Their footsteps on the wooden walkway sounded like distant thunder. It seemed like a whole army of Two-Legs was approaching.

'Return!' he cried. 'Return! Quickly!'

They all scampered back down to the giant's foot, where they huddled together again, their hearts pounding.

'We're trapped!' Small Face wailed.

The youngsters began to wail, too. And Bone-Cruncher resumed her mourning cries.

'What now, Master?' Slayer whispered into Twisted Foot's ear, but Twisted Foot didn't have an answer for him.

Chapter Thirty-Three

It was eleven o'clock, and the sun was still shining. A chill breeze was blowing in from the estuary, but it didn't seem to bother the mass of people who thronged the esplanade. Nor was it deterring the many others who were flocking to the place from every direction. The loudspeakers were booming out over the noise of the crowd to announce the first event of the day.

The procession could be heard before it was seen, faintly at first and then louder by the moment as it marched from the town to the esplanade. At its head, with bagpipes skirling and drums beating, was a pipe band in full Highland regalia. A short interval behind was a military brass band, its trumpets and trombones and tubas all blaring simultaneously. More bands followed: a jazz band, a calypso band, bands from the local schools; all playing a different, rousing tune, all fronted by rows of twirling majorettes. Then came the floats, each one depicting a scene from the hundred years' history of the town's famous bridge. And finally came the street performers, a whole circus of them. There were stilt-walkers, fire-eaters, jugglers and acrobats to wow the crowd, and there was a gang of clowns of all sizes and descriptions to jostle it. The shouts and whoops from the clowns, and the delighted cries of children in response, added to the general racket of the place. The celebrations had begun.

Just when the footsteps of the Two-Legs army above them had disappeared completely, just when they thought that it was safe again, they heard the din coming from the far shore. From where they squatted under the giant, they had a direct view of the esplanade and the sea of Two Legs massed on it. The number of Two-Legs over there was many, many times the size of their own society. Could there really be that many of them on the world above? The thought of it, the sight of it, the sounds of it were frightening, unnerving.

They became even more unnerved when the Two-Legs creatures suddenly zoomed into the sky above the waters. There were only six of them, but the noise that they made was deafening, unbearable. Keeping in formation, the creatures sped up the way and then down and then up again, turning in loops through the air. Now they were flying upside down. Now they were all speeding away in different directions, each one leaving behind it a long stream of coloured smoke. Now they were back in formation, streaking up and over the giant and out of sight completely, their distant roar being quickly replaced by the thunder of the Two-Legs' clapping on the esplanade.

Twisted Foot had closed his eyes tight in an attempt to shut out the awful clamour of the creatures, but it had been to no avail. When the clamour had gone, when he opened his eyes again, it was only to see that the sky was filled with another set of creatures. These were larger and quieter. They seemed to drone and hover in the air. Then, astonishingly, Two-Legs in their scores began to tumble from the creatures and float down to the waters, their great arms extended like the wings of the white birds when they landed. He watched, mesmerised, as the Two-Legs dropped into the sea, where they were immediately picked up by the numerous Two-Legs vessels that had appeared there, as if from nowhere. In panic, he looked around him. There were many more vessels in the waters; they were coming from every direction, and they were all converging on the same place.

Twisted Foot had to shake his muzzle to make sure that he wasn't dreaming. What he was seeing, what he was hearing – it was all incredible, mindboggling. The Two-legs were everywhere: on the giant above them,

on the shore opposite them, flying through the air, dropping from the sky –
and now in the waters around them. They were surrounded by them. The
only place where the Two-Legs were absent was on the island below.
Perhaps that is it, he said to himself. We've tried and failed. We should
return to the island now and take our chances with the Scavengers, who
must surely have been the victors of the battle down there. Their society
could be no worse than the one we left, could it? And we would have their
own King with us to protect us, wouldn't we?

He looked at Slayer by his side and then at the rest of the group.
They were all still hypnotised by the sight of the Two-Legs in the air – all,
that is, except for Long Ears at the end of the group. He saw that his
companion was staring at him. He felt that Long Ears was trying to climb
into his thoughts again.

'Don't fail us now, Twisted Foot,' Long Ears seemed to be saying.
'Hold your nerve, comrade.'

Quickly turning his gaze away from Long Ears, he glanced down at
the island instead. He caught a glimpse of a shape among the rocks close to
the point of the island. It was standing erect on its hindquarters, immobile,
facing the giant, its back to the sun. The shape was only a silhouette, but a
chillingly familiar one.

Twisted Foot gulped. There was no choice now.

'We'll go up again as soon as darkness comes,' he announced to the
group suddenly and resolutely. 'Try to remain calm until then. And try to
keep still and quiet.

'The danger will soon be over,' he added, although not very
convincingly.

He was aware of everything that had been going on up here. In addition to
the reports that he had received regularly from Torn Coat, he had caught
snippets of information from the Protectors at the sacred tunnel. He knew
that the Two-Legs had gone from the island, leaving their creature
uncovered. He knew about the gangs of Two-Legs crossing the giant, and

about the great army of them on the far shore and the noise that they were making. He had been told about the creatures flying through the air – the sounds of them could be heard even in the Protectors' lair – and about the many vessels that were gathering in the waters. And he had just been told about the Two-Legs dropping from the sky like white birds. He wanted to see the last spectacle for himself. So for the second time that day he had ventured out on the world above.

Long Snout was at a loss. He had no idea why this evil kept occurring. From those tales of the past which he and the other elders often related in the Common lair, he knew that the society had faced many dangers and many tests. But surely never so many all at the one time! The constant intrusions by the Two-Legs here on the outside world, the glowing giant, the slaves' revolt, the decimation of the Inner Circle, the massacre of the Watchers, the flight of the traitors. And now all of this activity by the Two-Legs. It was never ending. But he must hold steady. He must take action to preserve the society...

He realised suddenly that he was staring across at the traitors, his eyes boring into them. Still there, he snarled, and looking small and lost and frightened. He was glad. Their time would come soon enough. But first there were the slaves to deal with. He would tell Torn Coat to return to One Eye as soon as it was dark. Torn Coat would convey his order to the Chief Hunter to begin the assault immediately. Once the Hunters charged, he himself would lead the counterattack by the Protectors.

Chapter Thirty-Four

When night fell, the party on the esplanade was still going strong. The number of visitors had increased steadily throughout the day, and many more were still arriving, swelling the already jam-packed crowd. They were all there to see the main event, the finale of the celebrations. Most of them had wrapped up well, so they didn't seem to notice the icy breeze that was now sweeping in from the estuary. The clear, starry sky above the esplanade was dominated by a large, bright, almost white moon. Looming over the scene, the silvery reflection of its immense structure shimmering in the black water of the estuary, the old bridge looked ghostly in the moonlight. Down to the left of the bridge, in front of the esplanade, the twinkling lights from a multiplicity of craft of all sizes seemed to dance on the water. On board one of those craft was the radio announcer who would shortly begin his broadcast not only to the waiting throng on the esplanade, but also to the many thousands of people who had gathered elsewhere along the shores of the Forth on this cold night. Also on board were the dignitaries who would set off the fireworks display by remote control and who would subsequently inaugurate the floodlighting of the bridge by the same means.

'Good evening, ladies, gentlemen and children!' the announcer's voice boomed out from the loudspeakers. 'Welcome all to the Firth of Forth! And welcome to the climax of many months of events to mark the hundredth anniversary of the opening of the graceful, the majestic, the world famous Forth Railway Bridge!'

As if those words had triggered the release of their pent-up excitement, a great roar of whoops and claps and cheers erupted from the multitude of spectators along both banks of the river.

He was so very relieved that they were moving at long last. They were already exhausted from their ordeal, as well as hungry and thirsty. Had they remained still any longer, some of them, especially the young ones, might have begun to succumb to the biting cold, perishing where they squatted. Apart from the fact that it was dark now, it seemed to be the right time to move. They hadn't heard any footsteps above them for a long time. Nor had any creatures rushed through the giant all day. As far as he knew, it was quiet and safe up there. Although still noisy, the army of Two-Legs on the far shore didn't seem to pose a threat. There were also still many Two-Legs vessels in the waters below, but for some reason they were all keeping a good distance from the giant. Yes, he was sure that it was a good time to go.

Twisted Foot began the climb. The others followed in the same formation as during the first, aborted attempt. As before, their progress was easy, and it was not long before Twisted Foot reached the top of the arch. He was on the point of stretching up to climb through the parapet above the arch when two explosions, one coming immediately after the other, split the air asunder and momentarily lit up the sky; even the giant itself seemed to tremble at the ferocity of the blasts. The line of fugitives froze in terror.

One Eye had been dozing again when Torn Coat re-entered the underworld to rouse him and pass on Long Snout's instructions. Now the two old warriors were squatting side by side at the head of the ranks of the Hunters. Both of them were very tired – One Eye from the long period of inactivity here at the pool, Torn Coat from the constant scurrying back and forth between the crest of the island and the sacred tunnel in the course of that long daylight watch – but both were also ready for the fray that was about to begin.

Although most of the Scavengers were in their lair, still sleeping off the effects of the battle and the great feast after it, a good number of them had returned to gorge themselves again on the corpses in the Common lair. They'll be gone soon enough, thought One Eye. Then he turned to regard his warriors.

'Let's go,' he said quietly.

As soon as he spoke, a detachment led by Torn Coat moved off quickly and silently round the wall of the Common lair to seal off the tunnel to the Scavengers' dungeon. The main force with One Eye at its head then spread itself across the floor of the Common lair and rushed forward with bloodcurdling shrieks.

From his position outside of the entrance to the Protectors' lair, with Broken Tail and his warriors hidden from view in the tunnel behind him, Long Snout heard the muffled echoes of the two explosions on the world above. He looked up to the roof of the lair and cursed the Two-Legs again. But there was no time to think about their latest evil; One Eye had begun the charge.

Chapter Thirty-Five

Still reeling at the sudden thunder of the detonations, the crowd gasped when, equally unexpectedly, the sky was lit up by the powerful beams of a battery of searchlights from a score of boats moored at intervals along the estuary. The beams crisscrossed the sky, each one travelling in a wide arc across it, some intermittently washing over and highlighting a section of the rust-coloured bridge.

'Now we enter the dark and ominous days of the Second World War,' the announcer continued his narration of the history of the bridge. 'On October 16ᵗʰ 1939, only months after the outbreak of the War, and almost exactly fifty-one years to this day, the Luftwaffe came to destroy the bridge. But it was truly her lucky day, for she emerged unscathed from that attack. And, of course, she survived the rest of the War to reign over the landscape for the next five decades.'

As the searchlights went out one by one and the large silver moon re-appeared still hanging in the black sky, the narration resumed:

'And here she is today, on her one hundredth birthday, still reigning supreme, as majestic as ever.'

There was a long pause.

'And now ladies, gentlemen and children,' the voice rang out, louder than before, 'to celebrate that birthday, the moment that we've all been waiting for ...'

Each time a beam had swept over that part of the bridge, it had exposed the twelve small bodies clinging to the top of the arch, their black fur erect, almost rigid, with cold and fright. Each time, too, twelve pairs of fear-filled eyes glinted and blinked in the glare of the beam. They had stayed as still as stones. Then the intervals between the beams had grown longer, until the lights disappeared altogether, and they could breathe again.

Twisted Foot was the first to move. He climbed up to the parapet, through its crisscross spars and onto the wooden floor of the walkway behind it. The others scrambled up to join him. In seconds, they were all on the walkway, huddled together again, nuzzling into each other. Even although they were now inside the belly of the giant, they felt safe for the first time in a long time.

That feeling was not to last, however. The walkway stretched away into the distance ahead of them. No sooner had they set off along it, the youngsters twittering excitedly, when they heard the first of a series of loud whooshing noises below them. They looked down through the parapet to see that the creature on the top of the island was enveloped in smoke and spitting fire in all directions. Bolts of fire from it were shooting high into the sky, where they were exploding in bursts of brilliant light and deafening noise. Soon the bursts filled the whole sky. The light and the noise from them were far more intense and prolonged than from the couple of detonations that they had heard earlier.

Unlike the crowds of sightseers gathered round the shores of the estuary, the fugitives had no desire to gape in wonder at the magic and colour of the pyrotechnic wizardry. Instead, terrified, acting on reflex, they scurried down from the walkway and retreated into the centre of the bridge. There, on the narrow, gravel-covered aisle between the two railway tracks, they cowered down, trembling, their eyes shut tight against this latest assault on their senses.

Twisted Foot tried to shout above the racket.

'We'll be safe here,' he was saying. But he was wrong again.

They could feel the creature before they heard it or saw it; the whole of the giant seemed to be shaking under the weight of it. It was coming from behind them, rushing towards them. Like the creature on the island, it was spitting bolts of fire.

'Oh, no!' squealed Small Face in utter despair.

The second battle of the underworld was just as ferocious and as noisy as the first one, but this time it was the Scavengers who were under attack. While the majority of them were trapped in their own lair, unable to pass the wall of Hunters at its entrance, several hundred had been in the Common lair when the charge came. A few had sought refuge in the abandoned lairs of the Hunters and Watchers, where they were systematically hunted down and slain. Others had decided to fight back from where they squatted on the floor of the Common lair, but they, too, had perished. The rest had chosen the lair's platform from which to defend themselves.

Standing on his hindquarters in the centre of the platform among the half-eaten corpses of the Rulers, Slasher rallied the latter defenders. After the disappearance of Slayer during the last battle, Slasher had claimed the throne. The whole of the lair recognised him as their fiercest fighter. He was their undisputed King-rat now. He was determined to maintain control of the underworld. He was determined to lead his warriors to victory again.

Long Snout towered over the melee. Slave-blood was dripping from his muzzle. Keeping his eyes fixed on Slasher, he leapt up to the platform and moved in for the kill. He recognised those signs of leadership and determination in the new slave-King; they had sealed the little Scavenger's fate.

Chapter Thirty-Six

When the creature sped past them, the blast of air caused by its passage was so violent that it almost lifted them up and sent them careering across the giant. But they clung desperately to the gravel beneath them until it had gone by. Then they saw the creature coming to a halt away in the distance. It looked much smaller over there. It was still spitting; the bolts of fire shooting from it were erupting in huge balls of light all around the giant. Now it was growing bigger. It was making the giant shake again. Its whining roar was becoming louder. It was rushing straight at them!

It wasn't Small Face who squealed out this time. It was one of the youngsters, the son of Narrow Back and Timid One. His nerve having gone completely, he sprang away from the group and leapt onto the adjacent railway track in an attempt to get back to the walkway. In his panic, he didn't see the gap between the track and the walkway. Having inherited his father's skinny frame, as well as his nervous disposition, the youngster's small, thin body simply fell through the narrow gap to plunge into black space. The splash made by the body when it hit the water far below went unheard amidst the combined din of the spouting creature on the island and the whining, spitting monster inside the giant.

The rest of the group held fast and braced themselves for the next blast from the creature. The creature whizzed past them again. They held their breath and hoped upon hope that it had gone from the giant this time. Then they heard it returning behind them, and they braced themselves once more. After it roared past them for a third time, it stopped up ahead for a while, but only to prolong the fugitives' torment by beginning yet another charge. Just as it did so, the bursts of light in the sky above the island suddenly grew faster and larger and brighter.

The fireworks train had been the card up the sleeve of the organisers. They had never been totally convinced that the display from Inchgarvie would actually work. There had been the ferocious storm the day before, of course, and the scare about the rats before that, but it was the reliability of the electronic gadgetry that had worried them most. They had needed a backup. So they had come up with the idea of kitting out the old locomotive to fire rockets in all directions as it paraded back and forth across the bridge. In the event, the locomotive was being used to supplement, rather than to replace, the island display. Judging by the delighted reaction from the crowds on the esplanade and elsewhere, however, it was a resounding success.

With the cheers and claps of the crowds echoing around the estuary, the locomotive completed its last run and headed south to exit the bridge. As soon as it disappeared from view, there was a final and particularly deafening burst of fireworks from the display on the island. That was the trigger for the series of simultaneous events that would constitute the climax of the night's celebrations: the button to inaugurate the floodlighting of the bridge was pressed; a string of bonfires along both shores of the Forth were lit; and the multitude of horns on the flotilla huddled in the lee of the bridge sounded in one huge, discordant clamour.

Amidst much oohing and aahing from the crowds, the bridge started to light up. Bathed in an initial soft orange blush, she appeared ghostly at first, but soon her whole structure was glowing with a pink-hued brilliance. She looked magnificent, more radiant and more majestic than ever, in her shining, new birthday dress.

When the bonfires had burned down and the sound of the boat horns had petered out, the flotilla began to disperse. The crowds lingered for a little while longer, drinking in the sight of the floodlit bridge and its shimmering mirror image in the inky water, before they also embarked on the great exodus. The night was now bitterly cold. Everyone wanted to return to the warmth of their homes as quickly as possible. Very soon, quiet returned to the shores of the Forth. The Big Day was over.

Chapter Thirty-Seven

It wasn't just the brightness of the lights inside the giant that they were trying to get used to; it was the silence as well. Still crouched together on the aisle between the two railway tracks, they were peering in all directions, blinking furiously, waiting for the next explosion to come crashing out of the sky or the next Two-Legs monster to come thundering at them. But there were no sounds, no movements; only the light. The place seemed vast and eerie now. The silence itself was frightening.

They were still shaking, still trembling from the trauma of their experiences on the giant. Could it be? they wondered. Was it possible? Were they really safe after all this time? Could they dare to hope? They began to stir, moving away from each other, taking a few faltering steps on the gravel surface, keeping their eyes open for new dangers.

Like the others, Twisted Foot was looking around him, staring at the army of lights. The lights seemed to be everywhere – above him, below him, to his left and right. So this is what Narrow Back had been so excited about, he said to himself. 'The giant is awake!' he remembered Narrow Back shouting. He remembered, too, the stir that Narrow Back's revelation had caused in the underworld. Well, he thought, after everything that we've been through since leaving the island, the glowing giant doesn't appear to be much of a threat after all.

The thought of Narrow Back and his agonising death, and of Timid One and her unfortunate youngster, both drowned, suddenly made Twisted Foot wince. All gone, he shook his muzzle sadly. And Fat One as well. It was such a waste, such a loss. He sincerely hoped that this... this venture that they had embarked on would prove to be worth their loss. He shook his muzzle again, this time more forcibly. He needed to rouse himself from this depression, to get on. It was time to resume their journey. They were all cold and hungry and thirsty; but, most of all, they were exhausted. The sooner they left the giant and found land, the sooner they would be able to rest.

He led the group back across the railway track and up to the walkway. All of them studiously leapt clear of the gap between the two, gathering at the very point which they had reached when they were startled by the explosions from the creature on the island. They set off northwards along the walkway again, scurrying as quickly as they could through the dazzling, cavernous belly of the giant.

'Up ahead and down to our right,' Twisted Foot said to the group behind him.

Up ahead and down to our right, he repeated to himself. That was where it was: the land that he and Long Ears had spoken about ... how long ago now? It was only days, he knew. It seemed much, much longer. He thought that it was just a dream back then, but the dream had almost become reality.

It wasn't long before they emerged from the belly. In front of them was a long stretch of walkway that would take them to the end of the giant. Below them was the first in a series of gigantic stone legs which held up the giant. When Twisted Foot looked down through the parapet bordering the walkway, he could see that the leg was planted not in water, but in rock. They had reached land!

The group had come to a halt. Twisted Foot was still peering down at the giant's leg. If we continue, he reasoned with himself, the way ahead is bound to lead us straight to the Two-Legs. He could sense it. But if we descend here, we'll be on land more quickly. Besides, it's darker down there, safer.

'Down here,' he announced at last. 'We'll go down here.'

Small Face looked terrified.

'B-but it's straight down,' he wailed. 'W-we'll never make it.'

Slayer pushed through the group, crawled through the parapet and climbed onto the top of the leg.

'Watch me,' he said.

Accustomed to negotiating the near-perpendicular walls around the Scavengers' lair, Slayer clambered easily down the huge leg. He was almost halfway to the ground when Twisted Foot began to follow him.

'If I can do it with only three working feet,' he called to the others, 'then you can all do it.'

The rest followed him in turn. Even Small Face, after some hesitation, commenced a slow, nervous descent. Once again, Long Ears took up the rear.

As he had done on countless occasions before, Long Snout, ancient Chamberlain of the Secret World, stood erect in the centre of the platform in the Common lair and emitted a long, loud, piercing screech. His calls on those past occasions were intended to command the attention of the Assembly, to bring those assembled to order. His call this time had a different purpose. He was announcing to the underworld that the revolt was over, that he was back in control.

He looked around the platform at the brave warriors who had helped him to victory and at the many corpses piled around them. At his own feet lay Slasher's mangled body; the new slave-King had fought well, but his reign had been short-lived. He and the rest of them – all the slaves who had been foolish enough to linger outside of the Scavengers' lair – were all dead now.

Long Snout emitted another bloodcurdling screech and then leapt from the platform. He would forge a new society out of this massacre, this devastation. A society that was stronger and more vigilant and more loyal than before. He needed time to plan this new society, to work out the details. But first there was a long outstanding task to care of. And then he needed to rest; he hadn't slept for a long, long time.

'Come with me, Chief Protector!' he roared.

As he moved quickly to his nest in the sanctum of the Inner Circle, with Broken Tail limping behind him, he suddenly remembered the explosions on the outside world before the battle began. All of the warriors had been required for the assault on the slaves, so none had kept watch above, none would be able to relate the cause of the explosions. It's of no consequence, he decided.

Chapter Thirty-Eight

They had all descended safely from the giant's leg. They were huddled together below the giant now, gazing around them, feeling small and lost in this strange land, but happy to be squatting on hard ground again. Directly across from them was a steep hillside, which was covered with grass and bushes and a few trees. Only Twisted Foot, Long Ears and Small Face, as he-rats from the Watchers' lair, had seen those things before, and, even then, only at a distance.

If we are to get away from the lights on the giant and reach our new land, Twisted Foot reasoned to himself, the hillside is the right way to go. He started to lead the group in that direction, but he found that Long Ears was ahead of him.

'There's water over here,' Long Ears was shouting.

Before he had seen it or sensed it, Long Ears had heard the water bubbling in the tiny burn that ran along the foot of the hill.

'And it tastes good,' he added, raising his wet muzzle.

Soon, they were all lapping greedily at the edge of the burn, their backs to the giant. Long Ears had been correct: the water tasted good. In fact, it was the best water that they had ever lapped: cold and clear, and devoid of the muddy taste of the pool in the underworld.

Their thirsts slaked, they leapt over the burn and began their ascent of the hill. The soft ground below their feet felt odd at first, the long grass tickled their bodies, and the dark shapes of the bushes and trees seemed menacing, but the climb itself was easy. It was only when they had almost reached the top of the slope that some of them noticed Slayer's absence.

Twisted Foot looked back down the hill. Like a good Watcher, he systematically scanned the slope, the area around the burn and the ground below the giant's leg. There was no movement and no sign of the little Scavenger.

'Don't worry,' he said at length, 'he'll catch up.'

Then he turned round and continued to climb.

At the top of the slope, there was a strip of flat ground several feet wide, which curved away to their left and right. They crouched in the middle of the ground and looked about. On one side, they had a clear view of the giant, still glowing brilliantly; the ever-restless waters below the giant; and the familiar shape of the land from which they had escaped. On the other side, the ground gave way abruptly to a sheer rock face, at the foot of which was more water. The water this time was flat and still, and they could see the reflection of the moon in it. Its shape reminded them of the pool in the Common lair, only this pool was much, much bigger and deeper; like everything else on this new land, it was giant-sized.

It was while they were peering down at the pool that they were startled by the sounds of scraping behind them. The noise was coming from the slope below. They cringed back as it grew louder. Then Slayer suddenly appeared at the top of the slope. A large grey bird was clamped by the neck between his powerful jaws. The bird was almost as big as him. He dropped its limp body in front of them.

'Food, Master,' was all that he said.

There was no hesitation. They were all ravenous. He-rats and she-rats and youngsters alike tore noisily into Slayer's gift.

Twisted Foot remembered seeing these plump grey birds before. They frequently roosted high up on the giant, occasionally flying down to the rocks for a brief visit. He had often dreamed of tasting their succulent flesh. Now his dream had come true. Clear water and now bird flesh, he said to himself. He was liking this place already.

After the feast, they felt more tired than ever. They had no energy left to go any further, even to search for a proper shelter. In spite of the cold, they simply curled up together where they were on the soft, grassy ground. One of the youngsters, unused to the rich food, burped loudly, and everyone laughed. None of them noticed the lights on the giant dimming and then dying out completely; they were all fast asleep by then.

Broken Tail watched as they made their way through the waters towards the giant's foot. They were both strong swimmers. They would reach the foot in no time. Then they would climb up into the giant's belly, just as he had shown them. The traitors had gone from their perch on the foot, so they would have to go up after them. It was dark and quiet up there. Their passage should go unhindered.

'Sniff them out,' he had ordered the warriors. 'Follow them. Find them. Then kill them all except the cripple. Bring the cripple back alive. If you can't do that, bring his head instead, but be prepared for Long Snout's wrath.'

The Chamberlain had told him to select the two most able Protectors for the task. He had chosen Jagged Fangs and Neck-Snapper. Jagged Fangs was an experienced, ruthless and efficient killer, the warrior most likely to succeed him as Chief Protector. Neck-Snapper was younger and more hot-headed, but what he lacked in maturity he more than made up for in sheer grit and ferocity. He had recovered from the loss of his eye to fight courageously in the second battle of the underworld. Besides, ever since that time when he had prevented Sharp Claws from fleeing with the other traitors, Neck-Snapper had been Long Snout's favourite.

Almost simultaneously, two sleek black bodies emerged from the waters and began to crawl up the giant's foot. Good, nodded Broken Tail. He could go now. He turned back and crawled slowly across the rocks. He was limping badly and in great pain. The wound which he received when the Scavengers broke out of their lair hadn't healed. He knew that he was going to die soon. He would rest now and probably not wake up. But he had followed the Chamberlain's orders to the last.

Outside of the entrance to the sacred tunnel, Broken Tail stopped to sniff the air. There was an unfamiliar smell, a strange murkiness, hanging over the world above like a cloud. He grunted and disappeared into the tunnel. As soon as he did, a black shape slunk over the rocks and down to the point of the island. Slipping noiselessly into the waters, it, too, began to swim towards the giant.

Part Five:

A New Society

Chapter Thirty-Nine

The old quarry had been abandoned almost seventy years before. Its stone had been used in the construction of the Forth and Clyde Canal, the docks in Leith and the foundations of the nearby Forth Railway Bridge. But now it lay derelict and flooded by seawater, whose permanently smooth surface was strewn with debris. As the new day broke over the estuary, the first rays of the awakening sun glanced off that glassy surface to wash over the tight circle of black fur on the ridge overlooking the quarry.

The fugitives awoke slowly. They remained silent for some time, sleepy-eyed, not venturing out of their circle, staring in awe at the scenery below them: the vast pool on one side, the imposing giant on the other. They were suddenly in awe, too, of the scale of what they had achieved. They had braved so much over there – the waters, the storm, the giant, the many frightening Two-Legs creatures – to escape, to be free in this strange place. They felt exhilarated and apprehensive at the same time.

Then the cold began to set in. They were shivering now, needing to be on the move. After their recent feast of bird flesh, they were also very thirsty. They knew where to find water, so they automatically set off back down the slope to lap at the burn again. At that moment, the first Two-Legs creature of the day came thundering through the giant in their direction; its noise filled the air around them, its power shook the ground on which they squatted. When they looked down, they could see other creatures moving along the ground close to the waters; they were smaller and slower and quieter than the one on the giant, but they were Two-Legs creatures nevertheless.

'We should go the other way!' Long Ears shouted above the din. 'We're too close to the Two-Legs here!'

Motioning excitedly to Twisted Foot, he turned round.

'Over there,' he continued. 'That's where the land is. The land we saw during our watches on the world above. Our new land.'

They all swivelled round to follow Long Ears' gaze. Away in the distance, they could see another stretch of high ground. It was flat and covered with grass and trees, and it jutted out into the waters.

'Yes, of course,' said Twisted Foot.

Without further discussion, their thirsts forgotten for the time being, they immediately headed back along the ridge in the direction of the promontory.

The noise of the creature hurtling overhead was deafening. The giant's leg beside them seemed to be vibrating. Jagged Fangs was very relieved. We made it just in time, he said to himself. They had followed the scent of the traitors with great difficulty, zigzagging from one side of the giant to the other until they picked it up. Then they lost it completely. They had gone a long way, almost to the end of the giant, when they decided to double back. And all the time they knew that they were running out of time; that the light would come any moment and that the Two-Legs creatures would soon follow. Then they realised that the traitors had escaped down the first of the giant's legs. They were correct, of course, because the scent here was strong and it was leading them direct to the hillside.

One after the other, he and Neck-Snapper darted from under the bridge to the edge of the burn. Like the fugitives had done some hours earlier, they drank deeply of the cold, clear water. On the other side of the burn, they picked up the scent again. Both of them were tired and hungry. Although neither would admit it to the other, they were both also intimidated by the sights and sounds of this alien world. Not that it was important anyway: they had a mission to complete on behalf of the Secret World; that's all that mattered.

Their ears pricked, their muzzles close to the ground, they began their ascent of the hillside.

Chapter Forty

It was the day after the Big Day; another bright, fresh autumn morning. The usual lines of early Monday morning southbound traffic had begun to stream over the road bridge. After the disruption of yesterday's celebrations, traffic was also moving again in North and South Queensferry. Up on the rail bridge, the focus of those celebrations, train services had resumed, and the maintenance men had begun their first walk-through of the day. Life on the estuary was back to normal.

Down below the rail bridge, the two young men from the exhibition company had just stepped out of their dinghy on to Inchgarvie's jetty. As on their first visit to the island, both were wearing bright orange lifesaving jackets on top of shiny yellow anoraks. Unlike on that first visit, however, when the spectre of the rats had driven them away, both were looking very confident and very pleased with themselves. They were pleased because their fireworks display not only had worked, but had been widely acclaimed. And they were particularly pleased because this would be their final visit; once they were finished up here this morning, they could move on to their next big project.

They headed direct for the crest of the island, one carrying a plastic box and the other an empty satchel. When they reached the display platform, the former knelt down, opened the box and took out a large drill, to which he proceeded to fix a screwdriver bit. The latter began to search around the platform, picking up spent fireworks and other debris, which he dropped into the satchel. Once the platform was dismantled, the aluminium tubes making up its frame would also go into the satchel. The young men were determined to comply with the terms of their contract by leaving the place exactly as they had found it.

One of them began to whistle cheerfully. The other joined in. They were still whistling when the drill whined into action.

Long Snout was pacing the ground in front of his nest. He was still tired, not having slept for as long as he had wanted. Some of the oafs from the Protectors' lair had interrupted his sleep to inform him that Broken Tail had died. He had given them short shrift, of course. He had told them to be gone, to drag Broken Tail's corpse into the Scavengers' lair, as was the usual custom. Then he had tried to sleep again. But it had been impossible: there had been too much to think about it. And to add to all of his problems, now there was the question of the appointment of a new Chief Protector.

Still, he acknowledged, the rude awakening had given him more time to work out the details of the new society and the new regime that that society would be required to follow in order for it to survive. Dissent among the Watchers: that's what had been at the root of the insurrection by the slaves. The dissent had been rife; even old Sharp Claws had been in on it, it seemed. The Watchers felt that they were a lesser part of the society, treated less well than the Protectors and Hunters. Well, they were all gone now. All, that is, except for the traitors up there somewhere – and he had ensured that *their* so-called freedom would be short-lived, if it was not already over. The Watchers had been a bunch of misfits, anyway. They hadn't been real warriors like the rest of the Outer Circle. The new society would have no need for them. The Hunters would take on the Watchers' role; they would watch over the world above, as well as hunt for the white birds. And the Hunters' lair would be increased so that it was the same size as the Protectors' lair. Equality achieved. No dissent. But the Protectors would need to be rebuked and reminded about their responsibilities. After all, it was because of their complacency that the Scavengers had succeeded in breaking free from their dungeon to run riot in the underworld. From now on, many more Protectors would be assigned to guard the entrance to the dungeon, the tunnel from the Common lair to the outside world and the sacred tunnel. Yes, under the new regime, the Protectors would be kept busier – and more vigilant.

And then, of course, there were the Rulers to consider. Long Snout paused to survey the other nests around him. The Rulers were much fewer since the slaves' revolt. White Muzzle, the King-rat, had perished in the massacre, as had his older son, Red Coat. But Fire Eyes, his younger son, had survived. There he was: the princeling, the heir apparent, sleeping soundly, without a care, waiting to be announced as the new King-rat. But that was not going to happen. Yes, it was correct that the brown ones should still hold a higher place in the society, and that they should have others to fight and hunt and watch for them. But it was no longer acceptable for royalty to be hereditary, for kings and princes to be made simply because of their bloodline. In the past, it had always been the strongest and fiercest of the lair who had claimed the kingdom. Well, Long Snout was the strongest and fiercest, and he would make that claim!

Before resuming his pacing, he gave Fire Eyes' sleeping form a long, cold look of contempt. As soon as the cripple was back here, he would call the Assembly. There, in front of them all, he would kill Fire Eyes, declare himself as their new King-rat and announce the details of the new regime. Then they could watch the cripple suffer. He would reinforce his authority by inflicting the pain himself. First, though, he would send for One Eye. He wanted him to send the Hunters up when darkness came; white birds were needed for the Assembly, a great feast of them to celebrate the new epoch. He would also post guards outside of the sacred tunnel to watch for the return of Jagged Fangs and Neck-Snapper. Like sensible warriors, they were probably waiting until the light had gone before venturing back. Which reminded him about the matter of a new Chief Protector: Jagged Fangs appeared to be the most obvious choice; he was...

Long Snout stopped abruptly and looked up at the roof of the lair. The muffled whining sounds from above indicated the presence of Two-

Legs – again! Ill-tempered, cursing, he rushed into the Protectors' lair.

'You and you!' he ordered the first two Protectors in his path. 'Go to the outside world! Find out what the Two-Legs are up to now! Report back to me!'

It was only after he had returned to the Inner Circle lair that he suddenly realised his mistake. The two burly guards were just a couple of simple dung-heads. They wouldn't know how to conceal themselves among the rocks, not like the Hunters or even those wretched Watchers. They would go charging out into the open. But it was too late now; they had gone. Long Snout cursed again.

The little plum-coloured boat bobbed gently on the flat pool of water under the bridge's central arch. The boat had been shadowing the maintenance men as they made their slow progress northwards high above. It lay at anchor now, its skipper, Charlie McNulty, having decided that he needed a break. Charlie was outside of the cabin, standing aft, getting some air and nursing another hangover. Naturally, with all of those people about and all of those celebrations going on, it had been another boozy night in the old town. He had had a good time, but he was regretting it this morning.

Charlie lit a cigarette and looked across to Inchgarvie. He spotted the lime-green dinghy first and then the two whiz-kids clambering into it. Looking like a couple of parrots again, he sneered. He noticed that both of them were grinning broadly.

'Pair of smug-faced, little –' he began, but his words trailed off when he caught sight of the two rats. They were in plain view, almost nonchalantly climbing down from the top of the island and heading for the monastery. And both of them were as big as the one he had killed, the one that had begun to stink out the cabin.

'That's it!' he said out loud.

He was more determined than ever now; he would find the rat-catcher that evening.

Chapter Forty-One

They had travelled round the edge of the quarry and down the other side of the hill, where there was a small cove with a sandy beach which sloped down to the sea. They had crossed over the beach, the sand under their feet feeling uncomfortably soft and yielding. On the other side of the cove, they had climbed another steep slope to reach the top of the promontory. They hadn't encountered any Two-Legs on their journey. In fact, they had come across only one other creature, and then only briefly. It had been crouched on the short grass which fringed the beach, a Four-Legs like themselves, but grey-furred and fatter, with a short tail and enormous, pointed ears that were even bigger than those of Long Ears. It had stared at them with large, round eyes for a few moments before bounding off into the trees behind the cove.

Now they were on the flat ground among the grass and trees that they had seen from the top of the quarry. Twisted Foot hadn't been there before, of course, but the place felt oddly familiar and comforting to him. When they came out of the trees at the end of the promontory, the estuary was laid out before them. Down on their right, although farther away than before, the giant and the little island alongside it were still in clear view. And directly below them was a cliff-face that seemed to be alive with the movements and sounds of the white birds.

'Our food supply, Master,' growled Slayer, who then promptly disappeared over the edge of the cliff on another hunting expedition.

Twisted Foot looked back at this new land that they had escaped to. The mass of trees, which had seemed dark and threatening at first, now offered protection instead. Yes, he nodded to himself, they were secure here, far from the Two-Legs – and they were bound to find water close by.

'Welcome to our new home,' he said to the others.

Neck-Snapper was drooling. Long Ears and Small Face were backing away from him. Cowering and squealing, the mates and youngsters were behind the two terrified Watchers. And behind them was the cliff edge.

'Which one of you traitors shall I kill first?' asked Neck-Snapper. He had been looking forward to this encounter. He was enjoying the moment.

A similar drama was being played out on the other side of the promontory, where Jagged Fangs was closing in on Twisted Foot. Twisted Foot was looking around him in panic. With only the cliff behind him, there was nowhere for him to retreat to.

'You're coming with us, cripple,' Jagged Fangs spat out the words. 'The Chamberlain wants a word with you.'

Twisted Foot still couldn't believe it. Just when he had thought that everything was perfect, that they were safe at last, the Protectors had appeared from nowhere. They had separated him from the rest of the group. They wanted to take him back to the underworld to suffer the same fate as Narrow Back. But he had decided that he wasn't going with them; they were going to have to kill him here instead.

Jagged Fangs lunged at Twisted Foot, seized the young Watcher's left ear and pulled. Screaming in pain, Twisted Foot dug his heels into the earth, but the Protector was too strong for him, and he began to slide along the ground. Then he stopped resisting and sprang at Jagged Fangs instead. Taken off balance, the Protector let go of the ear and fell backwards with Twisted Foot on top of him. They were rolling on the grass, both growling deeply and scratching furiously, each with his fangs bared, trying to gouge the other, when Slayer re-appeared at the top of the cliff, a young white bird hanging limply between his jaws.

Instantly recognising his former Master's underling, Slayer

dropped the bird and flew into the fray. He clung on to Jagged Fangs' back and sought out the Protector's jugular. Having forgotten Twisted Foot for the moment, Jagged Fangs began to writhe about in an attempt to dislodge Slayer, but he writhed so violently that both he and the little slave-King tumbled over the edge of the cliff and out of sight.

Neck-Snapper had been too busy taunting his victims to see what had gone on behind him. Still drooling, his one eye fixed on Long Ears, the cripple's accomplice, he was moving in for his first kill when a loud, gruff voice came from the direction of the trees.

'Why don't you pick on me instead?' it challenged.

Neck-Snapper was slow to recognise the owner of the voice as he emerged into the open.

'You?' the Protector hissed eventually, although he was still not sure.

Then another voice came from behind him.

'And why don't you pick on me, too?' said Twisted Foot.

Neck-Snapper was surrounded by four warriors now; he should have been afraid. But instead he seemed to relish the situation. He felt invincible. His back to the cliff edge, he watched as the four of them crept closer to him.

'Come on, misfits!' he goaded them.

The stranger was first to move. He charged headlong at Neck-Snapper, searching for his throat. In the same moment, Twisted Foot attacked his right flank, and Long Ears his left. Even Small Face joined in by leaping on the struggling Protector's back. Despite his bravado, the fight was over in seconds for Neck-Snapper. As he lay gasping on the grass, blood spurting from his torn throat, the stranger gave him a powerful back-kick with both hindlegs, and he went hurtling over the cliff.

'That's how we rid ourselves of dung,' growled the stranger. Neck-Snapper's blood was on his fangs. Blood was also seeping from a long gash on his left flank.

There was a loud squeal from among the mates and youngsters, and then Bone-Cruncher rushed forward. She nuzzled into the stranger and licked at his wound.

'Is that you?' she asked. 'Is that really you?'

Before he had time to respond, the stranger was distracted by the sudden spectacle of the drenched figure at the top of the cliff. Slayer had materialised there once more. His fur was plastered to his body, accentuating the sleekness and muscularity of his small frame. His wide grin confirmed that Jagged Fangs had been disposed of.

Fat One looked at Slayer and then at the carcass of the white bird, which still lay where the slave-King had dropped it earlier.

'I could do with some of that,' he groaned. 'I'm starving!'

Although the whole group had participated in the feast, it was clear that Fat One had managed to eat the largest share. He looked much leaner and tougher than when they had last seen him, but he was still the same old Fat One as far as his appetite was concerned. It was only when there was nothing left but bones and feathers that he stopped to relate his tale.

'I know it was foolish of me,' he began, 'but I just couldn't come with the rest of you until I had at least tried to help Sharp Claws.'

'It wasn't foolish, Fat One,' interrupted Bone-Cruncher, nuzzling into him. 'It was a very brave thing to do.'

'Anyway,' he continued, 'by the time I went back down the escape tunnel, it was too late. The place was full of Rulers and Protectors. They had all escaped from the Common lair. Long Snout was there. I'm afraid that the old tyrant killed Sharp Claws ... just picked him up by the throat and bit his head off...

'When I saw that, I was terrified. I went as fast as I could up the tunnel, but I nearly didn't make it. I got this from the Protectors who came after you lot.'

He stopped to show them the wound along his flank.

'There was a Two-Legs at the other end of the tunnel. I managed to get out just in time, but its presence stopped the Protectors from coming any further. I found one of my hiding places among the rocks. That's when I saw the Two-Legs kill Digger... with a big rock. After that, everything went black. The next thing I knew it was light and there was a heck of a racket going on all around. After a while, I passed out, but only to be woken by the noise of the Two-Legs creature exploding above me. I thought the whole island was going to blow up. I really thought that I was going to die then...'

Fat One paused. He wondered why none of them seemed to be surprised about the exploding creature.

'Anyway, the explosions just went on for ever. Then they stopped, and everything went quiet. I could see that it was dark again. I waited for a long while before I came out of the hiding place and headed back down to the waters. That's when I saw those two thugs we've just dealt with. They were following you ... and I was following them... and... well, you know the rest.'

Twisted Foot didn't say much in response to Fat One's account. There would be plenty of time ahead to tell him about their own adventures. For the moment, there were important things to take care of before they could call this place their new home, before they could really feel safe. They still had to find water for a start. And then they needed to make a proper lair. Perhaps among the trees back there. Deep under the soft earth...

Long Snout was still angry; in fact, he was almost apoplectic now. He was standing on his hindlegs, glaring at the glowing giant. When the Two-Legs had come and removed their creature from the world above, he had thought that everything would return to normal. How wrong he had been! Here they were, practising their evil again. And it was because of that evil that the white birds had gone. One Eye's report of these matters only moments ago had forced him up here once more. To cap it all, there was still no sign of Jagged Fangs and Neck-Snapper. Without them and the cripple, there could be no Assembly. Without the white birds, there could be no feast afterwards, no celebration of his new regime. He snorted and continued to glare at the giant.

Chapter Forty-Two

Just as he had done when he first set foot on Inchgarvie, Tam Proudfoot stood on the jetty, lit his pipe and slowly surveyed the island. He had to admit that he was totally puzzled by this business of rats living and even breeding on the place. When Charlie had come to see him last night and had shown him the dead rat, he had immediately dismissed it as yet another stray visitor from a passing ship, especially given the size of it. But then Charlie told him about seeing others of a similar size. From the tone of Charlie's voice, he knew that the man's claim was no exaggeration. So he had agreed to come out here on Charlie's boat to look again. It was clear that a more thorough search than before was required if they were to get to the bottom of the mystery.

Tam stroked his short grey beard and took a long pull at his pipe, the billowing smoke from it momentarily enveloping his face.

'Okay, show me,' he said to Charlie.

'Come on, Nipper,' he added, motioning to the little Jack Russell prancing at his feet.

The two men and the dog set off round the island. When they entered the gloom of the monastery ruins, Charlie was nervous. It felt to him as if a thousand eyes were watching them from underneath those stones. Keeping to the edge of the ruins, he pointed roughly to the spot where he remembered hitting that first rat. Nipper understood immediately. Following the direction of Charlie's outstretched arm, the dog rushed towards the spot. In moments, it had sniffed out Fat One's hiding place and the trail of his blood spots. Excitedly, it followed the trail out of the monastery and down to the point of the island. Although the trail vanished at the water's edge, the dog picked up other scents there, some of which led it back across the rocks.

Tam and Charlie were clambering down from the monastery, still trying to catch up with Nipper. Hearing their approach, the dog stopped sniffing the ground, looked up and locked eyes with the large brown rat, which stood on its hindlegs, hissing and spitting, barely a yard away.

His anger had gotten worse as time went on. He hadn't slept because of it. He was impatient for his reign to begin, but it couldn't begin until the cripple had paid. So he had paced the lair, waiting for those two halfwits to return. But nothing. Nothing. He had watched as Fire Eyes continued to sleep soundly, unperturbed, safe. He had almost killed that soft, fat piece of dung there and then, but he had forced himself to stop, to come out here. Even though it was light again, there was still a chance that they could appear with the cripple. The thought of the cripple made him boil and seethe inside. Ever since his traitorous plot had been discovered, everything had gone wrong. It was his fault! All of it! That's why he had to pay!

Long Snout stood erect, glowering at the giant again. He felt like he was going to explode. He began to hiss and spit and snarl. That's when he saw the strangely coloured, yapping Four-Legs. He wanted to vent his rage on this noisy intruder.

Being roughly the same size and weight, and with equal degrees of unbridled aggression, Nipper and Long Snout were well-matched. Neither of them flinched when they rushed headlong at each other. In a split-second, they were transformed from two adversaries into a single growling, whirling ball of fury. But when the two Protectors outside of the sacred tunnel raced to the aid of their Chamberlain, the fight was suddenly weighted in Long Snout's favour. And when others streamed from the tunnel to join them, the fight was resoundingly lost by Nipper.

By the time Tam and Charlie saw the dog, it was surrounded by eight or more snapping black-furred assailants, and its fierce growls had turned into pleading yelps. The men shouted and stamped, but it was only when they began to throw rocks that the Protectors ceased their attack and retreated to the underworld along with an injured Long Snout.

Tam was in tears when he reached Nipper. The dog was lying on its side, whimpering softly. Every part of its body was torn and bleeding. Then it seemed to give out a final sigh before going completely still, its eyes wide open. Tam didn't say a word. He looked down at the place among the rocks into which the rats had disappeared; it was as if he was stamping that place on his memory. Then he knelt down, lifted up Nipper's body with both hands and carried it back to Charlie's boat. Charlie hurried after him, immensely relieved to be getting away from there.

Chapter Forty-Three

Twisted Foot knew the dream so well. There was a clearing among the trees. It was far away, deep in the woodlands. The sun was shining. They were basking in its warmth. Grey Eyes was there; and young Soft-Mover, his jet-black coat glistening as he moved through the tall grass. Fat One was dozing under a tree. His other companions were in the clearing with their mates and young ones. There was an aura about the place, a deep glow of happiness. It seemed that if he reached out from the dream he could touch the glow, let the warmth course through him.

Then he waited for the shadows to fall, as they always did. He waited for those familiar, cold, dark images to come and oust the brightness. He waited for those blurred, frightening scenes of Long Snout towering over the clearing, the blood of newly born young congealed on his enormous fangs; of Neck-Snapper hissing and spitting death, green pus festering in his ragged eyehole; of Grey Eyes surrounded by snarling Protectors, her small body lacerated and bleeding. But nothing came. The sun continued to shine. That warm glow persisted.

With a jolt, he snapped out of it. His mind had been wandering. He hadn't been dreaming at all. That clearing among the trees was real, and he was in it. Grey Eyes and Soft-Mover were there, too, and all the others. And the sun really was shining, as it had done during the last few days; it was as if the Cold Cycle had suddenly come to an end and the Warm Cycle had begun again. Their lair was at the edge of the clearing. It had been dug out a long time before by other creatures – probably by those Four-Legs with the short tails and large, pointed ears – and then abandoned. It was *their* lair now, their underworld. Here on the world above, a little spring trickled out from the rocks on the other side of the promontory, so they didn't have far to travel to lap water. And, of course, the teeming cliff-face beyond the trees provided a constant supply of bird flesh.

Twisted Foot sighed. For the first time in as long as he could remember, he felt at peace. This was their new home, their new society – and it was perfect. And those dark images that he had just seen in his mind: they were just shadows from the past. As he had done on many occasions since coming to the place, he wandered away from the clearing, through the trees and out to the end of the promontory. From there, he slowly scanned the waters below, the giant straddling the waters and the little island tucked in at the side of the giant.

There was a lot of commotion on the island today. He could see a gang of Two-Legs spread out along the length of it. Their bodies – even their heads and faces – were covered in white. It looked like most of them were searching among the rocks. Others were erecting a creature on the high ground, just like the Two-Legs had done before, although this new creature seemed much less elaborate than the one which exploded. He could also see a number of Two-Legs vessels on the other side of the island. Standing on the jetty beside the vessels was a familiar figure. It was the long Two-Legs with the silver fur on its face, the one which had come with the strangely coloured Four-Legs, the one which had used its cunning to kill the slave-rats when they escaped from the underworld. He wondered if all those Two-Legs and all that activity over there spelled discovery of the society; the end of it, perhaps.

'They'll never trouble us again, comrade.'

Long Ears was suddenly at his side. He didn't know if his companion had actually spoken those words or if he had crept into his thoughts again. It didn't matter either way; he just hoped that Long Ears was right.

They crouched at the edge of the cliff for a long time. Even after the Two-Legs had gone from the island, they remained there, scanning and re-scanning the terrain. They were Watchers, after all; it was in their blood.

Old One Eye was perplexed. He shook his muzzle in frustration as he came out of the Protectors' lair and began to pick his way through the rotting corpses which still littered the floor of the Common lair. He had told the Chamberlain about the many Two-Legs on the world above and about what they were doing up there, but all that Long Snout had done was to ask whether the cripple was back. There had been nothing else: no instructions; not even an angry outburst. One Eye shook his muzzle again. While the whole of the underworld trembled in fear, Long Snout was still obsessed about that wretched cripple! He would return to his own lair now, tell his warriors to stand down, to rest with their mates and young, to await the worst.

Back in the sanctum of the Inner Circle, with the other Rulers looking on anxiously, Long Snout remained in his nest and licked the wounds that the yapping Four-Legs had inflicted on him. They'll be here soon, he told himself. With the cripple. Then we'll begin the Assembly. Our new society will be born. And I'll become their new King-rat. Long Snout, the King-rat, after all these Cycles. Soon. Very soon. He didn't notice the fumes or the others dying around him. He felt drowsy. He yawned and settled down to sleep.

If you ever take the train across the Forth Bridge, look down as you pass the rocky, whale-shaped islet in the bridge's shadow. You'll see a crumbling monastery on one side and a Second World War gun emplacement on the other. You'll also see a big notice board sticking up from the crest of the island. If you peer at the notice, you'll probably see the bright red sign of the skull and crossbones, and you might just make out the letters underneath, which are also bright red and which declare: 'BEWARE POISON'. The notice was erected by the authorities in October

1990, a few days after the centenary of the old bridge, when they fumigated the island to rid it of a reported colony of rats. It seemed that the rats were in danger of wiping out the island's bird population – or at least that's what the authorities were told by the local rat-catcher.

The island's proper name is Inchgarvie. Nowadays, though, it's known to people on both sides of the Forth as Rat Island: a place to be avoided, a place of ghosts and demons and eerie, whispering winds.

About the Author

Brendan Gisby was born in Edinburgh, Scotland, halfway through the 20th century, and was brought up just along the road in South Queensferry (the Ferry) in the shadow of the world-famous Forth Bridge. He is the author of several novels and biographies and a mountain of short stories. He is also the founder of McStorytellers (http://mcstorytellers.weebly.com), a website which showcases the work of Scottish-connected short story writers.

5113732R00094

Printed in Great Britain
by Amazon.co.uk, Ltd.,
Marston Gate.

Allamah Mutahhari
Allamah Tabatabai
Imam Khumayni

IN THE NAME OF ALLAH MOST GRACIOUS MOST MERCIFUL

Mutahhari, Mortaza, 1920 – 1979.
Light Within Me/ by Mutahhari, Tabatabai, and Khumayni.-
Qum: Ansariyan, 2006.
207 P.
Includes bibliographical footnote.
ISBN: 964-438-301-X
1.Islam–Addresses, Essays, lectures.   2. Islam–Study and
Teaching.   I. Tabatabai, Mohammad Hussein, 1902 – 1981.
II. Ruhullah, Khomaeyni, Leader and founder of Islamic Rep. of
Islam, 1902 – 1989.   III. Title.
297.8   BP10.M650493

نور الضمير (باللغة الانجليزية)

LIGHT WITHIN ME

Author: Allamah Mutahhari, Allamah Tabatabai and Imam Khumayni
Publisher: Ansariyan Publications
Third Reprint: 1380 – 1422 – 2001
Forth Reprint: 1427 - 1385 - 2006
Sadr Press
Quantity: 2000
No of Pages: 216
Size: 143X205 mm
ISBN: 964-438-301-X

ANSARIYAN PUBLICATIONS
P.O. Box 187
22 Shohada St., Qum
Islamic Republic of Iran
Tel: 0098 251 7741744   Fax: 7742647
Email: ansarian@noornet.net
www.ansariyan.net & www.ansariyan.org

بســم الله الرحمن الرحيم

اُدْعُ اِلٰی سَبِیلِ رَبِّكَ بِالْحِكْمَةِ وَالْمَوْعِظَةِ
الْحَسَنَةِ وَجَادِلْهُمْ بِالَّتِی هِیَ اَحْسَنُ اِنَّ رَبَّكَ
هُوَ اَعْلَمُ بِمَنْ ضَلَّ عَنْ سَبِیلِهِ وَهُوَ اَعْلَمُ بِالْمُهْتَدِینَ

Call unto the way of your Lord with wisdom and good
exhortation, and reason with them in the best way. Lo!
your Lord best knows those who go astray from His path,
and He knows best those who are rightly guided.

(Qur'an, 16:125)

CONTENTS

PART ONE
(Allamah Murtaza Mutaharri)

PART TWO
(Allamah Muhammad Husayn Ṭabāṭabai')

PART THREE
(Ayatullah Ruḥullah Khumayni)

* * * * *

بِسْمِ اللهِ الرَّحْمٰنِ الرَّحِيمِ

اَلْحَمْدُ لِلّٰهِ الَّذِىْ عَلَّمَ بِالْقَلَمِ
عَلَّمَ الْإِنْسَانَ مَا لَمْ يَعْلَمْ
وَصَلَّى اللهُ عَلٰى مُحَمَّدٍ وَّآلِهِ وَسَلَّمْ

PREFACE

Although most people are preoccupied with earning their livelihood and pay little attention to spiritual matters, yet every man has an inherent desire to know the absolute truth. This dormant power, when awakened in some people and comes to surface, they gain a number of spiritual perceptions.

Despite the claim of the sophists and the atheists that every truth is an illusion, everybody believes in the existence of one eternal truth. When man with a pure heart and a pure spirit looks at the permanent factuality of the universe and at the same time observes the instability and transience of its various parts, he realizes that this world and its manifestations are a mirror which reflects the existence of one eternal truth. With this realization his joy knows no bounds and he is so elated that in his eyes everything else becomes insignificant and worthless.

This spectacle forms the basis of that impulse of the gnostics* which draws the attention of the godly people to a world beyond perception and cultivates the love of Allah in their hearts. The pull which they feel towards this spectacle makes them forget everything and removes many desires from their hearts. This pull leads man to the worship of the Invisible

---

* The Islamic esoterics known as *Irfān* or gnosis is sometimes associated with *Tasawwuf* or mysticism whose certain rites and rituals are repugnant to Islam. However Shi'aism considers Islamic acts of worship to be sufficient for gaining proximity to Allah.

1

Being who is more manifest than all that is visible or audible. It is this pull which gave birth to many a religion based on Allah's worship. The real gnostic is he who worships Allah not because he hopes for any reward or is afraid of any punishment, but only because he knows Him and loves Him.*

It is clear from the above that gnosis is not a religion like other religions. It is to be regarded as the central and the most vital part of all religions. Gnosis is a perfect way of worship, based on love, not on fear or hope. It is a way of understanding the inner facts of religion instead of being contented' with its outward and perceptible form. Among the followers of all revealed religions, even among those who believe in idol-worship there are individuals who follow the path of gnosis. The gnostics are found among the followers of polytheistic religions+ as well as among the Jews, Christians, Zoroastrians and Muslims.

Appearance of Gnosis in Islam

Out of the companions of the Holy Prophet Imam Ali is known for the eloquent description of gnostic truths and the stages of spiritual life. His sayings on this subject are a treasure of knowledge. As for the other companions of the Holy Prophet, their sayings which have come down to us do not contain enough material on this subject. The majority of the mystics and gnostics, whether Sunni or Shi'ah consider the chain of their spiritual leaders going to Imam Ali through such companions of his as Salmān Farsi, Uways Qarani, Kumayl bin Ziyād, Rashid Hujari, Mithām Tammār, Rabi' bin Khaytham and Hasan Basri.

---

* Imam Ja'far Sādiq has said: "There are three categories of the worshippers: 'Those who worship Allah out of fear; their worship is that of the slaves. Those who worship Allah for the sake of a reward; their worship is that of the wage-earners. Those who worship Allah out of love and earnestness; their worship is that of the freeman. This last is the best form of worship." (Biharul Anwār, vol. V, p. 208)

+ Here the learned author has in his mind the religions of India and the Far East in which different aspects of divinity are represented by gods and godesses in a mythical and symbolic form.

2

Next to this group some other persons like Ṭāus Yamāni, Shayban Ra'i, Mālik ibn Dinār, Ibrahim bin Adham and Sharif Balkhi appeared in the second century. They were considered holy men by the people. These persons were apparently ascetics. They did not talk openly of gnosis or mysticism, though they conceded that they introduced to spiritualism by the first group and trained by it.

Towards the end of the second century and the beginning of the third some other individuals like Bāyazid Bistāmi, Ma'rūf Karkhi and Junayd Baghdādi appeared. They openly talked of gnosis. Some of their esoteric sayings based on their spiritual intuition were apparently so obnoxious that they were strongly denounced and condemned by some jurists and theologians. Consequently several of these gnostics were imprisoned and flogged and a few of them were even put to death.* Nevertheless this group continued to flourish and maintained its activities despite all opposition. Thus the development of gnosis or mysticism continued till this system reached the zenith of its popularity and expansion in the seventh and the eighth centuries. During the later periods its popularity fluctuated from time to time, but it has been able to maintain its existence in Islamic world till today.

It appears that most of the mystic leaders whose names are found in biographies and memoirs belonged to the Sunni school of thought and the current sufi system that comprises some ceremonials and rituals not consistent with the teachings of the Qur'an and Sunnah, is the heritage transmitted by these gnostics and mystics, although their system has subsequently adopted a few Shi'ah rites also.

Some spiritual leaders hold that no mystic or gnostic system or programme was prescribed by Islam. The present gnostic system was invented by the mystics themselves; yet it has the approbation of Allah in the same way as monasticism was sanctioned by Allah after it had been introduced by the Christians into their religion with a view to propagate Christianity.

*Refer to the books on the biographies of the sages, such as the **Tazkiratul Awliyā'** by Attar and the **Tarāiqul Haqā'iq** by Ma'ṣūm 'Ali Shah.

3

Anyway the mystics trace the chain of their spiritual leaders to Imam Ali through their early preceptors. (This chain of spiritual descent resembles a genealogical tree). The account of the visions and intuitions of the early gnostics also which has come down to us, mostly contains those elements of spiritual life which we find in the sayings, and teachings of Imam Ali and other Imams of the Holy Prophet's Household *(Ahlul Bayt)*. We can clearly observe these facts provided we study their teachings patiently and calmly and are not carried away by their fascinating sayings which are often obnoxious and blasphemous.

(i)   The sufis (Muslim mystics) regard the holiness acquired by following the spiritual path as human perfection. According to the Shi'ah belief, this quality is possessed by the Imams* and through them can be acquired by their true followers.

(ii)   The sufi doctrine that there must always be a *Qutb*+ in the world and the qualities they attribute to him, correspond to the Shi'ah doctrine of Imamat. According to the "People of the Holy Prophet's Household" the Imam (in Sufi terminology the perfect man) is a manifestation of Allah's names‡ and is responsible for supervising and guiding all human activities. This being the Shi'ah conception of *Wilāyat*, the great sufis may be regarded as the proponents of the Shi'ah doctrine, though apparently they followed the Sunni school. What we mean to say is that the Shi'ites being the followers of an infallible Imam, already possess all that is indicated by the mystics. As a matter of fact the Qutb or the perfect man conceived by the mystics does not actually exist anywhere outside the Shi'ite world. Mere presumption is obviously quite a different thing.

*The twelve successors explicity expressed by the Holy Prophet of Islam through Divine Will.

+When a gnostic becomes totally oblivious of himself, in the Sufi parlance, he is said to have passed away in God, for he completely surrenders himself to the will and guidance of Allah.

‡The gnostics maintain that the world has derived its entity from the names of Allah and its existence and continuity depend on them. The source of Allah's all names is His most perfect and loftiest name. This name is the station of the perfect man, called the Qutb of the universe also. The world is never without a Qutb.

4

It may be mentioned here that some authentic Sunni books state that the outward form of the Islamic law and Islamic teachings does not explain how to perform spiritual journey.* On this basis the sufis say that they have individually discovered certain methods and ways which facilitate this journey. They also claim that their methods have gained Divine sanction in the same way as previously monkery had gained.+ As such the sufi leaders included in their programme of spiritual journey whatever rites, rituals and formalities they deemed fit, and asked their disciples to observe them. Gradually a vast and independent system came into being. This system included such items as total obedience, liturgy, special robes, music and ecstasy and rapture at the time of repeating the liturgical formulas. Some orders of the Sufis went to the extent of separating the *tariqah* (the sufi way) from the *shari'ah* (Islamic precepts). The adherents of these sufi orders practically joined hands with the Bātinites (Those who believe that in Islam everything is allegorical and has a hidden meaning). Anyhow according to the Shi'ah point of view the original source, of Islam, namely the Qur'an and Sunnah indicate what is absolutely contrary to all this. It is not possible that the religious texts would not guide to the truth or would ignore to explain an essential programme. Nor is anybody, whosoever, he may be, allowed to ignore his duty in regard to what is obligatory or is prohibited according to injunctions of Islam.

What do the Qur'an and Sunnah say about Gnosis?

At a number of places in the Holy Qur'an Allah has directed people to ponder over the contents of the Holy Book and not to pass by them cursorily In a large number of verses, the universe and the entire creation have been described as Allah's signs. They have been called so because they indicate a great truth. When a man sees red light as a sign of danger, his attention is

---

*In Islam spiritual journey is called *Sair wa Sulūk*, which signifies a journey towards Allah.

+Allah says: *But monkery the Christian invented, We ordained it not for them. We ordained only seeking Allah's pleasure, but they observed it not.* (Surah al-Hadid, 57:27)

5

concentrated on the danger and he ceases to pay attention to the light itself. If he still thinks of the shape, colour and nature of light, then these things will absorb his attention and he will not be able to attend to the impending danger. Similarly the universe and its manifestations are the signs of their Creator, an evidence of His existence and His power. They have no independent existence. We may look at them from any aspect, they indicate nothing but Allah. He who looks at the world and the people of the world from this angle under the guidance of the Qur'an, he will perceive Allah alone. He will not be fascinated by the borrowed charms of this world, but will see an infinite Beauty, a Beloved manifesting Himself from behind the curtain of this world. No doubt, as we have explained by citing the example of red light, what the signs indicate is not this world, but the person of its Creator. We may say that the relationship between Allah and this world is not that of $1 + 1$ or 1×1, but is that of $1 + 0$. In other words, this world in relation to Allah is a nonentity and does not add anything to His Essence.

As soon as man realizes this fact, his notion of having an independent existence is smashed and he suddenly feels imbibed with love of Allah. Obviously this realization does not come through eyes, ears or any other sensory organs or mental faculties, for all organs themselves are mere signs and cannot play any significant role in providing the guidance we are talking about.*

When a man having access to Divine manifestation and desiring to remember Allah alone, hears the following passage of the Qur'an, he comes to know that the only path of perfect guidance is that of knowing himself:

O you who believe, you have charge of your own souls. He who errs cannot injure you if you are rightly guided. (al-Mā'idah, 5:105)[1]

He understands that his true guide is Allah alone who enjoins upon him to know himself and to seek the path of self-knowing, leaving all other paths. He must see Allah through

---

*Imam Ali has said: 'Allah is not that who may be comprehended by knowledge. Allah is He Who guidess the argument to Himself.' (Biharul Anwar, vol. II, p. 186)

the window of his own soul and thus achieve his real objective. That is why the Holy Prophet has said: He who has known himself, has known Allah.*

He has also said: 'Those of you who know Allah better, better they know themselves.'+

As for the embarking on spiritual journey there are many verses of the Qur'an which urge the people to remember Allah. For example at one place the Qur'an says: *Remember Me, I will remember you.* (al-Baqarah, 2:152)[2]

Man has been ordered to do good deeds also, which have been explained in the Qur'an and the Sunnah. Mentioning the good deeds Allah says: *Surely in the Messenger of Allah you have a good example.* (al-Ahzāb, 33:21)[3]

How can it be imagined that Islam would declare that there was a path leading towards Allah without appraising the people what that path is?

And how can it be that Allah would mention a path without explaining how it is to be traversed?

Allah says in the Holy Qur'an: *Messenger, We have revealed this Book to you. It contains the details of every thing.* (Surah an-Nahl, 16:89)[4]

Allamah Muhammad Husayn Tabātabāi

---

* A well-known tradition repeatedly quoted in the books of both the Sunni and Shi'ah gnostics.

+ Another tradition cited in the books of the Sunni and Shi'ah gnostics.

SCIENCE OF GNOSIS

The science of gnosis is one of the sciences which were born and grew on the lap of Islamic culture.

This science can be studied and investigated from two angles, one of them being sociological and the other scientific. There is one important difference between the gnostics and the scholars of other Islamic sciences such as traditionalists, commentators of the Qur'an, jurists, theologians, men of letters and poets. Although the gnostics also belong to a scholarly class, have invented the science of gnosis and have produced great scholars who have written important books on the subject of gnosis, yet unlike other scholars they have chosen to form a separate social sect in the Islamic world. Other learned groups like the jurists etc. are only scholarly groups and are not considered to be separate sects.

From scientific point of view the adepts in gnosis *(Irfān)* are called gnostics *('Ārifs)* but from social point of view they are mostly known as sufis.

Anyhow, the gnostics and sufis are not an organized separate religious sect, nor do they claim to have formed any such cult. They are scattered over all Muslim sects. But from social point of view they form a separate group and a separate body, having its characteristic ideas and special manners of life. They wear a particular type of dress and grow their hair in a particular style. They live in hospices etc. Thus the sufis have to a certain extent become a separate sect from religious as well as social point of view.

9

Anyhow there have always been and there are still, especially among the Shi'ah, gnostics who are not apparently distinct from others, yet they are closely associated with gnosis and spiritual journey. In fact it is they who are the real gnostics, not those who have invented hundreds of rituals and innovations.

Here we propose to discuss gnosis only as a branch of Islamic sciences and have nothing to do with the sufis as a social sect or with the rituals they have adopted.

If we had intended to discuss the social aspect of mysticism, it would have been necessary to deal with the causes which originated this sect and would have told how it positively and negatively influenced Muslim society, how this sect and other Muslim sects reacted upon each other, what complexion it put on the Islamic sciences and what effects it produced on the propagation of Islam. But at present we are not concerned with these subjects and propose to discuss gnosis as a science only.

From scientific point of view gnosis has two aspects: one practical and the other theoretical.

The practical aspect of gnosis is that part of it which describes man's relation with the world and with Allah. It determines these relations and explains the duties which these relations devolve on man.

Being a practical science this part of gnosis resembles ethics. The difference between the two we will explain later.

This part of gnosis is called *Sayr wa Sulūk* (spiritual journey). It explains wherefrom the man desiring to attain to the goal of humanity, namely monotheism, should begin his journey, in what order he should traverse the intervening stages and 'stations' and what 'states' he is expected to undergo during his journey. For the purpose of journey it is essential that it is undertaken under the supervision of a fully experienced spiritual guide who may be conversant with the procedure of the journey and who himself might have passed through all its stages. Without the guidance of such a perfect preceptor (sometimes called Khizr) the *Sālik* (the traveller or the novice) may lose his way and go astray.

A poet says: 'Do not try to proceed without being accompanied by a Khizr. Dark is the track; so beware of losing your way.'

10

The monotheism or the Oneness of Allah which a gnostic seeks and which is the highest goal of humanity is quite different from the monotheism of the common people. To a philosopher unity of Allah means that there is only One Essential Being, not more than one.

The gnostic maintains that Oneness of Allah means that Allah is the only really existing Being. The existence of every thing else is illusory.

The monotheism of a gnostic lies in making a spiritual journey and by means of it reaching the stage where he may not see anything except Allah.

The oponents of the gnostics not only do not believe in any such stage, but they sometimes also call such an idea purely heretic. On the contrary, to the gnostics only attaining to this stage is the real monotheism and all other grades of belief in one God are heterodox. According to the gnostics man cannot reach this stage by means of intellectual thinking. He can reach it only through the cleansing and purification of his heart, by suppressing his base desires and undertaking a spiritual journey.

This is the practical side of the science of gnosis and in this respect it resembles ethics, which also deals with the question as to what one should do. The difference between these two sciences is that:

(i) Besides his relations with himself and with the world gnosis deals with man's relations with God, but no ethical system cares to deal with man's relation with Him. It is only the moral system of religion that deals with this aspect.

(ii) The spiritual journey of gnosis as these words indicate, is a moving condition, but the moral principles are static. Gnosis talks of a starting point and then mentions various stages which the novice has to traverse to reach the final stage.

From the viewpoint of a gnostic the spiritual path is a real path not a figurative or a phenomenal one. It is necessary to traverse every stage of it and it is not possible for anyone to reach the next stage without passing through the previous stage.

In the eyes of a gnostic human soul is like a child or a plant which has to be nurtured in accordance with a fixed system. On the other hand, in ethics only certain qualities are stressed, such as truthfulness, amity, justice, chastity, charity and sacrifice — the qualities that polish and beautify the soul. From moral point of view human soul can be compared to a house which is to be painted and decorated, but while doing so it is not necessary to observe any order and the work can be begun from any point.

In gnosis also morals are discussed, but in it the morals are moving elements.

(iii) The spiritual elements in ethics are limited. All know what they signify. On the contrary the spiritual elements of gnosis are comperatively quite vast.

In connection with spiritual journey such states and emotional phases are discussed in gnosis which are met with by the novice personally. His experience is not shared by others.

Another part of the science of gnosis explaining the nature of the universe. It deals with God, the world and man.

This part of gnosis resembles philosophy, for it tries to interpret the universe in a philosophical manner, where as the first part mentioned above had similarity to ethics, for it wanted to change man's moral condition. But just as the first part despite its close resemblance to ethics is different from it, similarly this second part is different from philosophy despite having some features in common with it. We will further elucidate this distinction later.

Theoretical Gnosis

We now come to the theoretical aspect of gnosis. The theoretical gnosis deals with the nature of the universe and discusses man, God and the world.

As such this part of gnosis has a close resemblance to theosophy, for both of them interpret the nature of the universe. Just as philosophy has its own problems and principles, similarly mysticism also has its own problems and principles. The difference between the two is that philosophy bases its arguments on its postulates whereas the science of mysticism or gnosis bases its arguments on visions and intuition and then enunciates its theories in a logical way.

The reasoning of philosophy may be compared to the

study of an essay in its original language and the reasoning of gnosis to the study of an essay translated from a different language.

What the gnostics themselves claim is that they state in the language of reason what they see with the eyes of their heart and their entire physical existence.

The gnostic conception of existence is quite different from its philosophical conception.

From the viewpoint of a philosopher the existence of the non-God is as real as the existence of God. The difference is that God is self-existing and essentially-existing Being, whereas everything non-God is neither self-existing nor essentially existing. It is the self-existing Being who brings it into existence. But according to the gnostics the existence of the non-God is absolutely insignificant in comparison to God's in existence even if it is admitted that it is Allah who is the bringer of the non-God into existence. From the viewpoint of the gnostics Allah's existence pervades everything and everything is a manifestation of His names and attributes. Nothing else exists at all as He exists.

The viewpoint of a philosopher is different from that of a gnostic. The philosopher wants to understand this universe. In other words he wants to have in his mind a correct, comparatively complete and comprehensive picture of the universe. In the eyes of a philosopher the highest attainment of man is to be able to perceive the world in such a way that in his own existence the existence of this world is set up and he himself becomes the world. That is why philosophy has been defined as: 'Man's becoming a mental world similar to the existing world.' But a gnostic is not interested in reason and intellect. He wants to have access to the reality of existence, that is Allah Himself. He wants to meet with this reality and to observe it.

According to the gnostic man's highest attainment is to return to his origin (that is from where he has come), to wipe out the distance between himself and Allah and to pass away of human attributes to seek survival in Allah.

A philosopher uses his reason and intellect whereas a gnostic for his purpose makes use of his purified heart and soul and constant spiritual effort.

13

Later when we discuss the gnostic conception of the universe, the difference between this conception and the philosophers' conception of the universe will become clear.

Gnosis and Islam

Both the practical and theoretical aspects of gnosis are closely related to Islam, for like every other religion or rather more than any other religion Islam determines and explains man's relation to Allah, to the universe and to other man.

Now the question arises as to what is the nature of the relation between what gnosis puts forth and what Islam says.

The Muslim gnostics do not admit that any of their views or practices is repugnant to Islam. They vehemently contradict it if anybody else imputes any such thing to them. On the other hand they claim to know Islamic truths better than anybody else and assert that actually only they are the true Muslims. The gnostics quote chapter and verse of the Qur'an, *Sunnah* and the life account of the Holy Prophet, the Imams and the prominent companions of the Holy Prophet.

But others hold opinions about the gnostics which are quite different from what they themselves claim. We mention below some of these opinions.

(i)   Some traditionalists and jurists hold that generally speaking the sufis do not abide by Islam and that they quote the Qur'an and the *Sunnah* only to deceive or cajole the Muslims. They say that basically mysticism has nothing in common with Islam.

(ii)   A group of the modernists is of the opinion — and these modernists are not much concerned with Islam and take delight in describing anything which they do not like as an anti-Islamic movement of the past deviation from Islam — that the gnostics practically do not believe in Islam and that mysticism was an anti-Arab and anti-Islam movement launched by the non-Arabs who used spirituality as a cover.

As far as opposition to mysticism and gnosis is concerned, this group holds the same view as the first one. The difference between the two is that the first group reveres Islam and out of respect for Islamic sentiments, looks down upon the sufis and wants to remove gnosis from the list of Islamic sciences. In contrast the second group criticizes and disparages some

14

worldly sufis simply to find a pretext to make propaganda against Islam itself. It thinks that a subtle and lofty spirituality does not befit Islam and as such must have been imported from outside. It believes that the level of Islam and Islamic ideology is too low for gnostic ideas.

According to this group the sufis and gnostics quote the Qur'an and Sunnah only to save themselves from the wrath of the masses.

(iii) The third group is of those impartial people who maintain that the practical form of mysticism, especially when it assumes the colour of a sect, is so full of abominable innovations and deviations that it cannot be reconciled with the Qur'an and Sunnah. Anyhow the sufis and the gnostics like other learned classes of the Muslims are sincere about Islam and do not want to say anything repugnant to Islam intentionally.

The sufis might have made some mistakes, but such mistakes have been committed by all scholarly classes including the scholastic theologians, philosophers, commentators of the Qur'an, jurists etc. This does not mean that they have any evil designs against Islam.

Only those who are hostile to Islam or mysticism and gnosis talk of the anti-Islamic sentiments of the gnostics and sufis. They do so only to serve their own nefarious objectives. Anybody who knows their language and special expressions if studies the books of the gnostics he may find many errors in their books, but cannot suspect their sincerity to Islam.

In our opinion this third view is the best because we are sure that the intention of the gnostics has not been bad. Anyhow, it is necessary that those who have a deep knowledge of gnosis and are at the same time proficient in other Islamic sciences also should impartially look into the theories and doctrines of the sufis and determine how far they conform to Islam.

Shari'at, Ṭariqat and Ḥaqiqat
(Islamic law, Spiritual path and Truth)

Another important cause of disagreement between the gnostics and others especially the jurists, is the special view that the gnostics hold about *shari'at*, *ṭariqat* and *ḥaqiqat*.

The gnostics and the jurists agree that the rules of Islamic

15

law are based on truth and good reason implying definite advantages. Generally the jurists interpret the good reasons as those things that ensure man's maximum material and spiritual well-being. But the gnostics believe that all paths go to Allah and all truths and good reasons pave the way for reaching Him.

The jurists say that all rules of Islamic law have certain implicit advantages which may be considered their rationale or spirit. These advantages can be gained only by acting according to these rules. The gnostics, on the other hand, say that these good reasons are a sort of stages which lead man to the station of proximity to Allah and guide him to having access to the Truth.

The gnostics believe that the inner side of the Islamic law is that spiritual path which is called *tariqat* and the end of this path is Truth, that is unity of Allah in the special sense we mentioned earlier. According to them, this position can be attained only by annihilating "self". The gnostic believes in three things: *shari'at, tariqat* and *haqiqat.* The *shari'at* is a means of reaching the *tariqat* and the *tariqat* is a means of reaching the *haqiqat.* Thus the *shari'at* is the husk in comparison with the *tariqat* and the *tariqat* is the kernal. Similarly the *tariqat* is the husk in comparison with the *haqiqat* and the *haqiqat* is the kernel.

From the view point of the jurists *(Fuqahā')* the Islamic teachings are divided into three parts. The first part consists of the fundamentals *('Aqā'id)* which are dealt with in scholastic theology. As far as the questions relating to the fundamentals are concerned, one must have a firm belief in all Islamic fundamentals and basic tenets at least intelectually.

Another part of Islamic teachings concerns with morals *(Akhlāq).* This part deals with good morals and bad morals which are discussed in ethics.

The third part of Islamic teachings deals with the rules of law which are mentioned in Islamic jurisprudence.

All these parts of Islamic teachings are independent of each other. The fundamentals are related to reason and thinking; the morals are related to the habits and leanings; and the rules of law are related to the limbs and organs. (Articles of Acts)

As far as the fundamentals are concerned, the gnostics do not consider the mere intellectual belief to be enough. They say

16

that it is necessary to ponder over the truths in which a man believes and also to do something to remove the curtain existing between him and these truths. Similarly the gnostics do not consider the limited range of good moral, enough. Instead of abiding by philosophical and scientific morals they suggest the undertaking of spiritual journey which has its own special characteristics.

As far as the rules of law are concerned, the gnostics are not opposed to them. There are only a few questions about which their opinions may be considered to be contrary to the accepted principles of Islamic law.

The gnostics call the above-mentioned three components of the Islamic teachings *shari'at*, *tariqat* and *haqiqat*.

They maintain that just as man is composed of three parts, body, soul and intellect, which cannot be separated from each other and in spite of each part having a separate entity, all the three parts form a unified whole, the same is the case with *shari'at*, *tariqat* and *haqiqat*. The relation existing between them is that of inside and outside. The *shari'at* is outside; the *tariqat* is inside and the *haqiqat* is inside of the inside. The gnostics also believe that the human existence has many stages and grades and that some of these grades are beyond human comprehension. We shall return to this question later and explain it further.

Material of Islamic Gnosis

To gain knowledge of a science it is necessary to know its history and the developments which took place in it from time to time. It is also necessary to be conversant with the basic books of that science and with the personalities who invented or developed it. Now we come to these questions.

The first question which may be mentioned here is whether the science of Islamic gnosis has developed in the same way as that of Islamic jurisprudence, principles of jurisprudence, Qur'anic exegesis and *Ahādīth* (traditions). The basic material of which was acquired by the Muslims from Islam and the principles and rules of which were subsequently discovered by themselves; or is the nature of Islamic gnosis similar to that of mathematics and medicine, the sciences which in the beginning

17

came to the Muslim world from abroad and then the Muslims developed them to the utmost? Or is there any third possibility?

As for the gnostics, they uphold the first alternative and totally reject all other possibilities. But some orientalists have been insisting and still insist that the subtle ideas of gnosis and mysticism have entered the Muslim world from outside.

Sometimes they allege that the origin of the gnostic ideas is Christian and they have penetrated the Muslim Circles as the result of a contact between the Muslims and the Christian monks. Sometimes they describe gnosis and mysticism as a reaction of the Iranians against the Arabs and Islam. Sometimes they call mysticism a by-product of neo-Platonic philosophy, which is an amalgam of the views of Aristotle, Plato and Pythagoras on the one hand and Judo-Christian tenets on the other. Sometimes these Orientalists assert that Islamic mysticism has taken its inspiration from Budhist ideas. Strange as it may seem in the Muslim world also the opponents of gnosis in Islam have been constantly trying to prove that its origin is non-Islamic and it is alien to Islam.

According to the third theory gnosis both in its theoretical and practical aspects has been basically derived from Islam only, although subsequently it has been influenced by other sources also, especially by scholastic theology, philosophy and illuminism, which all have considerably changed its complexion.

Now the question is whether like the jurists the gnostics also have been successful in arranging on correct lines the basic material which they originally obtained from Islam and whether they have been able to frame the working rules accordingly. If so how far have they been able to ensure that they do not deviate from the true Islamic principles? Has the outside influence on Islamic gnosis been limited to a reasonable extent?

Has Islamic gnosis assimilated the extraneous influences or have they turned it away from its original direction?

All these questions require deep thinking and thorough discussion. Anyhow, it should be admitted that Islamic gnosis owes its inspiration to Islam. The proponents and supporters of the first and to a certain of the second theory also, hold that Islam is a simple, plain and unequivocal religion. It does not contain anything mysterious or unintelligible.

18

Monotheism is the most fundamental belief of Islam, which maintains that as every house has a builder who is distinct and separate from the house itself, similarly this world also has a builder who is separate from this world and is totally independent of it.

In the eyes of Islam asceticism *(zuhd)* is the basis of property and other worldly goods. Asceticism means to shun transitory luxuries of this world for the sake of ever lasting spiritual and next worldly benefit. For this purpose one has to abide by certain rules of law mentioned in Islamic jurisprudence.

This group is of the opinion that what the gnostics mean by unity of Allah is quite different from Islamic monotheism for according to the gnostics unity of Allah means unity of existence. In other words they believe that there exists nothing except Allah, His names and attributes and their manifestations.

The spiritual journey of the gnostics is also different from Islamic asceticism, for in connection with their spiritual journey the gnostics talk of certain things such as love for Allah, annihilation of self and abiding in Allah and the revelation of Allah's glory on the heart of the gnostics, the things of which there is no trace in Islamic asceticism.

The *tariqat* of the gnostics is also different from the *shari'at* (Islamic law). The rules of personal behaviour and life style discussed in the *tariqat* are not found in Islamic jurisprudence.

This group holds that the virtuous companions of the Holy Prophet whom the gnostics and mystics claim to follow, were only ascetics and they knew nothing of the gnostics' spiritual journey nor were they conversant with the gnostic unity of Allah. All that they did was that they were indifferent to the worldly goods and concentrated their attention on the other world. They feared the punishment of Hell and hoped for the reward of Paradise. But the theory of this group is not acceptable in any way. The early period of Islam is more profound than these people intentionally or out of ignorance suppose. Islamic Monotheism is not so simple or so hollow as they think, nor is Islam limited to dry asceticism. Neither the Holy Prophet's virtuous companions were so simple as these people assert, nor are the Islamic injunctions limited to external acts of devotion.

19

Here we would like to point out briefly that in the original teachings of Islam there are many things which hint at the lofty and nice points of both practical and theoretical gnosis.

As for the question as to how far the Muslim gnostics and mystics have benefited from these teachings and what mistakes they have committed, it is not possible to deal with these points in this brief discourse.

As for the unity of Allah, the Holy Qur'an has not anywhere compared Allah and His creation to a house and its builder. The Qur'an declares that Allah is the Creator of the whole world and that He is everywhere and with everything.

The Qur'an says: *Wherever you turn your face, Allah's face is there.* (Surah al-Baqarah, 2:115)[5]

We are closer to you than yourselves. (Surah Qāf, 50:16)[6]

He is the First and the Last (every thing begins from Him and ends at Him), and the Manifest and the Hidden. (Surah al-Hadid, 57:3)[7]

It is obvious that such verses of the Qur'an draw the mind to a form of monotheism better and higher than the monotheism of the masses. There is a tradition in the Kāfi which says that Allah knew that during a later period there would be people who would go deep into monotheism, and that is why he revealed the surah, al-Tawhid and the initial verses of the surah al-Hadid.

To prove the validity of spiritual journey and gaining proximity to Allah, it is enough to keep in mind the verse speaking about "meeting Allah" and "gaining His good pleasure". Moreover there are verses which speak of revelation and inspiration or say that the angels talked with some persons other than the Prophets, for example with Maryam (Mary). In this connection the verses relating to the Holy Prophet's ascension to heaven are also important.

In the Qur'an the appetitive soul, the admonishing soul and the contented and calm soul have been mentioned. There is also a mention of the knowledge imparted direct by Allah as well as of guidance as the result of one's striving. *Those who strive for our sake, We guide them to Our paths.* (Surah al-Ankabut, 29:69)[8]

Similarly the Qur'an has described the purification of the soul as the cause of success. *Indeed he is successful who causes*

the soul to flourish; and indeed he is a failure who stunts it.
(Surah ash Shams, 91:7 - 8)[9]

At several places in the Qur'an the love of Allah has been described as superior to all human relations and affections.

The Qur'an says that every particle of the universe glorifies Allah. This has been stated in a way that suggests that if man perfects his *'tafaqquh'* (understanding) he can understand their glorification. Furthermore, in connection with human nature it has been said that Allah has breathed His spirit in man.

These things are enough to draw attention to the existence of vast spiritual relations, especially to the relation between man and Allah.

As mentioned earlier the question is not whether the Muslim gnostics used this material rightly or wrongly. What is important is that this material exists and it is potentially capable of suggesting very fine ideas. Even if it is admitted that the Muslim gnostics did not use this material rightly, some other people, not known as gnostics or mystics have correctly used it.

Furthermore, the Muslim traditions, reports, sermons, supplications, 'protests'* and the life accounts of eminent personalities of Islam clearly indicate that dry asceticism and mere worship in the hope of the next worldly reward were not considered enough in the early period of Islam.

These reports, sermons, supplications and 'protests' contain highly sublime points. The life accounts of early eminent Muslim personalities throw enough light on their lofty spirituality, enlightened heart, burning passion and spiritual love. Here we relate only one story:

There is a report in the Kāfi that one day after performing his prayers the Holy Prophet saw a weak and lean young man whose colour had turned pale, whose eyes were sunken and who could balance himself with difficulty. The Holy Prophet asked him who he was. He said: 'I carry conviction.' 'What is the sign of your conviction?', said the Holy Prophet. In reply he said: 'It is my conviction that has grieved me, that keeps me awake during the night (night vigil) and that keeps me thirsty during

---

* The books composed in protest against wrong tenets and views like al Ihtijāj by Tabrasi.

21

the day (on account of fasting). It has made me oblivious of every thing in the world. I see as if the Throne of Allah was set up for the purpose of reckoning the deeds of the people who were assembled in the Assembly Square, I being one of them. I see the dwellers of Paradise enjoying themselves and the dwellers of Hell undergoing punishment. It appears as if even now I was hearing the blast of Hell flames with my own ears.' The Holy Prophet turned to his companions and said: 'He is the man whose heart Allah has enlightened with the light of faith.' Then the Holy Prophet turned to that young man and said: 'Keep up this state of yours, lest you lose it.'

The young man said: 'Please pray to Allah to grant me martyrdom.' Before long a battle took place. The young man took part in it and was martyred.

Even the life account of the Holy Prophet himself and his sayings and supplications are full of spiritual fervour and gnostic hints. The gnostics often quote his prayers as their authority.

Imam Ali's sayings also are replete with spirituality and almost all mystics and gnostics trace the origin of their orders to him. Here we quote two passages from Nahjul Balâghah:

'There is no doubt that Allah the Almighty has made His remembrance the polish of the hearts. By means of it the deaf begin to hear, the blind begin to see and the arrogant become submissive. In every age and period Allah the Almighty has created men in whose minds He puts His secrets and through whose intellect He talks to them.' (Sermon — 220)[10]

'A godly person enlivens his heart and annihilates his ego till what is coarse becomes soft. A bright light like lightning shines in front of him, shows him the way and helps him in advancing towards Allah. Many doors push him forward till he reaches the gate of peace and safety and arrives at the destination where he has to stay. His feet are firm and his body contented, for he uses his heart and pleases his Lord.' (Sermon — 218)[11]

Islamic supplications, especially those which have been taught by the Imams of the Holy Prophet's Progeny are a source of knowledge. The Supplication of Kumayl, the Supplication of Abu Hamzah Thumali, the Munajât Sha'baniyyah and the Sahifah Sajjadiyyah contain most sublime and heart warning spiritual expressions.

Is it necessary in the presence of all these sources that we roam about looking for alien sources?

A similar question arises in connection with the protest campaign launched by the holy Prophet's prominent companion Abu Ẕar Ghifāri, against the tyrants of his time. He strongly criticized tyranny and discrimination committed by them and as a result under went many hardships. At last he was exiled and he died in exile.

Some orientalists have raised the question as to what Abu Ẕar's motive was. They look for the motive of his campaign outside the Muslim world.

An Arab Christian George Jordaq in his book Imam Ali — The Voice of Human Justice, says:

'We are surprised at these people. Will it be reasonable if we see a man sitting at the bank of a river or at the coast of a sea and then try to find out from which stream he got that water with which he filled his pot? If we do so, we will be overlooking the river or the sea and will be looking for a stream from where he might have brought water."

Evidently Abu Ẕar could have no motive other than Islam. What other motive could have persuaded him to agitate against the tyranny of Muʻāwiyah etc.?

Exactly the same case is with gnosis. The Orientalists have shut their eyes to the great source of Islam and are looking for some other source which they may describe as the motivating force of the spirituality of Islam.

Can we reject the sources of the Qur'an, traditions, sermons, supplications and the lifestyle of the Holy Prophet and the Imams simply to authenticate the theory of the Orientalists and their Eastern disciples?

In the beginning the pseudo-orientalists were bent upon proving something extraneous to Islamic teachings as the source of Islamic gnosis. But later some genuine orientalists such as Nicholson, the Englishman and Massignon, the French who had made a vast study of Islamic gnosis and mysticism and were not unaware of Islam also frankly admitted that the Qur'an and sunnah were the fountain-head of Islamic gnosis.

Here we quote a few sentences from Nicholson. He says:
We find in the Qur'an that Allah says:

(i)   Allah is the Light of the heavens and the earth.

(ii) He is the First and He is the Last.

(iii) There is no god but He.

(iv) Everything other than Allah is transitory.

(v)   I breathed in man My spirit.

(vi) We created man and We know what his soul says, because We are closer to him than his jugular vein.

(vii) Wherever you turn, Allah's face is there.

(viii) He whom Allah has not provided light, has no light.

There is no doubt that the roots of gnosis lie deep in these verses. For early gnostics the Qur'an was not only Allah's word but it was also a means of gaining proximity to Him. By pondering over the Qur'anic verses, especially the verses hinting at the Holy Prophet's Ascension, the mystics tried to absorb the Holy Prophet's spiritual quality.

The principle of unity found in mysticism is also mentioned in the Qur'an. In addition to that there is *Hadith al-Qudsi* (tradition quoting Allah's words) according to which the Holy Prophet has said that Allah says: 'When My bondman comes close to Me by means of his acts of worship and good deeds; I begin to love him, and when I love him, become his ears with which he hears, his eyes with which he sees, his tongue with which he speaks and his hand with which he holds.'

As we have repeatedly pointed out, the question is not whether the gnostics have or have not properly utilized these verses, traditions and reports. The question is whether the original source of gnostic ideas is Islamic or non-Islamic.

Brief History

The leaders of Islam whose life replete with Islamic ideas and spiritual manifestations has given birth to deep spirituality in the Muslim world, were not technically mystics or gnostics.

Now we propose to give a concise account of the development of this branch of Islamic sciences. For this purpose it appears to be proper to give first of all a brief history of gnosis and mysticism from the first century of Hijri era to the tenth century. After that we shall discuss some questions relating to gnosis as far as the space at our disposal allows us and then we shall analyse these question.

It is an admitted fact that in the early period of Islam, and at least during the first century there existed among the Muslims no group known as the gnostic or the sufi. The word sufi came into existence during the second century.

It is said that Abu Hāshim of Kufah was the first man to be called by this name. He lived in the second century, and is reputed to have founded the first monastery *(khānqah)** at Ramlah in Palestine for the exclusive use of a group of ascetics and worshippers. It is not known when Abu Hāshim died but we know that he was the teacher of Abu Sufyān Thawri who died in 161 A.H. The well-known gnostic and sufi Abu al-Qāsim Qushayri says that the word, sufi was not in vogue prior to 200 A.H. Nicholson is of the opinion that this word came into use towards the end of the second century.

There is a report in the Kāfi, vol. V which indicates that during the time of Imam Ja'far Sadiq, that is during the first half of the second century there were some persons who were known as sufis.

If it is true that the name sufi was first applied to Abu Hāshim of Kufa and if it is also true that he was Sufyān Thawri's teacher, that means that this epithet came into vogue in the first half of the second century, not towards the end of the second century as claimed by Nicholson and others. It also appears to be certain that the sufis were named so because they wore woolen garments (garments of sūf).

Being ascetics the sufis (mystics) avoided soft dress and preferred coarse woolen garments.

Nothing can be said for certain since when these people assumed the epithet 'Ārif (gnostic). Anyhow there is no doubt that this term was in vogue in the third century as the sayings of Sari al-Saqati (d. 243) indicate. An utterance of Sufyān Thawri quoted in the Kitab al-Lum'ah by Abu Nasr Sarrāj Ṭusi, an

---

* Dr. Qasim Ghani in his book, **Tarikh-e-Tasawwuf Dar Islam** has quoted a report from Ibn Taymiyyah's **al-Mutasawwifun wa al-Fuqara'** which says that it was a disciple of Abdul Wahid ibn Zayd who first founded a small monastery. Abdul Wahid was one of the companions of Hasan of Basrah. Should Abu Hāshim Sufi be one of the followers of Abdul Wahid, then there is no contradiction between these two reports.

25

authentic book of tasawwuf or mysticism, shows that this term appeared in the second century.

At any rate there was no class named sufi in the first century. The sufis appeared in the second century and apparently in this very century they became an organized group. It is not correct, as some people suggest, that this event took place in the third century.

Although in the first century there existed no group bearing the name of Sufi (mystic) or 'Ārif (gnostic), yet it is not correct to say that the Holy Prophet's eminent companions were simple ascetics and had no spiritual life.

Perhaps some of the virtuous companions were ascetic only, but some others enjoyed the spiritual life to the utmost. Even all these were not alike. Salmān Farsi and Abu Zar Ghifāri did not have the same degree of faith. The degree of faith which Salmān Farsi had, was unbearable to Abu Zar Ghifari.

Several traditions say: "If Abu Zar had known what was in Salman's heart, he would have killed him (thinking him to be an infidel).*

Now we talk about the mystics and gnostics of the period from the second century to the tenth century.

Gnostics of Second Century

Hasan Basri: Like that of scholastic theology the history of gnosticism and mysticism also begins with Hasan Basri who died in 110 A.D.

Hasan Basri was born in 62 A.H. and died at the age of 88. He passed 90 per cent of his life in the first century.

Hasan Basri was not known as a sufi, but he is counted among the sufis because he is the author of a book named Ri'āyat Huqūq Allah, which is considered to be the first book on *tasawwuf* or mysticism. The Oxford Library has the only extant copy of this book. Nicholson says: "Hasan Basri is the first Muslim who wrote about the sufi way of life. The programme of sufism proposed by the later authors for reaching high spiritual positions consists of repentance *(taubah)* followed by some other rituals. Each ritual is performed to reach a position higher than the preceding one."

* Safinatul Bihār by Muhaddith Qummi, root SLM.

It is important to note that certain orders of the sufis, for example that of Abu Sa'id Abul Khayr, trace the chain of their preceptors to Hasan Basri and through him to Imam Ali. Ibn Nadim traces Abu Muhammad Ja'far Khadi's chain of preceptors to Hasan Basri and says that Hasan met the Holy Prophet's 70 such companions who had taken part in the Battle of Badr.

Another point worth mentioning is that certain stories show that Hasan Basri practically was a member of the group which was subsequently known as the sufis. We shall relate some of these stories.

Malik ibn Dinar: He was one of those who practised a very high degree of asceticism and austerity. In this connection many stories are related of him. He died in 135 A.H.

Ibrahim bin Adham: The story of his life which resembles that of Mahatma Budh is well-known. In the beginning he was a ruler of Balkh. Then as the result of certain events he repented and joined the sufi order.

The gnostics and sufis attach great importance to him. In the Mathnawi of Mawlana Rum his story has been related in a very fascinating way. He died approximately in 161 A.H.

Rabi'ah 'Adwiyyah: She was a wonder of her age. Being the fourth daughter of her parents she was named Rābi'ah. She is different from Rābi'ah Shamiyyah who is also counted among the sufis. Rābi'ah Shamiyyah was a contemporary of Jāmi and belonged to the ninth century.

Rābi'ah Adwiyyah's utterances are lofty and her verses are a masterpiece of gnosis. The events of her life are prodigious.

Abu Hāshim Sufi of Kufah: The date of his death is not known. All that we know about him is that he was a teacher of Sufyān Thawri who died in 161. It appears that he was the first to become known as sufi in the history of Islam. Sufyān Thawri says: "If there had not been Abu Hāshim, I would not have been able to understand the subtle points about ostentation and pretended piety.

Shaqiq Balkhi: He was a disciple of Ibrahim ibn Adham. Quoting the Kashful Ghummah by 'Isa Arbali and the Nur al-Absār by Shablanji, the author of the book Rayhānatul Adab says that Shaqiq Balkhi met Imam Musa ibn Ja'far on his way to Makkah. Several miracles of the Imam are reported by him. The year of his death is either 153 or 174 or 184 A.H.

Ma'ruf Karkhi: He is one of the most renowned gnostics. It is said that his parents were Christian and he himself embraced Islam at Imam Riza' hands. The chain of the preceptors of many sufi order goes up to Ma'ruf Karkhi, from him to Imam Riza, through him to the preceding Imams and from them to the Holy Prophet. This chain is called the 'golden chain'. At least so is claimed by the adherents of his sufism.

Fuzayl bin Ayâz: He was an Iranian of Arab origin and lived in Marv. He is said to have been a bandit in the beginning. One night when he climbed the wall of a house with evil intentions, he heard someone who was keeping vigil, reciting a verse of the Qur'an. Fuzayl was so moved that he at once repented. A book named Misbâh al-Shari'ah is ascribed to him. This book is said to be the collection of the lessons imparted to him by Imam Sâdiq.

The late Haji Mirza Husayn Nuri, erudite scholar of tradition *(hadith)* of the last century regarded this book as reliable. Fuzayl bin Ayâz died in 187 A.H.

Gnostics of Third Century

Bâyazid Bistâmi: His name was Tayfur ibn 'Isa and he is one of the most prominent sufis. He is said to be the first who talked about the doctrine of 'fana' (dying to self and staying in Allah)

Bâyazid Bistâmi once said: "I came forth from Bayazidness as a snake from its skin." Some people have declared him an infidel on account of his ecstatic utterances. The sufis themselves admit that he is a "man of intoxication" and that he made heretical and outwardly un-Islamic statements and false claims in a state of ectasy and unconsciousness.

Bayazid died in 261 A.H. Some people assert that he served Imam Ja'far Sâdiq as a water carrier, but this is historically wrong because he was not alive during the time of Imam Ja'far Sâdiq.

Bishr Hafi: He is one of the most prominent sufis. In the beginning he was a libertine and lax in morals. Then he repented.

The late Allamah Hilli in his book, Minhâjul Karâmah has related a story, according to which he repented at the hand of

28

Imam Musa ibn Ja'far. As he was without shoes at that time, he came to be known as Hafi or bare foot. Some other people give some other reason as to why he is called Hafi. Bishr Hafi died in 226 or in 227.

Sari Saqati: He was one of the companions and friends of Bishr Hafi. Sari Saqati was very kind-hearted. He was always willing to help others and to make sacrifice for them.

In his book Wafiyāt al-A'yān Ibn Khallikan says: "Sari Saqati once said: 'Some thirty years ago I once said 'Alhamdu lillah, (Thank God) and since then I have been seeking Allah's forgiveness for that." "How was that", people asked. Sari Saqati said: "One night fire broke out in the market. I went there to see if my shop was safe. Somebody told me that the fire had not reached my shop. I involuntarily exclaimed Alhamdu lillah. At once I realized my mistake. It was all right that my shop was not damaged, but should I be indifferent to the fate of other Muslims?"

Sa'di has narrated this story with a slight variation.

"One night owing to the heat caused by the lamenting sighs of the people fire broke out. I have heard that as a result half of Baghdad was gutted by fire. While this destitution was going on one man said: Thank God. My house has not been damaged. Thereupon a wise man exclaimed: "Greedy man, you are too selfish. You want your own house to be safe and do not care if the whole town is burnt."

Sari was Ma'ruf Karkhi's pupil and disciple and Junayd Baghdadi's uncle and spiritual guide. Many of his utterances about unity of Allah and Divine love are quoted. Once he said: "The gnostic shines all the world over like the sun; he bears the weight of the virtuous and the wicked on his shoulders like the earth. He is like water; on him depends the life of hearts. Like fire his light reaches all."

Sari Saqati died at the age of 98 years in 245 or 250 A.H.

Harith Muhāsibi: He was one of Junayd Baghdadi's friends and disciples. He is called Muhāsibi because he was very keen on contemplation and self-checking. He was Ahmad bin Hambal's contemporary and friend. But Ahmad bin Hambal turned him away because Ahmad bin Hambal was opposed to scholastic theology while Muhāsibi was very fond of it. As a result people were estranged from him. Hārith Muhāsibi died in 223 A.H.

Junayd Baghdadi: Originally he was a resident of Nahāwand. The sufis call him Sayyid al-Tā'ifah (Chief of the tribe) just as Shi'ah jurists call Shaykh Tusi Shaykh al-Tā'ifah. Junayd is considered to be a moderate sufi. From him such ecstatic remarks have not been reported as from others. He did not wear the garb of the sufis and was always dressed like the jurists. Somebody asked him to wear the cloak of the sufis at least to please his friends. He said: 'If I had believed that the style of dress was of any significance, I would have worn the garments of molten iron. But the voice of the truth says: 'What is important is a burning heart and not a patched cloak.' Junayd was Sari Saqati's disciple, nephew and pupil. He was a pupil of Hārith Muhāsibi also. It is said that he died in 297 A.H.

Zun Nūn al-Misri: He was a native of Egypt and was a pupil of the renowned jurist, Malik ibn Anas. Zun Nūn was the first to use allegorical and symbolic language. Some people hold that it was he who introduce Neo-Platonic philosophy in Islamic mysticism. He died between 240 and 250 A.H.

Sahl bin Abdullah Tustari: He is counted among the great sufis. A sect of the sufis maintaining that the keynote of gnosis is self-mortification or a struggle against lower self, is called Sahliyyah after him. In Makkah he came into contact with Zun Nūn of Egypt. He died in 283 or 293 A.H.

Husayn bin Mansur Hallāj: Among the Muslim mystics his personality is most controversial. Many ecstatic utterances and impious sayings are attributed to him. He was accused of heresy, apostasy and claiming himself to be a God incarnate. The jurists declared him to be an infidel. Accordingly he was crucified during the reign of Caliph Muqtadir. The sufis accuse him of betraying the spiritual secrets.

Some people think that he was nothing but a trickstar. Anyhow the sufis try to give an explanation on his behalf and say that his and Bāyazid's utterances smacking infidelity were made by them in an ecstatic and unconscious state.

The sufis call him martyr. He was executed in 306 or 307 A.H.*

* In the preface of his book 'Causes of Inclination to Materialism' Allamah Mutahhari has repudiated the statement of some materialists that Hallaj was a materialist.

30

Gnostics of Fourth Century

Abu Bakr Shibli: He was Junayd Baghdadi's pupil as well as his disciple, and was acquainted with Hallāj also. He is one of the renowned sufis. Originally he belonged to Khurasan. In the Rawzatul Jannah and other biographical memoirs a large number of his verses and mystic sayings have been quoted.

Khwāja Abdullah Ansari says: "Zun Nūn Misri was the first to talk in symbolic terms and in an allegorical way. Junayd arranged this science and developed it further. When Shibli's turn came, he carried it to the pulpits." Shibli died at some time between 334 and 337 A.H. at the age of 87.

Abu Ali Rūdbāri: He came of the Sāsānian stock, and claimed to be a descendant of Nushirwān. He was one of the disciples of Junayd. He learned jurisprudence from Abul 'Abbās bin Shurayh and received education in literature from Tha'lab. He is known as the one who combined in himself the knowledge of the Shari'at (law), Tariqat (the mystic way) and Haqiqat (truth). He died in 322.

Abu Nasr Sarrāj Tusi : He is the author of the celebrated book Lum'ah, which is one of the earliest and reliable books of mysticism. He died in 378 A.H. Many of the prominent mystics are his direct or indirect pupils.

Abul Fazl Sarkhasi: He was Abu Nasr Sarraj's pupil and disciple and the renowned gnostic, Abu Sa'id Abul Khayr's preceptor and teacher. Abul Fazl died in 400 A.H.

Abu Abdillah Rūdbāri: He was a nephew of Abu Ali Rūdbāri and a leading mystic of Syria. He died in 396 A.H.

Abu Tālib Makki: His fame rests on his book Quwwatul Qulūb, which has been published and is counted among the earliest and the most authentic books of sufism. Abu Tālib Makki died in 385 or 386 A.H.

Gnostics of Fifth Century

Shaykh Abul Hasan Khirqāni: He is one of the most renowned sufis. Many astonishing stories are related of him. It is said that once he went to Bāyazid Bistāmi's grave, made a contact with Bāyazid's spirit and got his difficulties solved by Bāyazid direct.

This story has been related in his celebrated Mathnawi

31

by Mawlawi, who has mentioned Khirqani at a number of places in his Mathnavi and appears to be especially devoted to him. It is also reported that Khirqani was personally acquainted with the renowned philosopher, Abu Ali Sina and the well-known gnostic Abu Sa'id Abul Khayr. Khirqani died in 425 A.H.

Abu Sa'id Abul Khayr: He is one of the most famous sufis and is reputed to have possessed a very fine spiritual condition. His quatrains are distinguished by elegance. Once somebody asked him what *tasawwuf* was. He said: "*Tasawwuf* means that you remove what is in your head; give away that which is in your hand; and do all that you can." One day Abu Ali Sina attended his sermon meeting. Abu Sa'id was talking about the necessity of obeying Allah and doing good deeds. Abu Ali recited a quatrain which said: "We love Your forgiveness and rely on that, we have nothing do with obedience or disobedience. Wherever there is Your benevolence, the deeds done and the deeds not done are all alike."

Abu Sa'id at once retorted reciting a couplet saying: "Dont rely on forgiveness. The deeds done and the deeds not done can never be the same." He died in 440 A.H.

Abu Ali Daqqāq Nishāpuri: He was proficient in both *shari'at* and *tariqat*, and was a preacher and a commentator of the Qur'an too. His orisions are full of lamentation. Hence, he is known as the lamenting shaykh. He died in 405 or 412 A.H.

Abul Hasan Ali bin Uthmān Hujwiri: He is the author of the celebrated book of *tasawwuf*, Kashful Mahjub, which has recently been published. He died in 470 A.H.

Khwāja Abdullah Ansāri: He was one of the renowned and the most devoted sufis. His fame rests on his brief sayings, orisions and his beautiful and elegant quatrains. One of his sayings is: "You are immature in childhood, intoxicated in youth and weak in old age. Then when will you adore Allah?" Another saying of his is: "To return unkindness for unkindness is dog-like; to return kindness for kindness is donkey-like; Abdullah Ansāri returns kindness for unkindness."

In one of his quatrians he says: "It is very bad to brag or to be self-conceited. One should learn a lesson from the pupil of the eye, which sees everything but does not look at itself."

Khwāja Abdullah was born in Herat and died there in

481 A.H. That is why he is known as the Pir-e-Herāt.

He is the author of many books, including his well-known and magnificent book Manzilus Sā'irin, which is a text book of sufism and gnosis. On this book many commentaries have been written.

Abu Hāmid Muhammad Ghazāli: He is one of the most outstanding scholars of Islam and is well-known throughout the East and the West. He was well-versed in all rational and trans-mitted sciences. For some time he was the head of the celebrated Nizāmiyyah College which was the highest religious post of his time. After some time he felt that neither his knowledge nor his post was enough to provide him spiritual satisfaction. Therefore he retired to seclusion and engaged himself in the purification of his soul.

He passed 10 years in Jerusalam away from his friends and acquaintances. During this period his attention was absorbed by Islamic mysticism. After that till the end of his life he did not accept any post or position. The Ihyā' Ulum ad-Din is his most famous work. He died in his native town Tus in 505 A.H.

Gnostics of Sixth Century

'Aynul Quzāt al-Hamdāni: He was one of the most enthu-siastic sufis and was a disciple of Muhammad Ghazāli's younger brother Ahmad Ghazāli, who was also a leading sufi. 'Aynul Quzāt was the author of many books. His verses are pleasing and beautiful, but contain many ecstatic statements, for which he was accused of infidelity and put to death. His dead body was burnt and ashes were scattered. He was executed at sometime between 525 and 533 A.H.

Sanā'i Ghaznavi: He is a famous poet and in his verses he has alluded to the delicate questions of mysticism. In his mathnavi Mawlavi has quoted his sayings and explained them. Sanā'i died in the first half of the sixth century.

Ahmad Jāmi Zhindah Pil: He is one of the renowned sufis and gnostics. His grave is in a town named Turbat-i-Jām on the border of Iran and Afghanistan.

In a four-line poem he says:

"Do not be proud for it has so often happened that a fine rider was taken to a difficult tartarean track to tumble down.

At the same time do not lose heart for many a wicked person has unexpectedly been carried to destination."

Ahmad Jāmi died sometime about 536 A.H.

Abdul Qādir Jilāni: He is a controversial figure of the Muslim world. The sufi order known as Qādiriyya is attributed to him. His mausoleum in Baghdad is well-known. Abdul Qādir Jilāni was a descendant of Imam Hasan. He died in 560 or 561 A.H.

Shaykh Ruz Bahān Baqli of Shiraz: Because of his frequent ecstatic utterances he is known as Shaykh Shattāh. The Orientalists have recently published some of his books. He died in 606 A.H.

Gnostics of Seventh Century

In this century also there were many eminent sufis. We mention here some of them in the order of the year of their death:

Shaykh Najmuddin Kubra: He is one of the well-known great sufis. Several sufi orders branch off from him. He was Shaykh Bahān Baqli's pupil, disciple and son-in-law, and himself had many disciples. One of his disciples was Maulavi's father, Bahā'uddin.

While Shaykh Najmuddin Kubra was living in Khawārazm, the Mongols invaded that city. They sent a message to the Shaykh asking him to leave the city for safety along with his family. In reply Shaykh Najmuddin said: "I have lived with the people of this city during the days of peace and security. Now I cannot leave them alone at the time of a calamity." After that he took up arms and died bravely fighting along with the other people of Khawārazm. This event took place in 616 A.H.

Shaykh Fariduddin Attār: He is one of the first grade and most eminent sufis. His works are both in prose and poetry. He compiled a book named Tazkiratul Awliya, which contains the life-accounts of the sufis. The book begins with the biography of Imam Ja'far Sadiq and ends with that of Imam Muhammad Baqir (peace be on both of them). This book has served as a source-book for the subsequent books on the subject and is considered to be a reference book. His book Mantiqut Tayr is also a master piece of *tasawwuf* or *sufi'ism*.

In respect of him Mawlavi says:

Attār was the spirit and Sanā'i his two eyes;
We follow in the footsep of Sanā'i and Attār.

He has also said:

Attār has walked through seven cities of love;
We are still at the corner of a lane.

By seven cities Mawlavi means the seven vallies explained by Attār himself in the Mantiqut Tayr.

Mahmud Shabistari in his Mathnawi, Gulshan-e-Rāz says:

"I am not ashamed of my poor poetry:
Such wonderful men as was Attār are born only once in thousands of years."

Attār was Majduddin Baghdadi's pupil and disciple and Majduddin was a disciple of Shaykh Najmuddin Kubra.

Attār also received some gnostic training from Qutbuddin Haydar who was a great sufi of that time, and who is buried at Turbat-e-Haydariya a town named after him.

Attār was killed during the Mangol disturbances. According to a report he was killed by the Mongols at some time between 626 and 628 A.H.

Shaykh Shihābuddin Suhrawardi Zanjani: He is the author of the celebrated book of Tasawwuf, 'Awariful Ma'ārif, and is a direct descendant of Abu Bakr. It is said that he visited Makkah and Madina every year for pilgrimage. He was aquainted with Shaykh Abdul Qādir Jilāni and was his companion too.

Shaykh Sa'di Shirazi and the well-known poet Kamāluddin Isfahani were his disciples.

About him Sa'di says:

"My spiritual guide, Shaykh Shihābuddin, who was aware of spiritual mystics, gave me two counsels while travelling aboard a boat:

(i)   Do not be self-conceited, and
(ii) Do not be fault-finding."

This Surhrawardi is different from his name sake Shaykh Shihābuddin Suhrawardi, who was a philosopher known as "Shaykhul Ishrāq"* and who was killed in Alapps some time between 581 and 590 A.H.

---

* Ishraq signifies a school of philosophy known as the school of illumination.

The gnostic Suhrawardi died in about 630 A.H.

Ibnul Fāriz of Egypt: He is counted among the first rate sufis. His mystic verses in Arabic are exquisite. His Diwān (collection of poetical verses) has been published several times. One of those who have written a commentary on his Diwān is Abdur Rahman Jāmi, a well-known sufi of the ninth century.

His poems in Arabic can be compared to the lyrics of Hāfiz in Persian. Muhyuddin 'Arabi once asked Ibn Fāriz to write a commentary on his own verses. In reply he said: "Your book al-Futuhāt al-Makkiyyah is a commentary on my verses."

Ibn Fāriz is one of those whose spiritual condition may be described as extraordinary. Perhaps he was possessed by a state of rapture and ecstasy and he composed most of his verses while he was in that state. Ibn Fāriz died in 632 A.H.

Muhyuddin Ibn al-'Arabi: He was a descendant of Hātim Tā'i. Originally he belonged to Andalus, but it appears that he passed the greater part of his life in Makkah and Syria. He was a pupil of the sixth century sufi, Shaykh Abu Madyan Maghribi. The chain of his spiritual preceptors goes with one intervening link to Shaykh Abdul Qādir Jilāni, mentioned by us earlier.

Muhyuddin who is also known as Ibnul 'Arabi, was un-doubtedly the greatest gnostic of Islam. No gnostic in Islam has ever reached that position which he occupies. That is why he is called al-Shaykh al-Akbar (the grand master).

Islamic gnosticism made progress century by century. In every century there were some people who made significant contribution to its development and promotion. But in the seventh century Muhyuddin brought about a complete revolution and gnosis and mysticism suddenly reached their zenith. He set a new goal for gnosis and laid the foundation of the scientific and philosophical aspect of mysticism. His personality was a wonder of his time. It is because of his marvellous personality that contradictory opinions have been expressed about him.

Some say that he was a perfect *wali* (saint) and favourite of Allah whereas some others degrade him so much that they say that he was an infidel. They distort even his name and call him Mumituddin or Māhiyuddin (suppressor of faith). The great Muslim philosopher, Mulla Sadra attached great importance to him. In his opinion he was higher in rank than Abu Ali Sina and Fārābi.

The number of the books composed by him is more than two hundred and almost all those books the manuscripts of which are extant, have been published. The number of these published books is about 30. The most important of his books is al-Futuhât al-Makkiyyah, which is a voluminous book and is in fact an encyclopedia of tawsawwuf or mysticism.

Another book of his is Fusûsul Hikam, which is a very important and valuable book though small in size. This book is difficult to understand and that is why many commentaries on it have been written. Perhaps at no time there have been more than two or three persons who could understand its text. Muhyuddin died in 638 A.H. in Damascus where his tomb still stands.

Sadruddin Muhammad Qunawi: He was a disciple and stepson of Muhyuddin Ibn al-Arabi and a contemporary of Khwaja Nasiruddin Tusi and Mawlavi. Khwaja Tusi has had correspondence with him and Khwaja Nasiruddin held him in great respect. His relations with Mawlavi were very good and sincere. Qunawi used to lead the prayers and Mawlavi used to offer his prayers behind him. Mawlavi is said to be his pupil also.

It is related that Mawlavi one day came to the meeting place of Qunawi. Qunawi rose from the mattress on which he was sitting and offered his seat to Mawlavi who said: "If I sit on your mattress, what explanation shall I give to Allah?" Qunawi threw away the mattress and said: "If it is not fit for you, it is not for me also."

Qunawi is the best interpreter of Muhyuddin Ibnul 'Arabi's ideas. Perhaps without him it would have been too difficult to comprehend Ibnul 'Arabi. Even Mawlavi became conversant with Ibn al-'Arabi's school of thought through Qunawi.

It appears that Mawlavi is called Qunawi's pupil only because he got to Ibnul 'Arabi's ideas through him. Ibnul 'Arabi's thinking is reflected in Mawlavi's Mathnawi as well as his Diwân known as the Diwân of Shams Tabriz. For the past six hundred years Qunawi's books have been used as text books in the teaching centres of Islamic philosophy and tasawwuf.

The most well-known of his works are Miftâhul Ghayb, Nusûs and Fukûk. Qunawi died in 672 or 673 A.H. Mawlavi and Khwaja Nasiruddin Tusi also died in 672 A.H.

Mawlana Jalaluddin Muhammad Balkhi Rumi: He is known by his epithet Mawlavi. Among the Muslim gnostics he was gifted with an extraordinary intelligence. He is a direct descendant of Abu Bakr. His Mathnawi is an ocean of philosophy and gnosis. It is replete with subtle points, spiritual, social and gnostic. He is counted among the most eminent poets of Iran. Originally he belonged to Balkh. When he was still a boy he went on a pilgrimage to Makkah along with his father. On his way he met with Shaykh Fariduddin Attār in Nishapur.

On return from Makkah he and his father migrated to Qoniya where they settled.

In the beginning Mawlavi was a religious scholar and like other religious scholars occupied himself with teaching and passed a respectable life. Then he met the famous gnostic Shams Tabriz and was impressed by him so much that he lost interest in every thing worldly.

The anthology of his lyric poems is known as the *Diwān-e-Shams Tabriz*. In the Mathnawi also he has mentioned Shams Tabriz at several places with great pathos. Mawlavi died in 672 A.H.

Fakhruddin Iraqi of Hamdan: He is a well-known sufi poet of lyrics. He was Sadruddin Qunawi's pupil and the above mentioned Shahābuddin Suhrawardi's disciple. In 688 A.H. he departed this world.

Gnostics of Eighth Century

'Alā'uddin Simnāni: In the beginning he was a senior government official. Later he relinquished that job and joined the fraternity of the gnostics. He spent all his riches in the way of Allah. Alā'uddin Simnāni who is the author of a number of books, has a special theory of gnosis which is discussed in the books of *tasawwuf*. He died in 736 A.H. The famous poet Khwajwi Kirmāni was one of his disciples. He composed a poem in his praise.

Abdur Razzāq Kāshāni: He was a great gnostic scholar of the eighth century. He wrote commentaries on Muhyuddin Ibnul 'Arabi's Fusus and Khwaja Abdullah's Manāzilus Sā'irin. Both these commentaries have been published and are used by the scholars.

In the course of giving a life account of Abdur Razzāq Lāhiji the author of the **Rawzātul Jannāt** has said that the Shahid Thāni has paid glowing tributes to Abdur Razzāq Kāshāni. Heated discussions took place between Kāshāni and 'Alā'uddin Simnāni regarding the questions of theoretical gnosis advanced by Muhyuddin Ibnul 'Arabi.

'Abdur Razzāq Kāshāni died in 735 A.H.

Khwāja Hāfiz Shirazi: Although he enjoys world fame, we know scarcely anything about his life. Anyhow it is an undisputed fact that he was a scholar, gnostic, memorizer of the Qur'an and a commentator of it. He has alluded to these facts at a number of places in his poetry.

He has referred to his preceptor and spiritual guide also, but it is not known who that spiritual guide was. The gnostic poetry of Hāfiz is of the highest quality, but it is not easy for every one to get to its subtleties. All the subsequent gnostics admit that Hāfiz himself passed through the high stage of gnosis personally.

Some distinguished scholars have written commentaries on some of the verses of Hafiz. For example the famous philosopher of the ninth century Jalāluddin Dawāni compiled a whole book explaining one couplet of his. Hāfiz died in 791 A.H.*

Shaykh Mahmud Shabistari: He composed an excellent mathnawi named **Gulshan-e-Rāz** devoted to the subject of gnosis. This book is regarded as one of the best books of Tasawwuf, and it has made the name of Shabistari immortal. Several commentaries on it have been written. The best of them is perhaps that of Shaykh Muhammad Lāhiji. It has been published and is available. Shabistari died in about 720 A.H.

Sayyid Haydar Āmuli: He is an eminent gnostic scholar. One of his books is **Jāmi'ul Asrār**, which is a deep study of Muhyuddin 'Arabi's theoretical gnosis. This book has been recently published. Another of his books is the **Naṣṣun Nuṣūṣ**, which is a commentary on the Fusūs. Sayyid Haydar was a

---

* Hafiz is the most favourite poet of the modern Iranians. Some opportunists have tried to prove him to be a materialist or at least not a strict believer in Islam. We have repudiated this mischievous idea in our book, 'The Causes of Inclination to Materialism.'

contemporary of Allāmah Hilli. The exact year of his death is not known.

Abdul Karim Jili: He is the author of the well-known book, al-Insān al-Kāmil (Perfect Man). Ibnul 'Arabi was the first to advance the theory of perfect man. Later it became an important doctrine of Islamic gnosis.

Ibnul 'Arabi's pupil and disciple, Sadruddin Qunawi has elaborately discussed this doctrine in his book, Miftāhul Ghayb. As far as we know two gnostics have independently written two books each named al-Insān al-Kāmil. One of them is Azizuddin Nasafi and the other is 'Abdul Karim Jili. Both the books have been published. Abdul Karim Jili died at the early age of 38 in 805 A.H.

Gnostics of Ninth Century

Shāh Ni'matulah Wali: He is a direct descendant of Imam Ali and is one of the famous sufis and gnostics. At present the Ni'matuullah order is one of the most well-known sufi orders. His tomb at Māhān in the region of Kirmān is a place of pilgrimage for the sufis.

He is said to have died at the age of about 95 years in 820 or 827 or 837 A.H.

Sā'inuddin Ali Tarkah Isfahāni: He is a learned gnostic well-versed in Ibnul 'Arabi's system of theoretical gnosis. His book Tamhidul Qawā'id, which has been published testifies to his erudity. Well-known scholars appreciate this book and regard it as authentic.

Muhammad ibn Hamzah Fannāri Rumi: He was a scholar of the Uthmāni Empire. He had the knowledge of many sciences and was the author of a large number of books. His fame in gnosis and mysticism rests on his book, Misbāhul Uns, which is a commentary on Qunawi's Miftahul Ghayab.

It is not easy to write a commentary on Muhyuddin Ibnul 'Arabi's books or those of Sadruddin Qunawi, but Fannāri has successfully done this job and his work has been appreciated by the later gnostic scholars. This book has been published with the late Mirza Rashti's notes by litho in Tehran. Unfortunately some of the notes are not legible owing to bad printing. Mirza Rashti was a gnostic scholar of the last century.

40

Shamsuddin Muhammad Lahiji Nurbakhshi: He is a commentator of Mahmud Shabistari's Mathnawi, Gulshan-e-Râz, and was a contemporary of Sadruddin Dashtaki and Allamah Dawâni. He lived in Shiraz. In the Majâlisul Mu'minin Qâzi Narullah says that Sadruddin Dashtaki and Allamah Dawâni who were distinguished scholars of their time held Muhammad Lâhiji in great respect.

He was a disciple of Sayyid Muhammad Nur Bakhsh, who was a pupil of Ibnul Fahd Hilli. The chain of his preceptors, as mentioned by him in his commentary on the Gulshan-e-Râz, goes from Sayyid Muhammad Nur Bakhsh up to Ma'rûf Karkhi and then through Imam Riza and his forefathers to the Holy Prophet. Shamsuddin Muhammad Lâhiji calls this chain the "Chain of gold." *(Silsilatuz Zahab)*.

Lâhiji's fame rests largely on his commentary on the Gulshan-e-Râz. This book is regarded as one of the best books of sufism. As he has mentioned in the preface of his book, he started the compilation of it in 877. The exact year of Lâhiji's death is not known. Apparantly he died before 900 A.H.

Nuruddin 'Abdur Rahmân Jâmi: His ancestral line goes to Muhammad bin Hasan Shaybâni, an eminent Jurist of the second century. Jami was an outstanding poet, and is regarded as the last great poet of sufi poetry in Iran.

In the beginning his nom de plume was Dashti. Later he changed it to Jâmi, first because he was born at Jâm, a town in the province of Mashad and secondly because he was a disciple of Ahmad Jâmi known as Zhindah Pil. He himself says: "I was born at Jâm and my writings are inspired by Shaykh al-Islam Jâmi. For these two reasons my nom de plume is Jâmi."

Jâmi was the master of several sciences, such as syntax (grammar), morphology, theology, principles of jurisprudence, logic, philosophy and *tasawwuf*. He was the author of a large number of books, including a commentary on Muhyuddin's Fususul Hikam, a commentary on Fakhruddin 'Iraqi's Lam'ât, a commentary on Ibn Fâriz's Ode rhyming in 'tâ', a commentary on Qasidatul Burdah, a hymn in praise of the Holy Prophet, a commentary on Farazdaq's panagyric on Imam Zaynul 'Abidin, the Lawâ'ih, the Bahâristan, in which he followed Sa'di's style and the Nafahâtul Uns, a memoir of the sufis' lives.

41

Jāmi was a disciple of Bahā'uddin Naqshband, the founder of the sufi order known as the Naqshbandiya. Just as Muhammad Lāhiji's personality was superior to that of his preceptor, Sayyid Muhammad Nur Bakhsh, similarly Jāmi was a more distinguished and better scholar than his preceptor, Bahā'uddin Naqshband. As at present we are discussing the scientific aspect of gnosis and are not concerned with sufi orders, we have mentioned Muhammad Lāhiji and Abdur Rahmān Jāmi, but not their preceptors. Jāmi died at the age of 88 in 898 of the hijrah.

This is a brief account of the development of mysticism in Islam from its beginning up to the end of the ninth century. In our opinion after that the history of mysticism and gnosis underwent a complete change. So far sufi scholars were considered to be the eminent sufis themselves. They were attached to regular orders and their books were standard books of mysticism and gnosis. But with the beginning of the 10th century the situation changed.

(i)   Now even the most prominent sufis did not possess that amount of knowledge and capability as their predecessors did. Perhaps it would be correct to say that after the ninth century mysticism became a mixture of hollow rituals and self-made innovations.

(ii)   Secondly some persons who did not belong to any sufi order acquired more proficiency in the gnostic ideas of the Muhyuddin school than regular sufis.

For example Mulla Sadra Shirazi (d. 1050 A.H.), his pupil, Fayz Kāshāni (d. 1091 A.H.) and his pupils' pupil Qāzi Sa'id Qummi (d. 1103) had more knowledge of the theories and ideas of the Muhyuddin's school than the most prominent sufis of their age, although none of them belonged to any sufi order. Such examples still exist.

The late Agha Riza Qamsha'i and the late Āgha Mirza Rashti were not practising sufis, but were among those philosophers and scholars of the past 100 years who were experts in theoretical gnosis.

It may be said that this practice has started since the time of Muhyuddin Ibn al-Arabi when theoretical gnosis was founded and it acquired the shape of a philosophy.

We mentioned earlier Muhammad bin Hamzah Fannāri.

Perhaps he was also one of those who were not practising sufis, but were highly proficient in theoretical gnosis. Such a practice has become conspicuous since the 10th century onward when a class of such people came into existence who were experts in the theory of gnosis, but were not practising sufis or at least did not belong to any regular order of the sufis.

From the 10th century onward we meet many individuals who were really devoted gnostics and sufis, but not only they did not belong to any regular sufi order, but were indifferent to these orders and either denounced them totally or criticized some of their practices.

A characteristic of this group was that they were mostly jurists and divines and as such they were very particular about maintaining harmony between the mystic beliefs and practices and the rules of external religion and morality. This story also has a history, but this is not a proper occasion to narrate it.

Stages and Stations

The gnostics say that in order to attain to true gnosis it is necessary to pass through certain stages and stations, without passing through which, it would not be possible to attain to gnosis.

Gnosis and theosophy have one common feature, but each of them is distinct from the other in many respects. The feature which they have in common is that both of them in a way aim at gaining the knowledge of Allah, although the basic objective of theosophy is to gain the knowledge of the universe. Yet in its own way it aims at gaining the knowledge of Allah also, though that is not its sole aim.

On the contrary to the gnostics the knowledge of Allah is all that they want. They believe that in the light of Allah's knowledge from the angle of monotheism they perceive everything in its true perspective. In other words according to them, the perception of everything else depends on the knowledge of Allah.

Another difference between theosophy and gnosis is that a theosophist or a philosopher seeks mental and intellectual knowledge which can be compared to the knowledge that a mathematician gains through pondering over the mathematical problems. But the knowledge which a gnostic seeks is based on his personal and inner experience and his inward feeling and

43

observation, and may be compared to the knowledge gained by a researcher in his laboratory. The philosopher seeks that may be certain and definite knowledge but the gnostic seeks true and absolute knowledge.

The third difference is that the philosopher uses reasoning and arguments whereas the gnostic gains knowledge by the purification of his heart and changing his self. The philosopher wants to study the universe by using the telescope of his mind, whereas the gnostic stimulates his entire existence to reach the truth, and wants to pass away from his self by joining the Truth just like a drop of rain that passes away into the river.

From the view-point of a philosopher understanding the truth is the natural perfection that man is expected to attain, but in the eyes of a gnostic man's perfection is to gain access to the Truth. According to the philosopher the imperfect man is he who is ignorant, whereas according to the gnostic the imperfect man is he who is away from his origin and does not have access to the Truth.

The gnostic regards gaining access as perfection, not knowing and understanding. He considers it necessary to pass through several stages and stations in order to reach his goal and obtain true gnosis. It is passing through these stages which is called "spiritual journey".

In the books of tasawwuf these stages and stations have been elaborately discussed. To throw a brief light on the subject we here quote a summary of the ninth chapter of Abu Ali ibn Sina's book al-Isharat.

Abu Ali Sina is a philosopher, not a gnostic. Yet he is not a dry philosopher. Towards the end of his life he was drawn to gnosis and in al-Isharat, which is apparently his last book, he has devoted one whole chapter to the description of the stations of the gnostics.

Instead of citing any passages from the books of the gnostics we deem it better to give a summary of the ninth chapter of al-Isharat, which is an exceptionally high standard work.

Definition of Zahid, 'Abid and Ārif
"An ascetic (zāhid) is he who renounces wordly goods and pleasures and a worshipper ('ābid) is he who is strict in perform-

ing such acts of worship as prayers, fast etc. He who diverts his attention from every thing other than Allah and concentrates his mind on the world of divinity with a view to illuminate his soul in the radiance of Divine light, is called gnostic *('ārif)*. In many cases one can simultaneously have all these three qualities or two of them."

Although Abu 'Ali Sina here has defined ascetic, worshipper and gnostic only, yet by implication he has also defined asceticism, worship and gnosis.

This definition shows that asceticism means the renunciation of worldly desires and vanities; worship means the performance of such acts as prayers, fast and recitation of the Qur'an; and gnosis means the diversion of mind from everything other than Allah and its concentration on Him with a view to enlighten the heart. The last sentence of Abu Ali Sina alludes to an important point, that is that one can simultaneously be an ascetic and a worshipper or an ascetic and a gnostic. One can also be an ascetic as well a worshipper and a gnostic both. Ibn Sina has not further elucidated his point, but what he means to say is that one can be an ascetic and a worshipper without being a gnostic but one cannot be a gnostic without being an ascetic and a worshipper.

To make this point more clear it may be mentioned that every gnostic is necessarily an ascetic and a worshipper also, but every ascetic or every worshipper is not necessarily a gnostic.

Ibn Sina points out that the asceticism of a gnostic is different from that of a non-gnostic, for each of them has a different philosophy of asceticism. Similarly the philosophy of a gnostic's worship is different from that of a non-gnostic's worship. The nature and spirit of the asceticism and worship of a gnostic are different from those of a non-gnostic.

Ibn Sina says that the asceticism of a non-gnostic is a sort of barter trade for he buys other worldly benefits in exchange for this worldly goods. On the other hand the asceticism of a gnostic means purging of his heart of everything that may obstruct his attention to Allah. The non-gnostic's worship also is a sort of business. He is a workman who works for wages. He adores Allah in this world so that he may be recompensed in the next. But to a gnostic the worship which he performs is a sort of spiritual exercise and a constant practice of being attentive to the Divine essence and inattentive to the world.

Gnostic's Goal

Ibn Sina says: 'The gnostic seeks Allah alone. He is not concerned with anything else. In his eyes there is nothing more important and more valuable than gnosis. He worships Allah because worship is due to Him and because it is an appropriate and decent way of expressing man's relation to Him. The worship of the gnostic is free from any element of fear or hope of reward.'

In other words the gnostic is an absolute monotheist in his objective. He seeks Allah alone. He does not seek Him for the sake of gaining any benefits in this or the next world, for if he does so, his main aim would be these benefits and he would be seeking Allah only as a means of obtaining them, not as his sole objective. In this case his real deity would be his lower self to please and satisfy which he requires all the bounties and pleasures.

A non-gnostic seeks Allah for the sake of His bounties, and a gnostic seeks His bounties for the sake of Himself.

Here a question arises. If it was true that the gnostic did not seek anything except Allah, then why did he worship Him? He must have some objective. In reply to this question Abu Ali Sina says that the gnostic worships Allah for two reasons: Firstly because Allah deserves to be worshipped. It is a common practice that when a person finds any conspicuous good quality in another person or thing he automatically praises that person or thing, not in the hope of getting any benefit, but simply because that person or thing is praiseworthy. This rule applies to all commendable persons in all walks of life.

Another reason for the gnostic's worship is that worship in itself is a good thing, for it represents the relation between man and Allah. It is a job worth doing. Therefore it is not necessary that a hope of any reward or a fear of any punishment should be the motive of worshipping Allah.

Imam Ali has said: "Allah, I do not worship You because I am afraid of Your Hell or because I hope for Your Paradise. I worship You because I have found You worthy of being worshipped."

46

In this saying the worthiness of the worshipped has been mentioned as the reason of worship.

The gnostics stress the point that if man's objective in life, especially in acts of worship is anything other than Allah, then he is guilty of duality. The gnostics have stated this point in a very fascinating manner and elucidated it by quoting attractive stories. We give just one example here. This story of Mahmud and Ayāz has been related by Shaykh Sa'di in the Bostān.

Sa'di says: Somebody criticizing Sultan Mahmud of Ghazni once said that Ayāz was not handsome at all. It was surprising that the Sultan still loved him. Was there any sense in being enchanted by a flower having neither beautiful colour nor good smell? Somebody reported this incident to Mahmud. He said: "I love him because of his lovely habits and good manners, not because of his fine figure." Sa'di says: "I have heard that once upon a time a camel passing through a narrow passage lost its balance and fell. A box full of gold and jewelry which was on its back came down tumbling and was smashed. The Sultan did not care for the precious goods and left the place hastily. His retinue busied themselves with collecting and picking up the scattered gold and jewelry. No one except Ayāz went with the Sultan. The Sultan was pleased to see him and asked him what he had picked up out of that booty. Ayāz said: "I am following your Majesty. Being at Your Majesty's service I paid no attention to the precious stuff."

After relating this story Sa'di comes to his main point and says: "You are really selfish if you have an eye to the generosity of your friend and not to your friend himself. For the saints of Allah it is against the rules of "spiritual path" to wish Allah to grant them anything other than Allah."

First Stage

The first stage of the spiritual journey is called by the gnostics "*irādah*" (intention). *Irādah* means emergence of a strong desire and wish to hold fast to the path that leads to Truth and stimulates the soul to attain to its real goal. This desire may be created by an argument or by faith.

This first stage of spiritual journey, which is the keystone of the entire structure of gnosis requires some explanation.

The gnostics have a maxim enunciating that the end is the return to the beginning.

Obviously there are only two ways, in which the end can exactly be the beginning. In one case the motion should be along a straight line and the moving thing should after reaching a particular point change its direction and come back to the point from which it had started. It has been proved in philosophy that a change of direction always involves a pause, though it may be very slight and imperceptible. Moreover these two movements would be in the opposite directions. According to the other hypothesis the motion should be along a curved line equidistant all along from a particular point. In other words the motion should be circular.

Obviously the circular motion will end at the same point from which it had begun. Anything moving along a circular line will at first be moving away from its starting point and will at last reach a point farthest from the starting point. This point will be the point at which the diameter of the circle drawn from the starting point will end. After reaching this point the moving thing will begin to return to its starting point without a pause.

The gnostics call the line of motion that goes from the starting point to the farthest point the 'descending curve' and the line of motion that comes from the farthest point to the starting point "the ascending curve". There is a special philosophy of the movement of things from the strarting point to the farthest point. It is called by the philosophers the principle of causation and by the gnostics the principle of manifestation. When the things move along the descending curve it appears as if they were being pushed from behind. This philosophy is based on the doctrine that everything wants to return to its origin. In other words everything away from its home wants to come back to it. The gnostics maintain that this tendency exists in every particle of the universe including human beings, though in them this tendency sometimes is not very conspicuous, for they are often engrossed in other things which divert their attention from it. In man this dormant tendency is usually awakened only when his attention is repeatedly drawn to it. It is the awakening of this tendency that is called intention.

In his treatise named *"Istilāhāt"* which has been published on the margin of 'Sharh Manazilul Sā'irin', Abdur Razzāq Kāshāni defines intention as under:

"Intention is a flame of the fire of love. When it is kindled in his heart man begins to respond to the call of Truth."

In his book Manazilus Sā'irin Khwaja Abdullah Ansāri defines intention as follows:

"Intention means responding to the call of Truth of one's own accord."

It is necessary to point out that although intention has been described as the first stage, in reality it is the first stage following a few preliminary stages of development known as 'Bidāyat' (beginnings), Abwāb (doors), Mu'āmlāt (dealings) and Aakhlāq (good moral qualities). After the beginning of the state of real gnosis the first stage is intention. The gnostics call it and the subsequent stages the principles.

Mawlavi explains the maxim, "the end is the return to the beginning" in the following words:

"The parts turn to the whole like a nightingale longing for a flower. Anything that comes out of the sea and then goes back to it, returns to its origin."

Mawlavi in the preface of his Mathnawi has included a short poem entitled "the complaint of a flute". This poem which represents the pain of longing and a sense of nostalgia illustrates intention, the first stage of gnosis in the language used by the gnostics. Mawlavi says:

"Listen to what the flute says. It is complaining of separation. It says that since it has been cut off the jungle and brought here people are tired of its loud wailing. It wants its chest to burst open so that it could express the pain of its home-sickness. Whatever is separated from its origin is always in the quest of the meeting time."

Ibn Sina defining intention says: "Intention is that longing which man feels when he finds himself lonely and helpless and wants to be united with the Truth so that he may not have a feeling of lonliness or of helplessness".

Riyāzat (Spiritual Exercise)

Ibn Sina says that next to intention riyāzat is essential for a gnostic. Riyāzat has three aims:

(i) To remove every thing other than Allah from the path;

(ii) To make the appetitive soul submissive to the contented soul;

(iii) To soften the inner self with a view to make it fit for receiving enlightenment.

Thus the first stage is intention, which is the beginning of spiritual journey. The second stage is that of preparation, which is called *riyāzat*. According to certain schools of thought *riyāzat* means treating oneself harshly or inflicting physical pain on oneself as is practised by the jogis in India, but Ibn Sina has used the word in its real sense.

In Arabic *riyāzat* originally meant breaking and training a young horse. Later this word was used and is still being used in Arabic in the sense of physical and athletic exercise. The gnostics apply it to the spiritual exercise done for preparing the soul for gnostic enlightenment.

In any case here *riyāzat* means spiritual exercise, aiming at three objectives: The first objective is to get rid of all the causes of diverting attention from Allah; the second objective is to set the inner and spiritual faculties in a proper order with a view to gain inward composure. It is this process which is termed as subordinating the appetitive soul to the contented soul. The third objective is to change the inner condition of the soul, which is described as softening the inner ground of the soul *(taltifus sirr)*.

Ibn Sina says that correct type of asceticism helps in achieving the first objective, for it removes all barriers and distractions. There are several factors which contribute to the achievement of the second objective, that is subordinating the appetitive soul to the contented soul. One such factors is the acts of worship provided they are performed with one's whole heart. Another factor is good voice used for the delivery of heart-warming spiritual words, such as Quranic verses, supplications or gnostic verses. The third factor is preaching and counselling provided the preacher or the counsellor has a pure heart, eloquent expression and effective voice and is able to lead the people to the right path.

Pure thoughts and platonic love are the things which help in the achievement of the third objective, that is softening the inner self and purging the soul of all impurities. Love must be spiritual and intellectual aroused by moral qualities of the beloved, not by lust and cupidity.

Ibn Sina further says that when intention and *riyāzat* of the gnostic have progressed to a particular extent, he beholds the glimpses of divine light and feels a reflection of the glory of Allah on his heart which he finds very pleasing but it passes away very quickly like a flash of lightning.

This state is called *'awqāt'* (times) by the gnostics. The more a gnostic does *riyāzat* the more often he is seized by this state. When he has made further progress this state may overcome him even without any *riyāzat*. Whenever he thinks of the Divine world he is seized by a state in which he sees the manifestation of the glory of Allah in everything. At this stage sometimes the gnostic feels restless from within and his restlessness is felt by those sitting by him. Thereafter with further *riyāzat* that occasional condition is changed into composure. The gnostic gets familiar with his 'state' and he does not feel restless or uneasy. He feels as if he is in permanent communion with Allah. The gnostic fully enjoys this condition and when this condition occasionally disappears he feels distressed and grieved. Perhaps up to this stage others around him also can know his inward feeling of happiness or grief. The more the gnostic becomes familiar with this state, the less perceptible become his inward feelings. At last a stage comes when people see him among themselves, but he is actually somewhere else, his soul at that time being in another world.

The last sentence reminds us what Imam Ali said to Kumayl bin Ziyād Nakha'i about the *walis* (Muslim saints, friends of Allah). Imam Ali said:

"Springs of knowledge and wisdom gush out of their hearts. What appears to be difficult to those who live in ease and luxury, seems to be easy to them. They are familiar to what scares the ignorant. Their bodies are with the people, but their souls are in the higher world."

Ibn Sina says that so long as the gnostic is at this stage, perhaps this state comes over him occasionally but gradually he becomes able to bring it over him of his own accord whenever he likes. Then he goes a step further. He no longer needs to bring this state over him, as he begins to see the manifestation of Allah's glory everywhere and in everything. This state becomes a permanent feature for him though the people around him remain completely ignorant of it and notice nothing queer to draw their attention.

So long this state of the gnostic mostly depended on spiritual exercises and the acts of self-mortification, but after passing this stage even without performing any act of self-mortification he finds his heart shining like a polished mirror in which he beholds the manifestation of Allah's glory every moment. He enjoys this position and feels happy and delighted at the establishment of his connection with Allah. In this position he has an eye to Allah and an eye to himself (like a man with a mirror who sometimes looks at the mirror and sometimes at his own reflection. At the next stage even his own existence gets out of his sight. He has an eye to Allah only. If he sees himself, he sees in the same way as a man looking into a mirror sees the mirror while his attention remains fixed on the reflection, for at this time he is not expected to pay attention to the beauty of the mirror. At this stage the gnostic attains proximity to Allah and thus his journey from the creation to the Creator ends.

This was a summary of a part of the chapter 9 of al-Ishārāt.

It may be mentioned here that the true Muslim gnostics believe in four journeys: (i) A journey from the creation to the Creator; (ii) A journey with the Creator in the Creator,; (iii) A journey from the Creator to the creation; and (iv) A journey in the creation with the Creator.

In the second journey the gnostic or the novice gets acquainted with the Divine Names and Attributes and himself gets invested with these attributes. In the third journey he comes back to the creation for their guidance but is not separated from Allah. In the fourth journey he makes a journey among the people but accompanied by Allah. In this last journey the gnostic remains with the people and among the people and helps them gain proximity to Allah.

The summary which we have reproduced from Ibn Sina's Ishārāt relates to the first journey only. He has briefly discussed the other three journeys also, but we do not find it necessary to reproduce any more extracts.

In his commentary on the Ishārāt Shaykh Nasiruddin Tūsi says that Ibn Sina has described the first spiritual journey in nine stages. Out of them three stages are related to the beginning of the journey, three stages to the journey itself and three stages to the end of the journey. These stages become clear if we carefully study the description given by Ibn Sina.

Riyāzat literally means exercise. Ibn Sina means by it the rituals, liturgy and the acts of self-mortification carried out by gnostic. These rituals and acts are numerous and the gnostic has to traverse different stages while performing them. Ibn Sina has treated the matter briefly, but the gnostics have very detailed discussions on the subject, which can be seen in the books on sufism, for example al-Asfār al-Arba'ah by Mulla Sadra.

STAGES OF SPIRITUAL JOURNEY

A materialist passes his life in the dark valley of materialism. He is plunged in the sea of evil desires and always is tossed from this side to that side by the waves of material relations of wealth, wife and children. He cries for help, but in vain and in the end gets nothing but disappointment.

Sometimes in this sea a breath of enlivening breeze (divine impulse) pats him and kindles in him a hope that he may reach the shore safely. But this breeze does not blow regularly. It is only occasional.

"In your life you get some pleasant breaths from your Lord. Make a point of being benefited by them and do not turn away from them."

Under the divine impulse the novice decides to somehow or other pass the world of plurality. This journey is called by the gnostics *sayr wa suluk* (spiritual journey).

Suluk means to traverse the path and *sayr* means to view the characteristics and prominent features of the stages and stations on the way.

Riyàzat and acts of self-mortification are the provisions required for this spiritual journey. As it is not easy to renounce the material relations, the novice slowly breaks the snares of the world of plurality and cautiously begins his journey from the material world.

Before long he enters another world called 'barzakh'. This is the world of his evil desires and inner thoughts. Here he finds that material relations have accumulated a lot of impurities in his heart. These impurities which are an offshoot of his material relations, are a product of his voluptuous thoughts and sensual desires.

These thoughts obstruct the novice in the pursuit of his spiritual journey with a result that he loses peace of mind. He wants to enjoy the recollection of Allah for some time, but these thoughts suddenly interrupt him and foil his efforts.

Somebody has well said that man is always engrossed in his petty thoughts and haunted by the ideas of gain and loss. As a result he not only loses his composure and peace of mind, but can also not pay attention to his spiritual journey to a higher world. It is obvious that mental unrest is more harmful than any physical loss or pain. Man can avoid the clash of external relations and interests, but it is difficult for him to get rid of his own ideas and thoughts because they are always with him.

Anyhow, the true seeker of Allah and traveller in his way is not distressed and discouraged by these obstacles and continues to boldly proceed to his destination with the help of his divine impulse, till he safely gets out of the world of petty and conflicting ideas called *barzakh*. He has to be very vigilant and watchful lest any vicious thought may remain lurking in some hidden corner of his mind.

When these vicious thoughts are turned out, they usually hide in some hidden corner of the mind. The poor spiritual traveller wrongly thinks that he has got rid of their mischief, but when he has found the way to the fountain of life and wants to drink from it, they suddenly reappear to ruin him.

This spiritual traveller may be compared to a person who has built a tank of water in his house but has not used it for long. In the meantime the impurities and pollutions have settled down in the bottom of the tank although water appears to be clear from above. He thinks that water is clean, but when he gets down into the tank or washes something in it, black patches appear on the surface and he finds that water is dirty.

For this reason it is necessary for the *sālik* (spiritual traveller) to concentrate his thoughts with the help of *riyāzat* and acts of self-mortification so that his attention may not be diverted from Allah. At last when after passing through the *Barzakh* the spiritual traveller enters the spiritual world, he still has to traverse several more stages, the details of which we will describe later.

In short the spiritual traveller watching his own lower self and the Divine Names and Attributes gradually advances till ultimately he reaches the stage of total *fanā* (self-annihilation) that is passing away from his own perishable will and then the station of *baqā* (abiding in the everlasting Will of Allah). It is at this stage that the secret of eternal life is revealed to him.

We can infer this doctrine from the Holy Qur'an also if we ponder over certain verses of it.

Think not of those who are slain in the way of Allah, as dead. Nay, they are living. With their Lord they have provisions. (Surah Āli Imrān, 3:169).[12]

Everything will perish save His Countenance. * (28:88)[13]

That which you have is wasted away, and that which is with Allah remains. (Surah an Nahl, 16:96)[14]

These verses put together show that the countenance of Allah are those "who are living and who have provisions with their Lord." According to the text of Qur'an they never perish. Certain other verses indicate that the countenance of Allah signifies Divine names which are imperishable.

In one of its verses the Qur'an itself has interpreted the Countenance as the Divine names and Characterizes the Countenance of Allah as of glory and honour: *Everyone who is living will pass away, and there will remain the countenance of your Lord of glory and honour.* (Surah ar Rahmān, 55:27)[15]

All the commentators of the Qur'an agree that in this verse the phrase "of glory and honour" qualifies the countenance, and it means the countenance of glory and honour. As we know, the countenance of everything is that which manifests it. The manifestations of Allah are His names and attributes. It is through them that the creation looks at Allah, or in other words, knows Him. With this explanation we come to the conclusion that every existing thing perishes and wastes away except the glorious and beautiful names of Allah. This also shows that the gnostics to whom the verse, *Nay, they are living*

---

* Countenance of Allah signifies the Divine names and attributes through which Allah manifests Himself in all existing things. All things will perish but their countenance will remain because that is the manifestation of Allah. In simpler words it may be said that the 'basis' on which depends the existence of things does not perish.

and have their provisions with their Lord, applies, are the manifestations of the glorious and beautiful names of Allah.

From the above it is also clear what the Holy Imams meant when they said: "We are the names of Allah" Obviously to be the head of a government or to be the highest religious and legal authority is not a position which could be described by these words. What actually these words denote is the state of passing away in Allah, abiding permanently with His countenance and being a manifestation of His glorious and beautiful names and attributes.

In connection with the spiritual journey another important and essential thing is meditation or contemplation *(muraqabah).* It is necessary for the spiritual traveller not to ignore meditation at any stage from the beginning to the end. It must be understood that meditation has many grades and is of many types. In the initial stages the spiritual traveller has to do one type of meditation and at later stages of another type. As the spiritual traveller goes forward, his meditation becomes so strong that if ever it was undertaken by a beginner, he would either give it up for good or would go mad. But after successfully completing the preliminary stages, the gnostic becomes able to undertake the higher stages of meditation. At that time many things which were lawful to him in the beginning get forbidden to him.

As a result of careful and diligent meditation a flame of love begins to kindle in the heart of the spiritual traveller, for it is an inborn instinct of man to love the Absolute Beauty and Perfection. But the love of material things overshadows this inherent love and does not allow it to grow and become visible.

Meditation weakens this veil till ultimately it is totally lifted. Then that innate love appears in its full splendour and leads man's conscience towards Allah. The mystic poets often figuratively call this divine love "wine".

When the gnostic continues to undertake meditation, for quite a long time, divine lights begin to be visible to him. In the beginning these lights flash like lightning for a moment and then disappear. Gradually the divine lights grow strong and appear like little stars. When they grow further, they appear first like the moon and then like the sun. Sometimes they appear like a burning lamp also. In the gnostic terminology these lights are known as the gnostic sleep and they belong to the world of *Barzakh.*

When the spiritual traveller has passed this stage and his meditation grows stronger, he sees as if the heaven and the earth were all illuminated from the East to the West. This light is called the light of self and is seen after the gnostic has passed the world of *Barzakh.* When after coming out of the world of *Barzakh* primary manifestations of self begin to occur, the spiritual traveller views himself in a material form. He often feels that he is standing beside himself. This stage is the beginning of the stage of self-stripping.

Allamah Mirza Ali Qāzi used to say that one day when he came out from his room into the veranda he suddenly saw himself standing quietly beside himself. When he looked carefully, he saw that there was no skin or flesh on his face. He went back into his room and looked into the mirror. He found his face was as empty as it had never been.

Sometimes it happens that the gnostic feels as if he did not exist at all. He tries to find himself, but he does not succeed. These are the observations of the early stages of self-stripping, but they are not free from the limitations of time and space. In the next stage with Allah's help the spiritual traveller can rise above these limitations also and can view complete reality of his self. It is reported that Mirza Jawad Malaki Tabrizi passed full fourteen years in Akhund Mulla Husayn Quli Hamdani's company and took from him lessons in gnosis. He says:

"One day my teacher told me about one of his pupils that thence forward his training was my responsibility. This pupil was very pains-taking and diligent. For six years he kept himself busy with meditation and self-mortification. At last he reached the stage of knowing his self and having been stripped of his evil self (passion and lust). I deemed it proper that the teacher himself should tell that fact to this pupil. So I took him to the house of the teacher whom I told what I wanted. The teacher said: "That's nothing." At the same time he waved his hand and said: "This is stripping." That pupil used to say: "I saw myself being stripped of my body and at the same time felt as if another person just like me was standing beside me."

It may be mentioned here that to see the things existing in the world of *Barzakh* is comparatively of small account. It is of greater significance to view one's own lower self *(nafs)* in an absolutely stripped state, for in this case self appears as a pure reality free from the limitations of time and space. The viewing of the earlier stages was comparatively preliminary and partial and this viewing is so to say the perception of the whole.

Agha Sayyid Ahmad Karbalā'i, another well-known and prominent pupil of the late Akhund says: "One day I was sleeping somewhere when all of a sudden somebody awakened me and said to me: 'Get up at once if you want to see the 'eternal light.' I opened my eyes and saw an immensely bright light shining everywhere and in all directions."

This is a stage of the enlightenment of self. It appears in the shape of an infinite light.

When a lucky spiritual traveller has passed this stage, he passes other stages also with a speed in proportion to the attention he pays to meditation. He views Allah's Attributes or becomes conscious of Allah's Names as an absolute quality. On this occasion he suddenly feels that all existing things are only a unit of knowledge and there exists nothing but one single power. This is the stage of the vision of the Divine attributes. The stage of the vision of Divine names is still higher. At this stage the devotee sees that in all the worlds there exists only one knower and only one omnipotent and living being. This stage is far higher than that of the conciousness of the Divine Attributes, a state which appears in the heart, for now the spiritual traveller does not find any being knowing, powerful and living except Allah. This degree of vision is usually achieved during the recitation of the Qur'an, when the reader feels that somebody else, not he is reading the Qur'an. Sometimes he also feels that there is somebody else who is listening to his recitation.

It may be remembered that recitation of the Qur'an is very effective in securing this state. The devotee should offer the night prayers and should recite in them those surahs during the recitation of which prostration is obligatory, namely the Surah Sajdah, Surah Hāmim Sajdah, Surah al-Najm and Surah al-'Alaq, for it is very pleasant to fall prostrating while reciting a surah.

Experience has also proved that it is very effective for this purpose to recite the Surah Sâd in the Thursday night prayers *(wutairah)*. This characteristic of this surah is indicated by the report concerning the merits of this surah also.

When the devotee has completed all these stages and visions, he is surrounded by divine impulses and every moment he goes closer to the stage of real self-annihilation, till he is so seized by a divine impulse that he is totally absorbed in the beauty and perfection of the "True Beloved." He no longer pays heed to himself or to any body else. He beholds Allah everywhere. *There was Allah and nothing was with Him.*

In this condition the devotee is plunged in the fathomless sea of divine vision.

It must be remembered that this does not mean that everything in the material world loses its existence. Actually the devotee sees unity in plurality. Otherwise everything continues to exist as it is. A gnostic has said: "I was among the people for 30 years. They were under the impression that I was taking part in all their activities, but actually throughout this period I did not see them and did not know anyone but Allah."

The coming about of this state is of great importance. In the beginning it may come about only for a moment, but gradually its duration grows longer, first it may last for about 10 minutes or so, then for an hour and subsequently even for a longer period. This state may even become permanent by the grace of Allah.

In the sayings of the gnostics this state has been termed as 'abiding in Allah' or "the ever lasting life in Allah". Man cannot attain to this stage of perfection unless he passes away from self. On attaining to this stage the devotee does not see anything except Allah.

It is said that there was an enraptured sufi who was seized by a divine impulse. His name was Bâbâ Farajullah. People asked him to say something about the world. He said: "What can I say about it? I have not seen it since I was born."*

---

* The biography of Baba Faraj, the enraptured is available in Târikh Hashari. It is about the learned men and the sufis and gnostics of Tabriz. There is a couplet in it regarding the above words of Baba Faraj. There are similar versified sayings of Hâfiz and the renowned Arab mystical poet, Ibn Fâriz.

In the beginning when the vision is weak, it is called a state and its occurance is beyond the control of the devotee. But when as a result of continued meditation and by the grace of Allah this state becomes a permanent feature, then it is called a station. Now the state of vision gets under the control of the spiritual traveller or devotee.

Obviously a strong spiritual traveller is he who along with viewing these states keeps an eye to the world of plurality also and maintains well his relations to the world of unity and to the world of plurality at the same time. This is a very high position and cannot be attained easily. Perhaps this position is reserved for the Prophets and some other chosen people who are favourites of Allah and who can say: "The state of my relation to Allah is such that the most favourite angel cannot attain to it"* and at the same time declare: "I am a human being just like you."+

Somebody may say that only the Prophets and the Imams can attain to these high positions. How is it possible for others to attain to them? Our replay is that Prophethood and Imamate are undoubtedly the special assignments to which others cannot reach. But the station of 'absolute Oneness' and passing away in Allah which is called *wilāyat* is not exclusively reserved for the Prophets and the Imams, who have themselves called upon their followers to try to attain to this station of perfection. The Holy Prophet has asked his *Ummah* (Muslim nation) to follow in his footsteps. This shows that it is possible for others also to advance to this position, or else such an instructions would have no meaning.

The Qur'an says: *Surely in the Messenger you have a good example for him who looks to Allah and the Last Day, and remembers Allah much.* (Surah al-Ahzāb, 33:21)[16]

There is a report in the Sunni books that once the Holy Prophet said: "Had you not been talkative and of uneasy hearts you would have seen what I see and would have heard what I hear."

---

* A tradition of an Imam.

+ In the Qur'an Allah asks the Holy Prophet to tell the pagans: "I am a human being just like you, except that I receive revelation."

This report shows that the real cause of not attaining to human perfection is fiendish thoughts and vicious acts. According to a report from the Shi'ah source also, the Holy Prophet has said: "Had not the satans been roaming around their hearts, the human beings would have seen the whole kingdom of the heavens and the earth."

One of the characteristics of this high human position is that it enables the individual holding it to comprehend the divine kingdoms according to his capacity. He gains the knowledge of the past and the future of the universe and can dominate and control everything, everywhere.

The famous gnostic, Shaykh Abdul Karim al-Jili writes in his book, the 'Perfect Man' that once he was overcome by such a condition that he felt as if he had been unified with all other existing things and could see everything. This state did not last more than a moment.

Obviously it is because of the devotees' preoccupation with their physical needs that this state does not last long.

A well known sufi says that a man gets rid of the traces of material development only 500 years after his death. This period is equivalent to half a day of the divine days. Allah has said: *Surely a day with your Lord is like one thousand years of your reckoning.* (Surah al-Hajj, 22:47)[17]

It is evident that the next worldly blessings and divine bounties and favours are innumerable and unlimited. The words expressing them have been coined on the basis of human needs and new words continue to be coined with the expansion of human requirements. That is why it is not possible to express all divine truths and favours by words. Whatever has been said is only symbolical and metaphorical. It is impossible to express the higher truths in words. It has been said: "You are in the darkest world". According to this tradition man is living in the darkest of the worlds (earth) created by Allah.

Man coins words to meet his daily requirements on the basis of what he sees and feels in this material world. He has no knowledge of the relations, blessings and spirits of the other worlds and therefore he cannot coin words for them. That is why there do not exist proper words in any language of the world which may express the higher truths and concepts. Now when our knowledge is limited and our thinking faulty, how can this problem be solved?

There are two groups of people who have talked about higher truths. The first is that of the Prophets. They have direct contact with the non-material worlds, but they also say: "We the Prophets have been ordered to talk to the people according to their intellectual capacity." That means that they are compelled to express the truths in a way intelligible to the common people. Therefore they have avoided to describe the nature of the spiritual lights and their brilliance. They have not talked about the truths unintelligible to man. They have only used such words as paradise, houries and palaces for the truth about which it has been said: "No eye has seen, no ear has heard and no one has thought about it,". They have even admitted that the truths of the other worlds are indescriable.

The second group is of those who advance along the path prescribed by the Prophets and perceive the truths according to their capability. They also use a figurative style.

Sincerity of Devotion

It must be remembered that without being sincere in the way of Allah it is not possible to attain to spiritual stations and stages. Truth cannot be unravelled to a spiritual traveller unless he is fully sincere and single-minded in his devotion.

There are two stages of sincerity. The first stage is of carrying out all religious injunctions for the sake of Allah only. The second stage is of devoting one's entire self exclusively to Allah. The first stage is indicated by the following verse:

They are ordained nothing but to worship Allah keeping religion pure for Him. (Surah al-Bayyinah, 98:5)[18]

The second stage is indicated by the following verse: *Save single minded slaves of Allah.* (Surah aṣ Ṣäffät, 37:128)[19]

There is a well-known Prophetic tradition to the effect that he who has kept himself pure for Allah for 40 days, fountains of wisdom flow from his heart to his tongue.

This tradition also alludes to the second stage of sincerity.

The Qur'an has at certain places described a deed as ṣälih (virtuous and pious). For example it said: "Whoever did a ṣälih (virtuous and pious) deed". And at some other places it

64

describes some men as *ṣālih*. For example at one place it says: *Surely he was one of the ṣālih (pious)*. Similarly it has sometimes described a deed as sincere and sometimes a man as sincere. It is obvious that man's sincerity depends on his deeds and he cannot be sincere unless he is sincere in all his deeds and in all that he does or says. Allah says: *To Him ascends good word and the good deed raises it*. (Surah al-Fātir, 35:10)[20]

It may be remembered that a man who attains to the grade of personal sincerity, is endowed with certain other characteristic qualities which are not possessed by others.

An important characteristic which he acquires is that according to a text of the Qur'an he becomes immune from the domination of Satan. The Qur'an quotes Satan saying: *My Lord, I swear by Your honour, I shall adorn the path of error for them in the earth and shall mislead all of them, except such of them as are your sincerely devoted slaves.* (Surah al-Hijr, 38:82)[21]

It is clear that Allah's sincerely devoted slaves have been excluded here not because Satan was forced by Allah to do so. They have been excluded because owing to their attaining to the station of 'unity', Satan can no longer gain control over them. As these people have made themselves pure for Allah, they see Allah wherever they cast their eyes. Whatever shape Satan may assume, they see the manifestation of Allah's glory in it. That is why Satan has admitted from the beginning his helplessness against them. Otherwise it is his job to seduce the children of Adam and to lead them astray. He can have no mercy on anyone.

The second point is that the sincerely devoted slaves of Allah will be exempted from reckoning on the Day of Judgement. The Qur'an says: *And the trumpet is blown and all who are in the heavens and the earth swoon away, save him whom Allah wills*. (Surah az-Zumar, 39:68)[22]

This verse definitely shows that an unspecified group of people will be saved from the horrors of the Day of Judgement. When we match this verse with another verse which reads: *They will surely be produced save sincerely single-minded people*, (Surah aṣ-Ṣaffāt, 37:39 - 40)[23] it becomes clear what that group will be. The sincerely devoted people need not be brought up for reckoning. They have already secured eternal life as the result of their meditations, self-annihilation and ceaseless acts of devotion. They have already passed the reckoning and judgement and as having been slain in the way of Allah, they have provision with their Lord.

Think not of those who are slain in the way of Allah as dead. Nay, they are living. With their Lord they have provision. (Surah Āli Imrān, 3:169)[24]

Moreover, only that one is produced who is not present. These people are already present even before the beginning of the Day of Resurrection, for Allah says that they have provision with their Lord.

The third point is that on the Day of Judgement people will generally be rewarded and recompensed for their deeds. But these sincerely single-minded people will be favoured with rewards beyond their deeds. Allah says:

You are not requited but what you did, save sincerely single-minded slaves of Allah. (Surah az-Zumar, 39:40)[25]

If it is claimed that this verse means only that the sinners will be punished for their sins, but the reward given to the virtuous will purely be a favour bestowed on them by Allah, we will say that this verse is general in its connotation and does not exclusively refer to the sinners. Moreover, there is no contradiction between Allah's favour and His recompense, for Allah's favour means that He sometimes rewards a great deal for small deeds. In spite of this kind of favour the reward still remains for the deeds performed. But what this verse says is quite a different thing. It says that what Allah will bestow on His sincerely single minded slaves, will be a pure favour, not a reward for any deeds at all.

Another verse says: *There they have all that they desire and there is more with Us.* (Surah Qāf, 50:35)[26]

This verse means that the inmates of Paradise will have all that man can desire or wish. Not only that, but Allah will bestow on them what they cannot imagine or think of. This point is worth considering.

The fourth point is that this group holds such a high position that its members can glorify Allah in the most appropriate manner.

Allah says: *Glorified be Allah from what they attribute to Him, except what the sincerely single-minded slaves of Allah say of Him.* (Surah aṣ Ṣaffāt, 37:159 - 160)[27]

This is the highest position that a man can occupy.

The above mentioned details show what the blessings of this last stage of gnosis are. But it must be kept in mind that these blessings can be obtained only when the spiritual traveller's ceaseless devotion reaches the stage of self-annihilation so that he may be called to have been slain in the way of Allah and may become eligible for the reward reserved for the martyrs. Just as in the battlefield the sword cuts off the connection between the body and the soul of a martyr, similarly a spiritual traveller snaps off the connection between his body and his soul by fighting against his appetitive soul. For this purpose he acquires the help of his spiritual power instead of using his physical force.

In the beginning of his spiritual journey a devotee should lead an ascetic life and should constantly contemplate on the worthlessness of the vanities of the world and thus should break off his relation to the world of plurality. When he would cease to be interested in the world, no material gain will ever please him nor will any material loss grieve him.

So that you grieve not for what you have missed and exult not for what you have been given. (Surah al-Hadid, 57:23)[28]

Indifference to the happiness and sorrow does not mean that the spiritual traveller does not feel happy even about the bounties of Allah or does not grieve at anything which may distress Him, for happiness about Allah's favours is not the result of his love for worldly trivialities such as wealth, rank, honour, fame etc. He loves the bounties of Allah because he finds himself overwhelmed by His mercy.

After passing this stage the devotee feels that he still loves himself ardently. Whatever spiritual effort and exercises he makes is the result of his self-love. Man is selfish by nature. He is always ready to sacrifice everything else for his own self. He would be willing to destroy anything for the sake of his own survival. It is difficult for him to do away with this natural instinct and to overcome his selfishness. But so long as he does not do so, he cannot expect the divine light to manifest itself in his heart. In other words unless a spiritual traveller annihilates his individual self he cannot establish his connection with Allah. Therefore it is necessary for him first to weaken and ultimately to smash the spirit of selfishness so that whatever he may do, is done purely for the sake of Allah and his sense of self-love may turn into love for Him.

For this purpose ceaseless effort is necessary. After passing this stage the devotee's attachment not only to his body and every other thing material ceases to exist, but even his attachment to his soul is finished. Now whatever he does, he does for Allah alone. If he eats to satiate his hunger or provides for the bare necessities of life, he does so only becaue his Eternal Beloved wants him to continue to live. All his wishes become subject to the Will of Allah. That is why he does not seek any miraculous power for himself. He believes that he has no right to undertake any sort of spiritual exercise with a view to know the past or predict future events or to practise thought-reading or to cover very long distances in a very short time or to make any changes in the universal system or to invigorate his libidinous faculties, for such acts are not performed for pleasing Allah, nor can they be motivated by sincere devotion to Him. They mean only self-worship and are performed for the satisfaction of one's licentious desires, although the person concerned may not admit this fact and although he may apparently be sincerely devoted to Allah. But according to the following verse he only worships his desire. *Have you seen him who makes his desire his god?* (Surah al-Jāthiyah, 45:23)[29]

Therefore the spiritual traveller should pass all these stages cautiously and do his best to gain complete control over his vanity. We shall further talk on this subject later.

When the devotee reaches this final stage, he gradually begins to lose interest in himself and ultimately forgets himself totally. Now he sees nothing except the eternal and everlasting beauty of his True Beloved.

It must be borne in mind that it is essential for the spiritual traveller to gain complete victory over the fiendish horde of licentious desires, love for wealth, fame and power, pride and conceit. It is not possible to attain perfection if any trace of self-love is left, that is why it has been observed that many a distinguished man even after years long spiritual exercise and ceaseless acts of devotion could not attain perfection in gnosis and was defeated in his battle against his phenomenal self. The reason was that his heart was not fully purified, and petty desires still lurked in some corner of his heart, though he was under the impression that all his evil qualities had been uprooted. The result was that at the time of test the suppressed desires once again raised their head and began to thrive, with the result that the poor devotee fell on evil times.

Success against the lower self depends on the favour of Allah and cannot be achieved without His help.

It is said that one day the late Bahrul 'Ulūm was very cheerful. On being asked about the reason of that, he said: "After performing ceaseless acts of devotion for 25 years now I find my deeds free from ostentation." The lesson in this story is worth being remembered well.

It is to be remembered that a spiritual traveller must abide by the Islamic injunctions from the very beginning of his embarking on the path of gnosis to the end of it. Even the slightest digression from the law is not allowed. If you find that anyone in spite of claiming to be gnostic, does not follow all the rules of Islamic law and is not strictly pious and virtuous, he may be regarded as a hypocrite and impostor. But if he commits a mistake and has some valid reason to justify his wrong action, then it is a different thing.

It is a big lie and calumny to hold that the Islamic code of law may be disregarded by a *wali* (Muslim saint). The Holy Prophet held the highest position among all living beings, but he still abided by the injunctions of Islam till the last moments of his life. Therefore it is absolutely wrong to say that a *wali* is not obligated to observe the law. Anyhow, it is possible to say that an ordinary man worships Allah in order to consummate his potentialities, but a *wali* worships Him because his high position requires him to do so. Ayeshah is reported to have said to the Holy Prophet: "When Allah has said about you: *So that Allah may forgive you of your sin, that which is past and that which is to come,* (Surah al-Fath, 48:2)[30] then why do you exert yourself so much to perform the acts of worship?" The Holy

Prophet said: "Should I not be a thankful slave of Allah?"

This shows that certain individuals worship Allah not for the consummation of their personality, but to show their gratitude to Allah.

The states which a spiritual traveller experiences and the lights which he beholds, should be a prelude to his acquisition of certain traits and qualities. Otherwise a simple change in his condition is not enough. The spiritual traveller must completely get rid of all remnants of the lower world in himself by means of meditation and ceaseless acts of devotion. It is not possible to acquire the position of the virtuous and the pure without acquiring their qualities. A little slip in the matters of meditation and acts of devotion may cause a spiritual traveller a tremendous loss. The following verse throws light on this point: *Muhammad is but a messenger. Other messengers have passed away before him. Will it be that, when he dies or is slain, you will turn back on your heels?*. (Surah Āli Imrān, 3:144)[31]

Therefore the spiritual traveller must cleanse his heart and purify himself inwardly and outwardly so that he may be graced with the company of the pure souls.

Allah says: *Forsake outward as well as inward sins.* (Surah al-An'ām, 6:120)[32]

Acting according to this verse the spiritual traveller must pass all those stages which enable him to arrive at the stage of sincere devotion. These stages have been briefly enumerated in the following verse:

Those who believe, and have left their homes and strive with their wealth and their lives in Allah's way, are of much greater worth in Allah's sight. These are they who are triumphant. Their Lord gives them good tidings of mercy from Him, and acceptance, and Gardens where enduring pleasures will be theirs. There they will abide for ever. Surely with Allah there is an immense reward. (Surah at-Tawbah, 9:20 - 22)[33]

According to this verse there are four worlds preceding to the world of sincere devotion: (i) World of Islam, (ii) World of faith, (iii) World of emigration, and (iv) World of *Jihād* in the way of Allah. According to the Prophetic tradition in which it has been said: "We have returned from a minor holy war to a major holy war", the spiritual traveller's struggle is a major

70

holy war (major *jihad*), and as such his Islam also should be a major Islam and his faith also a major faith. After passing the stages of Islam and faith he should muster enough courage to be able to emigrate in the company of the inward messenger with the help of the outward messenger or his successor. Thus he should undertake self-mortification, so that he may gain the status of a person slain in the way of Allah.

The spiritual traveller must keep it in mind that from the beginning of his spiritual journey till the stage of self-mortification he has to face many obstacles, which are created either by man or the Devil. He has to pass through the worlds of major Islam and major faith before reaching the stage of self-mortification and gaining the status of a martyr. In the spiritual journey major Islam, major faith, major emigration and major holy war are preliminary stages preceding the final stage. The Major obstacles in the way to these stages are called major infidelity and major hypocrisy. At this stage the junior devils can do no harm to the spiritual traveller, but Satan who is their supreme head still tries to obstruct his progress. Therefore while passing through these stages he should not think that he is out of danger. So long as he does not pass out of above-mentioned "major worlds", Satan will continue to obstruct his way. The spiritual traveller should keep up his spirit and beware of Satan, lest he be involved in major infidelity or major hypocrisy. After passing through the worlds of major Islam and major faith the spiritual traveller undertakes major emigration and then by means of self-mortification he passes through major self-resurrection and then passes into the valley of those who are sincerely devoted to Allah. May Allah grant us all this success?

THE TWELVE WORLDS

On the basis of what has been said above, a devotee, making a spiritual journey has to pass through 12 Worlds before reaching the world of sincerity. The names of these worlds are: minor Islam, major Islam, greater Islam, minor faith, major faith, greater faith, minor emigration, major emigration, greater emigration, minor *jihād*, major *jihād* and greater jihād. It is necessary to know the characteristics of these worlds and to be aware of the obstacles and barriers which a devotee has to face while advancing towards them. To make our point clear we describe these worlds briefly.

Major Islam means complete submission to Allah, not to criticize any action of His and to believe with full conviction that what is happening is not without some advantage and what is not happening was not advisable. Imam Ali hints at this point when he says that 'Islam means submission and submission signifies conviction.' A devotee not only should have no objection against any Divine directives or decrees but also should not feel even in his heart unhappy about any of them. Allah says: *But nay, by your Lord, they will not be faithful unless they make you judge of what is in dispute between them and find within themselves no dislike of that which you decide, and submit with full submission.* (Surah an-Nisa, 4:65)[14]

This is the stage of greater Islam. At this stage Islam should infiltrate the soul of the devotee and truly overwhelm his heart and life.

73

When the devotee's heart is illuminated by the light of greater Islam, not only his heart testifies that everything is from Allah, but he also physically observes this truth. In other words, he often sees with the eyes of his heart that Allah is omnipresent and omniscient. This stage is called that of vision and greater Islam. But as the spiritual traveller has not yet attained to perfection, he has to face many material obstacles, especially when he is busy with his natural needs, a state of unmindfulness overcomes him. Therefore it is necessary for him to use his will power so that the state of vision may become a permanent feature for him and may not be disturbed by his other activities. For this purpose it is necessary to push the state of greater Islam from the heart to the soul so that this elementary state may become a fully developed state governing all internal and external faculties. This is the stage which is called by the gnostics the station of well-doing *(ihsan)*. The Qur'an says: *As for those who strive in Us, we surely guide them to Our path. Surely Allah is with those who do well.* (Surah al-Ankabut, 29:69)[35]

As such a striver in the way of Allah cannot find the way of guidance and proximity of Allah until he reaches the stages of well-doing. An eminent companion of the Holy Prophet Abu Zar Ghifāri once asked him what well-doing signified. The Holy Prophet said: "That you worship Allah as though you see him. If you do not see Him, He surely sees you". In other words, man should worship Allah as if he was seeing Him. If he is unable to worship Him in this way, then there is a lower grade of worship. He should worship Allah as though Allah was seeing him. So long as the devotee does not reach the stage of greater faith, he is only occasionally invested with the state of well-doing. In this state he performs the acts of worship with zeal and fervour. His soul having been imbued with faith, puts all his organs and faculties on their proper job. The organs and faculties once controlled cannot disobey the soul even for a moment. Concerning the devotees who have attained to the stage of greater faith Allah says: *Successful indeed are the believers, who are humble in their prayers and who shun all that is vain.* (Surah al-Mu'minun, 23:1 - 3)[36]

Only that man will busy himself with trivial things who is

interested in them. A spiritual traveller who has attained to the stage of greater faith and for whom well-doing has become a habit, cannot be fond of anything vain, for no heart can love two contradictory things at one and the same time. Allah Himself has said: *Allah has not assigned to any man two hearts within his body.* (Surah al-Ahzāb, 33:4)[37]

If we find any devotee flittering away his time in amusements, we can easily conclude that he is not fully devoted to Allah and that his heart is not free from the hypocrisy which is called in this context greater hypocrisy and which is the opposite of greater faith. As a result of this hypocrisy man does not act according to his inner incitement, but is guided by reason, expediency or apprehensions. The following verse refers to this kind of hypocrisy: *When they stand up to offer prayers, they perform it languidly.* (Surah an-Nisā', 4:142)[38]

When the spiritual traveller attains to the stage of greater faith, no trace of hypocrisy is left in him. His actions and deeds are no longer guided by unreliable directives of reason nor by any apprehension, expediency or conservatism. All his actions are then motivated by inner zeal, hearty inclination and real love. Once the spiritual traveller attains to the stage of greater faith, he should be ready for greater emigration. There are two sides of this emigration: one is bodily emigration which means giving up social dealings with the wicked, and the other is emigration of heart which means not making friends with them. A spiritual traveller not only has to abandon all habits, customs and usages which prevent him from pursuing the path of Allah, but has also to dislike them from the core of his heart. Such customs and usages have been mostly imported from the countries of the infidels. A man living in a material society becomes a prisoner of many customs and habits prevalent among the worldly people forming the basis of their social dealings. For example it has become customary to regard a person keeping quiet at an academic discussion as ignorant. Many people consider it a mark of their eminence to sit at the head of a meeting or to go ahead of others while walking in company. Fine talk and flattery are called good manners, and a behaviour contrary to these customs is described as bad manner and vulgarity. The spiritual traveller should with the help of

Allah ignore such odd customs and whimsical ideas. In this regard he should not fear anybody and pay no attention even to the criticism of those who call themselves great scholars. There is a report in Kulayni's Jāmi' on the authority of Imam Ja'far Sādiq that the Holy Prophet has said: "There are four pillars of infidelity: greed, fear, resentment and anger". In this tradition fear means an apprehension that people would be angry if their wrong ideas and wrong customs were opposed.

In short the spiritual traveller should say good-bye to all those habits and traditions, customs and usages which obstruct his advancement towards Allah. The gnostics call this attitude 'madness', because mad people also take little interest in and pay little attention to the popular habits and traditions and do not care what the other people would say. A mad man sticks to his own ways and does not fear any opposition.

Following his success in emigration and getting rid of the prevailing customs, the spiritual traveller enters the field of major jihād, which means a fight against the devilish hordes. Even at this stage the spiritual traveller is still a captive of his lower self, overwhelmed by his passions, and low desires and perplexed by apprehensions and worries, anger and disappointments. If anything that is not to his liking happens, he is upset and feels hurt. In order to overcome all his worries, griefs and pains, the spiritual traveller should seek Divine aid and crush the forces of apprehension, anger and lust. On getting rid of worldly botherations and worries he will enter the world of greater Islam. Then he will feel as if he was prevailing over the whole world, was safe from death and effacement and was free from every kind of conflict. He will find in himself a purity and glamour not connected with this humble world. At this stage the devotee becomes totally unconcerned with this transient world, as if he was dead. Now he begins a new life. He lives in the world of humanity, but sees everythng in the shape of the angelic world. Material things can no longer do him any harm. As he has reached the middle stage of self-resurrection, veil is gradually lifted from before his eyes and he can see many hidden things. This station is called that of greater Islam. The Qur'an clearly refers to it in the following words:

Is he who was dead and We have raised him to life, and set for him a light wherein he walks among men, like him who is in utter darkness whence he cannot come out? Thus is their conduct made fair-seeming for the disbelievers. (Surah al-Anfāl, 6:122)[39]

Whosoever does right, whether male or female, and is a believer, we shall surely quicken him with good life and We shall pay them a recompense in proportion to the best of what they used to do. (Surah an-Nahl, 16:97)[40]

It should be kept in mind that what the devotee views in this state may create in him a sense of false pride and as a result of that his worst enemy, that is his lower self may begin to resist him. There is a tradition which says: "The most deadly enemy of yours is your lower self which is within you."[41]

In these circumstances the devotee is in danger of being involved in greater infidelity unless he is helped and protected by Allah. The following tradition refers to this kind of infidelity. "The lower self is the greatest idol". It was this idol-worship for being protected from which the Prophet Ibrāhim prayed to Allah when he said: "Save me and my sons from worshipping idol".[42] Evidently it is unimaginable that Prophet Ibrahim would ever worship any fabricated idols. It was this kind of idol-worship from which the Holy Prophet also sought to refuge when he said: "Allah, I seek refuge in you from hidden polytheism".[43]

Therefore the devotee should whole-heartedly acknowledge his humbleness and completely do away with the idea of self-conceit from his heart so that he may not commit greater infidelity and may succeed in attaining to greater Islam. Some gnostics have throughout their life avoided even the use of the word 'I'. Some others attributed all that is good to Allah and only what could not be attributed to Allah, they attributed to themselves. They used first person plural pronoun while talking of a thing that could be attributed to themselves and to Allah both. They derived this method from the story of the Prophet Musa and Khizr. Khizr said: *As for the boat, it belonged to poor people working on the river, and I wished to mar it, for there was a king behind them who was taking every boat by force.* (Surah al-Kahf, 18:79)[44]

As the act of marring could not be attributed to Allah, he

77

attributed it to himself and used a first person singular pronoun.

And as for the lad, his parents were believers and we feared lest he should oppress them by rebellion and disbelief. And therefore we intended that their Lord should change him for them for one better in purity and nearer to mercy. (Surah al-Kahf, 18:80 - 81)[45]

In this case as the act of slaying the lad could be attributed both to Allah and Khizr, the plural pronoun was used.

And as for the wall, it belonged to two orphan boys in the city, and there was beneath it a treasure belonging to them. Their father had been righteous, and your Lord intended that they should come to their full strength and should bring out their treasure as a mercy from their Lord. (Surah al-Kahf, 18:82)[46]

As the intention of doing good to someone is attributable to Allah, it has been attributed to Him.

We find Prophet Ibrāhim also employing this style of speech. He said: *It is He Who created me and Who does guide me, and who feeds me and waters me, and who heals me when I get sick.* (Surah ash-Shu'ara, 26:78 - 80)[47]

Here Prophet Ibrāhim attributes sickness to himself and healing to Allah.

A devotee should leave no stone unturned to attain to the stage of major Islam and to do away with self-conceit.

Hāji Imām Quli Nakhjawāni was the teacher in gnosis of Agha Sayyid Husayn Āghā Qāzi, the father of the late Āghā Mirza Ali Qāzi. He completed his training in morality and gnosis at the hands of Sayyid Quraysh Qazwini. He says that when he got aged, one day he saw that he and Satan were standing on the top of a hill. He passed his hand on his beard and said to Satan: "Now I am an old man please spare me if you can." Satan said: "Look this side". Sayyid Qazwini says that when he looked that side, he saw a ditch so deep that it sent a cold wave into his spine. Pointing to that ditch Satan said: "I have no sympathy or mercy for anybody. If I could lay my hands on you once, you would fall into the bottom of this ditch from which you would never have an escape."

Next to greater Islam is the stage of greater faith, which means such an intense upsurge of major Islam that it may transform the knowledge of truth into a clear view of it. In the meantime the spiritual traveller moving from the angelic world *('Ālam Malakūt)* enters the souled world *('Ālam Jabarūt)*. For him greater self-resurrection would have already taken place and he can now see the sights of the souled world.

Thereafter the spiritual traveller should emigrate from his own existence which is to be totally rejected by him. This journey of his will be from his own existence to the absolute existence. Some saints have expressed this idea by saying: "Leave your self and come." The following verses of the Qur'an hint at it: *O contented soul, return to your Lord in His good pleasure. Enter among My bondmen! Enter My Garden.* (Surah al-Fajr, 89:27 - 30)[48]. In this verse the soul has been described as contented and addressed as such. It has been asked to join the ranks of the chosen people of Allah and enter the paradise.

The spiritual traveller has now completed the stage of major *jihād* and entered the world of victory and conquest which is the headquarters of contentment, but as some traces of his existence still remain, he has not yet completed the process of self-annihilation and hence needs embarking on greater *jihād*. Because of this deficiency he is not yet absolutely free. His place is still in the compound hinted at in the Qur'anic verse, *"in the nice sitting place with the Powerful Potentate"* (Surah al-Qamar, 54:55)[49]. Here 'Powerful Potentate' refers to Allah.

After this stage the spiritual traveller should wage a war against the remaining traces of his existence and remove them completely, so that he may step forward into the field of absolute 'unity'. This world is called the world of victory and conquest. The spiritual traveller has to pass through twelve such worlds before he succeeds in passing the stages of greater emigration and greater *jihād* and enters the field of sincerity. Then he will be called successful and victorious and will enter the world of sincerity and the compound of *We belong to Allah and We will surely return to Him.* (Surah al-Baqarah, 2:156)[50]. For him the greater self-resurrection will already have taken place. He will enter the stage of total passing away from self after crossing the curtains of bodies, souls and every thing fixed and appointed. He will have one foot in the world of divinity, and he will have passed the stage of *Every body has to taste death.* (Surah Āli Imrān, 3:185)[51] . Such a person being at the stage of passing away from self though consciously alive, yet in one sense will be dead. That is why concerning Imam Ali the Holy Prophet said: "Whoever wants to see a dead man walking, let him see Ali ibn Abi Tālib."

Explanation: The spiritual excellences and their signs and consequences which have been briefly mentioned above, are the favours which have been bestowed by Allah exclusively on the followers of the Last Prophet, Muhammad, peace be on him. The merits and the perfections which the spiritual travellers of the previous *ummahs* (nations) could gain, were of limited nature. After reaching the stage of passing away from self they could view the Divine names and attributes, but could not advance any further. The reason was that the highest stage of their gnosis was the maxim, "There is no deity, but Allah" which meant the version of Allah's most beautiful names and attributes. On the other hand the spiritual travellers of the Islamic ummah have reached several higher stages which cannot be described in words. The reason is that the guiding light of all Islamic rules is the maxim, *"Allah is far above being described".* The spiritual progress of a Muslim devotee being connected with this maxim, the stages which he can traverse, are too high to be explained. That is why even the former Prophets could think of no station higher than that of the vision of the Divine names and attributes, with the result that they had to face many difficulties and hardships, and were able to get rid of them only by invoking the station of the spiritual guardianship of the Holy Prophet, Imam Ali, Fatimah Zahra and thier progeny. It was the spiritual guardianship of these personalities that delivered the former Prophets from their worries and griefs. Although the former Prophets were to a certain extent conscious of the high position of the Imams and that is why they invoked it, but till the end of their life they did not know all its characteristics. Some Qur'anic verses show that only Prophet Ibrāhim once or twice viewed these higher truths, but only momentarily. The permanent vision of them will be in the other world only.

Before quoting the Qur'anic verses in support of our point it may be mentioned that the text of the Qur'an clearly shows that the position of sincerity also has several grades, for a

80

number of Prophets who held this position to a certain extent, could not attain to its higher grades, for which they used to pray to Allah. For example the Qur'an says about Prophet Yusuf that *Surely he was of Our single minded slaves.* (Surah Yusuf, 12:24)[52] Still he prayed to Allah saying: *You are my protecting friend in this world and the Hereafter. Make me to die submissive to you and join me to the righteous.* (Surah Yusuf, 12:101)[53]

The prayer shows that he did not attain the position he was praying for during his life time and so he prayed that he might be granted it after his death. Whether his prayer would be fulfilled in the hereafter, the Qur'an is silent on this point. Prophet Ibrāhim held a high position in the station of sincerity, yet he prays saying: *My Lord, vouchsafe me wisdom and unite me to the righteous.* (Surah ash-Shu'arā, 26:83)[54].

This shows that the station of the righteous is higher than that of sincerity. That is why Prophet Ibrāhim wanted to be joined to those who occupied this position. Allah did not accede to his prayer in this world, but promised to grant him the position he asked for in the hereafter: *Surely We chose him in this world and he will be among the righteous in the hereafter.* (Surah al-Baqarah, 2:130)[55].

It may be noted that the position of righteousness for which the former Prophets craved, is different from that which was conferred on Prophet Ibrāhim and his descendants according to the following verse: *We bestowed upon him Ishaq and Ya'qub as a grandson. Each of them We made righteous.* (Surah al-Ambiya, 21:72)[56]

This kind of righteousness they all enjoyed including Prophet Ibrāhim himself. But he was still praying to be joined to the righteous. That shows that he wished something higher than what he had already been granted.

As for the fact that the Holy Prophet and some other persons during their lifetime occupied this higher position, is clear from the following verse:

Surely my Guardian is Allah who revealed the Book. He befriends the righteous. (Surah al-A'rāf, 7:196)[57]

According to this verse, first the Holy Prophet admits that Allah is his Guardian and then declares that his guardian is He who befriends and protects the righteous. This shows that at that time there existed certain individuals occupying the position of righteousness, whom Allah befriended. This also shows why the former Prophets made their prayers through the medium of the Imams and what a high position was held by those righteous individuals whom even great Prophets like Ibrāhim wished to join.

As for the fact that the great Prophets attained to the position of sincerity, it can be inferred from a number of Qur'anic verses in different ways. The Qur'an expressly says that only the people of sincerity can eulogize Allah in a befitting manner. Allah says: *Glorified be Allah from what they attributed to Him, except the single minded slaves of Allah, whose case is different.* (Surah aṣ Ṣāffāt, 37:160)[58].

Ordering the Holy Prophet to eulogize Him, Allah says: *Say: Praise be to Allah and peace be on His slaves whom He has chosen. Is Allah best or all that they ascribe to Him as partners?* (Surah an-Naml, 27:59)[59].

The Qur'an cites Prophet Ibrāhim praising Allah in the following words: *Praise be to Allah who has given me in my old age Ismā'il and Ishaq. My Lord is indeed the hearer of prayer.* (Surah Ibrahim, 14:39)[60].

Prophet Nūh was ordered to glorify Allah in the following words: *Then say: Praise be to Allah who has saved us from the wrong doing people.* (Surah al-Mu'minun, 23:28)[61].

Concerning certain eminent Prophets the Qur'an expressly says that they held the position of sincerity. About Prophet Yusuf the Qur'an says: *Surely he is of Our single minded slaves.* (Surah Yusuf, 12:24)[62]

About Prophet Musa it says: *And make mention in the Book of Musa. He was single minded, and he was a messenger of Allah, a Prophet.* (Surah Maryam, 19:51)[63]

About Prophets Ibrāhim, Ishaq and Ya'qub the Qur'an says: *And make mention of Our slaves, Ibrahim, Ishaq and Ya'qub, men of parts and vision. We purified them with a pure thought, remembrance of the Home of the hereafter.* (Surah Ṣād, 38:45)[64]

According to the following verse Satan can do no harm to the men sincerily devoted to Allah: *He said: Then by Your might, I surely will beguile every one of them, save Your single-minded slaves among them.* (Surah Ṣād, 38:82)[65]

Only those who are not thankful to Allah are seduced by Satan: I shall come upon them from before them, and from behind them and from their right hands and from their left hands, and You will not find most of them thankful to You. (Surah al-A'rāf, 7:17)[66]

Concerning several Prophets the Qur'an says that they were chosen by Allah: *We bestowed upon him Ishaq and Ya'qub, each of them We guided; and Nuh We guided before. From among his descendants We guided Dāwud, Sulaymān, Ayyub, Yusuf, Musa and Hārūn. Thus do we reward the good, And We guided Zakariyah, Yahya, Isā and Ilyās. Each one of them was righteous. And We guided Ismā'il, alyasa', Yunus and Lūt. We gave each of them precedence over the rest of the people. And We guided some of their forefathers, children and brothers. We picked them and guided them to a straight path.* (Surah al-An'ām, 6:84 - 87)[67]

From these verses it may be inferred that all the Prophets held the position of sincerity, whereas in the verses mentioned earlier only a few Prophets were mentioned. In these verses Allah has said that He 'picked them', that is He chose them from so many people.

Those who are beguiled and seduced by Satan are those who are not thankful to Allah. Therefore we can say that those who are thankful to Him cannot be entrapped by Satan for they are sincerely devoted to Allah. Whenever the Qur'an describes anyone as thankful, we can easily conclude that he is one of Allah's single-minded and sincere slaves. For example, the Qur'an says about Prophet Nuh: *They were the descendants of those whom We carried (in the ship) along with Nuh. Surely he was a thankful slave.* (Surah Bani Isrā'il, 17:3)[68]

About Prophet Lut it says: *We sent a storm of stones upon all of them, except the family of Lut whom We rescued in the last watch of the night as a grace from Us. Thus we reward him who is thankful.* (Surah al-Qamar 54:34 - 35)[69]

About Prophet Ibrāhim it says: *Surely Ibrāhim was a nation, obedient to Allah, by nature upright and he was not one of the idolaters. He was thankful for Allah's bounties. Allah chose him and guided him to a straight path.* (Surah an-Nahl, 16:120)[70]

All the other Prophets who have been described as thankful are in principle men of sincerity.

In the above verse Allah says: *We picked them* from amongst all men as if they were taken up carefully and put somewhere safely. On this basis the case of those who have been picked is different from all other men. They are the people who are exclusively devoted to Allah and are especially favoured by Him. This picking by Allah applies to the people of sincerity only because they have attached themselves exclusively to Him and have severed their relations from everything else. Besides, picking in this verse is not related only to those mentioned in it by name, for Allah says: "We guided some of their forefathers, children and brothers. We picked them and guided them to a straight path". Here the word brothers means moral and spiritual brothers, of these Prophets, that is those who share spiritual knowledge with them. Therefore the statement appears to be applying to all Prophets, and it may safely be argued that all Prophets are the people of sincerity.

SEEKING ALLAH'S GUIDANCE

The first thing that a spiritual traveller has to do is to inquire into various religions as far as possible so that he may become conversant with the unity and guidance of Allah. He should try to acquire at least as much knowledge as be enough for practical purposes. Having carried out this kind of investigation into the unity of Allah and the Prophethood of the Holy Prophet he will come out of the domain of infidelity and enter that of minor Islam and minor faith. This is the knowledge about which there is a unanimity of opinion among the jurists that its acquisition is essential for every obligated person for the purpose of acknowledging the fundamental beliefs on the basis of proofs and arguments. If a person cannot get the required degree of satisfaction despite his best efforts he should not lose heart and should pray for obtaining it with humility and submissiveness. This is the method that is reported to have been followed by the Prophet Idris and his followers.

The prayer with humility means that the spiritual traveller should admit his weakness, and earnestly seek guidance from Allah who always helps those who seek the truth earnestly. The Qur'an says: *Those who strive in Us We will surely guide them to our path.* (Surah al-Ankabut, 29:69)[71]

I remember when I was in Najaf receiving spiritual and moral training from Hāji Mirza Ali Qāzi, one morning I fell dozing while I was sitting on the prayer rug. All of a sudden I saw as if two persons were sitting in front of me. One of them was Prophet Idris and other was my brother, Muhammad

Husayn Tabatabai. Prophet Idris began talking. He was speaking to me, but I was hearing what he said through the medium of my brother. He said: "During my life I faced many knotty problem which appeared to be too difficult to be resolved, but they were resolved automatically. It seemed that they were resolved by some supernatural hand from the unseen world. These events for the first time revealed to me the connection between this world and the metaphysical world, and established my relation to what is beyond this world."

I felt at that time that the problems and difficulties to which Prophet Idris was referring were the events which he experienced during his childhood. What he meant was that if any body sought guidance from Allah earnestly, Allah would surely help him. While seeking help from Allah chanting of some appropriate verses of the Qur'an repeatedly will be very useful. Allah says: "Remember that with the remembrance of Allah the hearts are satisfied." The repeated chanting of 'Ya Fattahu' 'Ya dalilal Mutahayyirin' will also be found useful. Anyhow, the chanting must be with full attention and concentration.

One of my friends relates that once he was going by bus from Iran to Karbala. A sturdy young man was sitting near him. No conversation had taken place between them. Then all of a sudden the young man began to cry. My friend was astonished. He asked the young man what was the matter. He said: "I will certainly tell you my story. I am a civil engineer. Since my childhood I was so brought up that I became an atheist. I did not believe in resurrection, but I had a feeling of love for the religious people, whether they were Muslims, Christians or Jews. One night I was attending a party of my friends where some Bahais* were also present. For some time we all took part in games, music and dance, but soon I began to feel ashamed of myself and so I went upstairs and began to weep. I said: 'O God! Help me if you really do exist! After a few moments I came downstairs. At dawn we all dispersed. In the evening while I was going on some professional duty along with my team incharge and some officers, I suddenly saw a religious scholar with an illuminated face coming towards me. He greeted me and said

---

* A hundred year old religious community like Qadyanis.

86

that he wanted to have some talk with me. I told him that I would see him next day in the afternoon. After he had left some people objected to my giving a cold reception to quite a well-known holy man. I said that I thought he was some needy person, who wanted my help. By chance it so happened that my team incharge asked me to be present next day in the afternoon at a particular place and do a certain job. The time which he gave me was exactly which I had given to that religious scholar. I said to myself that there was no more any possibility of going to him. Next day at the appointed time I felt that I was not feeling well. In a few moments I had a high fever and it became necessary to call a doctor. Naturally I was unable to go for the job entrusted to me by my incharge. But as soon as the representative of the incharge went away, I felt myself relieved. My temperature had become normal. I thought over my condition and was convinced that the incident had some secret. Therefore I got up immediately and went to that scholar's place. When I saw him, he began to talk of fundamental principles and proved each one of them to my entire satisfaction. Then he asked me to come to him next day again. For several days I went to him daily. Each day when I visited him he told me so many things in detail about my private affairs about which no body other than me alone knew at all. A lot of time passed in this way. One day my friends pressed me to attend one of their parties. There I had to take part in gambling also. Next day when I called on that scholar he at once said: "Don't you feel ashamed? How come that you committed such a grave sin?" Tears flowed down from my eyes. I admitted my mistake and said that I was sorry. He said: "Have a bath for repentance, and don't do such a thing again". Then he gave me some other instructions. Thus he changed the programme of my life. All this happened in Zanjān. Later when I was going to Tehran he asked me to call upon certain scholars there. At last he asked me to go on a pilgrimage to the holy places. Now I am going on the journey which he asked me to undertake."

My friend said: "When we approached Iraq. I saw that young man weeping again. On my inquiry he said: "It appears that we have entered the land of Iraq, for Abu Abdillah (Imam Husayn) has welcomed me.''

This story has been narrated to show that any body seeking guidance from Allah earnestly is bound to succeed in his objective. Even if he is sceptical about Monotheism — the unity of Allah, he will receive guidance.

Having successfully completed this stage the spiritual traveller should strive for attaining to major Islam and major faith. In this connection the first thing to do is to know the rules of Islamic law. This knowledge should be acquired from some competent jurist. Next to acquiring the knowledge of law comes the turn of practising it. It is very necessary to always act according to Islamic law, for knowledge is the best incentive to action, and action produces conviction. If a person is certain about the veracity of his knowledge, he is bound to act according to it . If he does not, that means that he is not convinced of the correctness of what he knows, and that his knowledge and belief are no more than a sort of mental impression. For example, if somebody is sure of Allah's absolute providence, he will never desperately try to earn money at all costs. He will be satisfied with what the Islamic injunctions allow him and will try to earn with tranquil happiness what is necessary for him and his family. But if a man is always worried about his livelihood, that means that he does not believe in the absolute providence of Allah or thinks that it is conditional on his trying hard, or he believes that providence is limited to earning cash or salary. That is what is meant when it is said that knowledge is an incentive to action. The following similitude shows how action enhances knowledge. When a person says from the core of his heart: "Glory and praise be to my exalted Lord", he acknowledges his helplessness and humbleness. Naturally, power and glory cannot be conceived without there being a conception of humbleness and helplessness.

Conversely no one can be powerless without there being a powerful. Therefore the mind of the person saying: "Glory and praise be to my exalted Lord" while prostrating himself in prayers, is naturally diverted to the absolute power and glory of Allah.* This is what is meant by saying that action promotes

---

* The supplications which have come down to us from the Holy Prophet and his Household provide the best means of our moral and spiritual train- ing. They strengthen faith; create a spirit of self- sacrifice and promote a

(Contd. . . .)

knowledge. The Qur'anic verse, *The good deed He promotes it* (Surah al-Fātir, 35:10)[72] also refers to this fact.

It is necessary for the spiritual traveller to do his best to abide by all that is obligatory and to refrain from all that is forbidden, for doing anything against Islamic injunctions is absolutely contrary to the spirit of his spiritual journey. It is no use to perform commendable deeds and spiritual exercises if the heart and soul are polluted, just as it serves no useful purpose to apply cosmatics if the body is dirty. Besides being very particular about performing what is obligatory and abstaining from what is forbidden, it is also imperative for the spiritual traveller to take interest in performing commendable deeds and avoiding obnoxious ones, for attaining to major Islam and major faith depends on doing that. It is to be remembered that every deed has a corresponding effect and contributes to the completion of faith. The following tradition reported by Muhammad bin Muslim refers to this point: "Faith depends on the deeds for the deeds are essential part of faith. Faith cannot be firmly established without good deeds."

Therefore the spiritual traveller must perform every commendable act at least once so that he may attain that part of faith also which depends on the performance of that particular act. Imam Ali has said that it is deeds that produce perfect faith. Hence it is necessary for the spiritual traveller not to overlook commendable deeds while advancing towards the stage of major faith, for his faith will be incomplete in proportion to his lack of interest in the performance of good deeds. If a devotee purified his tongue and his other organs but at the time of spending money was negligent of his duty, his faith would not be perfect. Every bodily organ must get that part of faith which is related to it. The heart which is the chief of all organs should be kept busy with remembering the names and attributes of Allah and pondering over the Divine signs in men and

(Contd. . . .)
taste for performing acts of worship and praying to Allah. The Supplication of Mujir, the Supplication of Kumayl, the Supplication of Abu Hamzah Thumali and the Supplication of 'Arafah may be mentioned in this connection.

the universe. That is the way how man's heart imbibes the spirit of faith. The Qur'an says: *It may be noted that with the remembrance of Allah the hearts become satisfied.* (Surah ar-Ra'd, 13:28)[73]

When every organ has obtained its due share of faith, the devotee should intensify his spiritual effort and enter the domain of certainty and conviction by completing the stages of major Islam and major faith.

Those who believe and obscure not their belief by wrong doing, theirs is safety; and they are rightly guided. (Surah al-An'ām, 6:82)[74]

As a result of doing spiritual exercises the spiritual traveller will not only be placed on the right path, but will also become safe from the assaults of Satan.

Remember that no fear shall come upon the friends of Allah, nor shall they grieve. (Surah Hud, 10:62)[75]

Fear means apprehension of impending danger or evil that causes worry and alarm. Grief means mental distress and sorrow caused by the occurrence of something evil and unpleasant. The spiritual traveller has no apprehension nor sorrow, for he entrusts all his affairs to Allah. He has no objective other than Allah. Such people as they enter the domain of certainty have been described by Allah as His friends. Imam Ali hinted at this stage when he said: "He sees Allah's path, walks on His way, knows His signs and crosses the obstacles. He is at such a stage of certainty that it seems as if he was seeing everything by the light of the sun".

Imam Ali has also said: "Knowledge has given them real insight; they have imbibed the spirit of conviction; they consider easy what the people living in ease and luxury consider difficult; they are familiar with what the ignorant have aversion to; their bodies are in the world but their souls are in high heaven."

At this stage the doors of vision and inspiration are opened before the spiritual traveller.

Evidently there is no inconsistency between passing through these stages and the spiritual traveller's being busy with his basic necessities in the world. His inner experience has nothing to do with his external activities such as his marriage, earning his livelihood and being engaged in trade or cultivation. The spiritual traveller lives bodily in this mundane world and takes part in worldly activities, but his soul goes round the angelic world and talks with its inmates. He is like a bereaved person whose some close relative has died recently. Such a person lives among the people, talks to them, walks to various places, eats and sleeps, but his heart is always lamenting over the memory of his relative. Whoever looked at him, could understand that he was in a wretched state of mind. Similarly a spiritual traveller despite his being engaged in fulfilling his natural needs, maintains his contact with Allah. A fire of love is always burning in his heart. The pain of separation keeps him restless, but no one except Allah knows his inner condition, though the onlookers also can in general discern that love for Allah and for truth has befallen him. It is clear from this explanation that the wailing, weeping and prayer of the Imams were not fake, nor were the supplications which have come down from them purely for instructional purposes. Such a notion is based on the ignorance of facts. It is below the dignity of the Imams to say anything unrealistic or to call people to Allah by means of fake prayers. Will it be proper to say that the heart rending wailings of Imam Ali and Imam Zaynul 'Ābidin were fake and had no reality or they were for teaching purpose only? Not at all. This group of the leaders of religion have attained to the stage of passing away from self and abiding in Allah after completing all the stages of spiritual journey and hence combine in themselves the qualities relating to the world of unity as well as the world of plurality. They receive Divine light in every walk of life and are required to maintain their attention to the higher world and not to violate any rule relating to that world even slightly.

When the spiritual traveller has traversed all the above mentioned worlds successfully and overcome Satan, he enters the world of victory and conquest. At that time he will have passed the material world and entered the world of souls. Hence forward his great journey will be through the angelic world and the spiritual world and ultimately he will succeed in reaching the world of Divinity.

RULES OF ATTAINING SPIRITUAL PERFECTION

To be able to advance on this spiritual path it is necessary for a spiritual traveller to appoint some righteous man his preceptor (spiritual guide). The preceptor must have passed away from self and reached the station of ever lasting abode in Allah. He should be fully aware of all the points which are to the advantage or disadvantage of a spiritual traveller and should be capable of undertaking the training and guidance of other spiritual travellers. Moreover, remembrance and recollection of Allah and prayer to Him with humility are also necessary for a spiritual traveller.

Besides, to be able to pass all the stages of spiritual path successfully it is necessary for him to observe certain rules:

(i) Renunciation of customs, usages and social formalities

It means to refrain from all those formalities which are related to mere customs or stylish living and which are a hindrance in the way of the spiritual traveller, who is required to live among the people but to lead a simple and balanced life. Some people are so absorbed in social formalities that they always observe them too minutely in order to maintain their position in society and often indulge in useless and even harmful practices, which cause nothing but inconvenience and worry. They give preference to unnecessary usages over the real and important necessities. Their criterion for judging what is proper and what is improper is the appreciation and disapproval of the common people. They do not have any opinion of their own, and simply follow the common trend. At the other end there are some other people who lead an isolated life and ignore all rules of society and thus deprive themselves from all social benefits. They do not mix with other people and come to be known as cynics.

To be successful in his objective the spiritual traveller should follow the middle way. He should mix up with the people neither too much nor too little. It does not matter if he looked different from other people because of his distinct social behaviour. He should not follow others and should not care for any criticism in this connection. Allah says: *They do not fear the criticism of any critic in the way of Allah.* (Surah al-Mā'ida, 5:54)[76]. That means that the true believer sticks to what he thinks to be right. As a principle it may be said that the spiritual traveller should weigh every matter seriously and should not follow the wishes of other people or their opinion blindly.

(ii) Determination

As soon as the spiritual traveller begins his spiritual exercises, he is bound to face many unpleasant events. He is criticized by his friends and acquaintances who are interested only in their selfish desires and current social customs. They taunt and unbraid the spiritual traveller in order to bring a change in his behaviour and to turn him away from his objective. When these worldly people find that the spiritual traveller has a new style of life and his ways and manners have become different from their own, they feel upset and try their best to remove him by means of mockery and taunt from the line recently chosen by him. Thus at every stage of his spiritual journey the devotee has to face fresh difficulties which he can resolve only by means of his determination, perseverance, will power and trust in Allah. *Let the believers place their trust in Allah.* (Surah Āli Imrān, 3:122)[77]

(iii) Moderation

It is one of those important principles which the spiritual traveller must follow, for a little negligence in this respect not only hampers his progress, but often as a consequence of a lack of attention to this principle he may get tired of the spiritual journey itself. In the beginning the spiritual traveller may show much zeal and fervour. In the middle he may see wonderful manifestations of Divine light, and consequently may decide to spend most of his time in acts of worship and make himself busy with prayer, bewailing and weeping. Thus he may try to undertake everything good and pick up a morsel of every spiritual dish. But this practice is not only not beneficial but is also in many cases definitely harmful. Under too much pressure he may get fed up, leave the work incomplete and cease to take interest in commendable acts. Too much enthusiasm in the beginning leads to too little interest in the end. Therefore the spiritual traveller should not be misled by momentary zeal, and keeping in view his personal circumstances should shoulder only as much burden, or even less, as he is sure to be able to carry permanently maintaining due interest in it. He should perform acts of worship when he is really inclined to them and should withdraw from them when his desire to perform them has not still completely faded away. He may be compared to a man who wants to eat something. Such a man first of all should choose a dish that agrees to his temperament, and then should stop eating it before his belly is full. This principle of moderation is derived from that tradition also according to which Imam Ja'far Sādiq said to Abdul Aziz Qarātisi: "Abdul Aziz, faith has ten degrees like the steps of a ladder which are climbed one by one. If you find anyone below you by one step, pull him up to you gently and do not burden him with what he cannot bear, or else you will break him."

This tradition shows that in principle only those acts of worship are beneficial which are performed with zeal and eagerness. The following saying of Imam Sādiq also means the same thing: "Do not force yourselves to worship."

(iv) Steadiness

It means that after feeling penitence about a sin and asking Allah's forgiveness for it, it must not be committed again. Every vow must be fulfilled and every promise made to the pious preceptor must be kept.

(v) Continuance

Before explaining this point it is necessary to make some preliminary remarks. The Qur'anic verses and religious reports show that everything we perceive by our senses, everything we do and everything that exists or occurs has a corresponding truth transcending this material and physical world and not subject to any limitations of time and space. When these truths descend to this material world, they assume a tangible and palpable form. The Qur'an expressly says: *There is not a thing the treasures of which we do not have with Us. But we send down everything in an appointed measure.* (Surah al-Hijr, 15:21)[78]

This verse essentially means that everything in this world has had an existence free from estimation and measurement prior to its material existence. When Allah intends to send a thing to this world, He appoints its measure and so it becomes limited: *No disaster befalls in the earth or in yourselves, but it is in a Book before We bring it into being. Surely this is easy for Allah.* (Surah al-Hadid, 57:22)[79]

As the external shape of everything is fixed and limited and everything is subject to all the changes that are the characteristics of matter such as coming into a shape and being disfiguared, everything in this world is temporary, transient and subject to decay. Allah says: *Whatever is with you is to be exhausted and whatever is with Allah is to stay.* (Surah an-Nahl, 16:96)[80] In other words, those abstract truths which are not subject to material characteristics and the treasures of which are with Allah. are not to come to an end. The following tradition, which is accepted by the Shi'ah and the Sunnis both, is also relevant in this connection: "We, the Prophets have been ordered to speak to the people according to their intellectual capacity."

This tradition relates to the description of the truths, not to their quantity. It says that the Prophets simplify the higher truths and describe them in a way comprehensible to their addresses. Human mind having been dazzled by the glamour of the world and being pre-occupied with the futile desires, has become dull and rusty and is not capable of comprehending the reality of the truths. The Prophets may be compared to a man who wants to explain some truth to the children. Naturally he will have to explain it in a way corresponding to the power of understanding and observation of the children. The same rule applies to the Prophets who are the custodians of the Divine teachings. Sometimes they describe the living truths in such a way that they appear to be lifeless, while as a matter of fact even the external rites such as prayers, fast, pilgrimage, zakāt, khums, urging that what is right and restraining from that what is evil are all living and conscious truths.

The spiritual traveller is he who by means of a spiritual journey and spiritual exercises seeks to purify his soul and intellect from all impurities to be able to view the higher truths by the grace of Allah in this very life and this very world. It often happens that a devotee views the ablution and prayers in their real form and feels that from the viewpoint of perception and consciousness, their real form is a thousand times better than their physical form.

The reports which have come down to us from the Imams show that the acts of worship will appear on the Day of Ressurection in their appropriate forms and will talk to the human beings. Even in the Qur'an it has been mentioned that the ears, the eyes and other organs will be speaking on that day. Similarly the mosques which appear to be composed of bricks and mortar, have a living and conscious reality. That is why some reports say that on the Day of Judgement the mosques and the Holy Qur'an will make complaints to their Lord. One day a gnostic was lying on his bed. When he turned from one side to the other he heard a shriek coming out of the ground. He could not immediately know the reason. Subsequently either he himself realized or somebody else pointed out to him that the ground, having been separated from him, was shrieking.

After these preliminary remarks now we come to our main point. By means of continuous practice the spiritual traveller should imprint on his mind an abstract figure of each act of worship he performs, so that his practice of it may turn into a permanent habit. He should perform each deed again and again and should not give it up till he begins to take delight in its performance. He cannot capture the permanent angelic aspect of a deed unless he continues to perform for quite a long time so that its impression on his mind may become indelible. For this purpose he should choose a deed consistent with his inclination and aptitude and then continue to perform it, for if a deed was abandoned prematurely, not only its good effects would be oblitrated, but a reaction also would begin to appear. As a good deed is luminous, the reaction of its abandonment involves

97

darkness and evil. The fact is that "there is nothing but good with Allah and all the evils, mischiefs and wrongs are attributable to us." Therefore man is responsible for all faults and defects. "My Lord, evil cannot be attributed to You." This shows that Allah's favour is common to all. It is not a prerogative of any particular class. Allah's infinite mercy is for all human beings, whether Muslims, Jews, Christians, Zoroastrians or idol-worshippers. But some men because of their wrong doing develop certain characteristics which make them unhappy, and so Allah's mercy make some people happy and some others distressed.

(vi) Meditation

This means that the spiritual traveller must at no time be forgetful of his duty and must always abide by the decision which he has taken.

Meditation or contemplation is very vast in its meaning and its sense differs according to the degrees and stages of the spiritual journey. In the beginning it means refraining from all acts not useful in this world or the hereafter and abstaining from saying or doing anything disliked by Allah. Gradually this meditation becomes stiffer and higher, and may sometimes mean concentration on one's silence, or on one's self or on a higher truth, that is the names and the attributes of Allah. The degrees and grades of this kind of meditation will be mentioned later.

Here it may be mentioned that meditation is an important factor in spiritual journey. The leading gnostics have laid great stress on it, and have described it as the foundation stone of spiritual journey on which the edifice of remembrance and recollection of Allah rests. Without meditation remembrance and recollection of Allah are not likely to produce any positive results. For a spiritual traveller meditation is as important as for a patient the prescribed course of diet, without which the medicines may be ineffective or may even produce counter effects. That is why the most outstanding spiritual guides do not allow any liturgies and recollection of Allah without meditation.

(vii) Checking

It means that the spiritual traveller should every day have a fixed time for checking and assessing what he had done during the past 24 hours. The idea of this checking has been derived from what Imam Musa ibn Ja'far has said: 'He who does not take account of himself once every day is not one of us.' If on checking the spiritual traveller finds that he has not done his duty, he should seek forgiveness from Allah and if he finds that he has performed his duty in every respect, he should be thankful to Him.

(viii) Censuring

If the spiritual traveller finds that he is guilty of some lapse or error, he should take some suitable action to reprimand or punish himself.

(ix) Hastening

This means that the spiritual traveller should be quick in implementing the decision he has taken. As he is likely to face many obstacles on his way, he should be vigilant and careful and should try to achieve his objective without wasting a moment.

(x) Faith and Reliance

The spiritual traveller must have love for and implicit faith in the Holy Prophet and his rightful successors.* Complete reliance and trust are especially necessary at this stage. The more the reliance, the more lasting the effect of good deeds.

As all the existing things are the creation of Allah, the spiritual traveller must love all of them and should have regard for them according to the grade of their dignity. A lover of Allah shows kindness to all men and animals. According to a tradition, affection for the creation is a part of faith in Allah.

* The rightful successors of the Holy Prophet are those who have complete knowledge of Islam and who have been designated to execute his mission after him. According to a tradition accepted both by the Shi'ah and the Sunnis the Holy Prophet said: 'There will be 12 Caliphs/amirs after me.' (al-Bukhari, al-Sahih, al-Tirmizi, Vol. II; Abu Dawud, al-Sunan, Vol. II, Ahmad ibn Hambal, al-Musnad, vol. V, al-Hakim, al-Mustadrak, vol. II)

Another tradition says: "Allah, I seek of You Your love and the love of him who loves You."

(xi) Observance of the Rules of Veneration

The observance of these rules of correct behaviour towards all and His vicegerents is different from the faith and reliance mentioned above. Here veneration means to be careful not to exceed one's limits and do anything inconsistent with the requirements of man's servitude to Allah. It is essential for man to observe his limits vis-a-vis his Creator, the essentially existing Being. This veneration is a requirement of this world of plurality, whereas faith and love naturally require attention to monotheism — the unity of Allah.

Faith and veneration stand in the same relationship to each other as an act obligatory and an act prohibited. While performing an obligatory act the devotee looks towards Allah and while abstaining from a prohibited act he looks towards his own limitations lest he should exceed them. Veneration means following a middle way between fear and hope. Not to observe the rules of veneration indicates too much familiarity which is extremely undesirable.

The distinctive characteristic of the late Hāji Mirza Ali Āgha Qāzi was his cheerfulness and faith rather than fear. The same was true of the late Hāji Shaykh Muhammad Bahār. On the contrary the predominent feature of Hāji Mirza Jawād Āgha Maliki was fear rather than hope and cheerfulness. That is what is indicated by their sayings. According to the gnostic parlance he who is dominated by chearfulness is called a "drunkard" and he who is dominated by fear is called a "hymist". The best thing is to adopt a middle way in between these two extremes. In other words the devotee should have the highest degree of both the qualities at one and the same time. This degree of excellence is found in the case of the Imams only.

In short, man who is a possibly existing being, should not forget his limits. That is why Imam Ja'far Sādiq used to prostrate himself on the ground whenever anything smacking extremism was uttered by anybody about him.

An absolutely dutiful devotee is he who always considers himself to be present before Allah and observes all the rules of property and deference while doing anything such as talking, keeping quiet, eating, drinking, sleeping etc. If the devotee kept the names and attributes of Allah in his mind, he would automatically observe all the rules of veneration and would always be conscious of his humility.

(xii) Intention

It means that the spiritual traveller should be single-minded and well-intentioned. The objective of his spiritual journey should be nothing but to pass away in Allah. The Qur'an says: "Worship Allah keeping worship purely for Him."

A number of reports say that there are three grades of intention. Imam Sādiq is reported to have said: "There are three kinds of worshippers: There are some who worship Allah because they are afraid of Him. Their worship is that of the slaves. There are some others who worship Allah for the sake of recompense. Their worship is that of the wage-earners. There are till others who worship Allah because they love Him. Their worship is that of freemen."

On deep thinking it appears that there are two kinds of worship. One of them is not worship at all in the right sense, because those who perform this kind of worship are actually self-worshippers. They are motivated by self-interest. As self-worshippers cannot be the worshippers of Allah, they may even be regarded as a sort of unbelievers.

The Qur'an has described the worship of Allah as man's nature. At the same time it has denied the possibility of any change in man's in-born qualities.

Set your purpose for religion as a man by nature upright — the nature in which Allah has created man. There is no altering in the nature framed by Allah. That is the right religion, but most men do not know 'even this fact.' (Surah ar-Rūm, 30:30)[81]

Therefore an act of worship actuated by self-interest is not only a deviation from the path of devotion to Allah, but is also a deviation from the path of monotheism, for these self-seekers appear not to believe in the unity of Allah in His actions and attributes because they associate some one else with Him. The Qur'an has everywhere proclaimed the unity of Allah and has denied the existence of any associate or partner with Him. The

101

first two groups of worshippers mentioned above consider Allah to be their partner in their objectives and do not refrain from the idea of self-aggrandizement even in worshipping Him. They have double objective and that is what is called polytheism which according to the Qur'an is an unforgivable offence.

Allah does not forgive that partners should be ascribed to Him. He pardons all save that to whom He will. (Surah an-Nisā', 4:48, 116)[82]

It is clear from the above that the worship performed by the first two groups is not fruitful and will not bring the worshipper closer to Allah.

As for the third group who worships Allah for the sake of love, their worship is that of freemen, and according to a report the most noble worship. "It is a hidden position to which only the pure attain." Love means attraction, or in other words to be drawn by some person or some truth.

The third group is of those who love Allah and are inclined towards Him. They have no objective other than being drawn to Him and gain His good pleasure. Their motive is their Real Beloved and they try to move towards Him.

Some reports say that Allah should be worshipped because He deserves being worshipped. He is fit and worthy of being worshipped because of His attributes. In other words He is to be worshipped because He is Allah.

Imam Ali says: "My Lord, I do not worship You because I am afraid of Your hell, nor because I want Your paradise. I worship You because I have found You fit for being worshipped. You Yourself have guided me to You and have called me to You. Had You not been I would not have known what You are."

In the beginning the spiritual traveller goes forward with the help of love, but after traversing a few stages he realizes that love is different from the beloved. Therefore he tries to give up love which was his means of progress so far, but which might prove a hindrance in his further advancement. Now he concentrates all his attention on the Beloved Whom he worships as his Beloved only. When he goes a few steps further he realizes that yet his worship is not free from duality for he still considers himself to be the lover and Allah the beloved, while it is inconsistent with absolute unity of Allah to think of a lover of Him. Therefore the spiritual traveller tries to forget about love so that he may step into the world of unity from the world of plurality. At this stage he ceases to have will and intention for his distinctive personality has already passed away.

Prior to this stage the spiritual traveller was seeking vision, viewing and sight. Now he forgets all these things, for when he has no intention, he can have no desire. In this state it cannot be said whether the eyes and the heart of the spiritual traveller are functioning or not. To see and not to see, to know and not to know all become irrelevant.

Bāyazid Bistāmi is reported to have said: 'First I renounced the world. Next day I renounced the hereafter. The third day I renounced everything other than Allah. The fourth day I was asked what I wanted. I said: I want that I do not want.' Perhaps taking a clue from this saying some people have fixed the following four stages:
(i) Renunciation of this world; (ii) Renunciation of the hereafter; (iii) Renunciation of the Lord; (iv) Renunciation of renunciation. This is a point which requires deep consideration for being understood properly. This is the stage at which the spiritual traveller gives up all desires. This is a great achievement, but difficult to realize, for even at this stage the spiritual traveller finds that his heart is not free from all desires and intentions. At least he aspires to gain perfection. It is of no use to make any conscious effort to get rid of the desires for such an effort itself involves a desire and an objective.

One day I spoke to my teacher, Mirza Ali Āgha Qāzi about this question and asked him what the solution of this problem was. He said that it could be resolved by adopting the method of "burning". The spiritual traveller should realize that Allah has created him in such a way that he must always have some desires and ambitions. That is a part of his inborn nature. Howsoever he may try, he cannot eliminate all desires. Therefore he should realize his powerlessness and give up all efforts to that effect. In that case he will entrust his case to Allah. The feeling of powerlessness will not only purify him, but will also burn the roots of all desire. Anyhow, it must be kept in mind that only theoretical knowledge of this point is not enough. The spiritual traveller must develop a real taste for it. If such a taste is developed, it can be more pleasure-giving than anything else in the world.

This method is called 'burning' for it burns out the very existence of will and intention and uproots them completely.

The Qur'an has used this method on a number of occasions. One instance is the use of the Divine expression: "We belong to Allah and to Him we shall return." Anybody who uses this method will find that it produces very quick results.

At the time of calamities, disasters and mishaps man consoles himself in different ways. For example he reminds himself that death and misfortunes are the destiny of all human beings. But Allah has suggested the burning method as a short cut by prescribing the above formula to be uttered on such occasions. If man realizes that he himself and all that he possesses and all that belongs to him in any way, are all owned by Allah who has full power and authority to dispose of them as He wills and pleases, he will not grieve for any loss and will feel relieved. Man should know that factually he is not the owner of anything. His ownership is only phenomenal. In reality everything belongs to Allah who gives whatever He will and takes away whatever He will. No body has a right to interfere in what He does. Man should know that he has been created wishful, ambitious and needy. All that is a part of his inborn nature. Therefore when the spiritual traveller is filled with any sort of yearning during his spiritual journey, he suspects that it is not possible for him to be totally free from desires, and that passing away in Allah, which is the basis of the worship of freemen, is inconsistent with his inmate propensities to will and desire. In these circumstances he is perplexed and feels helpless. But it is this feeling of helplessness that effaces his egoism, which is the basis of will and desire. Therefore after passing this stage no trace of will and desire is left. This point is worth understanding well.

(xiii) Silence

There are two kinds of silence: (i) general and relative; (ii) particular and absolute. Relative silence means to refrain from talking to people in excess to what is absolutely required. This kind of silence is necessary for the spiritual traveller at every stage. It is commendable for others also. Imam Ja'far Sādiq referred to this kind of silence when he said: "Our partisans (Shi'ah) are dumb." A report is mentioned in the Misbâhush Shari'ah according to which Imam Ja'far Sâdiq has said: "Silence is the way of the lovers of Allah because Allah likes it. It is the style of the Prophets and the habit of the chosen people."

According to another report Imam Ja'far Sâdiq said: "Silence is a part of wisdom. It is a sign of every virtue."

Particular and absolute silence means to refrain from talking during verbal recollection of Allah.

(xiv) Abstaining from Food or at least Observing Frugality

It is recommended on the condition that it should not disturb mental peace and composure. Imam Ja'far Sâdiq has said: "The believer enjoys hunger. For him hunger is the food of the heart and the soul."

Hunger illuminates the soul and makes it lighter whereas overeating makes it dull and tired and hampers its soaring to the heaven of gnosis. Out of the acts of worship fasting has been lauded a great deal. A number of reports concerning the Holy Prophet's Ascension to the Heavens have been mentioned in Daylami's Irshad and the Biharul Anwâr, vol. II. In these reports the Holy Prophet has been addressed as Ahmad. These reports underline the beneficial points of starvation, especially its wonderful effect in connection with spiritual journey. My teacher, the late Ali Âghâ Qâzi once related a wonderful story about starvation. In short he said: "Once during the days of the former Prophets three persons were travelling together. At the nightfall they set-out in three different directions with a view to get food, but agreed to assemble next morning at a particular place at an appointed time. One of them was already invited by some person. The second man also by chance became the guest of someone. The third man had no place to go to. He said to himself that he should go to the mosque to be the guest of Allah. He passed the night in the mosque, but could get no food. Next morning they assembled at the appointed place and each one of them related his story. At that time the Prophet of the time received a revelation to the following effect: "Tell Our guest that We were his host last night and wanted to provide him with sumptuous food, but found that there was no food better than hunger."

105

(xv) Solitude

There are two kinds of solitude also: general and particular. General solitude means not to mix with other people especially the ignorant masses and to meet them only as and when absolutely necessary. The Qur'an says: *And forsake those who take their religion for a pastime and a jest, and whom the life of the world beguiles.* (Surah al-An'ām, 6:70)[83]

Particular solitude means to keep away from all men. Such kind of seclusion is commendable at the time of performing all acts of worship, but is considered essential by the gnostics at the time of pronouncing certain liturgies. In this connection the following points must be observed:

For the spiritual traveller it is necessary to keep himself away from crowds and disturbing noises. The place where he performs acts of worship must be clean and lawful. Even the walls and the ceilings of his room must be tidy. His room should be a small one preferably accommodating only one person. A small room having no furniture and no decorating material is helpful in keeping the thoughts concentrated.

A man sought Salmān Farsi's permission to build a house for him. Till then Salmān had not built a house for himself. Still he refused to give the permission. That man said: 'I know why you do not give permission.' 'Say why', said Salmān. He said: 'You want me to build you a house only so long and so wide that it may accommodate you only.' 'Yes, that's the thing. You are right.', said Salmān. Subsequently that man built for Salmān with his permission a house of that small size.

(xvi) Vigil

It means that the spiritual traveller must make it a habit to wake up before dawn as early as he tolerably can. Denouncing the sleeping at dawn and praising the keeping awake at that time Allah says: *They used to sleep only a little while at night and at dawn used to seek forgiveness.* (Surah az-Zāziyāt, 51:18)[84]

(xvii) Continued Cleanliness

It means to be always ritually pure and to adhere to the performance of major ablution on Fridays and on all other occasions on which it has been recommended.

106

(xviii) Practising modesty and humility to the utmost degree

It includes weeping and wailing also.

(xix) Abstaining from Tasty Food

The spiritual traveller should abstain from tasty dishes and should be content with a little food as is absolutely necessary to sustain his life and energy.

(xx) Secrecy

It is one of the most important points to be observed by a spiritual traveller. The great gnostics have been very particular about it and have laid great stress on it. They advised their pupils to keep their spiritual exercises as well as their visions etc. secret. If simulation *(taqiyya)* is not possible, equivocation *(tawriyah)* must be resorted to. If necessary spiritual exercises may be abandoned for some time to maintain secrecy. "Try to fulfil your needs by maintaining secrecy."

At the time of sufferings and calamities simulation and secrecy make the things easier. If the spiritual traveller faces any hardships, he should go forward patiently.

Seek help in patience and prayers; truely it is hard except for the humble-minded. (Surah al-Baqarah, 2:45)[85]

In this verse the word *salāt* (prayers) has been used in its literal sense, that is attention to Allah. On this basis it may be inferred from this verse that patience in the remembrance of Allah makes the hardships less burdensome and paves the way to success. That is why it is often observed that the people who become extremely restless when their small finger is cut, do not worry in the least about losing their limbs and organs in the battlefield. According to this general rule the Imams have laid great stress on secrecy, and even have considered abandoning simulation a grave sin.

Shaykh Sadūq in his book, at-Tawhīd has quoted a report saying that one day Abu Basir asked Imam Ja'far Sadiq if it was possible to see Allah on the Day of Resurrection. He asked so because the *Ashā'irah*, the followers of the Sunni Imam Abul Hasan Ash'ari believe that all people will see Allah on the Day of Resurrection and in the hereafter, which is obviously not possible without incarnation. *Allah is far above what these wrong-doers say.* The Imam said: "It is possible to see Allah even in this world as you saw Him here just now." Abu Basir said: "Son of the Prophet, allow me to relate this event to others." The Imam did not allow him to do so and said: "Don't relate it to others; otherwise they will not be able to comprehend the truth and will go astray for no reason."

(xxi) Preceptor and Spiritual Guide

The preceptors are also of two types: General and special. The general preceptor is he who is not responsible for guiding any particular individual. People seek his guidance considering him to be a learned and experienced man. The Qur'an says: *Ask those who know if you do not know.* Such preceptors can be helpful only in the beginning of spiritual journey. When the spiritual traveller begins to view the manifestations of the glory of essence and attributes of Allah, he no longer needs to have a general preceptor. The special preceptor is he about whom a divine ordinance exists to the effect that he has been assigned the job of guidance. This position is held only by the Holy Prophet and his rightful successors. Their guidance and company are essential and indispensable not only at every stage of spiritual journey, but even after the spiritual traveller has reached his destination. The nature of this company is esoteric not physical for the real nature of the Imam is that station of his luminosity, the authority of which extends to everyone and everything in the world. Although Imam's body is also superior to the body of everyone else, yet the source of his authority over the universe is not his body. To explain this point it may be mentioned that whatever happens in this world, its source is the names and attributes of Allah, and the same Divine names and attributes are the essence of the Imam also. That is why the Imams have said: "Allah is known through us and he is worshipped through us." Therefore it may rightly be said that whatever stages the spiritual traveller traverses, he covers them in the light of the Imam, and every position to which he advances, that position is controlled by the Imam. Throughout his journey the spiritual traveller enjoys the company of the Imam and remains associated with him. Even after reaching his destination, he needs the company of the Imam, for it is the

Imam who teaches him the rules that are to be observed in the World of Divinity. Therefore Imam's company is essential at every stage of spiritual journey. In this connection there are many subtle points which are not easy to be explained. They may be discovered by the spiritual traveller through his own taste.

Once Muhyuddin Ibn 'Arabi went to a spiritual guide and complained to him that injustice was growing and the sins were rampant. The spiritual guide advised him to pay attention to Allah. A few days later he went to another spiritual guide and made the same complaint. That spiritual guide told him to pay attention to himself. Ibn 'Arabi was very much upset and began to weep. He asked the spiritual guide why the two answers were so different from each other. The spiritual guide said: "Oh dear! the answer is one and the same. He drew your attention to the companion and I to the path."

I have related this story to show that there is no difference between making a journey to Allah on the one hand and arriving at the station of the Imam while passing through the stages of the Divine names and attributes on the other. These two things are not only closer to each other but are almost identical. At this stage there is no conception of duality. There is nothing but the light of the glory of one Single Being, which is described in different words. Sometimes it is expressed as the Divine names and attributes and sometimes as the essence of the Imam or his luminosity.

To know whether a general preceptor is fit to be so, it is necessary to watch him closely and have contact with him for a considerable time. Such super-natural things as to know what others think, to walk on fire or water, to narrate the past events or to foretell the future, are not a sign of anybody's being a favourite of Allah. The performance of such things becomes possible at the beginning of spiritual vision, but the stage of proximity to Allah is far away from this stage. No one can be a preceptor in the true sense unless and until he receives the light of the glory of Divine essence. To receive the light of the manifestations of Divine names and attributes is not enough.

The spiritual traveller is said to be receiving the light of the manifestations of the Divine attributes when he feels that his knowledge, power and life are really the knowledge, power and life of Allah. At this stage when the spiritual traveller hears something, he feels that Allah has heard it and when he sees something, he feels that Allah has seen it. He may feel that Allah alone is the Knower, and the knowledge of every existing being is the knowledge of Allah Himself.

The spiritual traveller is said to be receiving the light of the glory of the Divine names when he views the Divine attributes in himself. For example he feels that Allah is the only Knower and his knowlege is also that of Allah. Or he feels that the only living Being is Allah and that he himself is not living, but his life is actually that of Allah. In other words he intuitively feels that "there is no knowing, living or powerful being except Allah." If a spiritual traveller receives the light of the manifestations of one or two Divine names, it is not necessary that he should receive the light of the manifestations of other Divine names also.

The spiritual traveller receives the light of the glory of Divine essence only when he forgets himself totally and can find no trace of himself or his ego. "There is none but Allah." Such a person can never go astray, nor can be seduced by Satan. Satan does not lose hope of alluring a spiritual traveller until he obliterates his very existence. But when he enters the sanctuary of the world of divinity after annihilating his personality and ego, Satan loses all hope of seducing him. A general preceptor must be such as to have reached this stage. Otherwise it is not safe for a devotee to submit himself to any Tom, Dick or Harry.

It is not advisable for a spiritual traveller to go at random to any shop for getting what he requires or to submit himself to any pretender. He should make complete investigations about the proposed preceptor and when it is not possible to do so, he should put trust in Allah, compare the proposed preceptor's teachings with those of the Holy Prophet and the Imams, and act only according to what conforms to the latter. If he does so, he will be safe from the wiles of Satan. The Qur'an says: *Satan has no power over those who believe and put trust in their Lord. His power is only over those who make a friend of him and those who ascribe partners to Allah.* (Surah an-Nahl, 16:99)[86]

110

(xxii) Daily Verbal Recitation of Liturgies:

The amount and the method of the recitation of the verbal liturgies depend on what the preceptor advises. The liturgies are just like a medicine which may suit some and may not suit others. Sometimes it so happens that a spiritual traveller begins more than one liturgies of his own opinion, while one liturgy pulls him towards plurality and another towards unity. Their mutual clash nullifies the effect of both and they become totally ineffective. It may be mentioned that the permission of the preceptor is necessary only for those liturgies which every body is not allowed to recite. There is no objection to the reciting of those liturgies for which general permission already exists.

The gnostics do not attach any importance to the mere repetition of liturgies without paying attention to their meaning which is far more important. Mere verbal repitition is of no use.

(xxiii, xxiv, xxv) Remembrance, Recollection, Evil thoughts

These three stages are of great importance for the purpose of achieving the objective. Many people who fail to reach their destination either stop at one of these stages or go astray while on their way to them. The dangers which these stages imply are idol-worship, star-worship, fire-worship and occasionally heresy, Pharaonism, claim of incarnation and identification with God, denial of being obligated to abide by religious injunctions and regarding everything lawful. We will discuss briefly all these dangers. Let us first talk about incarnation and identification with God, which is the greatest danger and is caused by devilish insinuation when the mind is not free from evil thoughts.

As the spiritual traveller is not out of the valley of ostentation, he may be led in the wake of the manifestation of Divine names or attributes to believe (God forbid) that Allah has dwelt in him. That is what is meant by incarnation, which amounts to infidelity and polytheism, while the belief in the unity of Allah nullifies every concept of pluralism, and considers every existence in comparison to the existence of Allah a mere fantasy and everything existing a mere shadow. When the spiritual traveller attains to this stage, he annihilates his existence and does not perceive anything existing except Allah.

Eradication of Devilish Insinuations

The spiritual traveller must have full control over himself so that no thought might enter his mind inadvertently and no action might be taken by him unintentionally. It is not very easy to secure the required degree of self-control and that is why it is said that the eradication of insinuations is the best means of purifying the soul. When the spiritual traveller attains to this stage he in the beginning finds himself overwhelmed by evil thoughts and devilish insinuations. Strange ideas come to his mind. He often thinks of old events which have already been forgotten and visualizes imaginary events which are not possible ever to materialize. On this occasion the spiritual traveller must remain steadfast and firm, and should eradicate every noxious thought by means of remembering Allah. Whenever any evil thought may come to his mind, he should concentrate his attention on one of the names of Allah and should continue to do so till that thought has vanished. The best method of eradicating the evil thoughts is to concentrate on the Divine names. The Qur'an says: *Whenever those who practise piety are throubled by an evil thought from Satan, they remember Allah and then they forthwith see the light.* (Surah al-A'rāf, 7:201)[87]

However, the treatise ascribed to the late Baḥrul 'Ulūm, does not allow this method to be adopted. This treatise lays stress on the necessity of banishing evil throughts before beginning the acts of remembering Allah and declares it to be extremely dangerous to use these acts for the eradication of evil thoughts and insinuations. We give below a summary of the arguments advanced by the treatise and propose to contradict them subsequently.

This treatise says that: Many preceptors ask the devotees to do away with insinuations by means of remembering Allah. Obviously here remembering means mental concentration, not verbal recitation of any liturgy. But this method is very dangerous, for remembering Allah in fact amounts to beholding the 'Real Beloved' and to fix eyes on His beauty, which is not permissible unless eyes are shut to all others, for the sense of the dignity of the Beloved does not allow the eye that sees him to see anyone or anything else. It will be a mockery to remove eye from the Beloved again and again to see something, and a

112

person who does that, is likely to receive a shocking blow. The Qur'an says: *He who ignores the remembrances of the Beneficent, We assign to him a devil who becomes his comrade.* (Surah az-Zukhruf, 43:36)[88]

Anyhow, there is one form of remembering Allah that is allowed for the purpose of getting rid of evil thoughts. According to this form the devotee should not have the beauty of the Beloved in mind. His purpose should be only to get rid of Satan, just like the man who calls his beloved only to dismay his rival and drive him away. Thus if the devotee comes across any evil thought from which he finds it difficult to escape, he should engage himself in remembering Allah in order to get rid of that evil thought. Anyhow, the experienced gnostics ask the beginners to clear away the evil thoughts first and then to undertake the remembrance of Allah. For this purpose they ask him to fix his eyes without blinking for some time on something like a piece of stone or wood and concentrate his attention on it. It would be better if this process was continued for 40 days. Meanwhile *'A'ūžu billah'*, *'Astaghfirullāh'* and *'Ya Fa'āl'* should continually be chanted, especially after morning and evening prayers. After the completion of 40 days' period the devotee for some time should concentrate on his heart and should not allow any other thought to enter his mind. If any evil thought came to his mind, he should chant the words, *'Allāh'* and *'Lā mawjuda illallāh'*, and continue to chant them till he feels somewhat enraptured. While pursuing this course he should chant a great deal *'Astaghfirullāh'*, *'Yā Fa'ālu'* and *'Yā Bāsiṭu'* also. When he has attained to this stage, the devotee is allowed to resort to mental remembrance, if he wants so, in order to eradicate all evil thoughts once for all, for once the devotee has reached the stage of remembrance, recollection and contemplation, the evil thoughts and the devilish insinuations disappear automatically. This was the summary of the discourse, ascribed to Bahrul 'Ulūm in the above-mentioned treatise.

Anyhow, it must be understood that this method of the eradication of evil thoughts has been derived from the method followed by the Naqshbandi, a sufi order found at some places in Turkey etc. This order has come to be known so after the name of its grand preceptor, Khwaja Bahauddin Naqshbandi.

But this is not a method approved by Akhund Mulla Husayn Quli Hamadani. Remembrance and recollection of Allah are an integral part of the method followed by him and his pupils also, but they lay greater emphasis on meditation and contemplation. We have already described meditation briefly and now propose to mention some details of its various stages.

First stage: The first stage of meditation is to abstain from everything unlawful and to perform everything obligatory. Any negligence or lethargy in this respect is not permissible.

Second stage: The devotee should intensify his meditation and try to do all that he does purely for the sake of gaining good pleasure of Allah. He should carefully refrain from all that is called pastime and fun. Once this habit has become firmly established, it will no longer be necessary for him to exert himself in this regard.

Third stage: He should believe and acknowledge that Allah is Omniscient and Omnipresent and that Allah who supervises all His creation is looking at him. This meditation should be observed at all times and in all circumstances.

Fourth stage: It is a higher degree of the third stage. At this point the devotee himself perceives that Allah is Omniscient and Omnipresent. He sees the manifestation of the Divine beauty. The Holy Prophet hinted at the third and the fourth stages of meditation when he said to his great companion Abu Zar Ghifāri: 'Worship Allah as if you were looking at Him, for if you do not see Him, He sees you.' This tradition indicates that the degree that Allah sees the worshipper is inferior to that of the worshipper's seeing Allah. When the devotee attains to this stage, he should get rid of the evil thoughts by means of some acts of worship. The Islamic law does not allow concentration of thought on any piece of wood or stone. Suppose the devotee died while concentrating on a piece of wood or stone, what would be his answer to Allah? It is commendable from religious point of view to get rid of evil thoughts by the weapon of remembering and recollecting Allah, which is itself is an act of worship. The best and the shortest way of getting rid of evil thoughts is to concentrate on one's self. This method is allowed and approved by Islam. The Qur'an says: *Believers, you have to take care of your own self. He who errs can do you no harm if you are rightly guided.* (Surah al-Mā'idah, 5:105)[89]

114

Concentration of thoughts on self is the method that was prescribed by Akhund Mulla Husayn Quli and has always been adopted by his pupils, who maintain that knowledge of self invariably leads to knowledge of Allah.

The chain of the teachers of gnosis goes back to Imam Ali. The number of the sufi orders which have taken part in imparting the mystic knowledge is more than 100, but the main orders are not more than 25. All these orders go back to Imam Ali. Almost all of them belong to the Sunni denomination. Only two or three of them are Shi'ite. Some of these orders are traced back through Ma'ruf Karkhi to Imam Ali Reza. But we belong to none of these orders and follow the directions of the late Akhund, who had nothing to do with these orders.

More than a hundred years ago there lived in Shustar a leading scholar and Qāzi (judge) named Agha Sayyid Ali Shushtari. Like other eminent scholars his occupation was teaching and administration of justice. Many people called on him to take counsel. One day all of a sudden somebody knocked at his door. When Agha Sayyid Ali opened it he saw a weaver standing there. On inquiry as to what he wanted, he said: 'The judgement given by you regarding the ownership of that particular property on the basis of the evidence produced before you was not correct. Actually that property belongs to an orphan little child and its deed is buried at such and such place. The course that is being followed by you is also wrong.' Ayatulllah Shushtari said: 'Do you mean to say that my judgement was wrong?' The weaver said: 'What I have told you is the fact.' After saying that the weaver went away. The Ayatullah began to think over who that man was and what he said. On further inquiry it was found that the said deed was actually buried at the place mentioned by the weaver, and that the witnesses produced were liars. The Ayatullah was alarmed, and said to himself: 'My other judgements also might have been wrong.' He was frightened. Next night the weaver again knocked at the door and said: 'The course being followed by you is not proper.' The same thing happened the third night. The weaver said: 'Do not waste time. Collect all your domestic effects and sell them out, and then set out for Najaf. Do as I have told you, and after six months wait for me in the Wadi'us Salām of Najaf. The late Shushtari left for

Najaf. As soon as he arrived there he saw that the weaver in the Wadius Salâm at sun-rise, as if he had emerged suddenly from the ground. He gave some instructions and then disappeared once again. The late Shushtari entered Najaf and began to act according to the weaver's instructions. At last he reached a position too high to be described.

The late Sayyid Ali Shushtari held Shaykh Murtaza Ansâri in great respect and attended his lectures on theology and jurisprudence. Shaykh Murtaza Ansâri also attended Sayyid Ali's lectures on moral law once a week. Following Shaykh Murtaza Ansâri's death, the late Sayyid Ali assumed his teaching functions and began to give lectures from where Shaykh Murtaza Ansâri had suspended them. But he did not live long and died after six months only. Anyhow, during this short period Sayyid Ali trained and guided Mulla Husayn Quli, one of Shaykh Murtaza Ansâri's distinguished pupils. Mulla Husayn Quli already had some contact with Āgha Sayyid Ali and from time to time used to ask him questions regarding moral and spiritual matters. When Sayyid Ali succeeded Shaykh Murtaza Ansâri, he sent a message to Mulla Husayn Quli, on which he wrote: 'The course that you are following presently is faulty. Try to attain to higher positions.' At last Āgha Sayyid Ali succeeded in persuading Mulla Husayn Quli to follow his method. Consequently before long Mulla Husayn Quli became a wonder of his time in morals, spiritual knowledge and self-mortification. Mulla Husayn Quli also trained some very distinguished and competent pupils, each of whom became a shining star on the sky of gnosis. His most prominent pupils included Haji Mirza Jawād Āgha Malaki, Āgha Sayyid Ahmad Karbalai Tehrani, Āgha Sayyid Muhammad Sa'îd Habbubi and Hāji Shaykh Muhammad Bahāri.

My preceptor was the late Hāji Mirza Ali Āgha Qāzi who was a pupil of Āgha Sayyid Ahmad Karbalai. This is the chain of my preceptors which goes back to the above-mentioned weaver through the late Shushtari. Anyhow, it is not known who that weaver was and from where he aquired his gnostic knowledge.

My preceptor Āgha Qāzi followed the method of knowing self like Akhund Mulla Husayn Quli and for the eradication of evil thoughts and devilish insinuations he called for paying attention to self first. He suggested that for this purpose the spiritual traveller should fix a time of day or night and should concentrate his attention on self for half an hour or a little more. This daily practice will gradually invigorate his heart and eradicate the evil thoughts. At the same time he will gradually acquire the knowledge of his soul and, Allah willing, will achieve his objective. Most of those who succeed in clearing their mind from evil thoughts and ultimately receive the light of gnostic knowledge, achieve this objective in either of the following two ways: Either while reading the Qur'an, their mind is suddenly diverted to the reader and it is revealed to them that the reader was really Allah; or the veils are lifted through the intercession of Imam Abu Abdillah (Imam Husayn — the grand son of the Holy Prophet of Islam), who is especially concerned with the lifting of veils and removing the barriers obstructing the way of the devotees.

There are two things which are especially helpful in receiving the light of gnostic knowledge: (i) Covering all the stages of meditation; and (ii) Concentrating attention on self. If the devotee paid full attention to secure these two things, he would gradually perceive that despite its variety the whole universe was being nurtured from one source, that is the source of all that happens in the world. Whatever perfection, excellence or beauty anything in the world possesses, it is a gift from that source. Everything has received a share of existence, beauty and grandure according to its capacity. The generosity of the Absolute Munificent is for all, but everything existing gets its share according to its capacity and nature.

Anyway, if the spiritual traveller adheres to complete meditation and attention to self, four worlds will gradually be revealed to him:

First World — Unity of Actions: In the beginning the spiritual traveller will feel that he himself is the source of all that his tongue says, his ears hear and his hands, feet and other limbs do. He will think that he does whatever he likes. Later he will feel that he himself is the source of all that happens in the world. At the next stage he will feel that his existence is closely connected with Allah and through this relationship the favours and bounties of Allah, reach the creation. Ultimately he will perceive that Allah alone is the source of all actions and occurrences.

Second World — Unity of Attributes: This world emerges after the first world. At this stage when the spiritual traveller hears or sees anything, he feels that Allah is the source of his hearing and seeing. Later he perceives that Allah is the source of all knowledge, power, life, hearing and sight found anywhere and in any form.

Third World — Unity of Names: This world emerges after the second world. At this stage the devotee feels that the Divine attributes are not in any way separate from the Divine essence. When he sees that Allah is the knower, he feels that his being knower is also Allah's being knower. Similarly he thinks that his having power, his sight and his hearing are Allah's having power, His sight and His hearing, for he is sure that on principle there is only One Being in the whole universe who is having power and who sees and hears. It is His power and His sight and His hearing that are reflected and indicated by everything existing according to its capacity.

Fourth World — Unity of Being: This world is higher than the third world. It is revealed to the spiritual traveller in consequence to the revelation of the glory of Divine Essence. He at this stage perceives that there is only One Being who is the source of all actions and attributes. At this stage his attention remains concentrated on the One Being and is not drawn to His names and attributes. He attains to this stage only when he has annihilated his transient existence completely and has passed away in Allah. It would be difficult and far from truth even to call this stage the station of Divine Essence or Divine Unity, for the Reality is far above any name that is uttered or written. No name can be given to the Divine Essence and no station of it can be imagined. Allah is even above the question of not being imagined for even negative expressions would mean that He has some limits whereas He is above all limitations. When the spiritual traveller attains to this stage, he will have annihilated his self and ego completely. He will recognize neither himself nor anyone else, He will recognize Allah alone.

While passing through each of these worlds the spiritual traveller annihilates a part of his self and ultimately annihilates himself completely.

In the first world he attains to the stage of passing away,

for he realizes that he is not the source of any of his doings and that everything is from Allah. Thus he annihilates the traces of his actions.

In the second world he as the result of attributive manifestation perceives that knowledge, power and all such qualities exclusively belong to Allah. Thus he effaces the signs of his own attributes.

In the third world the spiritual traveller receives the manifestation of Divine names and perceives that Allah alone is the knower, the doer etc. Thus he effaces the signs of his names and designations also.

In the fourth world he views the manifestation of the glory of Divine Essence. As a result he entirely loses his entity and feels that there exists nothing but Allah.

The gnostics call the revelation of the glory of Divine Essence at this stage the 'griffin', which cannot be hunted. They use this word for that Absolute Being and Mere Existence which is also described as the 'Hidden Treasure' and the Being having no name nor any description.

In his poems Hafiz Shirazi has described this point in an attractive style using beautiful metaphors. At one place he says: 'An old seer and sage told me the following story, which I shall never forget: One day a pious man was going somewhere. On his way he saw a drunkard* sitting, who said: 'Devotee, if you have some bait to offer, lay down your trap here. The devotee said: 'I have a trap but I want to catch a 'griffin'. The drunkard said: 'You can catch it only if you know where it is to be found. But its nest is not known.' 'That's right', said the devotee, 'but to be disappointed is a worse calamity.' Just see how this man did not lose heart. It is possible that the lonely man is led to the Peerless Being by a Divinely appointed guide.

Obviously it is not possible to catch the griffin when its nest is not known. But Allah can bestow His favour on the lovers of His everlasting beauty and can lead them to the world of Divine unity and passing away from self.

* We have already explained this term.

INTERPRETATION OF SURAH AL-HAMD

I have been asked to say something on the exegesis of Surah al-Hamd. The fact is that the exegesis of the Qur'an is not a thing of which we may be able to acquit ourselves well. In every period of Islamic history the top scholars including both the Sunnis and the Shi'ites have compiled a large number of books on this subject. But every scholar has written his book from the angle with which he was well conversant and has interpreted only one aspect of the Qur'an. Still it cannot be said whether even that aspect has been covered fully.

During the past fourteen centuries the gnostics such as Muhyuddin ibn Arabi, Abdur Razzāq Kāshāni, Mulla Sultan Ali etc. have written excellent commentaries on the Qur'an and dealt well with the subject in which they had specialized. But what they have written is not the exegesis of the Qur'an. At the most it can be said that they have exposed some aspects of it. The same case is with Tantāwi, Jawhari, Sayyid Qutb etc. They have compiled their exegeses in a different style, but their books are also not the exegesis of the Qur'an in every sense.

There are other interpreters of the Qur'an who do not belong to either of the above mentioned two groups. The Majma'ul Bayān by Shaykh Tabrasi is an excellent commentary and combines what the Sunni and Shi'ah authorities have said. There are so many other commentaries, but they all cover only certain aspects of the Qur'an. The Qur'an is not a book all aspects of which may be exposed by us or by any body else. There are some Qur'anic sciences which are beyond our comprehension. We can understand only one angle or one form of the Qur'an. Others are to be explained by the Imams who were the real exponents of the Holy Prophet's teachings.

121

For some time past there have appeared some interpreters of the Qur'an who are totally unfit for the task. They want to attribute their own wishes and desires to the Qur'an. Surprisingly enough even some leftists and communists pretend to be partisans of the Qur'an and show interest in its interpretation. In fact they do so only to promote their evil designs. Otherwise they have nothing to do with the Qur'an; let alone its interpretation. They just want to pass their doctrines under the name of the teachings of Islam.

That is why I say that those who do not possess enough knowledge of Islam and the young men who are not fully conversant with the Islamic problems, have no right to meddle in the exposition of the Qur'an. But if they still try to misinterpret it for some ulterior motive of theirs, our youth should ignore their interpretation and pay no attention to it. Islam does not allow anybody to interpret the Qur'an according to his personal opinion or private judgement. Anybody who tries to impose his own opinion on the Qur'an is either a materialist misinterpreting the Qur'an or is one of those who give some spiritual meaning to the Qur'anic verses. Both these groups interpret the Qur'an according to their own wishes. Therefore it is necessary to keep away from both of them. As far as the Qur'an is concerned our hands are tied. No body is allowed to attribute his opinion to the Qur'an and claim that the Qur'an says so.

The interpretation which I am going to give is only a possible interpretation. When I explain any verse of the Qur'an, I do not claim that the verse means only what I say. I do not say anything for certain. I am hinting a possibility only.

As some gentlemen have asked me to say something on the exegesis of the Qur'an, I have decided to speak briefly once a week about the Surah al-Hamd. I would like to repeat once again that the interpretation which I give is nothing more than a possibility. I do not want at all to interpret the Qur'an according to my own opinion or wish.

It is possible that the 'bismillah' in the beginning of each surah of the Qur'an is related to the verses following it. Generally it is said that the bismillah is related to a verb understood (omitted), but probably it is related to the surah following it. For example in the Surah al-Hamd it is related to *al-Hamdu lillah*. In this case the whole sentence would mean that: With the name of Allah all praises belong to Him. Now what does a name signify. It is a mark or a sign. When man gives a name to any person or thing, that name serves as a symbol for the recognition of that person or thing. If any person is named Zayd, people can recognize him by that name.

Allah's Names are the Symbols of His Person

Whatever little information man can get about the Divine Being, he can acquire it through His names. Otherwise man has no access to His Person. Even the Holy Prophet did not have, though he was the most learned and the noblest of all human beings. No one other than Him can know Him. Man can have access only upto the Divine names.

The knowledge of the Divine names has several grades. Some of them we can comprehend. Others can be grasped only by the Holy Prophet and some of his chosen followers.

The Whole World is A Name of Allah

The whole world is a name of Allah, because the name of a thing is its sign or symbol and as all the things existing are the signs of Allah, it may be said that the whole world is His name. At the most it can be said that very few people fully understand how the existing things are the signs of Allah. Most people know only this much that nothing can come into existence automatically.

Nothing, the existence of which is only possible, can come into existence automatically.

It is intellectually clear and every body knows it intuitively that anything the existence and non-existence of which is equally possible, cannot come into existence automatically and that there must be an external force to bring it into existence. The first cause of bringing into existence all possibly existing things must be an eternal and self-existing being. If it is supposed that the imaginary upper space, and it must be imaginary because it is a nonentity, has always existed, then it possibly can neither automatically turn into anything nor anything can come into existence in it automatically. The assertion of some people that in the beginning the whole world was an infinite vacuum (Anything being infinite is questionable in itself) in which subsequently appeared a sort of steam from which everything has originated, does not stand to reason, for without an external cause no new thing can appear nor can one thing change into another thing. For example, water does not freeze nor does it boil without an external cause. If its temperature remains constant and does not go below 0° nor above 100° it will always remain water. In short, the existence of an external cause is essential for every change. Similarly nothing the existence of which is only possible can come into existence without an external cause. These facts are self-evident truths.

All Existing Things are A Sign of Allah

This much can be easily understood by all that all existing things are a sign and a name of Allah. We can say that the whole world is Allah's name. But the case of this name is different from that of the names given to the ordinary things. For example if we want to indicate a lamp, or a motor car to someone, we mention its name. The same thing we do in the case of man or Zayd. But evidently that is not possible in the case of the Being possessing infinite sublime qualities.

Anything Which is Finite is A Possibly Existing Thing

If an existing thing is finite, it is a possibly existing thing. As Allah's existence is infinite, He should evidently possess all sublime qualities, for if he lacked even one quality, He would become finite and as such possibly existing. The difference between a possibly existing being and an essentially existing being is that the latter is infinite and absolute in every respect. If all the sublime qualities of the essentially existing being were not infinite, that being would not be the essentially existing being and the source of all existence. All the things caused by this source of existence are endowed with the qualities possessed by the essentially existing Being, but on a smaller scale and in varying degrees. What is endowed with these qualities to the utmost possible degree is called the Grand Name or *al-ism al-a'zam.*

124

What is the Grand Name?

The Grand Name is that name or sign that is somewhat endowed with all the Divine qualities to the greatest possible degree. As compared to other existing things it possesses the Divine qualities most perfectly, though no existing thing lacks them completely, for everything has been endowed with them according to its nature and capacity. Even those material things which appear to us to be totally devoid of all knowledge and power are not really so and possess some degree of perception and knowledge.

All Existing Things Glorify Allah

As we are veiled, we cannot perceive it, but it is a fact that the sublime qualities are reflected even in the things lower than man and animals. At the most these qualities are reflected in them according to the capacity of their existence. Even the lowest creations possess the quality of perception. The Qur'an says: *There is not a thing that does not praise Him, but you do not understand their praise.* (Surah Bani Isra'il, 17:44)[90]

As we are veiled and do not understand the praise of all existing things, the ancient scholars did not know that the imperfect beings also possessed perception. That is why they took this praise to mean the praise indicated by the creation of all things, but in fact this verse has nothing to do with that kind of praise, which is quite a different matter as we already know. According to a tradition once the people heard the pebbles in the Holy Prophet's hand praising Allah. They could understand the praise of the pebbles, but this praise was such that the human ears were quite unfamiliar with it. It was in the pebbles' own language, not in any human language. Hence, it is clear that the pebbles possess perception, although of course according to their existential capacity. Man who considers himself to be the source of all kinds of perception, thinks that other things are devoid of it, but that is not a fact, although it is true that man has a higher degree of it. Being veiled, we are unaware of the perception of other things and their praising Allah, and think that there is no such thing.

There are Many Things that We do not Know

There are many things about which man thinks that they do not exist, but in fact they do, though we may be unaware of them. Every day new discoveries are being made. Formerly it was believed that the plants were inanimate objects, but now it is said that they have a hearing system. If you put the tissues of a tree in hot water and pass a voice through them, there will be a reaction and you will hear some voices in response.

We do not know how far this report is correct. But it is certain that this world is full of voices and sounds. The whole world is living and is a name of Allah. You yourselves are a name of Allah. Your tongues and your hands are names of Allah.

All Movements are the Names of Allah

The praise you make of Allah is His name. When you go to the mosque after washing your feet, you go with the name of Allah. You cannot part with the name of Allah because you yourselves are His name. The beat of pulse, the throbbing of heart and the blowing of wind are all names of Allah. Perhaps that is what is meant by the names of Allah in this verse. There are many other verses in which the phrase: "With the name of Allah" has been used. As we have said, everything is the name of Allah, and the name has passed away in the named. We think that we have an independent existence, but that is not a fact. If that Being, who has brought everything into existence by means of His will and the reflection of the light of His glory withdrew His light for a moment all the existing things would be annihilated immediately and return to their pre-existing state. Allah has created the whole world by the light of His glory which is the true nature of existence and the name of Allah. The Qur'an says: *Allah is the light of the heavens and the earth.* Everything is illuminated by His light. Everything has appeared by dint of His light. This appearance itself is a reflection of His light. Man's appearence is also a light. Therefore man himself is a light. Animals are also a light of Allah's glory. The existence of the heavens and the earth is a light from Allah. This light has so passed away in Allah that the Qur'an has said: *Allah is the light of the heavens and the earth.*

It has not said that the heavens and the earth are illuminated by the light of Allah. The reason is that the heavens and the earth are a nonentity. Nothing in our world has an independent existence of its own. In other words there is nothing here that is self-existing. In fact there is no existent other than Allah. That is why the Qur'an says: *With the name of Allah all praise belongs to Allah. 'With the name of Allah say: He is Allah the One'.* Perhaps the Qur'an does not ask you to utter the words: *'With the name of Allah, the Compassionate, the Merciful.'* It actually mentions a fact. By asking you to say so with the name of Allah, it means that your saying so is also a name of Allah. The Qur'an has said: 'Whatever there is in the heavens and the earth glorifies Him.' It has not said whoever there is in the heavens and the earth glorifies Him. That means that everything whether animate or inanimate praises and glorifies Allah, for all are a reflection of the light of His glory and it is His glory that causes all movements.

Everything in the World is A Manifestation of His Glory

The cause of all that occurs in the world is the manifestation of Allah's glory. Everything is from Him and everything returns to Him. No creature has anything of its own. If any body claims to have anything of his own, he virtually wants to complete with the source of Divine light, while as a matter of fact even his life is not of his own. The eyes you have are not your own. The light of Divine manifestation has brought them into being. The praise of Allah that we or other people express, is a Divine name, or it is because of a Divine name. That is why the Qur'an says: *With the name of Allah and praise belongs to Allah.*

The Word Allah is a Comprehensive Manifestation of Divine Glory

It is a manifestation that includes all manifestations. Allah's names, *Raḥmān* (the Compassionate) and *Raḥīm* (the Merciful) are the manifestations of this manifestation.

Because of his mercy and benevolence Allah has bestowed existence in the existing things. This is itself is a show of mercy and kindness. Even the existence conferred on the harmful and obnoxious things is a show of His fevour, which is common to

127

all existing things. It is the manifestation of the glory of His name, Allah, which is a true manifestation of His glory in every sense. Allah is a station. It is a comprehensive name, which is itself a manifestation of Divine glory in every sense. Otherwise the Divine Being has no name apart from His Essence or Person. Allah His names including Allah, *Rahmān,* and *Rahīm* are only the manifestations of his glory. In the *'bismillah'* His names *Rahmān* and *Rahīm* have been added to His comprehensive name Allah, because they signify His self-sustaining attributes of mercy, favour and compassion. His attributes of retribution, anger etc. are subservient to these attributes. The praise of any kind of excellence is actually the praise of Allah. When a man eats something and says how delicious it is, he praises Allah unconsciously. When a man says about another man that he is a very fine man or that he is a great scholar or philosopher, he praises Allah because a philosopher or a scholar has nothing of his own. Whatever there is, it is a manifestation of Allah's glory. The man who understands this fact, he and his intellect are also a manifestations of Allah's glory.

No Praise is of Anyone Else's Praise

Whenever we praise anybody, we say that he has such and such good qualities. As every thing belongs to Allah, the commendation of any merit of any person or a thing virtually amounts to praising Allah. We, being veiled, do not realize this truth and think that we are praising Zayd or Amr, the sunshine or the moonlight. When veil is lifted we will come to know that all praises belong to none but Allah and that everything we praise is nothing but a manifestation of Allah's glory.

The Qur'an says: *Allah is the light of the heavens and the earth.* In other words, every excellence and every sublime quality, wherever it may be, is attributable to Allah. He is the cause of the whole world and the whole world is a manifestation of His glory. The things we do, are not actually done by us. Addressing the Holy Prophet Allah said in the Qur'an: *You did not throw (the pebbles), when you threw (them), but Allah threw (them).* (Surah al-Anfāl, 8:17)[91] Consider the words: *'You threw'* and *'You did not throw'.* Both of these phrases are a manifestation of *'but Allah threw'.*

There is another verse that says: *Those who swear allegiance to you, swear allegiance only to Allah.* (Surah al-Fath, 48:10)[92] Being veiled as we are, we do not understand the truth these verses imply. As a matter of fact we all are under a veil except the Holy Prophet who was educated direct by Allah and the Holy Imams of the Holy Prophet's Progeny who received training from him.

So there is a possibility that the preposition *'bi'* and *the* noun *'ism'* in *'bismillah'* may be related to *'al-Hamdu'*, meaning, 'With the name of Allah all praises belong to Him.' It is a manifestation of the glory of Allah that draws every praise to it and does not allow any praise to be a praise of anyone other than Allah, for howsoever you may try, you will not find anyone existing other than Him. Therefore whatever praise you express, it will be a praise of Allah. It may be noted that praise is always made of positive qualities. The defects and faults being negative qualities, do not actually exist. Everything that exists has two aspects. It is positive aspect that is praised and it is always free from defects and faults.

There exists only one excellence and one beauty and that is the excellence and beauty of Allah. We should try to understand this truth. Once we are convinced of this fact, everything else will be easy. As a matter of fact it is easy to acknowledge something verbally, but it is difficult to persuade oneself to believe even a rational thing firmly.

To Believe Something Intellectually is One Thing and to be Convinced of it is Another

To be convinced of the truth of a thing is different from believing it intellectually because of the existence of some scientific arguments to prove it. The impecability of the Prophets was due to their firm conviction. A man who is fully convinced of a truth, cannot act contrary to his conviction. If you were sure that somebody was standing near you with a drawn sword in his hand and that he would kill you if you uttered a single word against him, you would never say anything against him because your first concern was to save your life. In other words, as far as this matter was concerned, you were so to say infallible. A man who was convinced that if he slandered anybody behind his back, his backbiting would assume the shape of a dreadful animal with a long tongue stretching from the slanderer to the slandered and this animal would be crushing him, he would never indulge in backbiting anybody. If a man was sure that "slandering is the food of the dogs of hell" and the slanderer would be ceaselessly devoured by them, he would never stoop to this vice. We occasionally indulge in backbiting only because we are not fully sure of the consequences of this bad habit.

Man's Deeds Will Assume a Concrete Shape

If man was convinced that whatever deeds he performed would be embodied in the hereafter, the good deeds assuming a good shape and the bad one a bad shape, and that he would have to give an account of all that he did, he would not commit a bad deed even unconsciously. We need not go into the details of this affair. It is enough to say that everything will be reckoned. If a person slandered anyone else, he would be accountable for doing that. If anybody harassed or injured the faithful, he would go to Hell. The good men would get Paradise. One must be fully convinced and sure of this procedure. It is not enough to read the law in the books or to understand it rationally. Knowing and understanding are quite different from heart-felt conviction. By heart I mean the real heart, not an organ of the body.

Man often knows and understands a truth, but not being firmly convinced of it, does not act according to what a belief in it requires. He acts only when he gets fully and firmly convinced. It is this firm conviction that is called faith. Simply knowing a Prophet is of no use. What is beneficial is having faith in him. It is not enough to prove the existence of Allah. What is necessary is to believe in Him and to obey His commandments whole-heartedly. With the true faith, everything becomes easy.

If a man was convinced that there was a Being who was the source of this world, that man was accountable and that his death would not be his end but would only mean his shifting to a more perfect stage, he would surely be saved from all errors and slips. The question is how can he be convinced? I have already described one aspect of the verse saying: *'With the name of Allah all praises belong to Allah'.* I once again emphasize that what I say is only a possibility, not a definite interpretation of the Qur'an. Anyhow, it appears that a man fully convinced that all praises belonged to Allah, could never have any polytheistic ideas in his mind, for whomsoever anybody praises, he actually praises some manifestation of Allah's glory.

Anybody who composes or intends to compose an ode in honour of the Holy Prophet or Imam Ali, that ode of his is for Allah because the Holy Prophet and the Imam are not but a great manefestation of Allah, and therefore their eulogy is the eulogy of Allah and His manifestation. A man who is convinced that all praises are due to Allah, would never indulge in bragging, boasting and self-praise. In fact man is self-conceited because he does not know himself. 'He who knows himself, knows Allah.'

A man knows Allah only when he is firmly convinced that he himself has no significance and that everything belongs to Allah only.

In fact, we neither know ourselves nor Allah. We have faith neither in ourselves nor in Him. We are neither sure that we are nothing nor that everything is Allah's. So long as we are not certain of these things, all arguments to prove the existence of Allah are of little use, and all that we do is based on egoism. All claims to leadership and chieftaincy are the result of self-conceit and personal vanity.

Self-Conceit is the Cause of All Troubles

Most of the troubles man faces are the result of his vanity and empty pride. Man loves himself and desires to be admired by others. But that is his mistake. He does not realize that he himself is nothing and that he is the property of another Being. Man's self-conceit and love of power are the cause of most of his troubles, sins and vices, which ruin him and drag him to Hell. Because of his selfishness man wants to control everything and becomes the enemy of others whom he rightly or wrongly considers to be a hindrance in his way. He knows no limits in this respect and that is the cause of all troubles, misfortunes and calamities.

All Praises Belong to Allah

It appears that the Book of Allah begins with the question

that includes all questions. When Allah says: 'All praises belong to Allah', we feel that so many questions have appeared before our eyes.

The Qur'an does not say that some praises belong to Allah. That means that if somebody says to another person: 'I know that Allah is Almighty and Omnipotent, but still I am praising you, not Allah', even then his praise would go to Allah, because all praises are Allah's praises.

The Qur'an says: *'All praises belong to Allah'*. This means that all kinds of praises in all conditions belong to Him. This short verse resolves many problems. This verse is enough to cleanse man's heart from the impurity of all kinds of polytheism provided he is fully convinced of its truth. He who said that he had never committed any sort of polytheism, said so because he had intuitively discovered this truth and grasped it mentally. This state of conviction cannot be secured by any argument. I do not mean that argument is of no use. It is also required. But it is only a means of understanding the question of Allah's monotheism according to one's intellectual capacity. To believe in it is the next step.

Philosophical Reasoning is not much Effective

Philosophy is a means not an end. Philosophical arguments help in understanding the problems, but they do not lead to a firm faith, which is a matter of intuition and taste. Even faith has several grades.

I hope that we will not be contented with reading and understanding the Qur'an, but will have a firm faith in every word of it, because it is the Divine Book that reforms man and wants to turn him into a being created by Allah from His *'Ism A'ẓam'* (grand name). Allah has gifted man with all kinds of faculties but many of his potential capabilities are dormant. The Qur'an wants to raise man from this lower position to the high position worthy of him. The Qur'an has come for this very purpose. Allah the Prophets have come to help man in getting out of the depths of selfishness and seeing the Divine light so that he may forget everything other than Allah.

May Allah bestow this favour on us also!

DIFFERENCE BETWEEN BISMILLAH OF EACH SURAH

The 'bismillah' preceding one surah is different from that preceding another surah.

We were saying to which word the preposition and the noun it governs in the 'bismillah' are related. One of the possibilities is that the 'bismillah' of every surah is related to some appropriate word of that very surah; for example in the Surah al-Hamd it may be related to the word, al-Hamd. In that case 'bismillahi al-hamdu lillahi' would mean: With the name of Allah all praises belong to Allah. On the basis of this possibility 'bismillah' would signify differently in every surah, for in each surah it would be referring to a different word. If it was related to the word 'al-hamdu' in the Surah 'al-Hamd,' we would have to look for some other appropriate word, for example, in the Surah 'al-Ikhlās'. According to a rule of theology, if somebody pronounced the bismillah with some surah and then wanted to recite another surah, he would have to repeat the bismillah, and the previous bismillah would not be enough for him. This rule shows that 'bismillah' does not have the same meaning everywhere. It has a different significance with each surah, although there are some people who wrongly maintain that 'bismillah' is not the part of any surah and it is quite a separate verse revealed as a benediction. If it is accepted that 'bismillah' was related to 'al-Hamd', then 'hamd' might include everything to which the word 'hamd' applied, that is every kind of praise expressed by anybody on any occasion. Thus the verse would mean that every praise expressed is with the name of Allah, because he who expresses it is himself a name of Allah; his organs and limbs are a name of Allah and the praise he expresses is also a name of

Allah. From this point of view every praise is with the name of Allah. We all are His names, or manifestations of His names, because we all are His signs, He is our originator, who has brought us into existence. The Divine Originator is in several ways different from a natural cause or agent. One of the points of difference is that anything that is brought into existence by the Divine Originator, or in other words, anything that emerges from the Divine source disappears in that very source. To illustrate this point to some extent, let us take up an example, although this example falls too short of the relation between the Creator and the created. Anyhow, let us take up the example of the sun and its rays. The rays have no existence separate from the sun. The same is the case with the Divine Originator or the Creator. Anything coming into existence from this source depends on it for its existence as well as continuation. There is no existing being which can continue to exist if Allah withdraws from it even for an amount the light on which its existence depends. As no existing thing has any independent position, it is said to be lost in its source.

Every Possibly Existing Thing Depends on Allah for its Existence as well as Continuation

Every possibly existing being is Allah's name, His deed and a manifestation of His glory. He Himself says: *Allah is the Light of the heavens and the earth.* (Surah an-Nūr, 24:35)[93] Every possibly-existing being is a manifestation of the glory of Allah, but not Allah. Everything that appears in the world is so related to the source of its origin that it cannot have any independent existence. That is why it has been said in the Qur'an that: *'Allah is the light of the heavens and the earth.'*

If it is admitted that the definite article *'al'* in al-Hamdu indicated 'Comprehensiveness', the verse would mean that every praise by whomsoever it might be expressed, takes place with the name of Allah.

As he who praises Allah, is himself, one of Allah's names, it may be said that in a sense the praiser and the praised are one and the same. One is the manifestation and the other is the manifester. Some sayings of the Holy Prophet, such as: 'You are as You have praised Yourself', and 'I seek refuge from You in You', point in this direction. As the relationship between the praiser and the praised is that of passing away of the former in the latter, the former cannot claim that it is he who praises. In fact it is the 'praised' who praises Himself, for the praiser has passed in Him.

According to another possibility it may be said that the definite article in 'al-hamdu' is not for showing comprehensiveness, but it indicates that the word, 'hamd' signifies general praise without any qualification being attached to it. In this case the praise of Allah performed by us is not actually His praise. His praise is only that which He performs Himself. The reason is that Allah is the Infinite Being while all others are finite. Any praise expressed by a finite being will naturally be finite and limited and therefore it cannot be the praise of the infinite Being.

While mentioning the first alternative we said that every praise was Allah's praise. Even when you think that you are commending the merits of a beautiful handwriting, you are actually extolling Allah. Similarly when you believe that you are paying tributes to the world, in that case also you are praising none but Allah. That is why, while describing the first alternative or the first possibility, we said that every praise was that of Allah, whosoever might be the praiser, for nothing except Allah has an independent existence. Every excellence, every beauty and every perfection belongs to Him only. If Allah withdraws the manifestation of His glory, nothing would be existing any longer.

All Existing Things Are A Manifestation of Allah's Glory

The existence of eveything depends on Allah's glory. While discussing above the first possibility, we pointed out that everything existing is the outcome of a divine light. Allah Himself says that He is the light of the heavens and the earth. If He takes away this light, everything is bound to disappear and come to an end. As nothing except Allah has any excellence of its own, nothing except Him is worth praising. In fact there is no excellence except His. He excels in His essence, His attributes and the state of His manifestation. All the merits attributed to anything or anyone else are His merits. Anybody who praises anyone for his

135

excellence and merit, actually praises Him. This is true if we accept the first possibility mentioned above.

In the case of the second possibility, which is also no more than a mere guess or a possibility, the word 'al-hamdu' does not imply totality or comprehensiveness. It only signifies abosolute praise without any qualification, restriction or any conception of its opposite being attached to it. But the praise that we perform is definitely not absolute. It is a particular praise expressed by a particular to a particular. We do not have access to the Absolute, nor can we perceive Him. So how can we praise Him. Even at the time of saying, 'al-hamdu lillah', you do not perceive the Absolute Truth, and as such the question of praising the Absolute does not arise.

Whatever praise is expressed, that actually is not the praise of Allah, but is the praise of some manifestation of His glory. In the case of the previous possibility no praise was that of Allah except that expressed by Himself. In this case the word 'ism' (name) in 'bismillah al-hamdu lillah' will not have the same meaning as we stated earlier when we said that everybody is Allah's name including you and me. Now the name of Allah is a symbol for His absolute and unqualified manifestation, the meaning of which can neither be explained nor grasped. It is this name of Allah that is praised and this praise can be expressed only by Allah Himself. This is a possible explanation based on the assumption that 'bismillah' is connected with 'al-hamdu lillah'. In short there are two possibilities. According to one possibility every praise is the praise of Allah and according to the other, praise of Allah is only the absolute and unqualified praise pronounced and performed by Allah Himself.

According to the first possibility there is no praise that is not of Allah; and according to the second possibility a praise can be of Allah only in its limited sense, not in its absolute sense. In this case the 'hamd' (praise) in 'al-hamdu lillah' will mean an absolute and unqualified praise. Allah can be praised only by the name that is worthy of Him. This rule is also a mere possibility.

There is another possibility that 'bismillah' might have no link with the surah following it. We know that some scholars maintain that the preposition and the noun in 'bismillah' are linked with an omitted but understood verb, *'Zahara'* (appeared), meaning, existence appeared. Thus the sentence would mean: Existence appeared with the name of Allah. In other words the name of Allah is the source of everything existing. This name of Allah is the same that is alluded to in a Prophetic tradition in the following words: 'Allah created His will Himself and created all other things through His Will.'

Here Allah's Will means 'the first manifestation of His glory' that was created by Him direct. It is this manifestation that has been called existence in the ellipsis mentioned above, namely 'Existence appeared'. On the basis of the assumption that *'bismillah'* is not linked with the surah following it, some grammarians hold that some such elliptical phrase as 'We seek the help' exists before *'bismillah'*. These grammarians may not realize, but in fact, whoever seeks the help of Allah, he invariably seeks the help of His name. It is not possible to seek His help in any other way. Though it is not necessary to always use the words, 'with the name of Allah', the fact remains that in everything His appearance or presence is His name and thus the help of His name is invariably sought.

It is this appearance the help of which we seek and with the help of which everything is done. The grammarians may not be aware of this conception, but it is a fact that seeking help means turning to Allah. This much as to which word *'bismillah'* is linked with. We said earlier that a name is the sign of the named. But there is nothing which is not the sign of Allah. Whatever you see, you will find that to be a sign of Him. Of course signs also have degrees. There are some names which are perfect signs of Him in every respect. There are some others that cannot be said to be so perfect signs. Anyhow, all existing things are His signs and manifestations in varying degrees. A tradition says: 'We are the beautiful names of Allah'. Anyhow, at the stage of manifestation the loftiest and the most splendid names of Allah are the Holy Prophet and the Imams who, unlike us who are still lying in the abyss of base desires, have reached the highest stages of spiritual journey towards Allah.

Emigration

We have not yet started even moving, but there are some

people who have not only came out of the abyss but have also emigrated from that stage. The Holy Qur'an says:

He who leaves his home, emigrating for the sake of Allah and His Messenger and is then overtaken by death, shall surely to be rewarded by Allah. (Surah an-Nisa', 4:100)[94]

According to one possible interpretation 'emigration' here might have meant going from oneself to Allah and 'home' might have meant one's lower self. In this case the whole verse would mean that there were some people who came out of the dark and dingy home of their base desires and continued to move towards Allah till they were overtaken by death, that is they passed away from self to survive in Allah, who was to reward them. In other words Allah Himself is their reward, for they attach no importance to Paradise and the bounties found therein. Their sole objective is Allah, because for a person who undertakes the path of self-annihilation and proceeds towards Allah and His Prophet, nothing is left which he could call his own. For him everything belongs to Allah. He who reaches this stage is surely to be rewarded by Allah. It may be noted that there are some who have reached their desired goal after emigration, while there are some others who though they emigrated, yet they could not reach the stage of passing away in Allah. The third category is that of the people like us who could not emigrate at all and are still groping in darkness. We are not only lost in the labyrinth of the mundane things but are also a prey to selfishness and egoism so much that we cannot see anything beyond our self-interest. We want everything for our selves, for we think that nothing except us has any value. We have not yet thought of emigrating, because our thinking is limited to this world only.

Seventy Years Back

We do not discard the faculties with which Allah has equipped us, but we use them for mundane purposes as if we were to live in this world for ever. As the time passes, we continue to get away farther and farther from the source to which we should have emigrated. According to a report once the Holy Prophet was sitting along with his companions when a loud sound of something falling was heard. The Holy Prophet's companions were startled. They enquired what had happened. According to the report the Holy Prophet said: 'A stone was rolling down in the middle of Hell. Now after 70 years it has fallen into a well located at the other end of it. This was the sound of its fall.' This event is said to be an allegorical description of a wicked man who died at the age of 70. We are all rolling down towards the same hole. I may go there at the age of 80. You will also go to that side in a few years.

Worst Enemy

It is our selfishness and egoism that are responsible for our present condition. The following maxim expresses the same truth: 'Your worst enemy is your lower self that is within you.' It is this idol which man worships most and to which he is attached most. Man cannot become godly unless he smashes this idol, because an idol and God cannot go together. An egoist can never be a devout person. We may apparently be religious, but in reality are idol-worshippers unless we get rid of our selfishness and egoism, which are the root-cause of all our troubles and evils. While offering prayers we say: *'You alone we worship and You alone we ask for help'*, but unfortunately all our thoughts remain concentrated on ourselves. We offer prayers to serve our own selfish interests and thus in reality worship ourselves only.

Egoism the Cause of All Quarrels

All wars in the world are due to man's egoism. Believers are not expected to fight each other. If they do, they are not believers.

A dishonest and selfish man wants to seize everything for his own benefit. It is this attitude which gives rise to all sorts of troubles. I want a position for myself; you want it for yourself. As both of us cannot occupy it at one and the same time, a quarrel is bound to arise. I want to take this chair; you also want it. When I and you want to take the same thing, naturally there will be an altercation. If two persons attempt to occupy this country, a war would ensue. All wars and battles are the outcome of selfishness, the result of the conflict of personalities and their interests. As the holy men are not selfish, they do not fight each other. Even if all the holy men gather together at one place, there would be no fight and no quarrel among them, for whatever they do, they do for the sake of Allah. As they are neither selfish nor egoistic, they do not oppose each other.

They all have the same source and the same direction. It is we who are lying in a well that is as dark as possibly can be. This darkness is that of our egoism. So long as we do not give up our egoism, we cannot get out of this darkness. We are selfish and self-conceited. That is why we do not attach importance to others and consider ourselves alone to be all important. If a thing is advantageous to us, we accept it. If it is not, we reject it howsoever right it may be. We believe only that thing, which is in our favour. All this is egoism and selfishness. It is this attitude that is the cause of all our troubles and is responsible for all misfortunes of humanity. I want to pursue my interest and you want to pursue yours. There can be no godliness so long as selfishness persists. Then what is the remedy? Man has within himself an idol-temple. It is not easy for him to get out of it. He needs Divine help, a hidden hand which may take him out of this dungeon. The Prophets have come for this very purpose.

Aim of the Prophets

All the Prophets and the revealed Books have come only to smash this idol-temple and to take man out of it. The Prophets have come to set up a divine order in this fiendish world ruled by the Devil whom we all obey. Our base desires are the Devil's manifestation. The greatest Devil being our own appetitive soul, whatever we do become devilish. That is the reason why nothing that we do is free from selfishness. The Devil holds influence over us and we are dictated by the Devil. We can get out of this labyrinth only if we emigrate from our present stage, act according to the teachings of the Prophets and other holy men and cease to be selfish and egoistic. If we do so we will gain an inconceivable success. This emigration is essential for anybody who aspires to attain to perfection.

Major Jihād

He who wishes to get out of the dungeon of egoism, must

140

strive to emigrate from his present state. According to a Prophetic tradition once certain companions of the Holy Prophet came back from a Jihād (holy war). The Holy Prophet said to them: 'You have returned after carrying out a minor jihād, but still owe a major one". A major jihād is carried out against one's lower self. All other jihāds are subservient to this one. Any other jihād performed by us will be worth the name only if we succeed in the major jihād. Otherwise all other jihāds will be nothing more than a satanic act. If a person takes part in the holy war with a view to obtain a slave girl or to provide for his livelihood, these very things would be his reward. But if a person performs jihād for the sake of Allah, then it would be Allah's responsibility to reward him. In fact the reward depends on the quality of the job performed. Obviously there is a vast difference between the quality of our performance and that of the holy men and friends of Allah, for our aims and objects are quite different from theirs.

Devotion is the Criterion

Has it been said without any reason that at the war of Ditch (Khandaq) one stroke of Imam Ali's sword was more meritorious than all the acts of worship performed by the jinn and mankind? Apparently his stroke was no more than a blow to kill a person. But it had a far greater significance. At that time Islam was facing the combined forces of infidelity and if Muslims had been defeated in that encounter, the very existence of Islam would have been endangered. There is still another aspect of the question, and that is the dedication and devotion involved in Imam Ali's act. Once while Imam Ali was on the chest of an enemy, he spat on the Imam's face. Imam Ali at once got off so that his act might not be affected by the motive of personal vengeance.

The spirit of such a stroke is certainly superior to all acts of worship. It is this spirit which gives the acts of a true believer their proper meaning and significance. Outwardly the acts performed by the polytheists and the monotheists, the idolaters and these who do not worship the idols, look alike. Apparently there is no difference in them. Abu Sufyan also used to offer prayers. Mu'awiyah was himself the Imam of Congregational

141

prayers. They performed their religious acts like others. It is the spirit of prayer that accords sublimity to it. If the spirit is there, prayer is a devotional act. Otherwise it is nothing more than a mere show and a fraud. This principle applies to us also. We simply deceive each other.

Our Worship is For Paradise

All our devotional acts serve our own interests only. Those who are more pious among us perform them for the sake of Paradise. Take away the temptation of Paradise, then see who performs them. Imam Ali's case is different. He was in fact fond of the acts of devotion and worship. It is said about him that he loved the acts of devotion and embraced them. As a matter of principle it is not of much significance to perform acts of worship for the sake of Paradise. A person who has reached the stage of passing away in Allah, attaches no importance to Paradise. He actually does not care for it. Paradise and Hell are alike for him who has annihilated himself. He praises Allah because he believes that Allah deserves devotions. This position is attained by those who are fond of acts of worship. They worship Allah because they believe that He is fit for being worshipped.

There are many degrees of devotion. Anyhow, the first step is shunning the selfishness and getting out of the narrow hole of egoism.

For this purpose the first thing to be done is to wake up for the sake of Allah and not to remain sleeping. At present we are asleep, although apparently awake. Our waking is that of animals, not of man.

A tradition says that people are asleep; they will wake up when they will die. At that time they will realize that they were totally unconscious of the real situation. A Qur'anic verse says: 'Hell is surrounding the unbelievers'. It means that Hell is even now surrounding them but man being in a state of unconsciousness does not perceive that. When he will gain his consciousness, he will realize that there is a fire all round him. We all have to go by this path. Therefore it is better for us to wake up and walk along the 'straight path' shown to us by the Prophets.

Prophets Come to Reform Men

Reforming mankind is the mission of all Prophets. For this purpose they set up a just order. It is man who is just or unjust. To establish a just order means turning the wicked into the righteous and the unbelievers into believers. The Prophets' job is to transform the people. If people were left to do what they liked, they would certainly fall into the deep pit of hell. It is the Prophets who guide them to the right path. Alas! We are not yet following it. I am 70 years old, but am still where I was. I have not emigrated. Perhaps my condition will not change till the end of my life. Anyhow, it is essential for everybody to follow the straight path. There is no alternative.

An Appeal to the Youth

You are young and can adopt this path better. Do not worry about us, for we are already a spent force. You can purify your soul easily as you are closer to the world of divinity than we the old people. Comparatively you have deteriorated less but things are becoming worse day by day. The more delay will make the matter more difficult. It is difficult for an old man to be reformed, but a young man can be reformed quickly.

It is easier to reform thousands of young men than to reform an old man. Therefore do not postpone the task of reform to old age. Begin this work while you are still young. Follow the teachings of the Prophets. This is the starting point. The Prophets have shown us the way we should follow. While we are unaware of it, the Prophets are familiar with the way of safety and security. If you want safety, follow the way shown by them. Gradually pay less and less attention to your desires. You will not get the desired result immediately, but gradually you can get rid of your egoism. One day all our desires will come to nought. It is not in our interest to pay attention to them. Lasting is only that which relates to Allah. The Qur'an says: *What is with you will come to an end, what is with Allah will remain.* (Surah an-Nahl, 16:96)[95]

Man has that 'which is with you' as well as that 'which is with Allah'. All the things that keep your attention directed to yourselves, are that 'which is with you'. All these things will vanish. But those things that keep your attention directed to Allah, are lasting and permanent.

143

Continue Your Effort Till You Gain Complete
Victory Over Your Lower Self

You and we should make every effort to change our present state. Those who achieved success in their struggle against the unbelievers, never worried as to how many people were with them. After all it was he* who said that even if all the Arabs were combined against him, he would not give up. As he was doing the duty assigned to him by Allah, there was no question of failure in it, what to say of being repulsed. Then there is another question. Suppose you retreat, but where will you go to? Those who advanced in the jihāds, went forward without caring for their lives or their personal interests. They fought against their lower self to the utmost degree. The struggle of those who occupied a higher spiritual position was proportionately more intense. In fact man can achieve nothing unless he fights against his lower self. He cannot go forward unless he ignores his desires and keeps clear of this world, which is another name of base desires. The desires of every body are his world. It is this world which has been denounced, not the physical world.

This world is within you. When you pay attention to your lower self, you yourself become this world. Thus this world of everybody is within him. It is this world which has been condemned, not the sun, the moon or any other natural object. All the natural objects, being the signs and manifestations of Allah, have been praised.

It is this world in the above mentioned sense that deprives man from gaining proximity to Allah. May Allah grant us success in getting out of the deep dungeon of egoism. It is the friends of Allah who have gained success in being delivered from the catastrophe of egoism.

---

* Imam Ali (Peace be upon him).

144

RELATIONSHIP BETWEEN ALLAH AND CREATION

We were talking as to which word the word *'ism'* in *'bismillah'* is connected. In this regard there are several possibilities as I have mentioned.

The Creator and the Created

We cannot understand certain questions in this regard unless we know what sort of relationship there exists between Allah and the creation. We talk about this relationship either parrot-like and repeat some set words, or occasionally in addition to that advance some arguments also. A stage higher than this is the privilege of some other people. Anyhow the relationship between Allah and the creation is not of the sort that exists, for example, between father and son, that is between two things existing independently but related to each other. The sun and its rays are an example of a closer relationship. In this case also the sun and its rays are two different things, each having a separate existence to some extent. Man and his mental and physical faculties are an example of another kind of relationship. Even in this case man and his faculties are not identical, though they are closely related. Unlike all these examples the relationship between the existing things and Allah, Who is the source of their existence, is of quite a different kind and cannot be compared to any of the relationships mentioned above. At several places in the Qur'an and the traditions the relationship between Allah and His creation has been described as Allah's glory. The Qur'an says: *When his Lord revealed His glory to the mountain.* (Surah al-A'rāf, 7:143)[96] .

145

There is a sentence in the Samāt Supplication which says: 'By the light of Your glory You revealed to the mountain and thus sent it down crashing. . . '.

At another place the Qur'an says: *Allah takes away the souls at the times of their death.* (Surah az-Zumar, 39:42)[97] while it is known that taking away the souls is the job of the Death Angel. If somebody kills a person, in that case also it is said that he has put him to death. At another place the Qur'an says: *You did not throw when you threw (the pebbles), but Allah threw.* (Surah al-Anfāl, 8:17)[98] All this is the description of a light and a glory. If we ponder over this concept, certain questions occur to our mind.

Meanings of Al-Hamd

We said earlier that the first possibility about the definite article in *al-Hamdu* is that it might be denoting comprehensiveness. In that case *hamd* (praise) would mean all praises, and the word *'hamd'* as well as the word, *'ism'* will have a sense of multitude. From this point of view *'al-hamdu lillahi'* would mean that every praise that is made is that of Allah, for it is always the praise of some aspect of His manifestation or glory. The sun manifests itself in its rays. Man is manifested in his seeing and hearing faculties. Allah manifests Himself far more clearly in every creation of His. Therefore when anything is praised actually a manifestation of Allah's glory is praised. As all the existing things are the signs of Allah, they are His names. According to the second possibility we mentioned, the meaning would be diametrically different, and *'al-hamdu lillahi'* would signify that no praise made by any praiser was that of Allah, although in this case also His glory is revealed in all the objects which are praised. But our praise cannot be absolute, nor are we capable of praising the Absolute Being.

Anyhow, as all pluralities are lost and aborbed in the unity of the Absolute Being, it may be said that from one angle even in this case it is the Absolute Being that is praised. The only difference is of the angle from which you look at this issue. If you look at it from the angle of plurality, then every praise would be that of Allah, every existing thing would be His name and every name would be different from other names. Accord-

146

ing to this possibility the meaning of *bismillah* will be different from its meaning according to the other possibility. The main feature of this possibility is that a sense of numerousness is implied in the conception of *'ism'* or name. Allah is the name in which the stage of multitude and detail is taken into consideration. This name is the 'Exalted Name' in which Allah's glory is revealed.

Divine Glory in Everything

The glory of Allah's Exalted Name is revealed in everything. Allah's name *Rahmān* (Beneficent) is the reflexion of His beneficence in the state of action and His name *Rahīm* (Merciful) is the reflexion of His mercy in the state of action. The same applies to *'rabbil 'alamin'* (Lord of the Universe), *'iyyaka na'budu'* (You we worship) etc. According to the second possibility, *hamd* (praise) in *'al-hamdu lillah'* signifies absolute and unqualified praise. In this case the conception of *Allah, Rahmān* and *Rahīm* will also be a little different. According to the first possibility *'ism'* (name) means every existing thing with reference to its function. In other words, as the function of anything changes, it becomes a different *ism* or name. But according to the second possibility *'hamd'* in *'al-hamdu lillah'* signifies unqualified and absolute *hamd* with the names of *Allah, Rahmān* and *Rahīm.*

Allah alone can perform such a *hamd* or praise and He does so with a name that is the name of the manifestation of His glory at the stage of self. In other words He praises Himself with some of His names at this stage. Allah is the comprehensive name at the stage of self, not at the stage of manifestation. Allah's every name at this stage is His glory. *Rahmān* (Munificent) is the name of His munificence at the stage of self. *Rahīm* (Merciful) is the name of His mercy at the stage of self. The same is the case with such other names as *Rub* (Sustainer) etc. These conceptions can be proved by means of higher philosophy which is different from commonly known ordinary philosophy. But the case of the holy men, the friends of Allah is quite different. They have perceived and grasped these things by traversing the stages of spiritual journey.

147

Prophets' Observations and Experiences

The holy men cannot tell others what they see. Even in the Holy Qur'an many sublime truths have been mentioned in a simplified and diluted form so that they may be communicated even to the ordinary people not yet free from their low and base desires. In this respect the hands of the Holy Prophet himself were tied. He was not allowed to explain the truths to the people in clear terms and therefore he stated the truths in a weakened form. The Qur'an has many degrees of meanings and has been revealed in 70 or 70,000 layers. Having been reduced in intensity in each layer it has come to us in a form which we may be able to understand with our limited intellect.

Telling us about Himself Allah says: *Will they not regard the camels how they have been created?* (Surah al-Ghāshiya, 88:17)[99]

It is our bad luck that while describing lower creations like sun, sky, earth and man, the Prophets felt that there was a knot in their tongue and that they could not express the truth in clear words: *O my Lord! Open my chest for me; make the matter easy and untie the knot in my tongue.* (Surah Tāhā, 20:25)[100]

Other Prophets also had knots in their tongues as well as their hearts, and for that reason they could not express the truths exactly as they perceived them. They tried to a certain extent explain them to us through examples and illustrations. When an example of camel is used to explain to us the existence of Allah, it should not be difficult to understand where we stand. In fact we are no better than animals, and as such the knowledge we can obtain must be very defective.

As for the Prophets the Qur'an says at one place: *And when his Lord revealed His glory to the mountain, He sent it crashing down. And Moses fell down senseless.* (Surah al-A'rāf, 7:143)[101] When Allah imparted special spiritual training to Moses he said to Allah: *'My lord, let me see you.'* Obviously an eminent Prophet cannot ask for seeing Allah with his physical eyes. Therefore his request must have been for a kind of seeing appropriate to the seer and the object to be seen. But even this kind of seeing was not possible, Moses said to Allah: *'My Lord! Let me see you.'* The answer was: *'you will not see Me.'* Allah further said: *'But gaze upon the mountain.'* What is meant by the mountain here? Does it signify Mount Sinai? Was it that the glory that could not be revealed to Moses, could be revealed to this mountain? If some other people had been present at the Mount Sinai at that time, could they also see the revelation of Allah's glory? The sentence, *'Gaze upon the mountain'* implies a promise. Allah said: *'You cannot see Me. But gaze upon the mountain. If it stands still in its place, then you will see Me.'* (Surah al-A'rāf, 7:143)[102] There is a possibility that the mountain here might have meant the remnant of egoism still left in Moses. As the result of the revelation of glory the mountian was smashed. In other words egoism of Moses was completely done away with. *'And Moses fell down senseless.'* That means that Moses reached the stage of completely passing away of his human attributes.

What happened to Moses is a story for us, but for the Prophets it is an experience. This experience has been narrated to us in the form of a story because we are not yet free from egoism. The mention of the mountain or the Mount Sinai is only for our sake.

Meaning of Glory

People like us think that the glory revealed to Prophet Moses was a light seen by him. It might have been seen by others too. What a novel idea! As if it was a light that could be seen by everybody. Jibrā'il (Gabriel), — the Holy Ghost used to recite the Qur'an before the Holy Prophet. Could others hear him? We do not have the slightest idea of the reality and our knowledge is confined to hearsay.

The Prophets can be compared to a person who saw a dream or witnessed something, but is unable to describe what he saw and others are also not fit to understand what he says. The same is the case with the Prophets. Neither they can describe what they see, nor can we understand what they say. No doubt the Prophets have said something, but we can understand only that which is comprehensible to us. The Qur'an contains everything. It has the rules of law as well as the stories, to the underlying idea of which we do not have access, but we can understand what they apparently mean. There are certain things in the Qur'an by which everybody can be benefited to some extent, but in the real sense the Holy Qur'an could be understood only by him to whom it was addressed. Of course those Holy men who were either trained and instructed by the Holy Prophet direct or later imbibed his teachings, also understand the Qur'an.

Through the Holy Ghost the Qur'an was revealed to the heart of the Holy Prophet. The Qur'an itself says: *The Holy Ghost descended with it on your heart.* (Surah ash-Shu'ra, 26:193)[103]

The Qur'an was revealed many a time and each time it was revealed in a more diluted form. The Qur'an says: *We revealed it on the Night of Power.* (Surah al-Qadr, 97:1)[104] On each Night of Power the same glory is revealed, but on a reduced scale.

In short the Qur'an was revealed to the heart of the Holy Prophet many a time. It was revealed in stages, grades and layers till it finally assumed the form of words.

Nature of the Qur'an

The Holy Qur'an is not a collection of words, nor is it a thing that could be seen, heard or expressed in words. Nor is it a mode or a quality. It has been accorded an easy form for the benefit of us, who could neither hear it nor see it. Those who were really benefited by the Qur'an, were trained on different lines. Their method of deriving benefit from the Qur'an was quite different. They had a special way of attending to the source from which the Qur'an has emerged. Glory of Allah is revealed from the hidden world and reaches the physical world after having been reduced gradually in intensity. As there is a vast difference between the various grades of the hidden world and the corresponding grades of the physical world, similarly there is a vast difference between our perception and the perception of those who are superior to us and then between their perception and the perception of those who are still higher. The Prophets and the Imams enjoy the highest grade of perception. Only they can have that divine glory revealed to them which was witnessed by Prophet Musa and which is mentioned in the Qur'an when it says: *When his Lord revealed His glory to the mountain.* This even has been hinted at in the *Samāt*

Supplication also. The Qur'an says: *When Allah revealed His glory to the mountain,* a voice was heard saying: *'Moses, surely I am Allah'.* Each of these things is perfectly all right in itself. As for the question. What should we do if we want to learn the Qur'an, it must be remembered that these things are not a subject for learning and teaching.

Exegesis of the Qur'an

If we are interested in the interpretation of the Qur'an, we have to study those commentaries which are well-known and commonly available. Some of these commentaries occasionally mention some of these subjects, but all that they say amounts to leading the blind by the blind. The Qur'an deals with all these questions, but only for him who can understand them. It has been said: 'Only he to whom it is addressed, knows the Qur'an.' This fact has been alluded to in the following verses: *The Holy Spirit descended with it on your heart. We revealed it on the Night of Power.* Nobody can witness the reality of the Qur'an except the Holy Prophet, who was the first addressee of the Qur'an. Here there is no question of intellectual perception nor of any proof or argument. It is a question of witnessing the truth, not with the eye or with the mind, but with the heart, and for that matter, not an ordinary heart, but the heart of the Holy Prophet, who himself was the heart of the world. The Holy Prophet witnessed the reality of the Qur'an. As its first addressee he knew the Qur'an well. But even he expressed the truth in veiled words and by means of examples. How can we explain sunlight to a blind man. What language should we use for this purpose? Where can we find the appropriate words? All that we can say is that sight is possible in the light only. What can he who has seen the divine light tell the one who has not seen it? What can he who has a knot in his tongue tell him who has a knot in his ears. The Prophets had a knot in their tongues because their listeners lacked the capacity of understanding what they said.

The Holy Prophet's Embarrasment

This knot was causing a great deal of worry and inconvenience to the Holy Prophet who wondered to whom he

151

should explain the Qur'an which was revealed to his heart. Perhaps there were a good number of things which could not be told to anybody except the person who was occupying the position of absolute *Wilāyat*. The Holy Prophet is reported to have said: 'No Prophet has been tortured so much as I have been.' If this report is correct, it might have implied among other things that the Holy Prophet was unable to convey to others what he wanted to convey. His position in this respect was that of a father keen to show the sun to his blind child. His frustration can easily be imagined. The father wants to explain the sunlight to his child, but on account of child's blindness he is unable to do so. He does not find suitable words to convey what he wants to convey.

It is said that knowledge is a great hurdle. It prevents people from undertaking gnostic journey and instead involves them into intellectual questions and scientific theories. For the Holy men knowledge is the greatest barrier and veil. The more the knowledge, the bigger hurdle it will prove. Man being egoistic and self-centred, feels elated by his limited knowledge and thinks that there is nothing beyond what he knows. Only a few persons guided by the help of Allah refrain from such false notion and silly thinking.

Tendency of Monopolization in Knowledge

Everybody thinks that knowledge is confined to what he has learnt and all achievements depend on it. The jurist holds that the only branch of knowledge that exists is jurisprudence. The gnostic things that there is nothing except gnosis. The philosopher is of the opinion that everything other than philosophy is useless. The engineer maintains that only engineering is important. Now-a-days it is said that knowledge is only that which can be proved by experiment and observation. Everything else is unscientific. Thus knowledge is a big hurdle. There are other hurdles too, but this is the biggest.

Knowledge, which was expected to be a beacon light and a guide has became a hurdle, an obstacle. That is true of all kinds of formal knowledge. Formal knowledge does not allow man to become what he should. It makes him egoistic. Its adverse effect on an untrained mind leads man backward. As knowledge accumulates, its disadvantages and harmful effects grow. It is no use sowing seeds in a barren soil. A barren soil and untrained mind averse to the name of Allah are alike. Some people are scared by philosophical questions, although philosophy is a branch of formal knowledge. Similarly philosophers shy of from gnosis, while the gnostics consider all formal knowledge to be an idle talk.

Formal Knowledge is a Hurdle
in the Way of Remembering Allah

I do not know what we should become, but I know that our training should be such that our formal knowledge should not be a hurdle in the way of remembering Allah. This is an important question. Our pre-occupation with knowledge should not make us forget Allah. Our pride on account of our knowledge should not make us self-conceited and away from the source of all perfection. Such a pride is common among the scholars and intellectuals irrespective of the fact whether they are the scholars of medical sciences, Islamic sciences or rational sciences. If heart is not purified the emergence of such a pride is natural. It keeps man away from Allah.

How is it that the study of a book often absorbs man's entire attention, but prayer does not? I had a friend who is dead now. Whenever he forgot something and could not recollect it, he used to say: 'Let me stand up for offering prayers. I hope I'll immediately recollect it.' He thought as if while offering prayers man was not required to pay attention to Allah and was free to think of anything on the face of earth, even to try to solve any scientific question if he wanted. Knowledge which was meant to help man reaching his goal can thus prevents him from doing so. Religious law and other branches of religious knowledge are only a means, which enable us to act according to Islamic injunctions. Even action according to Islamic injunctions is not an end in itself. The real objective is to awaken our conscience so that we may be able to reach the veils of divine light after crossing the veils of darkness. According to a tradition there are 70,000 veils of divine light. The number of the veils of darkness is also stated to be the same. Further, the veils of divine light are also after all veils or screens. We have not yet

153

come out of the veils of darkness, to say nothing of the veils of light. We are still wriggling in the veils of darkness.

As the luck would have it, the sciences whether religious or rational, have affected us adversely.

Mental and Concrete

Some of those who are wandering about in darkness call the rational sciences mental sciences. Probably what they mean is that these sciences have no concerete existence. Anyway, all sciences are a means of reaching a goal. Any science that does not serve that purpose is not fit to be called a science. Any knowledge which does not allow man to achieve the objective for which the Prophets have come, is darkness and a barrier. The Prophets came to take the people out of the darkness of this world and to lead them to the sole source of light. They wanted man to pass away in absolute light. They want the drop of water to be mingled in the ocean and lose its existence. (It must be remembered that the simile does not represent the position fully.)

All Prophets came for this very purpose and all sciences are a means of achieving this goal. The real existence is of that Light only. We are but nonentity. All Prophets came to pull us out of all sorts of darkness and to lead us to the sole and absolute Light, the source of all existence.

Sometimes even scholastic theology becomes a hurdle and a barrier. In this branch of knowledge arguments are adduced to prove the existence of Allah, but in some cases even these arguments lead people away from Him. The method followed by scholastic theology is not that of the Prophets and the Holy men who never adduced arguments. Of course they were aware of the arguments, but did not use them, because they did not like this method of proving the existence of Allah.

Imam Husayn addressing Allah once said: 'When were You not there?' When Allah has always existed, where is the necessity of proving His existence? It is a different thing that a blind eye does not see Him.

Rising for Allah

The Qur'an mentions the first stage of rising in these

words: *Say: I advise you to do one thing: that you rise for Allah.* (Surah Saba, 34:46)[105]

The gnostics say that this verse describes the first stage of spiritual journey. The Manāzil al-Sā'irin* also says so. But what the verse mentions may be only a prelude, not a stage. Anyhow, what is important is that Allah through his well-beloved Prophet offers an advice and asks people to rise. This is the starting point. Those who are sleeping have been told to get up and rise for Allah only. This is the only piece of advice which we have not so far listened to. We have not yet begun walking for Allah. We do walk, but for our own sake. Those who are good and pious, are also good for their own sake only. Yes, there are some friends of Allah whose ways are different. The advice given in the verse is for us who are sleeping. Those friends of Allah have gone to the higher world. We will also be carried there. Nobody can claim that he would for ever stay here. We are being pushed away by the angels controlling our organs. We will go there, but shall we go with all our veils and darknesses?

Love of the World is the Root
Cause of all Troubles

Besides being the source of all things, love of the world is the main cause of all mistakes, as a well-known maxim says: 'Love of the world sometimes makes a man so irresponsible that if he feels that Allah has withdrawn something from him, he, in spite of being a believer, gets offended'.

It is said that when a person is about to die the devils who do not want him to die as a believer bring before him certain things to which he was very much attached. For example if he was a student and loved books, the devils would bring before him his favourite books and would threaten him to set them on fire if he would not deviate from his faith. The same way the devils threat the person who loves his child or is strongly interested in something else.

It is not correct to think that a worldly person is he who possesses wealth. One may possess a lot of wealth, but still may

* The name of a book.

155

not be worldly. On the other hand, a student possessing only one book may be worldly if he was too much attached to it. Attachment to worldly things is the criterion of being worldly. Because of this attachment a person may become hostile to Allah when he finds himself at the time of his death forced to quit his favourite things and thus may die as an enemy of Allah. Therefore we must lessen our attachment to worldly things. Obviously we have to quit this world one day or other. So it does not make any difference whether we are attached to the world or not.

Suppose you owned a book. Whether you were attached to it or not, it would remain with you. You could use it and could get benefited by it. Similarly if a house was yours, you could use it in every case. Therefore diminish attachment as much as you can, and if possible, give it up altogether, for it is this attachment that causes trouble. It is because of self-love that man gets attached to the world. Love of self, power and position ruins man. Love of chair and love of pulpit both show attachment to the world. All these are veils, 'some of them above others.' Instead of saying worldly people are those who possess such and such things, we should see how far we are attached to the things we possess. It is only because of this attachment that we criticize others.

Egoism

A man who is not egoistic, does not criticize others. If some of us find fault with others, it is because they consider themselves to be cultured and perfect and regard others imperfect and faulty. There is a couplet which I would not recite because it is liable to some objection. Anyway, it says: 'I am just what you say, but are you what you pretend to be!'

Here in the seminary we show that we have come here for the sake of Allah. We call ourselves 'Allah's troops'. Are we really so? At least we should not pretend to be what we are not.

Is hypocrisy something else? Hypocrisy is not merely that a man pretends like Abu Sufyan to be religious while he is not so. It is also hypocrisy that a man claims to be what he is not. Anyway, hypocrisy has degrees, some of which are more severe than others. Another important thing is that when a man departs this world it should not be said about him that he was merely inviting people to the next world and was indifferent to the present one. The Prophets invited people to the next world, but in this world also they used to set up justice and fair play.

The Holy Prophet was very close to Allah, but he used to say that he sought the forgiveness of Allah seventy times every day as he felt his heart somewhat perturbed. Naturally for a man who wants always to be with his beloved, it is perturbing to meet other people and talk to them. Suppose a man came to you to ask you about a rule of law. He is a very good man, and you know that it is your duty as well as a meritorious act to answer his question, but you still feel perturbed because at that time you wanted to be with your beloved.

'Because of the perturbation of my heart I seek the forgiveness of Allah seventy times every day.' The Holy Prophet is reported to have said some such thing. But for us it would not be proper to involve ourselves in such things. At least we should be as we give ourselves out. If we have a mark of prostration on our forehead, we must not be showy in our prayers. If we profess to be pious, we must not deceive anybody, we must not take usury. Those who say that spiritual sciences make a man idler, are mistaken. The man who taught these sciences to the people and who next to the Holy Prophet knew the spiritual truths more than anybody else, according to history, took up his shovel and went out to work the same day as he pledged his allegiance to the Holy Prophet. There is no contradiction between spiritual sciences and physical work.

Those who, in order to keep people busy with their worldly affairs, prevent them from praying and saying liturgy etc., are not aware of real facts. They do not know that it is prayer that builds human character and teaches man how to live in this world respectably. The Prophets prayed and said liturgy etc. and it were they who established justice in the world and rose against the wrongdoers. Imam Husayn also did the same thing. Just see his Supplication of the Day of Arafah and ponder over it.

All their achievements were due to this prayers. It is prayers that make man attentive to Allah. If man recites them properly, then as the result of divine favour brought about by them, his self-attachment is diminished, but his efficiency is in

157

no way affected adversely. Not only that but he becomes more active and ever ready to render service to his fellow human beings.

Some ignorant people criticize the books containing supplications. They do not know what kind of men these books build. Some of these supplications such as Munājat Sha'bāniyah, Dua' Kumayl, Dua' Yawmul 'Arafah, Dua' Samāt etc. have come down to us from our Imams. What kind of men do these prayers build. Those who recited the Munajāt Sha'bāniya, wielded the sword also.

According to reports all Imams recited Munājat Sha'bāniya. I have not read anywhere about any other prayer or supplication that it was recited by all Imams. Those who recited this prayer, also fought against the unbelievers. These prayers take man out of darkness and he who comes out of darkness becomes the real man. Then he does everything for Allah's sake. If he wields the swords, he does so for the sake of Allah; if he fights, he does so for the sake of Allah and if rises, he does so for the sake of Allah. It is absolutely wrong to say that prayers make man idle and useless. Those who say such things, to them this world is everything. They believe everything beyond this world to be fantastic. But one day they will find that the things they thought to be fantastic were real and the things they thought to be real were fantastic. In fact prayers, sermons and the books like Nahjul Balaghah and Mafātihul Jinān help man in building his personality.

When one becomes a real man, he automatically begins to act according to true Islamic principles. He cultivates land, but his cultivation is for Allah. He fights but only against the infidels and wrongdoers. Such people are the monotheists and pious prayerers. Those who accompanied the Holy Prophet and the Commander of the Faithful were devoted worshippers.

Imam Ali himself used to offer prayers while fighting was going on. Fighting and praying went on side by side. Once while fighting was going on somebody asked him a question. He immediately rose and delivered a sermon. Somebody said: 'Sermon even on this occasion?' He said: 'It is for what we fight.' According to a report he added: 'We do not fight against Mu'awiyah to capture Syria. Syria has no importance to us.'

The Holy Prophet and Imam Ali were not keen to conquer Syria and Iraq. They wanted to deliver the people from the oppressors and to reform them morally. It was they who were ardent worshippers. Dua' Kumayl was taught by Imam Ali to Kumayl, who himself was a warrior.

Effect of Prayer on Heart

To prevent people from praying and reciting prayer books one day some wicked people, the followers of Kasrawi etc. collected gnosis and prayer books and set them on fire. These people did not understand what prayer was and what effect it produced on heart. They did not know that all good things in the world were due to the pious prayerers who prayed and remembered Allah. Although some people repeat their prayer simply parrot-like, yet it produces some effect, for the people who pray are better than those who do not.

A man who offers prayers, of howsoever low quality his prayers may be, is better than a man who does not offer prayers. The former is more cultured. He does not commit theft. Look at the list of the offenders and criminals. How many of them are the students of religious sciences? How many mullas drink wine, commit theft or perpetrate other crimes? It is true that the smugglers include some unreal mullas and sufi-looking persons, but those wicked people neither offer prayers nor do they perform any other meritorious acts. They have assumed this disguise just to achieve their vicious ends. Among those who recite prayers and observe Islamic injunctions, there are few who have ever been charge-sheeted for any serious crime.

The world order rests on the people who pray. Praying must not be done away with. It will be wrong to divert the attention of our young men from prayer on the plea that instead of prayer the recitation of the Qur'an should be popularized. What paves the way for the Qur'an must not be given up. It is a diabolic insinuation that the Qur'an should be recited and the tradition and supplications to Allah should be abandoned.

The Qur'an Without Traditions and Prayer

Those who say that they do not want supplications, would never be able to popularize the Qur'an. Their deceptive ideas are mere devilish insinuations. The young men should consider who have rendered better service to society, those who took keen interest in traditions, supplication and liturgy or those who said that the Qur'an was enough for them. All these charitable institutions and religious endowments are the works of those who offered prayers and recited the Qur'an, not of others.

All the religious schools and hospitals were built by those members of the rich nobility of the previous era who offered prayers. This system should continue. People should be encouraged to keep their attention to the good works. Besides helping in the achievement of spiritual excellence, these prayers and supplications help in the administration of the country also. Those who attend the mosques and pray, do not violate the law of the country nor do they breach the public order. This in itself is a great service to society. Society consists of individuals. Even if fifty per cent individuals in a society, being busy with prayers and supplications, did not commit crimes, it would be a happy situation! A craftsman who does his job honestly and earns his livelihood, does not commit sins. Similarly those who commit murders and robberies, are not interested in spiritual matters. If they had been interested in them, they would not have committed such crimes.

Prayers and supplications play a significant role in training society. These supplications have been taught by Allah and His Prophet. The Holy Qur'an says: *Say: My Lord would not have cared for you, if you had not been calling Him.* (Surah al-Furqān, 25:77)[106]

If you read the Qur'an, you will find that Allah Himself urges people to pray to Him and says that *'He would not have cared for you if you had not been calling Him.'* It appears that those who oppose supplications, do not believe even in the Qur'an. If anyone says that he does not want supplications, that means that he is neither interested in the Qur'an, nor does he believe in it. He does not know that Allah says: *Call Me, I will respond to you.* (Surah Ghāfir, 40:60)[107]

May Allah include us among those who are keenly interested in supplications, prayer and the Qur'an.

ALLAH AND HIS GLORY

It is clear from what we have so far said about *'bismillah'* that the *'ba'* in it is not for causation, as some grammarians say. In fact in the matter of doings of Allah there is no question of cause and effect. The best way of expressing the relationship between the Creator and the created is that which is found in the Qur'an. At some places this relationship has been described as glorification: *'Your Lord revealed His glory'* and at some others as 'manifestation'. It has been said about Allah that *'He is the First and the Last, the Explicit and the Implicit'*. This relationship is different from that of cause and effect, which implies a sort of tendency that is not appropriate to Allah, and therefore it is not a proper expression of the relationship between Allah and the existing things.

For this purpose we have either to expand the meaning of causation to include glorification and manifestation or to say that the *'ba'* in *bismillah* is not for causation and that 'with the name of Allah' means with His manifestation or with His glorification. Therefore *Bismillah al-Hamdu lillah'* does not mean that Allah's name is the cause and his praise is the effect. Anyway, as far as I remember the words, *sababiyyat* or *'illiyat* (cause, effect, causation) are not mentioned anywhere in the Qur'an and the sunnah (traditions). These words are merely philosophical terms used by the philosophers. In this sense the Qur'an and the sunnah have used the words of *Khalq* (creation), *Zūhūr* (manifestation) *Tajalli* (glorification) etc.

There is another aspect of *bismillah*. We have a report about the dot under the *'ba'*. I wonder whether this report is mentioned in any authentic book. Apparently it is not. Anyway,

Imam Ali is reported to have said: 'I am the dot under the *'ba'* of *bismillah*. If this report is mentioned anywhere, it may be interpreted in the following way: The *'ba'* signifies absolute manifestation. The dot signifies its first specification or determination, which lies in the state of *wilāyat*. If this report was true, the Commander of the Faithful might have meant that as the dot determined the *'ba'*, similarly the state of universal *'wilayat'* is the first determination of the Absolute Manifestation. The name is synonym with absolute glory. It is primarily determined by the *Wilāyat* of the Holy Prophet, Imam Ali etc. This fact is true even if it is not mentioned in any authentic book. The first and primary determination of absolute glory is the highest stage of existence and this highest stage of existence is the same as the stage of absolute *wilāyat*. As a matter of fact a divine name is sometimes a symbol of the state of self. The comprehensive name of this state of self is Allah. Sometimes a divine name is the symbol of the manifestation of some divine attribute such as beneficence, mercy etc. All these names are the reflections of the Exalted Name. Some of these names are the names of the state of self, some of the reflections of the glory of names and some of the reflections of the glory of doings. The names of the first category are called the state of uniqueness; the names of the second category are called the state of oneness and the names of the third category the state of will. All these are the terms used by the mystics. The last three verses of the Surah al-Hashr (59:22 - 24)[108] perhaps hint at this division of the divine names:

(i)   He is Allah, there is no other deity but He, the Knower of the invisible and the visible. He is the Beneficent, the Merciful.

(ii) He is Allah, there is no other deity but He, the Sovereign Lord, the Holy One, Peace, the Keeper of Faith, the Guardian, the Majestic, the Compeller and the Superb. Glorified be Allah from all that they ascribe as partners to Him.

(iii) He is Allah the Creator, the Shaper out of nought, the Fashioner, His are the most beautiful names. All that is in the heavens and the earth glorifies Him and He is the Mighty, the Wise.

Possibly these three verses hint at the three states of the divine names as mentioned above. The first mentions the names

162

appropriate to the state of self. The second verse contains the names appropriate to the reflections of the glory of names. The third verse has the names suitable to the reflection of the glory of doings. Thus there are three stages of divine glorification: the stage revealing self-glory for self, the stage of revealing glory at the stage of divine names and the stage of revealing glory at the stage of manifestation. *He is the First and the Last* is perhaps the negation of the existence of any other being. *He is the First and the Last, the Explicit and the Implicit.* This shows that it is He who is manifestation, not that manifestation is from Him, for *'He is the First and the Last, the Explicit and the Implicit.'*

Glory is Not Separate From the Glorious

There are several degrees of the revealing of glory, but in no case glory is separate from the master of glory. It is an idea difficult to conceive, but once you conceive it, it is easy to believe it. It is also possible that Allah is the name of divine glory at the state of divine attributes. In this case *'ism'* in *bismillah* will denote the revealing of overall manifestation of glory. Even in this case it will not be difficult to apply the two possibilities mentioned by us earlier, for Allah's attributes are not separate from His self or essence. In this connection it is to be pointed out that sometimes we look at an event from the point of view as to what our perception says; sometimes from the point of view as to what our intellect says; sometimes from the point of view as to what impression our heart has formed; and sometimes we witness the event at the stage of its actual reality. This rule applies to all spiritual matters.

The farthest limit of our perception is either intellectual perception or argumentative or semi-argumentative perception. We perceive things according to our intellectual capacity. In spiritual matters the lowest degree of our perception should be that we come to understand that there is Allah and His glory. As a matter of fact whatever method of perception we use, we cannot go beyond this limit.

The utmost limit of our perception is either rational perception or argumentative and semi-argumentative perception. We perceive things according to our intellect only. As far as the questions relating to the knowledge of Allah are concerned, the main stage of knowing Him is just to understand that there is Allah and His glory. In fact whatever method of perceiving Him we employ, our perception cannot go beyond this limit.

His Being And His Glory Are the Real Truth

That is the main question. As for the nature of His glory at the various stages of His essence, His attributes and His actions, the verses we have quoted above indicate only that "He is the First and the Last and He is the Explicit and the Implicit". The real truth is only that there is no existence besides Allah. In fact it is meaningless to imagine that besides Allah there can be any existence. Sometimes we calculate according to our understanding what our perception is, what our intellect says, whether our rational perception has so firmly been established in our heart that it may be named faith, and whether we have started our spiritual journey in the right direction so that it may be called *irfān* or gnosis. Anyhow, it is all a matter of our perception rather than that of actualities.

The Real Truth Is Nothing But He

If we look into the question deeply, we come to the conclusion that there is nothing but Allah and that His glory is not but He himself. To illustrate this truth we cannot conceive of any example which may exactly fit in with it. The simile of shadow and the thing casting shadow is defective.

The relation between Allah and His glory can best be illustrated by the example of Sea and its waves.

Perhaps this is the closest similitude. As we know, the waves of the sea are not separate from the sea itself, but still the sea is not the waves, although the waves are the sea. When the sea vibrates, the waves rise in it. At that time the sea and its waves appear to us to be separate from each other. But the waves are a temporary phenomenon. They are again merged in the sea. In fact the waves do not exist independently. This world is also like a wave. Any how, even this similitude is not perfect, for no similitude can properly illustrate the relation between Allah and His creation. We talk only as we perceive. There are two aspects of this question. On the one hand there are some general conceptions like the names of Allah, the names of His attributes and His actions and some stages and stations. These are the conceptions we can perceive. The second stage is that of adducing arguments to prove that Allah and His glory are not separate from each other. To prove this it is said that Allah is pure and absolute existence that can in no way be qualified or limited, for an existence qualified or incomplete in any way cannot be absolute. The absolute existence must be perfect, unlimited and free from all restrictions and deficiencies. The attributes of Absolute Existence must also be absolute and unspecified. Neither Allah's mercifulness is specified or limited nor His compassionateness nor His divinity.

Lack of Any Excellence Means Limitation

As Allah is absolute light and unqualified existence, He must automatically combine in Himself all excellences, for the lack of any excellence would mean specification and restriction. If there were a slightest deficiency or defect at the stage of His essence, the term absolute would not be applicable to Him. He would be imperfect and as such would not be self-existing, because absolute excellence and absolute perfection are essential for being self-existent.

When we think about Allah according to our imperfect mental capacity, we find that Allah is the name of that Absolute Being who has all beautiful names and attributes and who combines in Himself all excellences, and that everything else is nothing but a reflection of His glory. He is Absolute and unqualified perfection. If there were slightest deficiency in Him, He would become a possibly existing being instead of being an essentially existing Being, as He is. He combines in Himself all the excellences and meritorious qualities. He is pure and unspecified existence. Every existence is His. He is everything but in an unspecified manner and by the way of absolute perfection. As His names are not separate from His Being, the names of His attributes are also the names of His essence. All the characteristics pertaining to Allah, pertain to Raḥmān (Merciful) also. Raḥmān being absolute perfection and absolute mercy, has all the excellences of existence. The Qur'an says: *Call Allah or call Raḥmān* (Surah al-Isrā', 17:110)[109] In another

165

verse it says: *Call Him by any name, for all the beautiful names are His.* (Surah al-A'rāf, 7:180)[110] Allah, *Raḥmān, Raḥīm* and all other names of Him are good and beautiful. Each of them combines all His attributes. He being Absolute, there is no disparity between Him and His names or between one of His names and another.

Allah's beautiful names are not like the names we give to different things for different considerations. His glory and His manifestation are not two different aspects of Him. His manifestation is exactly His glory and His glory exactly His manifestation. Even this expression is defective. Absolute existence means Absolute perfection and Absolute perfection must be absolute in every respect. Therefore all His attributes are absolute. No disparity of any sort can be imagined between His essence and His attributes.

Observation is a Step Further than All Arguments and Proofs

It is often said: "There is no proof of such and such thing" or "Reason says so". A gnostic is reported to have said: "Wherever I went, this blind man also arrived there with his stick. By 'the blind man' this gnostic meant Abu Ali Sina (Avicenna). What he wanted to say was that the person who perceived truth by means of his arguments and cold reasoning could be compared to a blind man who found out his way by means of his stick. This gnostic meant to say: "Wherever I reached by means of my vision and gnosis, this blind man (Avicenna) also reached there rattling his stick, that is by means of his logical arguments".

People Depending On Arguments Are Blind

The people depending on arguments are blind because they lack the power of vision. Although they have proved unity of Allah and other questions relating to it by means of their arguments and have also proved that the source of Existence is Absolute Perfection, yet what they say is still a matter of arguments, behind the walls of which these people are unable to see anything. With a great deal of effort the heart perceives that the Essentially Existing Being is pure existence and that He is everything. Still the heart remains like a child who needs to be spoon-fed at every step. He who perceives the rational questions

166

by means of arguments, need, repetition of these arguments and has to make strenuous struggle before his findings are firmly established in his heart.

Faith Means Cordial Perception

When it is cordially accepted that Allah is pure existence as well as all perfection, this conviction becomes a faith. Prior to that it was only a rational idea obtained by means of arguments. Later it produced a particular conception. When the heart accepted that conception as a truth either by means of rational arguments or through Qur'anic teachings, it became a faith. Intellect discovers the truth and teaches it to the heart. When as the result of repetition and mental exercise it is firmly established in the heart that there is nothing in this world except Allah, that idea becomes a faith or an implicit belief. Although the stage referred to in the Qur'an by the words: "so that my heart may be at ease", is a stage lower than the vision of the Prophets, yet it is a stage. But the vision of the beauty of Allah is a far higher stage. Glory of Allah was revealed for Prophet Musa. The Qur'an says: *When his Lord revealed His glory to the mountain.* In connection with the story of Prophet Musa the periods of 30 days and 40 days and the subsequent events are significant and worth consideration. When Prophet Musa departed from the house of his father-in-law, Shu'ayb, after traversing a little distance he said to his wife: "I feel that there is a fire". His wife and children did not see at all the fire which he felt. Prophet Musa said: "I am going so that I may bring a live coal from it for you."

When he approached the fire, he heard a call saying: "Surely I am Allah." He heard this voice from the fire which was ablaze in a tree. This sort of vision was acquired by the blind man by means of his stick and the gnostic by means of his heart. But Prophet Musa had that vision with his eyes.

The Truth is Higher Than What We Say and Hear

We speak about the truths, but they are higher than what we can say about them. "Surely I am Allah". Nobody except Prophet Musa could see the Light of the divine glory that was revealed to the tree. Similarly nobody could know the nature of the revelation that was received by the Holy Prophet, Muhammad. The whole Qur'an used to be revealed to his heart at one time. How? Who knows? If the Qur'an is what we have, consisting of 30 parts, then it cannot be revealed all at once to an ordinary heart.

Heart Also Means Something Quite Different from What We Understand

In this content heart is different from what we ordinarily understand. The Qur'an is a truth and this truth is revealed to the heart. The Qur'an is a secret — a guarded secret. It must descend from its high position so that it might be revealed to the heart of the Holy Prophet. Then it must come down further so that it could be understood by others also. The same is true of man. Man is also a closed secret. From what we can see man appears to be an animal and for that matter, an animal lower than many other animals. But the distinguishing feature of this animal is that it can attain humanity and by traversing various stages of perfection can reach the stage of absolute perfection. Man before his death can become what is difficult even to imagine.

What We Feel Are Qualities and Forms

The whole man is a secret. It is difficult to say what we apparently see in this world, for we cannot perceive bodies or substances. All that we peceive are forms and qualities only. For example, our eyes see a colour. Our ears hear a sound. Our tongue feels a sensation of taste. Our hands feel the things by touching them. All these are forms and qualities. But the actual body is nowhere. When we describe a thing, we mention its length, breadth and depth. Length, breadth and depth are all forms only. We say that such and such thing has attraction. But attraction is also a quality only. Whatever qualities of a thing we may describe, they are all mere forms. Then where is the body? The body is a secret — a shadow of the divine secret. What we know is only names and qualities, otherwise everything in this world in unknown. Perhaps it is this conception a degree of which has been described by the gnostics as "invisible though apparently visible", for in this world things are visible and invisible at one and the same time. Only those things are invisible which we can neither see nor can we perceive. If we want to describe a thing we can do no more than mentioning its name, qualities and characteristics. Man cannot perceive a thing which is a shadow of the Absolute Secret, for human perception is defective. Only that man can perceive things fully who through his 'Wilayat' has attained that position where glory of Allah is fully revealed to his heart. The question of visibility and invisibility is present everywhere. That is why such expressions as the invisible world, the angelic world and the world of the intellects are on the lips of everybody.

The Holy Prophet is the Exalted Name of Allah

All the names of Allah are a secret as well as a known thing. They are implicit and explicit. That is what the following Qur'anic verse means: "He is Explicit and Implicit." What is explicit is implicit as well and what is implicit is explicit as well. That is how all the names of Allah imply all the grades of existence. Every name covers the concepts of all other names. It is not that *Rahman* is a name or an attribute different from *Rahim*. The same is true of all other names of Allah. For example *Muntaqim* (Avenger) is not the opposite of *Rahman* (Merciful).

The Qur'an says: *Call Him by any name for He has all the beautiful names.* All these beautiful names are of *Rahman* as well as of *Rahim*. It is not that one name means something and some other name signifies something else. Had it been so *Rahman* would have signified one aspect of Allah and *Rahim* another aspect of Him, while the Absolute Existence cannot have many aspects. The Absolute Existence as such is *Rahman* as well as *Rahim*, *Nur* (Light) and Allah. His being *Rahman* is not different from His being *Rahim*. A person occupying that highest position of gnosis in which his heart is enlightened by Allah Himself, not by His glory, will himself be an 'exalted name' of Allah and at the same time will be enlightened by the light of the 'exalted name'. Such a person could only be he to whose heart the Qur'an was revealed and to whom Gabriel used to Come. The glory revealed to his heart comprised all glories. This person was the Holy Prophet who personally was the most exalted name of Allah. The Imams are also reported to have said: "We are the beautiful names of Allah."

Even Our Existence Is A Revelation of the Glory of Allah

The topics we have discussed today included the question of causation. We said that it was wrong to raise the question of causation in respect of Allah. In our authentic texts we do not find any mention of it. Some far-fetched examples do not serve any purpose. Another question we mentioned was that of a dot under the letter '*bā*'. I explained the meaning of this tradition in case it was really reported anywhere. Furthermore some such questions were also discussed as the name at the stage of divine essence, the name at the stage of attributes, the name at the stage of the revelation of glory of action, revelation of the glory of essence to essence, revelation of the glory of essence to attributes, and revelation of the glory of essence to all existing things. When we talk of the revelation of divine glory, we say that even our existence is the revelation of glory. To illustrate this fact it may be said that if you put 100 mirrors in a place all reflecting the light of the sun, it may be said that there are one hundred lights, but actually there would be only one light reflected in all mirrors. But the light of the sun being limited, even this example is far-fetched.

All Existing Things Are the Result of Divine Glory

It is the light of Allah's glory that is being reflected in all existing things. It is the same light that is reflected everywhere. For each and every thing there is no separate light. All the existing things are the concommitant result of the same one light. As such in '*bismillah*' the *ism* or the name means the name of divine essence and Allah is the glory of divine essence which includes all glories. It is this comprehensive glory the name of which is Allah, as well as *Rahmān, Rahīm* etc. It is wrong to say that *Rahmān* is the name of one divine attribute and *Rahīm* is the name of another attribute. In fact Allah, *Rahmān* and *Rahīm* are the names of the same divine glory. The whole of that glory is Allah as well as *Rahmān* and *Rahīm*. That is the only possibility. Otherwise Allah will become a limited being, and a limited being is a possibly existing being, not an essentially existing one.

170

According to the details we mentioned earlier, praise (*hamd*) will be of Allah and Allah is the name of the Comprehensive divine glory or divine manifestation. *Rahmān* and *Rahīm* are also the names of exactly the same glory. *Hamd* means either every praise or praise in general. There are three possibilities about the name, Allah. It can either be the name of the comprehensive divine glory at the stage of essence or at the stage of attributes (This is the stage of will. Every thing is produced by it) or at the stage of action. When we apply these possibilities to the verse of '*bismillah*', a different style of expression emerges in every case. We talked about Allah on this very basis and said that it is the Comprehensive name at the stage of essence as well as at the stage of attributes and at the stage of the revelation of divine glory producing action. While discussing '*bismillah*' we said a few things briefly about the letter '*bā*', its dot and the names of Allah, *Rahmān* and *Rahīm*.

The Belief Is Essential

We hope that it will be admitted that the discussion of such problems is necessary. Some people totally deny their importance. Not only that, there are some people who do not believe in gnostic questions at all. Those who are at the stage of animals cannot understand that there is something beyond what they know. We must have belief in spiritual matters. This is the first step. The foremost thing is that man should not deny everything he does not know. Shaykh Abu Ali Sina says that anybody who denies a thing without any reason, behaves against human nature.

Belief Must Be Based On Reason

As there must be a valid reason to prove a thing, there must also be a valid reason to deny a thing. If you do not have a reason in favour or against a thing, then simply say: "I don't know". But there are some obstinate people who deny everything. As these people do not understand, they behave inhumanly. Whatever you hear you should normally admit that at least there is some possibility of its being correct. Do not reject anything outright without any reason. We do not have access to what is beyond this world. Even about this world our knowledge is defective and limited. At present we have a certain amount of knowledge. In future we will know much more. So many things which we now know, about this world, were totally unknown till a hundred years ago. In future many more discoveries will be made. When man is still unable to know and perceive this world fully, how does he dare to deny what the saints *(Awliyā')* of Allah know and see. A man denies the spiritual truths, because his heart lacks the spiritual light. He says that spiritual truths do not exist, but does not admit that he is unaware of them. He alleges that what the believers in spiritual truths say are all fables. He dares to say so because he is ignorant. He does not know that the things he rejects as fables have been mentioned in the Qur'an too. What the Muslim gnostics say has been derived from the Qur'an and sunnah (traditions). Then how can he deny what the Qur'an confirms?

To Deny What One Does Not Know Is Unbelief

If not legally unbelief, at least it is a sort of unfaithfulness. The root-cause of man's misfortune is that he denies the truths he does not perceive. He rejects these truths because he has not reached the stage that has been reached by the 'Saints of Allah' This is the worst kind of negationistness. The foremost thing is that one must not deny what is contained in the Qur'an and sunnah, what is acknowledged by the Imams and what is admitted by the philosophers. If some body has not perceived the truth himself, he should frankly admit that he does not know. But it is all humbug if some idiot says that he would not believe in Allah unless he himself has disected Him with his sharp knife. The most important thing is that we must not deny what we have been told by the Prophets and the Imams. This is the first step. We cannot take the next step if we deny the things in the very beginning. If anybody wants to go forward he should as a first step admit that the spiritual things he does not know, may possibly he correct. Then he should pray to Allah to open for him a way that might lead him to the place where he should reach.

We Must Not Deny the Qur'an and Sunnah

If a man will not deny the Divine things and will pray to

Allah, Allah will certainly help him and will gradually open the way for him.

I hope that we will not deny what is in the Qur'an and sunnah. It often happens that a man believes in the Qur'an and sunnah, and does not deny even when he does not understand what is in them, but when somebody else tells him that the Qur'an and sunnah say so, he instead of admitting his lack of knowledge, rejects that outright as nonsense.

Total Denial Is A Stumbling Block

Total denial deprives man from acknowledging many truths and prevents him from proceeding on the right path. The veracity of the facts which have been affirmed by the saints of Allah should be acknowledged at least tacitly if not expressly. A man who denies them totally and describes them as nonsense, can never succeed in proceeding further.

We Must Do Away With Negative Attitude

I hope that we will give up the negative attitude and will pray to Allah to make us familiar with the diction of the Qur'an which is of a special type. Like man the Qur'an also has many potentialities. It is a large table on which many dishes of various tastes have been placed by Allah. From it everybody can have food of his choice, provided he has not lost his appetite, which happens in the case of heart patients. The Qur'an like this world is a vast dining table. This world is also used by different people differently according to their requirements and taste. Man utilizes it in one way, animals in another and the men who are on the same level as the animals in a third way. As the level goes up, the way of utilization improves. The same is true of the Qur'an. It is for all. Everybody can be benefited by it according to his taste and choice.

Its highest beneficiary is he who is its first addressee and to whom it was revealed. "Only he knows the Qur'an to whom it was addressed."

Denial of Prophethood

We need not be disappointed. Instead we must try to be benefited by the Qur'an. For this purpose it is essential that first of all we remove from our mind the idea that there exists nothing besides physical and material problems and that the Qur'an also has been revealed only to deal with these problems and is exclusively concerned with this worldly life. This way of thinking amounts to total denial of Prophethood. In fact the Qur'an has come to make man a real human being and all this is a means to an end.

Supplications and Worship Are Means

Worship is a means. Supplications are a means. They are a means to develop real human qualities and to awaken dormant human potentialities so that man becomes a real human being, a godly man, able to see what is right and understand what is right. Prophets have come for this very purpose. Prophets are also a means. They did not come merely to set up a government. The government has its own place, but the Prophets did not come only for the sake of obtaining power and administering worldly affairs. This is what the animals also do. They also have their own world and they administer the affairs of it.

Justice Is A Quality Appropriate to Allah

Those who have an insight look at the discussion of justice as the discussion of a characteristic of Allah. The administration of divine justice is one of the functions of the Prophets. They set up a government as a means of leading man to that position which is the real aim of the Prophets' coming. May Allah help us in all affairs!

Before dealing with the remaining points perhaps it is necessary and useful to point out that the scholars often disagree because they do not understand the language of each other properly. The reason is that each group of scholars has its own language.

A Dispute About Grapes Between An Iranian, A Turk And An Arab

I wonder whether you have ever heard this story. There were three men. One of them was an Iranian; another was a Turk and the third was an Arab. They were discussing what they should have for lunch. The Iranian said that *angur* would

174

be quite suitable. The Arab said: "No, we would have *inab.*" The Turk said: "No, I don't like either. We would have *uzum.*" As they did not understand the language of each other, they differed. At last someone of them went out and brought grapes. Then they realized that all of them wanted the same thing.

To express the same thing there are different words in different languages. For example, the philosophers have a particular diction. They have their own terminology. Similarly the sufis have their own language. The jurists have their own terms. The poets have their own poetic diction. The Imams have their own separate style. Now we have to find out which one out of these three or four groups has a language closer to the language of those who are infallible and to the language of revelation. I do not think that any sensible person will deny that Allah exists and that He is the source and cause of all that exists. Nobody believes that you with your coat and pants are God, nor can any sensible person imagine that any man with a turban, a beard and a staff is Allah. Everybody knows that all men are creatures.

Anyhow the way in which the cause and effect are described and the impression that such description creates, often gives rise to disagreement. We should find out what those who belonged to the gnostic class actually wanted to say and what induced them to use questionable words and a vague style.

How To Reconcile Different Groups And Their Ways Of Expression?

Now I want to reconcile these different groups for they all say the same thing. I do not want to condone all philosophers or to defend all gnostics or all jurists. That is not my intention. I know that many of them are shopkeepers. They say only that which may promote their business. What I mean to say is that in all these groups there are people who are pious. The differences which exist between them are due to the scholars of to which they belong. Their differences may be compared to the difference existing between the *Uṣūlis* and the *Akhbāris* (traditionalists). Sometimes some *Akhbāris* condemn the *Uṣūlis* as infidels and unbelievers, and *Uṣūlis* condemn the *Akhbāris* as ignorant. They do so despite the fact that the objective of both the groups is the same.

175

Now the main point of our discourse is that a group of philosophers uses such terms as the primary cause, first effect, second effect, causativeness etc. Such terms as causativeness, source and consequence are some of the favourite terms of the ancient philosophers.

Even our jurists do not refain from using terms like causativeness and effectiveness nor have they any objection against using such words as creatorness and createdness. There is a class of the Muslim gnostics, who because of difference they have with other classes, use quite different expressions, such as manifest, manifestations, glory etc. In addition, they use certain other words to which the literalists take exception. Now let us see why they use such words and why some of these words have been used by the Imams also. I do not remember to have seen such words as *illiyat, ma'luliyyat, sababiyyat* and *musabbibiyat* (causativeness and effectiveness) being used by the Imams, but other such words as *khallāqiyyat* (creatorness) *makhluqiyyat* (createdness) *tajalli* (revelation of glory) *zāhir* (manifest) and *mazhar* (manifestation) are found in what they have said. Now let us see why the Muslim gnostics and sufis have refrained from using the terminology of the philosophers as well as the language of the common people. They have invented a style of their own to which the literalists usually object. Let us know the reason.

Cause And Effect

On the basis of causation one thing is considered to be the cause and another to be the effect. As a rule the cause should be on the one side and the effect on the other. In other words they should be in two different places. Take the example of the sun and the sunlight. There is light in the sun, but it also emits light. The sun and its light have two separate identities and are located at two different places. As the sun emits its light, the sun is the cause and its light is its effect. But the question is whether it is possible in the case of the self-existing being also to imagine such relationship of cause and effect as is found in nature. For example, fire is the cause of heat and the sun is the cause of light. In nature the effect is a consequence of the cause and the cause and effect are usually found in two separate places.

In nature the cause and the effect are also usually located

at two different places. But we cannot say about the Creator and the created that they are in two separate places or exist at two different times. Even it is difficult to say how Allah exists, because He is Absolute and His existence is abstract. Whatever the way of expression you may adopt, it is impossible to say how Allah exercises His eternal and ceaseless power of creating and sustaining every thing. The Qur'an says: *He is with you wherever you are.* What does "with you" mean in this verse? Is Allah by the side of every man?

Meaning of "with you"

This way of expression has been chosen because it is impossible to express the truth exactly. Therefore, words as close to the reality as possible, have to be chosen. It is very difficult to understand where the Creator is and how He is with the created. Is the relation between the Creator and the created the same as between fire and its effect? Or is the relation between them is similar to the relation between soul and eyes, ears, nose and other organs? The second similitude may be closer to the reality. Anyhow it also cannot express the meaning clearly. The Creator is encompassing the whole creation and this encompassing is related to His eternal attributes of creation and sustenance. It is difficult to say anything more. All that may be added is that this encompassing is such that there is no place where Allah may not be. A tradition says: "If you were dropped to the lowest earth by means of a rope, you would find Allah even there." This is only a way of expression. For example if it is said: "All that exists is Allah". This does not mean that any particular man wearing a gown and a turban is Allah. No man who is mentally normal would ever say so. We can only use words which may be as close to the reality as possible. Only to draw the attention of a man not conversant with the reality, to the relation between the Creator and the created it is said that it is true that "All that exists is Allah". But that does not mean that any particular man or a particular thing may be called Allah. That is why the Muslim philosophers say that Allah is pure existence, and He is all things, but not any thing particular out of them. This statement may appear to be somewhat contradictory. But what is meant is that Allah is free from

177

every shortcoming. He is pure existence and has no deficiency or defect. He is characterized with every perfection, whereas all other things are defective.

Therefore He 'is not anything particular out of them'. As Allah is free from every defect and deficiency, He consequently enjoys every perfection. Any perfection found in any creation of His is a reflection of His own perfection. As every perfection is a revelation of His glory, He Himself is all perfection. In the above quoted tradition "all things" means all kinds of perfection and "not any thing particular out of them" means that He is free from every defect and deficiency. "All things" does not mean that you are also Allah.

That is why it is said that "He is not any thing particular out of them." In other words He is all perfection while no one else is characterized with every perfection. There is another example of this kind. There is a well-known Persian poetical line that means: 'Because non-attachment became confined to attachment.' This line has nothing to do with any question of divinity. But those who are not conversant with this topic, often confuse its meaning. This line in fact is concerned with the hostility between two persons. But those who do not understand its meaning say that it amounts to infidelity. In fact it has been misunderstood and misinterpreted. It actually deals with quite a different question, that is why the wars occur in the world.

Why Do the Wars Occur?

Why are the wars fought? What is the basis of the wars? In the above mentioned line and in Persian the word, 'rung' (colour) is used in the sense of attachment and 'berungi' (colourlessness) in the sense of non-attachment. Some other poets have also used these words in this sense.

If one is not attached to any thing, there can be no quarrel. All quarrels are caused by somebody's attachment to some thing, which he wants to obtain for himself. The poet who wrote the above mentioned line wants to say that attachment to any particular thing or things is not a part of real human nature and if this attachment to worldy things is done away with there will no longer be any quarrel.

In the story of Prophet Musa and Fir'awn if Fir'awn had

178

been as indifferent to worldly things as Prophet Musa was, there would have been no trouble. If all the Prophets gathered together at a place there would be no dispute at all, for all disputes and quarrels are due to attachment. Nature was unattached, but when it became a captive of attachment, quarrels arose. Even Prophet Musa and Fir'awn would make friends, if the sting of attachment was removed. This topic has no concern with divinity. It did not occur to him who objected to this line, that it related to two men quarreling between themselves.

Words in Imam's Supplications

You are already familiar with the words used in Imams' supplications. Now let us see whether the words and phrases used by Muslim gnostics for which they have been charged with unbelief by those who are unaware of reality, are similar to those used by the Imams or the gnostics have a different vocabulary. This topic relates to spiritual journey.

The following words have come in the *Sha'bāniyah* supplication:

"O my Lord! grant me complete withdrawal to You and enlighten the eyes of our heart with the light of looking towards You so that the eyes of heart may tear off the curtains of light and reach the source of granduer and our souls get suspended in the honourable chamber of your sanctity."

Further the text says: "O my Lord! grant me that I may be one of those whom you called and they responded, and at whom You looked and they were dumb-founded."[111]

What do these words signify? Now what do the critics of the gnostics say? The gnostics have not said anything different from what the Imams have said. Why did all our Imams use to recite this supplication? What does "complete withdrawal" mean?

Imams pray for complete withdrawal

The Imams ask Allah to grant them complete withdrawal to Him, while it was up to them to undertake the spiritual journey themselves, but still they prayed to Allah for it. Why so? They asked Allah to enlighten the eyes of their hearts. What did they mean by the eyes of the hearts with which they wished to see Allah? What does heart mean in this context, and what is the meaning of the eye of the heart? Thereafter the aim of all this has been stated in these words: "So that the eyes of our heart may tear off the curtains of light and may reach the source of majesty and our souls may become suspended in the honourable chamber of Your sanctity". Here the question arises what is meant by becoming suspended? The next prayer is: "O my Lord! Make me one of those whom you called and who responded to You and who were dumbfounded by Your majesty." The Qur'an also has said about Prophet Musa that he fell down senseless. Are these expressions different from what is called *fanā'* or passing away in the terminology of the Muslim gnostics. Thus climbing up higher and higher the spiritual traveller reaches the stage where the eyes of his heart tearing off all curtains reach the source of majesty. What is this source of majesty and what does reaching this source mean? Does this not mean gaining that proximity to Allah of which the gnostics talk? Can anything other than Allah be the source of majesty? Only that can be this source of majesty from whom all the favours and blessings can be contained. Only after reaching this source of majesty "our souls will become suspended in the honourable chamber of Your sanctity".

Anybody who looks over the relationship between Allah and His creation will never use the words, cause and effect for this relationship. The use of these words, wherever it has been made, shows only that this relationship is such that it cannot be expressed in exact terms. The use of the words Creator and creation is nothing but following the taste of the common people. A far better expression is revealing the glory. The Qur'an says: *Then his Lord revealed His glory to the mountain.* (Surah al-A'rāf, 7:143)[112] This is also only a way of using the closest words to state a relationship that cannot be expressed exactly.

A Question Difficult To Conceive, But Easy to Believe

The relationship between Allah and His creation is a question that is difficult to conceive but after having been conceived, is easy to be believed. The difficulty is how to conceive a Being who is everywhere, but still it cannot be said that He is at such and such place. He is outside of everything as well as the inside of everything. Everything is caused by Him. Nothing is devoid of Him. Now where can we find appropriate words to express these concepts? Whatever words we choose, they will be inadequate. All that can be done is that those who are fit to do so pray to Allah and pray in the style of the *Shābaniyah* Supplication that He may enlighten them on this subject. Anyhow, it is not a thing for which one group may declare another group infidel or ignorant, for it is not possible for anyone to express himself clearly on this subject. Try to understand the sentiments of others and what they want to say. Sometimes it happens that as light surges in the heart of somebody, he involuntarily exclaims that he is everything.

Imam Ali is the Eye of Allah, He is the Light of Allah's Eye

You read in the supplications that Imam Ali is the eye of Allah. What does that signify? Imam Ali is often described as the eye of Allah, light of Allah and the hand of Allah. What does the Hand of Allah mean? Such words are used by the Muslim gnostics also. It is reported in our traditions that the alms given to a poor-man reaches the Hand of Allah.

The Qur'an says: *You did not throw the pebbles, when you threw them, but Allah threw.* (Surah al-Anfāl, 8:17)[113] What does this mean? This is what you all repeat, but you do not allow the gnostics to mention the Hand of Allah. When these poor people cannot say expressly, they say the same thing in a roundabout way. But such expressions are common even in the Qur'an and especially in the Imams' supplications. Therefore there is no reason why we should suspect the gnostics especially. Try to understand what they mean and why they do not use the diction commonly used by other people. Although they have not used the familiar words and phrases, they have not sacrificed the truth, but have sacrificed themselves for the sake of truth. If we could understand that truth, we might have used the same diction.

The Qur'an has used the same way of expression. The Imams also have used similar words. If somebody says: "This is the truth", no sensible person will think that he means that this is Allah. Now just see how manifestation of Allah can be interpreted? In regard to the Imams in a supplication the following words have been used: "There is no difference between You and them, except that they are your bondsmen; their creation is in Your Hand and their restoration is in Your Hand." This sentence also shows the inadequacy of expression. That is why the Imams use the words which are closer to the Qur'an than to the words used by others.

About gnostics anyone could say that they were nobody. But there were some other people whom we knew intimately and knew that they had a thorough knowledge of all Islamic sciences. They also used similar words. For example they used to say: "That reveals Allah's glory". In the 'Samat' Supplication there is a word, 'tal'atuka'. This word also means glory. Similarly there is another word *nūr* (light) in the phrase, 'binūri wajhika' (by the light of Your Countenance). That is why I say: Make peace with the gnostics. I do not mean to say that all of them are good. What I mean is that all of them must not be rejected. When I support the scholars and jurists, I do not intend to support all kinds of scholars and what I mean is that all of them should not be rejected. The same is the case with the gnostics. Do not think that whosoever talks in gnostic terms is an infidel.

Every Thing Must Be Investigated

First of all it must be understood what the other man is saying. If that is understood, perhaps there will be no need of rejecting him. Eveywhere it is the same story of grapes — 'inab, angūr and uzūm. One man states a thing in one way;another man uses the terms of cause and effect while saying the same thing; the third man uses the word, mover and consequence; while the fourth man says manifest and manifestation. At some time or other all of them reach a stage where they realize how to describe the Being who is everywhere but is not any of the things we perceive. That is why sometimes someone ever says: "Ali is Allah's hand; Ali is Allah's eye."

The Qur'an says: *You did not throw when you threw, but Allah threw.* It also says: *Surely those who pledge their allegiance to you, really pledge their allegiance to Allah. Allah's hand is above their hands.* (Surah al-Fath, 48:10)[114]

Does this verse mean that Allah's Hand is literally placed

on their hands? Obviously it does not. 'Above' here means at a higher point spiritually. Actually we lack words to express this position properly.

As Allah is far above that he may be mingled with any-thing or that he may be related to anything in a general sense, similarly he is above that we may be able to understand the nature of His glory. His glory is unknown to us. But we believe that there is certainly something of this sort. We cannot deny its existence. When we believe that such things exist, we have to admit that they are mentioned in one way or another in the Qur'an and Sunnah. In the Qur'an wherever there is a mention of the glory of Allah, the words revealing or manifesting have been used. In the Surah al-Hadid a verse says: *He is Explicit and Implicit.*

A report says that the last six verses of the Surah al-Hadid are for the people who will appear "in the last era." Only they will be able to understand these verses which give some account of creation etc. It is in these verses that Allah says: *He is the First and the Last and the Explicit and the Implicit and He is with you wherever you are.* (Surah al-Hadid, 57:3-4)[115] Nobody can easily understand what is meant by 'the last era'. Only one or two persons in the world may be able to understand the significance of this phrase.

Misunderstandings Must Be Removed

The main point which I want to emphasize is that mis-understanding must be removed and there should be an end to the differences between the pedagogues and the scholars. The way to gnosis must not be blocked. Islam is not the name of the rules of law only. The basis of these rules is something else. The basis should not be considered to be superfluous, nor should it be sacrificed for the sake of derivatives. We must not say that gnosis is not required or has no importance. Someone told me that a person was mentioned before the late Shaykh Muhammad Bahâri. He says: "That man is a righteous infidel." 'How can that be' we said: 'Is he righteous and at the same time an infidel?' Shaykh Muhammad Bahâri said: 'Yes, he is righteous because he acts according to the law of Islam and does not commit any sin. And he is an infidel because the god which he worships is not true God.'

Even the Ant Loves Itself

According to our traditions perhaps the ant thinks that Allah has two horns. This is due to self love which an ant also apparently harbours. The ant is a very funny creature. It thinks that it is a mark of granduer to have horns. When we think about our virtues and merits, we also think almost in the same way. It is the same ant which thought that Prophet Sulaymān (Soloman) and his troop could not understand any thing. The Qur'an says: *An ant exclaimed: 'O ants: Enter your dwellings lest Sulaymān and his troops crush you because they do not understand.' 'And he (Sulaymān) smiled laughing at her speech. (Surah n-Naml, 27:17 - 19)*[116]

The case of the ant is not a solitary one. Everybody thinks the same way. Even the hoopoe, according to the Qur'an, said: *I know what you do not.* (Surah an-Naml, 27:22).[117] The hoopoe said so to Prophet Sulaymān who was a Prophet and who had a companion who brought to him the throne of Bilqis in the twinkling of an eye. How could he do that, is not known. Was there any electric system of transportation, or was it a case of annihilating a thing and then bringing it back into existence, or was the throne of Bilqis transported after having been converted into electric waves? According to a report one of the companions of Prophet Sulaymān knew a letter of Allah's Exalted Name and by virtue of it could bring anything desired to Prophet Sulaymān before the twinkling of an eye. To such a prophet the hoopoe said: 'I know what you do not.'

Anyway, what Shaykh Muhammad Bahāri meant to say was that that particular scholar said what he understood and he acted also accordingly.

It Is Bad Luck To Be Unaware of Some Important Questions

I think that it is unfortunate that a group of scholars which includes some very good and pious persons, is unaware of some important questions. When I came to Qum, Mirza Ali Akbar Hakīm was there. He had established an Islamic Academy at his house. The scholars used to receive education there. Such outstanding persons as the late Agha Khawānsāri and the late Agha Ishrāqi used to attend Mirza Ali Akbar's lectures. On that occasion a pious and prominent personality, who is no longer amongst us, remarked: 'Look, to what level has the condition of Islam gone down? Now the business of Islam is being transacted at the house of Mirza Ali Akbar.' He made this remark despite the fact that personally he was a pious man. Even after his death one of his representatives said on the pulpit: 'I have myself seen Mirza Ali Akbar reciting the Qur'an.' The late Agha Shāh Ābādi was very much offended by this remark. Such misunderstandings are regrettable, and keeping oneself aloof from good work is also deplorable. What a pity that this scholar did not take part in the meritorious act of setting up a learned academy! Philosophy is a common place thing, but some people object to it also. In fact these people do not understand each other and that is why all the disputes arise. A scholar declares another scholar infidel simply because he does not understand what the other man says. The fault of the other man is that he uses such terms as cause, effect etc., which in the eyes of the former are contrary to the facts. I said earlier that divine name is not separate from the named. The name is a manifestation and a sign, but not such a sign as a mile-stone is. Therefore it is difficult to say that such and such thing is a sign of Allah. The words used in the Qur'an are closest to the reality but still do not represent it fully. The difficulty is that better words do not exist.

I said earlier that the Qur'an was like a dining table with many dishes placed on it. Everybody can have food according to his choice. No group has a monopoly of the Qur'an. All have a right to be benefited by it equally. The supplications of the Imams are full of spiritual knowledge. But some individuals try to deprive the people of these supplications which impart knowledge and convey the views of the Qur'an. Imams' supplications interpret the Qur'an and explain the questions to which others do not have access.

It is Wrong To Persuade People To Give Up Supplications

It is wrong to say that as we want to concentrate on the Qur'an, the supplications are not required. People should cultivate a liking for the supplications so that they may develop an attachment to Allah. Those who do so, give no importance to worldly things. They are not self-conceited, and keep themselves busy with the tasks liked by Allah. Such people include those who used to fight for the sake of Allah, and at the same time used to recite the supplications. Their circumstances were not different from ours, but still they managed to wield the sword and pray at the same time. Just as the Holy Prophet and the Holy Qur'an are not separate from each other, similarly the Holy Qur'an and the supplications are also not separate from each other.

We cannot say that as we have the Qur'an, we do not need the Holy Prophet. The Qur'an and the Holy Prophet go togather. "They will always remain together till they arrive together at the Fountain of Kawthar." There is no question of their parting.

If some of us take them separately and want the Qur'an to be separate, the Imams to be separate and the supplications to be separate; or if some of us say that the books of supplication are not required, and as such they may be set on fire; or if some of us want the books of the gnostics to be burnt, the reason is simply that the people who say and do such thing are ignorant. A man who exceeds his limit always falls into error.

Kasrawi And Ḥāfiz

Kasrawi was an historian. His knowledge of history was good. He was a fine writer also. But he was self-conceited. In the end he began to claim to be a prophet. He, however, believed in the Qur'an, but he was totally against supplications. He lowered Prophethood and brought it down to his own level. As he himself could not rise up, he lowered Prophethood. The supplications and the Qur'an all go together. The gnostics, the sufi poets and the philosophers all say the same thing. Their points of view are not different. The difference is only that of their diction and the style of expression. Hafiz Shirāzi (the Celebrated Persian Poet) has his own individual style. He mentions the same points as others do, but in a different manner. Their choice of words may be different, but the people should not be deprived of the blessings of the subject matter. It is essential to call people to the vast treasure of knowledge contained in the Qur'an, sunnah and supplications so that everybody may be benefited by them according to his capacity.

This was a prelude to the points I intend to put forward later. If I am spared and mention any expression used by the gnostics as a possibility, it should not be said that I was trying to revive their expressions. In fact their expressions are worth being popularized. Some craftsmen used to call on the late Agha Shāh Ābādi, who used to narrate gnostic problems in front of them as in front of others. One day I said: 'Do you narrate these things in front of these people also?' He said: 'Never mind! Let these heresies be heard by them too'.

We also had some such people. I cannot say who they were. It will be wrong to mention anybody by name. Now the topic of discussion is that *"Bismillahir Rahmānir Rahim"* has *al-Rahmān al-Rahīm* and *"Al-hamdu lillahi Rabbil 'alamin"* is also followed by the same words, viz. *al-Rahmān al-Rahim*. The words *al-Rahmān* and *al-Rahim* may in *bismillah* either relate to *ism* or Allah. Both the possibilities are there. God-willing we will see later which of these two possibilities appears to be more reasonable.

THE INVOCATION OF SHA'BĀNIYAH

My Lord, bestow Your blessings on Muhammad and his descendants; respond to my prayer when I pray to You; listen to my call when I call You; and turn to me when I make my submission to You in confidence. I have come running to You and am standing before You imploring You in humility and hoping to get the reward You have for me. You know what is in my heart, and You are aware of what I need. You know my mind and are not unaware of my future and of my present, of what I want to begin my speech with; of the request I would utter, and of the hopes I have in regard to my ultimate lot.

My Lord, whatever You have destined for me up to the end of my life, whether concerning the open aspect of my life or the hidden aspect of it, is bound to come. What is to my advantage and what is to my disadvantage — all my losses and gains are in Your hand, not in the hand of anybody else.

My Lord, if You deprive me, who else will provide me; and if You let me down, who else will help me?

My Lord, I seek Your protection from Your anger and from earning Your displeasure. If I am not fit for gaining Your Mercy, You are certainly fit to be generous to me by virtue of Your Magnanimity.

My Lord, I see as if I am standing before You

اَلْمُنَاجَاتُ الشَّعْبَانِيَّةُ

اَللّٰهُمَّ صَلِّ عَلَىٰ مُحَمَّدٍ وَّالِ مُحَمَّدٍ. وَاسْمَعْ دُعَائِى اِذَا دَعَوْتُكَ . وَاسْمَعْ نِدَائِى اِذَا نَادَيْتُكَ وَاَقْبِلْ عَلَىَّ اِذَا نَاجَيْتُكَ فَقَدْ هَرَبْتُ اِلَيْكَ وَوَقَفْتُ بَيْنَ يَدَيْكَ مُسْتَكِينًا لَّكَ مُتَضَرِّعًا اِلَيْكَ رَاجِيًا لِّمَا لَدَيْكَ ثَوَابِى وَتَعْلَمُ مَا فِى نَفْسِى وَتَخْبُرُ حَاجَتِى وَتَعْرِفُ ضَمِيرِى وَلَا يَخْفٰى عَلَيْكَ اَمْرُ مُنْقَلَبِى وَمَثْوَاىَ وَمَا اُرِيدُ اَنْ اُبْدِئَ بِهٖ مِنْ مَّنْطِقِى وَاَتَفَوَّهُ بِهٖ مِنْ طَلِبَتِى وَاَرْجُوهُ لِعَاقِبَتِى وَقَدْ جَرَتْ مَقَادِيرُكَ عَلَىَّ يَا سَيِّدِى فِيمَا يَكُونُ مِنِّى اِلٰى اٰخِرِ عُمْرِى مِنْ سَرِيرَتِى وَعَلَانِيَتِى وَبِيَدِكَ لَا بِيَدِ غَيْرِكَ زِيَادَتِى وَنَقْصِى وَنَفْعِى وَضَرِّى اِلٰهِى اِنْ حَرَمْتَنِى فَمَنْ ذَا الَّذِى يَرْزُقُنِى وَاِنْ خَذَلْتَنِى فَمَنْ ذَا الَّذِى يَنْصُرُنِى اِلٰهِى اَعُوذُ بِكَ مِنْ غَضَبِكَ وَحُلُولِ سَخَطِكَ اِلٰهِى اِنْ كُنْتُ غَيْرَ مُسْتَأْهِلٍ لِّرَحْمَتِكَ فَاَنْتَ اَهْلٌ اَنْ تَجُودَ عَلَىَّ بِفَضْلِ سَعَتِكَ اِلٰهِى كَاَنِّى بِنَفْسِى وَاقِفَةٌ بَيْنَ يَدَيْكَ

189

protected by my trust in You. You said what befitted You and covered me with Your forgiveness.

My Lord, if You forgive me, then who is more suited than You to do that? If the time of my death has come near and my deeds have not still brought me close to You, I make this confession of my sins a means of approaching You. I have been unjust to my soul for I have not looked after it. It will certainly be doomed if You do not forgive it.

My Lord, You have always been kind to me during my life time. Therefore do not cut off Your favour from me at the time of my death.

My Lord, how can I lose the hope, of Your looking kindly, in me after my death, when you have always been good to me during my life.

My Lord, in my case do what befits You and bestow Your favour on me — a sinner enwrapped in his ignorance.

My Lord, You have concealed many of my sins in this world. I am in a greater need of their being conceded in the next. As You have not revealed my sins even to any of Your pious bondmen, do not expose me on the Day of Resurrection before everybody.

My Lord, Your generosity has expanded my aspiration, and Your forgiveness is superior to my deeds. Therefore gladden my heart by allowing me to meet You on the day You administer justice to Your bondmen.

My Lord, my apology to You is the apology of him who cannot afford his apology being not accepted. Therefore accept my apology, You the Most Magnanimous of those to whom the evil-doers tender their apology.

My Lord, do not turn down my request; do not foil my desire; and do not cut off my hope and expectation of You.

My Lord, if You had wanted to disgrace me, You would

وَقَدْ اَظْلَهَا حُسْنُ تَوَكُّلِي عَلَيْكَ فَقُلْتُ مَا اَنْتَ اَهْلُهُ وَ
تَغَمَّدْتَنِي بِعَفْوِكَ اِلهِي اِنْ عَفَوْتَ فَمَنْ اَوْلَى مِنْكَ بِذلِكَ
وَاِنْ كَانَ قَدْ دَنَا اَجَلِي وَلَمْ يُدْنِنِي مِنْكَ عَمَلِي فَقَدْ
جَعَلْتُ الْاِقْرَارَ بِالذَّنْبِ اِلَيْكَ وَسِيْلَتِي اِلهِي قَدْ جُرْتُ
عَلَى نَفْسِي فِي النَّظَرِ لَهَا فَلَهَا الْوَيْلُ اِنْ لَّمْ تَغْفِرْ لَهَا
اِلهِي لَمْ يَزَلْ بِرُّكَ عَلَى اَيَّامِ حَيَاتِي فَلَا تَقْطَعْ بِرَّكَ عَنِّي
فِي مَمَاتِي اِلهِي كَيْفَ اَيْسُ مِنْ حُسْنِ نَظَرِكَ لِي بَعْدَ مَمَاتِي
وَاَنْتَ لَمْ تُوَلِّنِي اِلَّا الْجَمِيْلَ فِي حَيَاتِي اِلهِي تَوَلَّ مِنْ اَمْرِي
مَا اَنْتَ اَهْلُهُ وَعُدْ عَلَيَّ بِفَضْلِكَ عَلَى مُذْنِبٍ قَدْ غَمَرَهُ جَهْلُهُ
اِلهِي قَدْ سَتَرْتَ عَلَيَّ ذُنُوْبًا فِي الدُّنْيَا وَاَنَا اَحْوَجُ اِلَى سَتْرِهَا
عَلَيَّ مِنْكَ فِي الْاُخْرَى اِذْ لَمْ تُظْهِرْهَا لِاَحَدٍ مِّنْ عِبَادِكَ الصَّالِحِيْنَ
فَلَا تَفْضَحْنِي يَوْمَ الْقِيَامَةِ عَلَى رُءُوْسِ الْاَشْهَادِ اِلهِي جُوْدُكَ
بَسَطَ اَمَلِي وَعَفْوُكَ اَفْضَلُ مِنْ عَمَلِي اِلهِي فَسُرَّ فِي بِلِقَائِكَ
يَوْمَ تَقْضِي فِيْهِ بَيْنَ عِبَادِكَ اِلهِي اِعْتِذَارِي اِلَيْكَ اِعْتِذَارُ
مَنْ لَّمْ يَسْتَغْنِ عَنْ قَبُوْلِ عُذْرِهِ فَاقْبَلْ عُذْرِي يَا اَكْرَمَ مَنِ
اعْتَذَرَ اِلَيْهِ الْمُسِيْئُوْنَ اِلهِي لَا تَرُدَّ حَاجَتِي وَلَا تُخَيِّبْ
طَمَعِي وَلَا تَقْطَعْ مِنْكَ رَجَائِي وَاَمَلِي اِلهِي اَرَدْتَّ هَوَانِي لَمْ

191

not have guided me; and if You had wanted to expose my faults and vices, You would not have kept me safe and sound.

My Lord, I do not think that You will turn down my request for that in asking You for which I have spent my whole life.

My Lord, all praise is due to You, always and for ever, growing not diminishing, as You like and please.

My Lord, if You condemn me for my crimes, I will cling to Your forgiveness, and if You hold me for my sins, I will cling to Your granting pardon. If You haul me into the hell, I will tell its inmates that I love You.

My Lord, if my deeds are too small in relation to how I should obey You, my aspirations are high enough as compared to what I should expect of You.

My Lord, how can I go away from You unsuccessful and disappointed, when I had a high hope that You will be kind enough to send me away enjoying safety and deliverance.

My Lord, I have wasted my life committing the crime of forgetting You and played havoc with my youth, intoxicated with keeping myself away from You.

My Lord, I did not wake up when I was under a delusion about You and was inclined to earn Your displeasure.

My Lord, I am Your bondman, son of Your bondman. I am standing before You, trying to use Your own magnanimity as a means of approaching You.

My Lord, I am a bondman of Yours, I want to rid myself of the sins I used to commit in Your presence because I lacked the sense of feeling ashamed that You were looking at me. I request You to forgive me, because forgiveness is a characteristic of Your Kindness.

My Lord, I was not strong enough to move away from Your disobedience, except when You awakened me to Your love. I was exactly as You wanted me to be. I am thankful to You for introducing me to Your Kindness and purging my heart

تَهْدِنِي وَلَوْ اَرَدْتَ فَضِيحَتِي لَمْ تُعَافِنِي اِلٰهِي مَا اَظُنُّكَ
تَرُدُّنِي فِي حَاجَةٍ قَدْ اَفْنَيْتُ عُمْرِي فِي طَلَبِهَا مِنْكَ اِلٰهِي
فَلَكَ الْحَمْدُ اَبَدًا دَائِمًا سَرْمَدًا يَزِيدُ وَلَا يَبِيدُ كَمَا تُحِبُّ
وَتَرْضٰى اِلٰهِي اِنْ اَخَذْتَنِي بِجُرْمِي اَخَذْتُكَ بِعَفْوِكَ وَاِنْ
اَخَذْتَنِي بِذُنُوبِي اَخَذْتُكَ بِمَغْفِرَتِكَ وَاِنْ اَدْخَلْتَنِي النَّارَ
اَعْلَمْتُ اَهْلَهَا اَنِّي اُحِبُّكَ اِلٰهِي اِنْ كَانَ صَغُرَ فِي جَنْبِ طَاعَتِكَ
عَمَلِي فَقَدْ كَبُرَ فِي جَنْبِ رَجَائِكَ اَمَلِي اِلٰهِي كَيْفَ اَنْقَلِبُ مِنْ
عِنْدِكَ بِالْخَيْبَةِ مَحْرُومًا وَقَدْ كَانَ حُسْنُ ظَنِّي بِجُودِكَ اَنْ
تَقْلِبَنِي بِالنَّجَاةِ مَرْحُومًا اِلٰهِي وَقَدْ اَفْنَيْتُ عُمْرِي فِي شِرَّةِ
السَّهْوِ عَنْكَ وَاَبْلَيْتُ شَبَابِي فِي سَكْرَةِ التَّبَاعُدِ مِنْكَ اِلٰهِي
فَلَمْ اَسْتَيْقِظْ اَيَّامَ اغْتِرَارِي بِكَ وَرُكُونِي اِلٰى سَبِيلِ سَخَطِكَ
اِلٰهِي وَاَنَا عَبْدُكَ وَابْنُ عَبْدِكَ قَائِمٌ بَيْنَ يَدَيْكَ مُتَوَسِّلٌ
بِكَرَمِكَ اِلَيْكَ اِلٰهِي اَنَا عَبْدٌ اَتَنَصَّلُ اِلَيْكَ مِمَّا كُنْتُ اُوَاجِهُكَ
بِهِ مِنْ قِلَّةِ اسْتِحْيَائِي مِنْ نَظَرِكَ وَاَطْلُبُ الْعَفْوَ مِنْكَ اِذِ
الْعَفْوُ نَعْتٌ لِكَرَمِكَ اِلٰهِي لَمْ يَكُنْ لِي حَوْلٌ فَاَنْتَقِلَ بِهِ عَنْ
مَعْصِيَتِكَ اِلَّا فِي وَقْتِ اَيْقَظْتَنِي لِمَحَبَّتِكَ وَكَمَا اَرَدْتَ اَنْ
اَكُونَ كُنْتُ فَشَكَرْتُكَ بِاِدْخَالِي فِي كَرَمِكَ وَلِتَطْهِيرِ قَلْبِي

193

of the impurities of being inattentive to You.

My Lord, look upon me as the person whom You called and he responded to You, whom You helped by using his services, and he obeyed You. You Near One, Who is not far from one who is away from You. You Munificent, Who does not withhold His reward from one who hopes for it.

My Lord, provide me with a heart, the passion of which may bring it near You, with a tongue the truth of which may be submitted to You, and with a vision the nature of which may bring it close to You.

My Lord, whoever gets acquainted with You, is not unknown; whoever takes shelter under You, is not disappointed; and one to whom You turn, is not a slave. One who follows Your path is enlightened; and one who takes refuge in You, is saved.

My Lord, I have taken refuge in You. Therefore do not disappoint me of Your Mercy and do not keep me secluded from Your Kindness.

My Lord, place me among Your friends in the position of one who hopes for an increase in Your love.

My Lord, inspire me with a passionate love of remembering You so that I may keep on remembering You, and by Your Holy Name and Pure Position cherish my cheerful determination into a success.

My Lord, I invoke You to admit me to the place reserved for those who obey You, and to attach me to the nice abode of those who enjoy Your good pleasure. . . I can neither defend my self nor do I control what is advantageous for me.

My Lord, I am Your powerless sinning slave and Your repentant bondman. So do not make me one of those from whom You turn away Your face, and whom his negligence has secluded from Your forgiveness.

My Lord, grant me complete severance of my relations with everything else and total submission to You. Enlighten the eyes of our hearts with the light of their looking at You

مِنْ أَوْسَاخِ الْغَفْلَةِ عَنْكَ اِلٰهِى اُنْظُرْ اِلَىٰ نَظَرِمَنْ نَّادَيْتَهٗ
فَاَجَابَكَ وَاسْتَعْمَلْتَهٗ بِمَعُوْنَتِكَ فَاَطَاعَكَ يَاقَرِيْبًا لَّايَبْعُدُ
عَنِ الْمُغْتَرِّبِهٖ وَيَا جَوَادًا لَّايَبْخَلُ عَمَّنْ رَجَا ثَوَابَهٗ اِلٰهِى
هَبْ لِى قَلْبًا يُّدْنِيهِ مِنْكَ شَوْقُهٗ وَلِسَانًا يُّرْفَعُ اِلَيْكَ صِدْقُهٗ
وَنَظَرًا يُّقَرِّبُهٗ مِنْكَ حَقُّهٗ اِلٰهِى اِنَّ مَنْ تَعَرَّفَ بِكَ غَيْرُ
مَجْهُوْلٍ وَمَنْ لَاذَ بِكَ غَيْرُ مَخْذُوْلٍ وَمَنْ اَقْبَلْتَ عَلَيْهِ
غَيْرُ مَمْلُوْكٍ اِلٰهِى اِنَّ مَنِ انْتَهَجَ بِكَ لَمُسْتَنِيْرٌ وَاِنَّ مَنِ
اعْتَصَمَ بِكَ لَمُسْتَجِيْرٌ وَقَدْ لُذْتُ بِكَ يَاۤ اِلٰهِى فَلَا تُخَيِّبْ
ظَنِّى مِنْ رَّحْمَتِكَ وَلَاتَحْجُبْنِى عَنْ رَأْفَتِكَ اِلٰهِى اَقِمْنِى
فِىۤ اَهْلِ وِلَايَتِكَ مَقَامَ مَنْ رَجَا الزِّيَادَةَ مِنْ مَّحَبَّتِكَ،
اِلٰهِى وَاَلْهِمْنِى وَلَهًا بِذِكْرِكَ اِلٰىٰ ذِكْرِكَ وَهِمَّتِى فِىْ رَوْحِ
نَجَاحِ اَسْمَاۤئِكَ وَمَحَلِّ قُدْسِكَ اِلٰهِى بِكَ عَلَيْكَ اِلَّا اَلْحَقْتَنِى
بِمَحَلِّ اَهْلِ طَاعَتِكَ وَالْمَثْوَى الصَّالِحِ مِنْ مَرْضَاتِكَ فَاِنِّىْ
لَاۤ اَقْدِرُ لِنَفْسِى دَفْعًا وَلَاۤ اَمْلِكُ لَهَا نَفْعًا اِلٰهِى اَنَا عَبْدُكَ
الضَّعِيْفُ الْمُذْنِبُ وَمَمْلُوْكُكَ الْمُنِيْبُ فَلَا تَجْعَلْنِى مِمَّنْ
صَرَفْتَ عَنْهُ وَجْهَكَ وَحَجَبَهٗ سَهْوُهٗ عَنْ عَفْوِكَ اِلٰهِى هَبْ
لِى كَمَالَ الْاِنْقِطَاعِ اِلَيْكَ وَاَنِرْ اَبْصَارَ قُلُوْبِنَا بِضِيَاۤءِ نَظَرِهَا

to the extent that they penetrate the veils of light and reach the Source of Grandeur, and let our souls get suspended by the glory of Your sanctity.

My Lord, make me one of those whom You call and they respond; when You look at and they are thunderstruck by Your majesty. You whisper to them secretly and they work for You openly.

My Lord, I have not allowed my pessimistic despair to overcome my good opinion about You, nor did I ever lose my hope of Your benevolence.

My Lord, if my errors have degraded me with You, You may forgive me in view of my unqualified reliance on You.

My Lord, if my sins have made me unfit to receive Your tender affection, my firm belief has reminded me of Your Compassion.

My Lord, if my disregard for preparations to meet You has put me to sleep, my knowledge of Your kind bounties has awakened me.

My Lord, if Your severe punishment calls me to Hell, the abundance of Your reward invites me to Paradise.

My Lord, I ask You and pray to You earnestly, I desire and request You to show Your favour to Muhammad and his descendants, make me one of those who always remember You and never violate the pledge they make to You, who do not fail to show You their gratitude and do not take Your orders lightly.

My Lord, let me be attached to the Light of Your Majestic Glory, so that I may know You alone, be away from others, and have a heart fearful of You and an eye watchful of You. May Allah's blessing and peace be on Muhammad and those of his descendants who are pure.

إِلَيْكَ حَتَّى تَخْرِقَ أَبْصَارَ الْقُلُوبِ حُجُبَ النُّورِ فَتَصِلَ إِلَى
مَعْدِنِ الْعَظَمَةِ وَتَصِيرَ أَرْوَاحُنَا مُعَلَّقَةً بِعِزِّ قُدْسِكَ
إِلَهِى وَاجْعَلْنِى مِمَّنْ نَادَيْتَهُ فَأَجَابَكَ وَلَاحَظْتَهُ فَصَعِقَ
لِجَلَالِكَ فَنَاجَيْتَهُ سِرًّا وَعَمِلَ لَكَ جَهْرًا إِلَهِى لَمْ أُسَلِّطْ
عَلَى حُسْنِ ظَنِّى قُنُوطَ الْإِيَاسِ وَلَا انْقَطَعَ رَجَائِى مِنْ جَمِيلِ
كَرَمِكَ إِلَهِى إِنْ كَانَتِ الْخَطَايَا قَدْ أَسْقَطَتْنِى لَدَيْكَ فَاصْفَحْ
عَنِّى بِحُسْنِ تَوَكُّلِى عَلَيْكَ إِلَهِى إِنْ حَطَّتْنِى الذُّنُوبُ مِنْ
مَكَارِمِ لُطْفِكَ فَقَدْ نَبَّهَنِى الْيَقِينُ إِلَى كَرَمِ عَطْفِكَ إِلَهِى إِنْ
أَنَامَتْنِى الْغَفْلَةُ عَنِ الِاسْتِعْدَادِ لِلِقَائِكَ فَقَدْ نَبَّهَتْنِى الْمَعْرِفَةُ
بِكَرَمِ الْآيكَ إِلَهِى إِنْ دَعَانِى إِلَى النَّارِ عَظِيمُ عِقَابِكَ فَقَدْ
دَعَانِى إِلَى الْجَنَّةِ جَزِيلُ ثَوَابِكَ إِلَهِى فَلَكَ أَسْأَلُ وَإِلَيْكَ
أَبْتَهِلُ وَأَرْغَبُ وَأَسْأَلُكَ أَنْ تُصَلِّىَ عَلَى مُحَمَّدٍ وَآلِ مُحَمَّدٍ
وَأَنْ تَجْعَلَنِى مِمَّنْ يُدِيمُ ذِكْرَكَ وَلَا يَنْقُضُ عَهْدَكَ وَلَا يَغْفُلُ
عَنْ شُكْرِكَ وَلَا يَسْتَخِفُّ بِأَمْرِكَ إِلَهِى وَأَلْحِقْنِى بِنُورِ عِزِّكَ
الْأَبْهَجِ فَأَكُونَ لَكَ عَارِفًا وَعَنْ سِوَاكَ مُنْحَرِفًا وَمِنْكَ خَائِفًا
مُرَاقِبًا يَا ذَا الْجَلَالِ وَالْإِكْرَامِ وَصَلَّى اللهُ عَلَى مُحَمَّدٍ رَسُولِهِ
وَآلِهِ الطَّاهِرِينَ وَسَلَّمَ تَسْلِيمًا كَثِيرًا .

ARABIC TEXT

The readers are requested to note that the Arabic text reproduced below refers to the corresponding English translation given inside the book in numerical order.

١ — يَاأَيُّهَا الَّذِيْنَ آمَنُوْا عَلَيْكُمْ اَنْفُسَكُمْ لَايَضُرُّكُمْ مَّنْ ضَلَّ اِذَا اهْتَدَيْتُمْ.

٢ — فَاذْكُرُوْنِيْ اَذْكُرْكُمْ.

٣ — لَقَدْ كَانَ لَكُمْ فِيْ رَسُوْلِ اللهِ اُسْوَةٌ حَسَنَةٌ.

٤ — وَنَزَّلْنَا عَلَيْكَ الْكِتَابَ تِبْيَانًا لِّكُلِّ شَيْءٍ.

٥ — فَاَيْنَمَا تُوَلُّوْا فَثَمَّ وَجْهُ اللهِ.

٦ — وَنَحْنُ اَقْرَبُ اِلَيْهِ مِنْ حَبْلِ الْوَرِيْدِ.

٧ — هُوَ الْاَوَّلُ وَالْاَخِرُ وَالظَّاهِرُ وَالْبَاطِنُ.

٨ — وَالَّذِيْنَ جَاهَدُوْا فِيْنَا لَنَهْدِيَنَّهُمْ سُبُلَنَا.

٩ — قَدْ اَفْلَحَ مَنْ زَكَّاهَا وَقَدْ خَابَ مَنْ دَسَّاهَا.

١٠ — قَالَ اَمِيْرُ الْمُؤْمِنِيْنَ عَلِيٌّ عَلَيْهِ السَّلَامُ :

اِنَّ اللهَ سُبْحَانَهُ وَتَعَالَى جَعَلَ الذِّكْرَ جِلَاءً لِّلْقُلُوْبِ تَسْمَعُ بِهِ بَعْدَ الْوَقْرَةِ وَتُبْصِرُ بِهِ بَعْدَ الْعَشْوَةِ وَتَنْقَادُ بِهِ بَعْدَ الْمُعَانَدَةِ وَمَا بَرِحَ لِلهِ عَزَّتْ آلَاءُهُ ـ وَفِيْ اَزْمَانِ الْفَتَرَاتِ عِبَادٌ نَاجَاهُمْ فِيْ فِكْرِهِمْ وَكَلَّمَهُمْ فِيْ ذَاتِ عُقُوْلِهِمْ

١١ — قَالَ اَمِيْرُ الْمُؤْمِنِيْنَ عَلِيٌّ عَلَيْهِ السَّلَامُ :

قَدْ اَحْيَا عَقْلَهُ وَاَمَاتَ نَفْسَهُ حَتَّى دَقَّ جَلِيْلُهُ وَلَطُفَ

غَلِيظُهُ وَبَرَقَ لَهُ لَامِعُ كَثِيرُ البَرْقِ فَأَبَانَ لَهُ الطَّرِيقَ وَ
سَلَكَ بِهِ السَّبِيلَ وَتَدَافَعَتْهُ الأَبْوَابُ إِلَى بَابِ السَّلَامَةِ
وَدَارِ الإِقَامَةِ وَثَبَتَتْ رِجْلَاهُ بِطُمَأْنِينَةِ بَدَنِهِ فِي قَرَارِ
الأَمْنِ وَالرَّاحَةِ بِمَا اسْتَعْمَلَ قَلْبَهُ وَأَرْضَى رَبَّهُ .

12 — وَلَا تَحْسَبَنَّ الَّذِينَ قُتِلُوا فِي سَبِيلِ اللهِ أَمْوَاتًا بَلْ أَحْيَاءٌ
عِنْدَ رَبِّهِمْ يُرْزَقُونَ .

13 — كُلُّ شَيْءٍ هَالِكٌ إِلَّا وَجْهَهُ .

14 — مَا عِنْدَكُمْ يَنْفَدُ وَمَا عِنْدَ اللهِ بَاقٍ .

15 — كُلُّ مَنْ عَلَيْهَا فَانٍ وَيَبْقَى وَجْهُ رَبِّكَ ذُو الجَلَالِ وَالإِكْرَامِ

16 — لَقَدْ كَانَ لَكُمْ فِي رَسُولِ اللهِ أُسْوَةٌ حَسَنَةٌ لِمَنْ كَانَ يَرْجُو اللهَ
وَاليَوْمَ الآخِرَ وَذَكَرَ اللهَ كَثِيرًا .

17 — وَإِنَّ يَوْمًا عِنْدَ رَبِّكَ كَأَلْفِ سَنَةٍ مِمَّا تَعُدُّونَ .

18 — وَمَا أُمِرُوا إِلَّا لِيَعْبُدُوا اللهَ مُخْلِصِينَ لَهُ الدِّينَ .

19 — إِلَّا عِبَادَ اللهِ المُخْلَصِينَ .

20 — إِلَيْهِ يَصْعَدُ الكَلِمُ الطَّيِّبُ وَالعَمَلُ الصَّالِحُ يَرْفَعُهُ .

21 — فَبِعِزَّتِكَ لَأُغْوِيَنَّهُمْ أَجْمَعِينَ إِلَّا عِبَادَكَ مِنْهُمُ المُخْلَصِينَ

22 — وَنُفِخَ فِي الصُّورِ فَصَعِقَ مَنْ فِي السَّمَوَاتِ وَمَنْ فِي الأَرْضِ إِلَّا
مَنْ شَاءَ اللهُ .

23 — فَإِنَّهُمْ لَمُحْضَرُونَ إِلَّا عِبَادَ اللهِ المُخْلَصِينَ .

24 — وَلَا تَحْسَبَنَّ الَّذِينَ قُتِلُوا فِي سَبِيلِ اللهِ أَمْوَاتًا بَلْ أَحْيَاءٌ
عِنْدَ رَبِّهِمْ يُرْزَقُونَ .

200

وَمَا تُجْزَوْنَ إِلَّا مَا كُنْتُمْ تَعْمَلُوْنَ . إِلَّا عِبَادَاللهِ الْمُخْلَصِيْنَ — 25

لَهُمْ مَا يَشَاءُوْنَ فِيْهَا وَلَدَيْنَا مَزِيْدٌ . — 26

سُبْحَانَ اللهِ عَمَّا يَصِفُوْنَ إِلَّا عِبَادَ اللهِ الْمُخْلَصِيْنَ . — 27

لِكَيْلَا تَأْسَوْا عَلَىٰ مَا فَاتَكُمْ وَ لَا تَفْرَحُوْا بِمَا آتَاكُمْ . — 28

أَفَرَءَيْتَ مَنِ اتَّخَذَ إِلَهَهٗ هَوٰىهُ . — 29

لِيَغْفِرَ لَكَ اللهُ مَا تَقَدَّمَ مِنْ ذَنْبِكَ وَمَا تَأَخَّرَ . — 30

وَمَا مُحَمَّدٌ إِلَّا رَسُوْلٌ قَدْ خَلَتْ مِنْ قَبْلِهِ الرُّسُلُ أَفَإِنْ مَّاتَ — 31
أَوْ قُتِلَ انْقَلَبْتُمْ عَلَىٰ أَعْقَابِكُمْ .

وَذَرُوْا ظَاهِرَ الْإِثْمِ وَبَاطِنَهٗ . — 32

اَلَّذِيْنَ اٰمَنُوْا وَهَاجَرُوْا وَجَاهَدُوْا فِيْ سَبِيْلِ اللهِ بِأَمْوَالِهِمْ وَ — 33
أَنْفُسِهِمْ أَعْظَمُ دَرَجَةً عِنْدَاللهِ وَأُولَٰئِكَ هُمُ الْفَائِزُوْنَ .
يُبَشِّرُهُمْ رَبُّهُمْ بِرَحْمَةٍ مِّنْهُ وَرِضْوَانٍ وَّجَنَّاتٍ لَّهُمْ فِيْهَا نَعِيمٌ مُّقِيمٌ
خَالِدِيْنَ فِيْهَا أَبَدًا اِنَّ اللهَ عِنْدَهٗ أَجْرٌ عَظِيْمٌ .

فَلَا وَرَبِّكَ لَا يُؤْمِنُوْنَ حَتّٰى يُحَكِّمُوْكَ فِيْمَا شَجَرَ بَيْنَهُمْ ثُمَّ — 34
لَا يَجِدُوْا فِيْ أَنْفُسِهِمْ حَرَجًا مِّمَّا قَضَيْتَ وَيُسَلِّمُوْا تَسْلِيْمًا .

وَالَّذِيْنَ جَاهَدُوْا فِيْنَا لَنَهْدِيَنَّهُمْ سُبُلَنَا وَ اِنَّ اللهَ لَمَعَ — 35
الْمُحْسِنِيْنَ .

قَدْ أَفْلَحَ الْمُؤْمِنُوْنَ الَّذِيْنَ هُمْ فِيْ صَلَاتِهِمْ خَاشِعُوْنَ وَ — 36
الَّذِيْنَ هُمْ عَنِ اللَّغْوِ مُعْرِضُوْنَ .

مَا جَعَلَ اللهُ لِرَجُلٍ مِّنْ قَلْبَيْنِ فِيْ جَوْفِهِ . — 37

وَإِذَا قَامُوْا إِلَى الصَّلٰوةِ قَامُوْا كُسَالَىٰ . — 38

٣٩ — اَوَمَنْ كَانَ مَيْتًا فَاَحْيَيْنَاهُ وَجَعَلْنَا لَهُ نُورًا يَمْشِى بِهِ فِى
النَّاسِ كَمَنْ مَثَلُهُ فِى الظُّلُمَاتِ لَيْسَ بِخَارِجٍ مِّنْهَا كَذَلِكَ
زُيِّنَ لِلْكَافِرِينَ مَا كَانُوا يَعْمَلُونَ .

٤٠ — مَنْ عَمِلَ صَالِحًا مِّنْ ذَكَرٍ اَوْ اُنْثَى وَهُوَ مُؤْمِنٌ فَلَنُحْيِيَنَّهُ
حَيَاةً طَيِّبَةً وَلَنَجْزِيَنَّهُمْ اَجْرَهُمْ بِاَحْسَنِ مَا كَانُوا يَعْمَلُونَ

٤١ — قَالَ رَسُولُ اللهِ صَلَّى اللهُ عَلَيْهِ وَآلِهِ :
اَعْدَى عَدُوِّكَ نَفْسُكَ الَّتِى بَيْنَ جَنْبَيْكَ .

٤٢ — وَاجْنُبْنِى وَبَنِىَّ اَنْ نَعْبُدَ الْاَصْنَامَ .

٤٣ — قَالَ رَسُولُ اللهِ صَلَّى اللهُ عَلَيْهِ وَآلِهِ :
اَللّٰهُمَّ اِنِّى اَعُوذُ بِكَ مِنَ الشِّرْكِ الْخَفِىِّ .

٤٤ — اَمَّا السَّفِينَةُ فَكَانَتْ لِمَسَاكِينَ يَعْمَلُونَ فِى الْبَحْرِ فَاَرَدْتُ
اَنْ اَعِيبَهَا وَكَانَ وَرَآءَهُمْ مَلِكٌ يَاْخُذُ كُلَّ سَفِينَةٍ غَصْبًا.

٤٥ — وَاَمَّا الْغُلَامُ فَكَانَ اَبَوَاهُ مُؤْمِنَيْنِ فَخَشِينَا اَنْ يُرْهِقَهُمَا
طُغْيَانًا وَّكُفْرًا فَاَرَدْنَا اَنْ يُبْدِلَهُمَا رَبُّهُمَا خَيْرًا مِّنْهُ زَكَاةً
وَّاَقْرَبَ رُحْمًا.

٤٦ — وَاَمَّا الْجِدَارُ فَكَانَ لِغُلَامَيْنِ يَتِيمَيْنِ فِى الْمَدِينَةِ وَكَانَ
تَحْتَهُ كَنْزٌ لَّهُمَا وَكَانَ اَبُوهُمَا صَالِحًا فَاَرَادَ رَبُّكَ اَنْ يَبْلُغَا
اَشُدَّهُمَا وَيَسْتَخْرِجَا كَنْزَهُمَا رَحْمَةً مِّنْ رَّبِّكَ .

٤٧ — اَلَّذِى خَلَقَنِى فَهُوَ يَهْدِينِ وَالَّذِى هُوَ يُطْعِمُنِى وَيَسْقِينِ وَ
اِذَا مَرِضْتُ فَهُوَ يَشْفِينِ .

٤٨ — يَآيَّتُهَا النَّفْسُ الْمُطْمَئِنَّةُ ارْجِعِى اِلَى رَبِّكِ رَاضِيَةً مَّرْضِيَّةً

فَادْخُلِى فِى عِبَادِى وَادْخُلِى جَنَّتِى .

49 ـــ فِى مَقْعَدِ صِدْقٍ عِنْدَ مَلِيكٍ مُقْتَدِرٍ .

50 ـــ اِنَّا لِلَّهِ وَاِنَّا اِلَيْهِ رَاجِعُوْنَ .

51 ـــ كُلُّ نَفْسٍ ذَآئِقَةُ الْمَوْتِ .

52 ـــ اِنَّهُ مِنْ عِبَادِنَا الْمُخْلَصِيْنَ .

53 ـــ اَنْتَ وَلِيِّى فِى الدُّنْيَا وَالْاٰخِرَةِ تَوَفَّنِى مُسْلِمًا وَّاَلْحِقْنِى بِالصَّالِحِيْنَ .

54 ـــ رَبِّ هَبْ لِى حُكْمًا وَّاَلْحِقْنِى بِالصَّالِحِيْنَ .

55 ـــ وَلَقَدِ اصْطَفَيْنَاهُ فِى الدُّنْيَا وَاِنَّهُ فِى الْاٰخِرَةِ لَمِنَ الصَّالِحِيْنَ .

56 ـــ وَوَهَبْنَا لَهُ اِسْحَاقَ وَيَعْقُوْبَ نَافِلَةً وَكُلاًّ جَعَلْنَا صَالِحِيْنَ .

57 ـــ اِنَّ وَلِيِّى اللَّهُ الَّذِى نَزَّلَ الْكِتَابَ وَهُوَ يَتَوَلَّى الصَّالِحِيْنَ .

58 ـــ سُبْحَانَ اللَّهِ عَمَّا يَصِفُوْنَ اِلاَّ عِبَادَ اللَّهِ الْمُخْلَصِيْنَ .

59 ـــ قُلِ الْحَمْدُ لِلَّهِ وَسَلَامٌ عَلَى عِبَادِهِ الَّذِيْنَ اصْطَفَى اللَّهُ خَيْرٌ اَمَّا يُشْرِكُوْنَ .

60 ـــ اَلْحَمْدُ لِلَّهِ الَّذِى وَهَبَ لِى عَلَى الْكِبَرِ اِسْمَاعِيْلَ وَاِسْحَاقَ اِنَّ رَبِّى لَسَمِيْعُ الدُّعَاءِ .

61 ـــ فَقُلِ الْحَمْدُ لِلَّهِ الَّذِى نَجَّانَا مِنَ الْقَوْمِ الظَّالِمِيْنَ .

62 ـــ اِنَّهُ مِنْ عِبَادِنَا الْمُخْلَصِيْنَ .

63 ـــ وَاذْكُرْ فِى الْكِتَابِ مُوْسَى اِنَّهُ كَانَ مُخْلَصًا وَّكَانَ رَسُوْلاً نَّبِيًّا .

64 ـــ وَاذْكُرْ عِبَادَنَا اِبْرَاهِيْمَ وَاِسْحَاقَ وَيَعْقُوْبَ اُولِى الْاَيْدِى وَالْاَبْصَارِ اِنَّا اَخْلَصْنَاهُمْ بِخَالِصَةٍ ذِكْرَى الدَّارِ .

٦٥ ــ قَالَ فَبِعِزَّتِكَ لَأُغْوِيَنَّهُمْ أَجْمَعِينَ اِلَّا عِبَادَكَ مِنْهُمُ الْمُخْلَصِينَ

٦٦ ــ ثُمَّ لَآتِيَنَّهُمْ مِنْ بَيْنِ اَيْدِيهِمْ وَمِنْ خَلْفِهِمْ وَعَنْ اَيْمَانِهِمْ
وَعَنْ شَمَآئِلِهِمْ وَلَا تَجِدُ اَكْثَرَهُمْ شَاكِرِينَ .

٦٧ ــ وَوَهَبْنَا لَهُ اِسْحَاقَ وَيَعْقُوبَ كُلًّا هَدَيْنَا وَنُوحًا هَدَيْنَا مِنْ
قَبْلُ وَمِنْ ذُرِّيَّتِهِ دَاوُدَ وَسُلَيْمَانَ وَاَيُّوبَ وَيُوسُفَ وَمُوسَى
وَهَارُونَ وَكَذَلِكَ نَجْزِى الْمُحْسِنِينَ وَزَكَرِيَّا وَيَحْيَى وَ
عِيسَى وَالْيَاسَ كُلٌّ مِّنَ الصَّالِحِينَ وَاِسْمَاعِيلَ وَالْيَسَعَ وَ
يُونُسَ وَلُوطًا وَكُلًّا فَضَّلْنَا عَلَى الْعَالَمِينَ وَمِنْ اَبَآئِهِمْ
وَذُرِّيَّاتِهِمْ وَاِخْوَانِهِمْ وَاجْتَبَيْنَاهُمْ وَهَدَيْنَاهُمْ اِلَى
صِرَاطٍ مُّسْتَقِيمٍ.

٦٨ ــ ذُرِّيَّةَ مَنْ حَمَلْنَا مَعَ نُوحٍ اِنَّهُ كَانَ عَبْدًا شَكُورًا .

٦٩ ــ اِنَّا اَرْسَلْنَا عَلَيْهِمْ حَاصِبًا اِلَّا اَلَ لُوطٍ نَجَّيْنَاهُمْ بِسَحَرٍ
نِعْمَةً مِّنْ عِنْدِنَا كَذَلِكَ نَجْزِى مَنْ شَكَرَ .

٧٠ ــ اِنَّ اِبْرَاهِيمَ كَانَ اُمَّةً قَانِتًا لِلّٰهِ حَنِيفًا وَلَمْ يَكُ مِنَ الْمُشْرِكِينَ
شَاكِرًا لِأَنْعُمِهِ اِجْتَبَاهُ وَهَدَاهُ اِلَى صِرَاطٍ مُّسْتَقِيمٍ.

٧١ ــ وَالَّذِينَ جَاهَدُوا فِينَا لَنَهْدِيَنَّهُمْ سُبُلَنَا .

٧٢ ــ وَالْعَمَلُ الصَّالِحُ يَرْفَعُهُ .

٧٣ ــ اَلَا بِذِكْرِ اللّٰهِ تَطْمَئِنُّ الْقُلُوبُ .

٧٤ ــ اَلَّذِينَ اٰمَنُوا وَلَمْ يَلْبِسُوا اِيمَانَهُمْ بِظُلْمٍ اُولٰئِكَ لَهُمُ الْاَمْنُ
وَهُمْ مُّهْتَدُونَ .

٧٥ ــ اَلَا اِنَّ اَوْلِيَآءَ اللّٰهِ لَا خَوْفٌ عَلَيْهِمْ وَلَا هُمْ يَحْزَنُونَ .

76 — وَلَا يَخَافُونَ لَوْمَةَ لَائِمٍ .

77 — وَعَلَى اللهِ فَلْيَتَوَكَّلِ الْمُؤْمِنُونَ .

78 — وَإِنْ مِّنْ شَيْءٍ إِلَّا عِنْدَنَا خَزَائِنُهُ وَمَا نُنَزِّلُهُ إِلَّا بِقَدَرٍ مَّعْلُومٍ

79 — مَا أَصَابَ مِنْ مُّصِيبَةٍ فِي الْأَرْضِ وَلَا فِي أَنْفُسِكُمْ إِلَّا فِي كِتَابٍ مِّنْ قَبْلِ أَنْ نَّبْرَأَهَا إِنَّ ذَلِكَ عَلَى اللهِ يَسِيرٌ .

80 — مَا عِنْدَكُمْ يَنْفَدُ وَمَا عِنْدَ اللهِ بَاقٍ .

81 — فَأَقِمْ وَجْهَكَ لِلدِّينِ حَنِيفًا فِطْرَتَ اللهِ الَّتِي فَطَرَ النَّاسَ عَلَيْهَا لَا تَبْدِيلَ لِخَلْقِ اللهِ ذَلِكَ الدِّينُ الْقَيِّمُ وَلَكِنَّ أَكْثَرَ النَّاسِ لَا يَعْلَمُونَ .

82 — إِنَّ اللهَ لَا يَغْفِرُ أَنْ يُّشْرَكَ بِهِ وَيَغْفِرُ مَا دُونَ ذَلِكَ لِمَنْ يَّشَاءُ

83 — وَذَرِ الَّذِينَ اتَّخَذُوا دِينَهُمْ لَعِبًا وَّلَهْوًا وَّغَرَّتْهُمُ الْحَيَاةُ الدُّنْيَا .

84 — كَانُوا قَلِيلًا مِّنَ اللَّيْلِ مَا يَهْجَعُونَ . وَبِالْأَسْحَارِ هُمْ يَسْتَغْفِرُونَ.

85 — وَاسْتَعِينُوا بِالصَّبْرِ وَالصَّلَوةِ وَإِنَّهَا لَكَبِيرَةٌ إِلَّا عَلَى الْخَاشِعِينَ

86 — إِنَّهُ لَيْسَ لَهُ سُلْطَانٌ عَلَى الَّذِينَ آمَنُوا وَعَلَى رَبِّهِمْ يَتَوَكَّلُونَ. إِنَّمَا سُلْطَانُهُ عَلَى الَّذِينَ يَتَوَلَّوْنَهُ وَالَّذِينَ هُمْ بِهِ مُشْرِكُونَ.

87 — إِنَّ الَّذِينَ اتَّقَوْا إِذَا مَسَّهُمْ طَائِفٌ مِّنَ الشَّيْطَانِ تَذَكَّرُوا فَإِذَا هُمْ مُّبْصِرُونَ .

88 — وَمَنْ يَّعْشُ عَنْ ذِكْرِ الرَّحْمَنِ نُقَيِّضْ لَهُ شَيْطَانًا فَهُوَ لَهُ قَرِينٌ.

89 — يَا أَيُّهَا الَّذِينَ آمَنُوا عَلَيْكُمْ أَنْفُسَكُمْ لَا يَضُرُّكُمْ مَّنْ ضَلَّ إِذَا اهْتَدَيْتُمْ.

٩٠ ــوَإِنْ مِنْ شَيْءٍ إِلَّا يُسَبِّحُ بِحَمْدِهِ وَلَكِنْ لَا تَفْقَهُونَ تَسْبِيحَهُمْ

٩١ ــوَمَا رَمَيْتَ إِذْ رَمَيْتَ وَلَكِنَّ اللهَ رَمَى .

٩٢ ــإِنَّ الَّذِينَ يُبَايِعُونَكَ إِنَّمَا يُبَايِعُونَ اللهَ .

٩٣ ــاَللهُ نُورُ السَّمَوَاتِ وَالْأَرْضِ .

٩٤ ــوَمَنْ يَخْرُجْ مِنْ بَيْتِهِ مُهَاجِرًا إِلَى اللهِ وَرَسُولِهِ ثُمَّ يُدْرِكْهُ الْمَوْتُ فَقَدْ وَقَعَ أَجْرُهُ عَلَى اللهِ .

٩٥ ــمَا عِنْدَكُمْ يَنْفَدُ وَمَا عِنْدَ اللهِ بَاقٍ .

٩٦ ــفَلَمَّا تَجَلَّى رَبُّهُ لِلْجَبَلِ .

٩٧ ــاَللهُ يَتَوَفَّى الْأَنْفُسَ حِينَ مَوْتِهَا .

٩٨ ــوَمَا رَمَيْتَ إِذْ رَمَيْتَ وَلَكِنَّ اللهَ رَمَى .

٩٩ ــأَفَلَا يَنْظُرُونَ إِلَى الْإِبِلِ كَيْفَ خُلِقَتْ .

١٠٠ ــرَبِّ اشْرَحْ لِي صَدْرِي وَيَسِّرْ لِي أَمْرِي وَاحْلُلْ عُقْدَةً مِنْ لِسَانِي يَفْقَهُوا قَوْلِي .

١٠١ ــفَلَمَّا تَجَلَّى رَبُّهُ لِلْجَبَلِ جَعَلَهُ دَكًّا وَخَرَّ مُوسَى صَعِقًا .

١٠٢ ــقَالَ لَنْ تَرَانِي وَلَكِنِ انْظُرْ إِلَى الْجَبَلِ فَإِنِ اسْتَقَرَّ مَكَانَهُ فَسَوْفَ تَرَانِي .

١٠٣ ــنَزَلَ بِهِ الرُّوحُ الْأَمِينُ .

١٠٤ ــإِنَّا أَنْزَلْنَاهُ فِي لَيْلَةِ الْقَدْرِ .

١٠٥ ــقُلْ إِنَّمَا أَعِظُكُمْ بِوَاحِدَةٍ أَنْ تَقُومُوا لِلهِ .

١٠٦ ــقُلْ مَا يَعْبَأُ بِكُمْ رَبِّي لَوْلَا دُعَاؤُكُمْ .

١٠٧ ــوَقَالَ رَبُّكُمُ ادْعُونِي أَسْتَجِبْ لَكُمْ .

١٠٨ ___ هُوَ اللهُ الَّذِى لَا إِلٰهَ إِلَّا هُوَ عَالِمُ الْغَيْبِ وَالشَّهَادَةِ هُوَ الرَّحْمٰنُ الرَّحِيمُ هُوَ اللهُ الَّذِى لَا إِلٰهَ إِلَّا هُوَ الْمَلِكُ الْقُدُّوسُ السَّلَامُ الْمُؤْمِنُ الْمُهَيْمِنُ الْعَزِيزُ الْجَبَّارُ الْمُتَكَبِّرُ سُبْحَانَ اللهِ عَمَّا يُشْرِكُونَ هُوَ اللهُ الْخَالِقُ الْبَارِئُ الْمُصَوِّرُ لَهُ الْأَسْمَاءُ الْحُسْنَى يُسَبِّحُ لَهُ مَا فِى السَّمٰوَاتِ وَالْأَرْضِ وَهُوَ الْعَزِيزُ الْحَكِيمُ .

١٠٩ ___ قُلِ ادْعُوا اللهَ أَوِ ادْعُوا الرَّحْمٰنَ .

١١٠ ___ وَللهِ الْأَسْمَاءُ الْحُسْنَى فَادْعُوهُ بِهَا .

١١١ ___ إِلٰهِى هَبْ لِى كَمَالَ الْإِنْقِطَاعِ إِلَيْكَ وَأَنِرْ أَبْصَارَ قُلُوبِنَا بِضِيَاءِ نَظَرِهَا إِلَيْكَ حَتَّى تَخْرِقَ أَبْصَارُ الْقُلُوبِ حُجُبَ النُّورِ فَتَصِلَ إِلَى مَعْدِنِ الْعَظَمَةِ وَتَصِيرَ أَرْوَاحُنَا مُعَلَّقَةً بِعِزِّ قُدْسِكَ، إِلٰهِى وَاجْعَلْنِى مِمَّنْ نَادَيْتَهُ فَأَجَابَكَ وَلَاحَظْتَهُ فَصَعِقَ لِجَلَالِكَ.

١١٢ ___ فَلَمَّا تَجَلَّى رَبُّهُ لِلْجَبَلِ .

١١٣ ___ وَمَا رَمَيْتَ إِذْ رَمَيْتَ وَلٰكِنَّ اللهَ رَمَى .

١١٤ ___ إِنَّ الَّذِينَ يُبَايِعُونَكَ إِنَّمَا يُبَايِعُونَ اللهَ يَدُ اللهِ فَوْقَ أَيْدِيهِمْ .

١١٥ ___ هُوَ الْأَوَّلُ وَالْآخِرُ وَالظَّاهِرُ وَالْبَاطِنُ وَهُوَ بِكُلِّ شَئْ عَلِيمٌ هُوَ الَّذِى خَلَقَ السَّمٰوَاتِ وَالْأَرْضَ فِى سِتَّةِ أَيَّامٍ ثُمَّ اسْتَوَى عَلَى الْعَرْشِ يَعْلَمُ مَا يَلِجُ فِى الْأَرْضِ وَمَا يَخْرُجُ مِنْهَا وَمَا يَنْزِلُ مِنَ السَّمَاءِ وَمَا يَعْرُجُ فِيهَا وَهُوَ مَعَكُمْ أَيْنَمَا كُنْتُمْ .

١١٦ ___ قَالَتْ نَمْلَةٌ يَا أَيُّهَا النَّمْلُ ادْخُلُوا مَسَاكِنَكُمْ لَا يَحْطِمَنَّكُمْ سُلَيْمَانُ وَجُنُودُهُ وَهُمْ لَا يَشْعُرُونَ فَتَبَسَّمَ ضَاحِكًا مِنْ قَوْلِهَا .

١١٧ ___ فَقَالَ أَحَطُّ بِمَا لَمْ تُحِطْ بِهِ .